Bruce,

Happy Running

8-8-95

Gloria

The Runner's Literary Companion

THE RUNNER'S LITERARY COMPANION

Great Stories and Poems About Running

EDITED BY GARTH BATTISTA

Breakaway Books
New York City
1994

The Runner's Literary Companion:
Great Stories and Poems About Running

ISBN: 1-55821-335-X
Library of Congress Catalog Card Number: 94-71686

For permissions acknowledgments:
see a continuation of this page on pages 321-323.

Published by:
BREAKAWAY BOOKS
P.O. Box 1109
Ansonia Station
New York, NY 10023

Breakaway Books are distributed by:
LYONS & BURFORD, Publishers
31 West 21st Street
New York, NY 10010

Second printing: January 1995.
First printing: August 1994.

[A note on spelling conventions: in stories from the British Commonwealth, where the original text contained British spelling (colour, flavour, kerb, metre, etc.) I have left it as found, rather than altering the book to a uniform American spelling. This is an entirely personal preference: I like the "colour and flavour" of a British story, just as I would want American spelling left in Hemingway published in London. It enhances the nuances of location, character and diction. One exception to this odd rule, however, is the most British story of them all, the excerpt from Brian Glanville's *The Olympian*. It was published first in the U.S., a few weeks before its U.K. publication. The version from which the excerpt was taken contains the American spelling imposed upon it long ago. I was unable to locate a British edition, and wouldn't attempt to reconstruct one. But, fortunately, Ike Low's voice leaves no room for doubt as to his provenance. —G.B.]

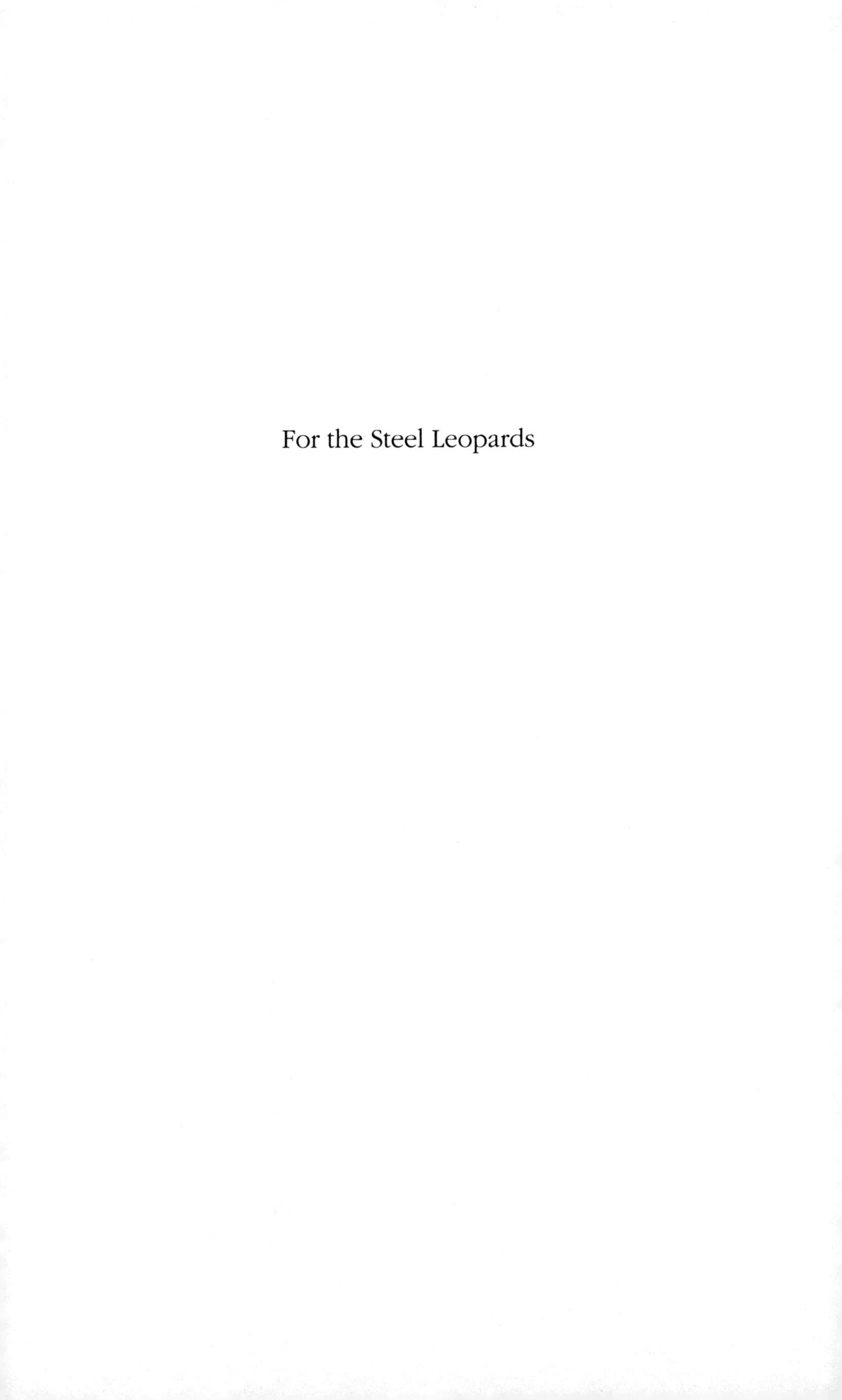

For the Steel Leopards

CONTENTS

POEMS

Introduction

The camera's eye
Does not lie,
But it cannot show
The life within,
The life of a runner
—W.H. Auden

Literature and sports are not mutually exclusive, though at times one may despair of finding their common ground. A flood of disposable writing on sports is published each year. But at the sublime high end, baseball has Roger Angell and Roger Kahn; basketball and tennis each received a visit from John McPhee; football has Peter Gent and Fred Exley; golf has P.G. Wodehouse and John *Updike*, by God.

Running's well-known literary pantheon is composed mostly of non-fiction writers. George Sheehan was the master essayist and philosopher. Other standouts whose work transcends journalism include Kenny Moore, Amby Burfoot, and Joe Henderson. But fiction and poetry about running are relatively rare. Some will know Sillitoe; the cognoscenti have read John L. Parker. Beyond that, the familiar names or stories usually dwindle. The only mildly familiar running poem is A.E. Housman's "To an Athlete Dying Young." As a group, we runners are strangely under-represented in literature. There are eight million serious runners in the U.S. alone (surely some of them are fiction writers), but a wildly disproportionate number of runners in novels and stories and poems. This anthology is an attempt to find and honor our bards; to bring the best of them together—both the writers of great renown who in the course of their distinguished careers have touched upon running (Walt Whitman, Evelyn Waugh, Joyce Carol Oates, W.H. Auden, A.E. Housman, Rudyard Kipling, Toni Cade Bambara), and the lesser known writers whose works (some hereby recovered from the dustbin of history) will also bring gladness, insight, or inspiration to any runner.

This book does not pretend, by any means, to establish a runner's literary canon. It omits as many great works as it includes, and for reasons of space and focus it includes only fiction and poetry, leaving out the best nonfiction writing on running (which could easily fill another volume). The main purpose of *The Runner's Literary Companion* is to provide runners with a source of aesthetic pleasure: seeing themselves reflected in these characters, and seeing the ephemeral truths and beauties of running distilled to lasting purity. It also provides the pleasure of concentrated wealth: if it is a rare joy to come across one running story, finding twenty-four in one place must be that much better. This book should be a solace on rainy days (after your run) or during travel, late nights, or illness. It should be inspiration for even more and better running, and for thinking and talking about running.

Coupling good writing with good running is an extraordinarily difficult task, as the sport is innately interior, and impossibly complex. Elvis Costello once said, "Writing about music is like dancing about architecture." In the same way, running—the total, exalted, painful, glorious, miserable, purifying, filthy, rhythmic, dreamy, transcendent, achy experience—for the most part defies rendition in words. In that light, what is gathered here seems miraculous by its very existence; and it is a wonder to see the various ways running has been fictionalized. Some of these stories and poems are brilliantly written, literary gems in the truest sense. Some of them contain uncannily perceptive descriptions of the act of running, or a great character who happens to run. Good writing and good running are present to varying degrees in every story here, and that is why they have been chosen. "The Winning Bug," by Jackson Scholz, gets a special nod, as Scholz was the 1924 Olympic gold medalist in the 200m (thus subsequently a filmic character in *Chariots of Fire*), and went on to write some fine stories.

Not all of these stories are about champions and victories: the place of running in average lives is as moving as any world record. The poems, as well, run the gamut: from traditional forms to modern; from light verse to the fiercely serious; and from those concerned with the mechanics of running to those seeking to illuminate the inner life of the runner.

The combined effect of everything included in this anthology, I hope, is to begin to reveal the ghost in the machine—the ineffable spirit of running which every runner knows intimately, but can't entirely explain.

—G.B., New York, May 1994

The Milers

ONCE A RUNNER

John L. Parker, Jr.

(1978)

[*Quenton Cassidy has been banned by meddlesome administrators from competing for his university, or even on its track. He leaves school—and his girlfriend—to train in isolation, and returns to race (incognito) against one of the world's greatest milers. Bruce Denton is his confidant and coach, and himself a world-class runner. The umbrella man is the girlfriend's new companion.*]

Saying something about walking off his macaroni and cheese, Cassidy escaped to the evening. There was a bit of marital uneasiness in the air, a strain that he may have had more than a little to do with, but for now all he could think of was closing the glistening, seamless orb, receptacle of his fiercest yearning.

In the afternoon they had gone to a deserted high school track for the last session, a nearly lightheaded tune-up; for the first time in months he was completely rested and strong and when Denton walked over and held up the watch grimly it said: 24.8. That was the fourth and final 220. Denton shook his head disgustedly.

"I couldn't help it," Cassidy said.

"Okay," Denton replied; he would have liked to have been able to show a little genuine anger at such a reckless display, but he knew how it felt and so remained quiet as they jogged a final slow mile around the battered old asphalt track.

During dinner there was none of the usual banter and Jeannie, after trying several times to relieve the tension, finally clammed up, allowing everyone to stew in the awful clink clank, chomp chomp of non-conversing diners who, when the pressure is on, cannot seem to keep their silverware and their own mastication under control. It was nerve-wracking for Denton and his wife, but Cassidy hardly noticed.

Now he was walking quickly, inexorably, towards the place he would complete the orb, set it gently adrift and leave it hard and shining until it was time.

It was one of the early balmy spring evenings when no one wanted to go inside. The campus was bustling; the lighted tennis courts were full and other players sat around waiting patiently, talking and laughing. Groups of three or four made their way to the nearer taverns, loaded cars roared to and fro, cyclists whirred by like mechanical butterflies, with books and Italian sandwiches strapped onto luggage racks.

It was the kind of scene Cassidy would have reveled in before, but the roar was now a tiny faraway buzz, growing by the minute, and as he walked on consumed by it, he was aware only that scenery was moving by as always, steadily and without apparent effort. He walked with the light, brisk, slightly pigeon-toed gait of an athlete, and though he walked very quickly, his breath would not have troubled the smallest candle. He took in even, deep measures of cool air with mechanical regularity, disinterestedly feeling inside his chest the huge heart muscle thumping its slow liquid drumbeat. His legs coiled and uncoiled with rhythm; sacks of anacondas. That part of it was done as well as he could humanly do it. Now he would see to the rest. He had made this pilgrimage many times before and though he would probably do so many times again, he never quite got over the eerie feeling that each time could be the last. Soon he was on the far side of campus where there were few dormitories and hence less activity, fewer lights, and none of the happy spring weekend noise.

Moths fluttered around the single streetlight as he went through the gate, and though the rubbery smell of wintergreen and sweat was as familiar to him as the musky woodiness of his room at Doobey Hall, his heart still jumped. The usual night joggers were out, and if they cast haughty glances at this mere stroller on their turf, the stroller paid no attention. He walked clockwise around the curve to the starting post at the beginning of the first turn, and stood there a few feet behind the parabolic bend of the starting stripe. He looked around and tried to imagine, in Hollywood-style flashes, the skeletal bleachers full, the now dark klieg lights burning down, the pageantry of the multi-hued sweatsuits from a thousand schools flashing by as athletes warmed up. He would be part of that faceless panorama too, until the announcement over the loudspeaker that never failed to twist his heart around with a spurt of adrenalized fear: FIRST CALL FOR THE MILE RUN. The all-consuming roar, the overwhelming psych would begin then and would build up until he stood ready on this line, at once controlled and near lunacy, fearless and terrified, wishing for the relief of the start, the misery of the end. Anything! Just let the waiting be done with! Cassidy toed the starting line there in street clothes and was able to get some of it: A few of the runners would run back and forth in their lanes, some would jiggle their fingers, some would jump up and down (all this more nervous than therapeutic). The orange-sleeved starter would walk among them with his pistol, saying, all right gentlemen, all right. He would talk gently, trying to somehow ease it for them, hoping to prevent a false start by calming them with the soft modulation of his voice. They were not as bad as sprinters, he knew, but they were still pretty skittish. The runners would gather nervously at the starting line, taking care not to look each other in the eye.

The starter would say: "There will be two commands, gentlemen, 'take your marks' and then the gun. All right, gentlemen, stand tall. Stand tall, gentlemen." He would sound a little like an executioner.

And Cassidy stood tall there in the dark, while a cool breeze ruffled the ragged lock of hair on his forehead, knowing that for that one instant there would be a kind of calm in the midst of all that pounding, roaring furor, a moment of serene calm before an unholy storm. There would be a single instant of near disbelief that it would finally be happening in a fraction of a second; finally happening after the months, the miles, the misty mornings; finally happening after the eighth or ninth now forgotten interval along the way somewhere that broke your heart once again. He would be leaning over tensely with the rest of them while the white lights burned down on them and for an awful split-second he would feel as if his legs had no strength at all. But then his heart would nearly explode when the pistol cracked. Cassidy felt a little of that now. He took a deep breath and began walking into the first turn, counterclockwise, the way of all races.

The first lap would be lost in a flash of adrenaline and pounding hooves. They would crash into the first turn in a bunch; the technical rule was that with a one-stride lead, a runner could cut in front. As with many such rules it was honored generally by the breach; the real-life rule of the first turn is exactly this: every man for himself. He would run powerfully into this turn, Cassidy thought, just like always, and he would use his elbows if he needed to make some space. Cassidy walked the turn, trying to imagine the sudden rasping of heavy breathing, the flashing of elbows and spiked feet all around. You had to be calm in the heavy traffic, he knew, hold back your impatience and control the panic; wait for opportunities. The first lap would be like that the whole way: fast, scary, with no pain or serious effort. The rampaging adrenaline and pent-up energy did that. The first lap was a process of burning it off; no one ever won a mile race on the first lap. Cassidy walked the far, dark straightaway. On the opposite side from the main bleachers, it was the loneliest part of the track. This was where the race-acute senses picked up the single calls of encouragement (usually from teammates), sometimes the idiotic suggestion called out by those who knew no better ("pick it up, pick it up"). There would be the occasional giggling of moronic teeny-boppers who did not quite know what they were laughing about. But those were the peripheral toys of a frenzied mind; the real work of the shining orb was monitoring the steadily droning pocketa pocketa of a human body hurtling along at a constant fifteen plus miles an hour. He walked through the far turn and up the straight to the starting post. Someone would be reading out times, probably around 57 or 58; assuming that no one went crazy during the first quarter. You'll hear the crowd again along here, he thought, particularly after we go through under 60; they won't be cheering for some godamned Finn, but you'll hear them just the same.

Whether a psychological thing or not, the second lap was when it always hit him, either right at the post or as they rounded the turn. The shocking enormity of the physical effort descended on him then and he knew from there on in it would be pretty grim business. At this point the carefully nurtured mental toughness, tempered by hours of interval work, would allow him to endure the shock to his system with relative ease and race on. He would be ready for it and he would know it was going to get far worse. He could be the best-conditioned athlete in the world but if his mind were not ready to accept the numbing wave at the start of the second lap, he would not even finish, much less hope to win. Cassidy walked through the turn, and again into the lonely back straight. By this time he would be concentrating on pace, not allowing himself to become frightened by the first hint of numbness and discomfort. It wouldn't be "pain" exactly, not at this point, but it would not be altogether pleasant either. It was here the pace might tend to slow, something he would have to watch, something he would damned well *prevent* if he had to. He would now go into his floating stride, the long ground-eaters, and he would think to himself: cover territory.

No one ever won a race on the second lap either but plenty of people lost them there. This would be the time for covering distance with as little effort as possible. Through the far turn and into the home straight again he tried for the feeling and thought he got it pretty well. Finally around at the starting post again he tried to get the awfulness of the start of the third lap, but could not. He had seen the drawn haunted look on his own face in mid-race photographs and still he could not get that feeling; it was contained there somewhere in the glistening orb, he knew, and would never get out. Denton was right about it, you could think about it all you want but you couldn't feel it until you were there again. He knew only that here, at the halfway point, he would be once again *in extremis.* It would flabbergast him to think (so he would do so only for an instant) that he was only half- way through it. He would have run the first half-mile faster than he could run a half mile flat out in high school (1:59.2) and he would have a long way to go.

He walked into the turn of the third lap. Here the real melancholy began, when the runner might ask himself just what in the hell he was doing to himself. It was a time for the most intense concentration, the iciest resolve. It was here the leader might balk at the pain and allow the pace to lag, here that positions shifted; those whose conditioning was not competitive would settle to the back of the pack to hang on, the kickers would move up like vultures to their vantage points at the shoulders of the front runners. It was a long, cruel lap with no distinguishing feature save the fact that it had to be run. Every miler knows, in the way a sailor knows the middle of the ocean, that it is not the first lap but the third that is farthest from the finish line. Races are won or lost here, records broken or forfeited to history, careers made or ended. The third lap was a microcosm not of life, but of the Bad Times, the times to be gotten through, the no-toys-at-Christmas, sittin'-at-the-bus-station-at-midnight blues times to look back on and, however weakly, laugh at if you can. The third lap was to be endured and endured and endured.

Cassidy reached the home straight again, thinking: No matter how bad it is, I can't let it lag here, whatever the cost. If I have to lead the whole mothering thing, I can't let it lag here. Then he was walking back by the post for what would be the gun lap. As soon as the pistol cracked, he would feel a tingling on the back of his neck and the adrenaline would shoot through his system again. A quarter of a mile to go and he would become a competitive athlete again, looking around to size up the situation, leaning a little into his stride and once again, even through the numbing haze then taking hold of his body, feeling pride in his strength.

Cassidy walked through the turn, pumping his arms a little, thinking of the nervous crowd noises as the pace began to pick up. Perhaps there would be only a small group left in it now; three, four maybe. But they would all have ambitions; no one ever ran down the back straight of the gun lap with the leaders without thinking he had a shot at it. On Cassidy walked along the lonely straight imagining the bristling speed as the pace heated up; there would be some last second evaluations, some positioning and re-positioning, and then finally the kicks, one by one or all at once, blasting away for the tightly drawn yarn across the finish line. Into the turn with only a 330 to go, everyone would be into it by then, everyone still in contention. Walton was known to kick from more than a 440 out, so surely his hand would be on the table. Coming out of the final turn just at the place Landy turned to look for the elusive Bannister, Cassidy walked into the final 110 straight and thought: Here, as they say, it will all be over but the shouting; you will fight the inclination to lean backwards, fight to keep the integrity of the stride, not let overeager limbs flail around trying to get more speed, just run your best stride like you have trained ten thousand miles to do and don't for god's sake let up here until the post is behind you. The die would be cast here, and no praying or cheering or cajoling or whimpering would change it. He had lost in this final straight before, but not as much as he had won here; neither held much in the way of fear or surprise once you were there. Such matters, as Denton had often said, were settled much earlier: weeks, months, years before; they were settled on the training fields, on the ten-mile courses, on the morning workout missed here or made up there. Other than maintaining and leaning at the tape, Denton had told him, there is not much you can do about it. Heart has nothing to do with it. In the final straight, *everyone* has heart.

Cassidy walked on past the finish line, across which someone would hold the taught yarn and blink as the runners flashed by. It was still more than 24 hours away, but standing there in the calm anonymous night five yards past the familiar white post, Quenton Cassidy knew at that instant the depth of his frenzied yearning to feel the soft white strand weaken and separate against his heaving chest.

The demons were in control; it no longer made him afraid.

The noise from the stadium carried out here but Cassidy didn't pay much attention. He liked doing most of the warmup ritual out on the cross-country course where he could think. The routine itself was automatic: four miles easy; then long, flowing striders, another mile easy, faster striders, then on with the spikes, some sprints on the track, then jog until time. It was the roar in his head he had to fight.

It had to be contained, suppressed, released only in that slow crescendo of calculated frenzy that would crest when the pistol cracked and he unleashed it all. The orb now floated gently in his mind, glistening, peaceful, hard as spun steel. It would hold all grief, all despair, all the race-woes of a body going to the edge; it would allow him to do what he had to do until there was nothing left.

Yes, he had decided long ago, it was better to get ready out here, where things were quieter, more normal, more like his everyday routine. Trying to warm up in the stadium, being close to the crowd, would make him jittery, causing the roar in his head to build in spurts, getting him there too early. It might upset the orb and when the despair descended he would have no place to put it. Or he might be in such a lunatic state as to turn the first 220 in 25 seconds out of sheer screaming hysteria. No, it was better out here, where it was quiet, where he could get ready in the same way he had done all the rest; it gave some comfort, this last bit of quietude.

He jogged slowly by the married student housing area, watching little children play under the trees. It was the eerie, almost magic, post-dinner hour when time stands still for a child, when all existence floats in a cool gray bath of dying day and Order is mercifully drawn from a chaotic infinity by a mother's come-home call.

"Erica! Jeremy!" Two little figures scuttled away in the shadows. He was getting farther and farther from the stadium, but he had plenty of time. Some other runners passed in pairs and threes, but no one spoke. One nodded at Cassidy but looked puzzled. What would they be thinking about this bearded Finn with the ragged blond hair?

Would they think they recognized him from some *Track and Field News* photo? Cassidy jogged on. It was early May; warm and subtropical flowers ruled the air dizzily: the kind of evening so heavy with promise as to make him wonder if his life could ever be quite the same again as it was now, while he was so vital, so quick, so nearly immortal; while his speed and strength was such that he could be called by only a handful of men on earth. Surely there could not be that many of us walking around like this, he thought.

He felt a strange brand of nostalgia now that it was so close; a nostalgia for this moment, for this next hour. The present was so poignant he had begun to reminisce already. He thought of Michelangelo's David pondering the stone: David, too, wondering if life would ever be the same.

Quenton Cassidy could be forgiven the solemnity of his mood. He was a young man about to go to the edge, a young man with every bit of the wherewithal to *get* to the edge. The inevitability of his journey there was never very far from his mind; he knew that before too very long he would be in mortal distress.

The time you won your town the race, we chaired you through the marketplace, he thought. Then a burst for twenty yards just to enjoy the sensation of sudden unleashed speed. He felt flushed and tired. That was common. You never really know how you feel, he thought, until the second lap. Sometimes not even then. Sometimes you don't even know until the last lap, *the stiller town.*

When he reached Lake Alice, he slowed to a walk and then stopped altogether. He stretched out on the grass and did hurdles and butterflies. Stretching was always a pleasant indulgence.

Then he undid the vertical zippers along the legs of his sweat pants and felt up and down both achilles tendons. All the knots and lumps were gone. Soft trails, he thought; godamn Denton and those beautiful soft trails. He had made it through the winter okay, only two colds and no real injuries. He was a man without an alibi.

Two runners in Villanova sweats went by, but he didn't recognize either of them. From far off the crowd yelled as someone cleared a height or broke the tape in a sprint preliminary, and his own body responded by dumping a shot of adrenaline into his system. He caught it quickly. Not yet, he thought, not even close yet.

It was a time for daydreams; the roar in his head was far off now and building, but it would grow on its own. The problem now was control.

Cassidy swooped into a strider, held it until the speed built to racing pace, held it, held it, then eased off, slowed to a stride, then a jog, and finally to a walk a hundred yards away. He was on the flat grass in the field across the street from the stadium; other athletes flashed by in blurs of color. He allowed himself some excitement on one of the striders and instantly felt the goose bumps on the back of his neck. He hadn't ever had it quite this bad before.

The noise from the stadium across the street added to the growing roar in his head but it didn't matter now; it was all right now. He allowed it to come, let it fuel his stride as he started up, slipped into it, and then built up speed until his legs seemed to come detached from him and he flew along without conscious effort. Other athletes were at it too, nervous, casting furtive glances at each other (never looking anyone in the eye). A lot of people talk themselves right out of races now, Cassidy thought. He looked at his watch: 7:38. The mile was scheduled for 8:20 but they were running behind. Still, a few minutes later he heard the call over the loudspeaker: FIRST CALL FOR THE MILE RUN. His heart twisted around in his chest like a wild animal; it was an absolutely wrenching shot of adrenaline. *They were going to run it after all! He was going to have to go through with it!* Then he got control again and steadied himself. Of course he was going to run this race. Take it easy. It was time to get into the infield and get used to being inside there, do the last touch-ups, put on the spikes: ritual, ritual, ritual. Then the last sprints, the final psyching. Jesus, he thought suddenly, why am I doing this? I ought to be in the three-mile. I've been doing all that bulk work and everything. I can't possibly be ready for a mile . . .

Then he steadied himself again; he thought of the last 220 the evening before and told himself: easy. He took a deep breath and walked over to pick up his bag. He had not spoken one word to anyone during the entire hour he had been out here. Runners flashed by. Everyone looked fast and fit as hell.

Then he caught himself again. Any of these mothers runs 3:58 in a godamn time trial in the dead of night and he'll damned well deserve to eat my lunch. Again he told himself: easy.

Inside the stadium a 178-pound lad who could bench press 300 pounds planted a 16-foot fiberglass pole in a tin box, inverted himself, and was tossed into the air a little more than 17 feet, 8 inches. When the crowd reacted to this feat with a roar, something flipped in Quenton Cassidy: His heart jumped so hard he thought his head was going to pop right off. The tumult in his head was like rush hour traffic in the bottom of a wishing well. He walked to the competitors' entrance and for a split second had a rush of ordinary civilian panic as well. He had forgotten completely about this disguise business.

But the little round face looked up from the clipboard and the cold stump of cigar went round and round.

"Well, let's see here, 242, why I guess that would be you, Seppo! Go right on in there boy and you have yourseff a good race, yuh hear? Say, that ain't true what they say about you Finn boys drinkin' reindeer milk, is it? Didn't think so."

Cassidy heard Brady Grapehouse cackling behind him as he went into the stadium.

How the hell did Denton arrange that, he wondered. But then he was on the inside and the special atmosphere, the blue-white lights, the wintergreen-laced, multi-colored carnival that is a major track meet sent his senses reeling, just as it always did. God, he thought, here I am again; here it all is and here am I with it all on the line one more time. He looked back uptrack to make sure it was clear and then jogged across the lanes to put his bag down. His heart skittered again, feeling the springy Tartan beneath his feet. Officials were running here and there, hurdle setters scurrying around, timers checking watches. No one noticed the tall runner in robin's egg blue as he began the methodical jogging on the inside grass lane. The infield was a mass of motion. Javelin throwers were slogging back and forth in their strange sideways gate, hurling imaginary spears at their long-extinct enemies, broad jumpers bounded around, high jumpers took their run-ups, and the runners of all sizes circled the track in various stages of their warmups. It made a three-ring circus look like a quilting bee.

SECOND CALL FOR THE MILE RUN. *Flash* went another shot of adrenaline through his veins—he took two gasping breaths that seemed wrenched from his body as if from one tossed suddenly into an icy sea. He got control again, this time with difficulty. Two laps, that's what the ritual called for. The roar inside his head drowned out the crowd altogether, except when they went wild over some performance. But Quenton Cassidy noticed nothing; he moved inside his own box. His gaze was starting to take on the trance quality, so that when he ran by Denton without seeing him, the older runner was not in the least surprised.

"Seppo!" he called. It took awhile to register. But then, of course it was all right. Denton would know an international runner, it would only be natural. Denton held out his hand when Cassidy circled back. He took it nervously.

"Sorry," Cassidy said. "He here yet?"

"Nope. But he will be. Best get your spikes on. How is it?"

"Banjo string. E flat."

Denton nodded.

"Bruce, I can hardly swallow."

"It's okay. It'll be like all the rest once you get moving. Beforehand's tougher. I would jog with you but I don't want to push our luck. Both Prigman and Doobey are here. Guess Walton's a big enough attraction to get even the football establishment. Anyone say anything to you?"

"No. Guess it's working. I'll be all right. I want to do it alone anyway." Denton noticed he was breathing fast, shallow, nearly gasping. It was not important he knew, so long as he had not torn himself all up inside over it already. It would be all right soon. He gripped Cassidy by the elbow.

"Cass, I . . ."

Cassidy looked Denton in the eye very briefly, then smiled. He gripped Denton's forearm and held it hard for a moment. Then he turned and ran off down the track. So, Denton thought to himself. He had seen the look in Cassidy's eye. *So there it is after all.*

Cassidy finished the rest of the ritual lap. Then it would be off with the flats, on with the spikes, off with the damp t-shirt, on with the nylon racing singlet: ritual ritual ritual. He had done it exactly this way hundreds of times.

A roar came from the crowd that he did not understand. Nothing was going on with the field events, and they were between races on the track. Then he looked over at the competitor's entrance and understood. A knot had formed, a chancre of humanity around the gate that suddenly opened up and expelled in a burst the fastest miler in history. The crowd went crazy as he ambled easily across the track with a wan smile, giving the stands a little wave. But Cassidy could tell, even from where he stood, the kind of look in his eye as he glanced quickly around the stadium and with a shudder dropped his bag to tug up the zipper on his turtleneck warmup. Little fluffs of hair on the back of Cassidy's neck went prickly again as Walton began his striders. He was nearly two inches shorter than Cassidy but looked as if he could run through a wall. He already had his spikes on. Every eye in the place followed him as he began doing his sprints on the back straight. The black suit of New Zealand, Cassidy thought, the silver leaf—*Baillie, Halberg, Snell.* His idols, his Gods! And now Walton.

Then he shook his head violently and swore under his breath at himself: *Godamn you!*

The roar had gone! He had been watching Walton slack-jawed like some high school kid and the roar in his own head had just gone! He jumped up, spikes on, and sprinted around the first turn, ignoring (not really seeing) Denton's bemused expression as he went by. When he slowed to a jog on the far side, calmer now, his jaw was set, his eyes fixed in a trance, and the orb rested inside a howling mindstorm. He did not realize that the figure flashing by on the turn had been Walton.

Now Cassidy took off his sweat bottoms, jogged around and left them at his bag; he kept the top on and jogged on. This was the way he always did it. They were getting ready to run off the high hurdles, the last race before the mile.

THIRD CALL FOR THE MILE RUN. ALL MILERS REPORT TO THE STARTER.

The last leap of his heart jounced him as he heard the announcement but by now he was accustomed to the shock. He made no move for the starting line, nor did any of the other milers. The high hurdles hadn't even been run and there would be several minutes of confusion afterwards while the timers sorted things out. The milers knew all these ancient rhythms, so they kept doing their striders and jogging. The gun cracked for the highs and they looked across the track at the race in the mildest sort of curiosity. After the hurdlers had swept past the finish line the announcer was after them again: ALL MILERS REPORT TO THE STARTER IMMEDIATELY. LAST CALL FOR THE ONE MILE RUN. It no longer jolted him because it was *all* jolt now. He barely heard the loudspeaker, such was the roar in his head. When he took off his sweat top he realized he had not put on his racing singlet. He was still in the wet t-shirt! Godamn it! How the hell could I have . . .

Then he got control again, jogged rapidly over to his bag and changed. There was still plenty of time even though most of the milers were on the track milling around. The timers were in disarray from the previous race and the starter was walking among the runners as Cassidy knew he would. All right, gentlemen, he was saying, all right, listen to the starting instructions gentlemen, as the runners paced back and forth, jiggling and jumping up and down, avoiding eyes, gasping their little shallow gasps, shaking out legs that didn't need shaking, and generally living their last few seconds of torment. Cassidy jogged out among them, feeling feathery light now in just racing nylon and spikes; he felt as though he weighed about 10 pounds. He wore the white and blue Adidas 9.9's that had never been second.

Cassidy, too, took up the jiggling and pacing. The announcer was making introductions, but no one seemed to be paying attention. Walton was in lane one, so naturally they started with the outside lane. All eyes were on just one person, the powerful looking Kiwi in the all black nylon with a little silver fern over the breast. There was polite applause for the Finn in lane three, but when the announcer started on the final introduction, he didn't get to the gold medals, the world records, the endless titles, before the place was a madhouse. Everyone knew it all already. Walton jogged out a few steps and waved. Denton stood by the first turn in his navy blue USA team sweats, watching. You have to learn the little smile and wave, he thought, that's one part of it maybe you don't think about beforehand. I'll bet that's the last thing old John wants to be doing right now. Even before a race like this.

Cassidy thought: easy easy easy. Be careful through the turn and get through the first lap. Then start *thinking*. Easy easy easy. Save your goodies.

"All right gentlemen," the starter was saying in his executioner's tone, gun hanging down at the end of his fluorescent orange sleeve, "a two-command start, gentlemen, 'take your marks' and then the gun. Is that clear? All right gentlemen, stand tall. Stand tall, gentlemen . . ."

The crowd hushed suddenly.

High up in the stands very nearly directly across from the starting post, Andrea sat beside the very excited umbrella man and thought: It's *him*.

The starter was backing out from among them now, still saying, "Stand tall, gentlemen, stand tall . . ."

And Quenton Cassidy stood tall in the night as a very slight breeze brushed his burning face. At last, he thought, at last it is here. It is really here.

The starter began backing off the track in quick little steps, raising his gun arm at the same time. For just an instant, Cassidy looked over to lane one and saw John Walton staring right back at him.

"TAKE YOUR MARKS!"

Cassidy's heart tried to leap out through his thin taut skin and hop into his wet hands. But outwardly it was all very calm, very serene, just as always, and it seemed to last a tiny forever, just like that, a snapshot of them all there on the curved parabola of a starting line, eight giant hearts attached to eight pairs of bellows-like lungs mounted on eight pairs of supercharged stilts. They were poised there on the edge of some howling vortex they had run ten thousand miles to get to. Now they had to run one more.

CRACK!

There was the tiny little flutter during which he thought his legs were going to fail completely, but then they were away, out of their crouches and fairly bolting, bounding out and away, not even smoothly yet, burning off the first rush of excitement and fear. But here Cassidy found himself about two yards in front already and probably right on schedule for his maniac 25-second 220. Standing on the inside of the curve, Denton flashed by and said quietly: tuck in. Cassidy tucked in.

He didn't recognize the green singlet, but it occurred to him that it had to be the runner in lane two. Walton was obviously behind them somewhere, unworried and unrushed. Then Cassidy glanced again and recognized the Irishman. Of course! He had hardly paid attention to anyone else in the race. The first 220 went by as always, giddily, And as they flashed by the white post someone gave them an unofficial split: 26.2 Yeeow! Too fast! No wonder Walton didn't hop right on up there. But there was no chance to look around. Cassidy could sense runners on his outside shoulder and twice he felt someone clipping his heel. He was running almost abreast of the Irishman, sharing the lead actually, but the real truth was that he was more surrounded than anything else. As they came out of the second turn he dared a quick glance to the inside and saw Walton, striding comfortably, head down, watching the feet flashing by in front of him; all business. Okay, thought Cassidy, stay right there. Right where you are.

It was an untenable attitude, he knew, but at this moment before it all got wild and bad it was easy to entertain such facile delusions of control. The crowd shrieked as they passed the starting post in a knot. But did he hear that? Probably not. He thought he heard one single shout: Go Cassidy.

". . . fifty SIX, fifty SEVEN, fifty EIGHT . . ." They were going by the post. Denton, flashing by again on the inside, said quickly: "Fifty seven five too fast." Remarkable, he said it almost in a conversational tone, but Cassidy heard it distinctly. All right Bruce, it's too godamn fast, what the hell am I supposed to do about it?

The announcer was saying: "O'RORK, THEN KAITAINEN, HARRIS, AND JOHN WALTON OF NEW ZEALAND . . ."

Then it started to come on him, as it always did here. He usually felt it in the gut first; a slow, acid kind of strain, systems beginning to panic down there; intestines, other organs closing down for the duration, preparing for whatever dire project was in progress. And the legs now started to get the first wave of lactic acid numbness, the start of a deep ache that would all too soon become the ambulatory paralysis of the final straightaway. Even this early he was getting all the old feelings, thinking: God here it is again! Back in it again and I had forgotten completely what it was like. Forgotten altogether. Shoulders and arms starting now. Pay attention godamn it!

The orb bobbed gently, taking it all in, retaining it, keeping it quiet inside the steely interior and allowing him to think. He concentrated on his task.

Even from the far straightaway he could hear the crowd grow uneasy and then erupt, but before he could react he sensed a body coming up on his shoulder and then flinging by to take the lead. A roar came from across the field. Cassidy pondered calmly. Who was it? It wasn't Walton. A short runner in all red. Wisconsin? St. Johns? He racked his brain, but came up with nothing. Was he a rabbit or just some guy looking for a few seconds of glory, leading John Walton in a mile? Cassidy hung where he was all through the turn coming into the home straight for the second time, then glanced back to the inside and saw Walton, this time a little more labored, but still running casually, eyes cast slightly downward, watching the feet in front of him. The roar was deafening as they went by, but this time he was sure he heard it, there was no mistake, several voices called out: Go Cassidy! ". . . one fifty SEVEN, one fifty EIGHT, one fifty NINE . . ."

Then two things happened almost at once. First Bruce Denton flashed by, said calmly: one fifty seven good. And a split second after that the crowd erupted again as a black-suited runner bolted by in a savage burst of speed: *WALTON!* What the hell is he doing, Cassidy thought.

The announcer, excited, came on: "AND NOW WALTON HAS TAKEN THE LEAD FROM HARRIS AS THEY WENT BY THE HALF IN . . ."

Cassidy couldn't hear the rest.

Jesus, what is he doing, Cassidy thought as he watched the black-suited figure easily slide by the runner in red, and keep on, showing no sign of slowing down. Cassidy was really feeling it now, starting the third lap, the old intestine-sliding-down-the-leg *extremis* that comes at the precise middle of a race when it dawns on you that there is a long melancholy way to go. But there was Walton, *pulling away*.

Quenton Cassidy did not know it, of course, but here was the decision for all time, the decision that led him up the path to the higher callings or off on a side road to end up in the bushes somewhere. There was really no thinking to it; his face now set firmly in the race mask, showing nothing more than a detached strained interest, he let out a surge and found himself fairly flying around the Irishman down the back straight. Red shirt was already fading badly from his burst and Cassidy was by him quickly too. He pulled into lane one and thought: that was too fast! You could have done that better. But it was too late for recriminations, he set about hauling in the black suit in front of him, even now blending into the night, spikes flashing in a blur ahead. And this: from across the field, the calls, more of them, louder, most positive, beseeching now: CASSIDY! CASSIDY! The announcer: ". . .WALTON OF NEW ZEALAND WITH KAITAINEN SEVEN YARDS BACK . . ."

His shoulders ached now with the heavy strain of lactic acid, so he pumped harder, concentrated on his form, trying to cover ground smoothly. Now was the time he wanted to be floating, covering ground with as little effort as possible, but he found himself straining just to hold pace. And Walton looked so easy! Was he of this earth? Could it really be this much of a joke to him, running this pace without a care in the world? Cassidy could not feel his legs but that was all right. He was flying along in the night concentrating so hard on the black-suited demon out there that he was actually surprised to hit the second turn. He cursed mentally when he found himself flung by his own momentum out into the second lane, then got it under control, leaned into the turn and got back on pattern. A stupid mistake, he thought, and it cost me two yards.

But coming out of the turn into the straight he felt it. He had contact. Walton had come back to him some and he had contact from five yards back. And he had the power. He knew that too as they sped down the straight, really feeling it now, the lactic acid aching through his body, but also starting the build-up, getting excited knowing that this time it would not be long, that it wasn't going to go on forever after all.

Down past the stand and this time Cassidy heard, unbelieving, what they were chanting as the two figures went by the white starting post: CASS-A-DAY! CASS-A-DAY! CASS-A-DAY! Even the announcer no longer played the game: ". . . IT'S WALTON FOLLOWED BY . . . CASSIDY OF SOUTHEASTERN . . ."

Dick Doobey, nearly blind with rage, blood vessels standing out on his soft red face, jumped up from his seat in the officials' section and started out the gate onto the track to do God only knew what when he ran smack into the really quite startlingly muscled arm of Mike Mobley, that was stretched across the opening, his huge hand holding the far post in a death grip. Mobley challenged him for an instant with a gaze full of contempt and pity, then the giant turned back to the race and the chant: CASS-A-DAY! CASS-A-DAY! CASS-A-DAY!

His face ashen, Doobey slumped into the nearest seat he could find. Up in the press box, in icy silence, Steven C. Prigman turned to look at the gentlemen of the press, some of whom waited for his reaction; he smiled ruefully, turned back to the race.

And Denton flashing by now: Two fifty five flat. Wait.

Then the gun: CRACK! And the hair on the back of his neck standing up as it always did. Cassidy thought: four hundred yards to go *jesus god what a cost just to be here and he's slipping away if I could just hold him now he's been flat out for . . .*

But Walton was not flat out at all. He suddenly looked back at Cassidy and Cassidy thought he saw a tiny flicker in those hard eyes: surprise. Not concern. Just a mild kind of surprise.

And that followed by a little burst so powerful and quick it broke Cassidy's heart. *God how can he do that?* Quenton Cassidy, sadly now, was starting to tie up halfway down the back straight and all he could think was: *son of a bitch what has he been doing running from the front?* He never does that. Now Cassidy's arms and shoulders getting worse and worse as the orb strains and bounces around inside, trying to hold it all, Cassidy feeling now the process of his form starting to degenerate involuntarily, he wanly remarks to himself that this must be how death is, *and look how easy dear god he looks up there. So this is how it is, this is exactly how it is, how he beats you and beats you and beats you.*

She had stood with everyone else the last time by and though she knew umbrella man was unobtrusively observing her reactions now, she studied Cassidy's face when he went by and saw in it the totally dispassionate look of the runner at his toil; alert but not excited, full of strain and some unnamed misery, but so obviously showing no emotion, masking darker secrets. What was it he had said about demons? She had some idea of what Cassidy and Walton were experiencing because the other runners, some twenty yards behind, did not hold it as well as these two. Walton to her looked simply intimidating, as if he had been born at full stride; his torso was powerful for a runner and his every stride suggested merciless strength held in reserve. He was haughty in his power and it was somehow chilling to watch.

But then she had looked at Quenton Cassidy, saw the same objective, emotionless look about him, watched the sleek, machinelike workings of legs that were longer than Walton's. And suddenly she had seen him from a different perspective: he too looked intimidating. And something very deep inside her turned a little as she realized that she was, after all, frightened for him, for this task he had taken upon himself. Her eyes had flooded and she stood there in her confusion and turmoil, not caring that umbrella man was staring at her.

CASS-A-DAY! CASS-A-DAY! CASS-A-DAY!

He was starting to get the white haze even this early; it would be very bad when it all caught up, but of course that was no consideration now. *Come on you son of a bitch*, he thought, but he knew he was just hanging on. It was all going slowly downhill and Walton had about eight yards on him still. Cassidy could feel the muscles in his neck start to tighten, pulling his lower lip downwards into an ugly grimace; he knew this was one of the last signs, this death sneer. *So this is what happens! You just don't get him, that's all! The son of a bitch just keeps on going and it ends and you don't get him ever!*

Cassidy adjusted his lean a little forward; that seemed to help some, but the neck was getting tighter and he felt his arms beginning to stiffen. By the time they got out of the turn and into the last straight, he knew they would be really bad. All down the back straight Cassidy tried to reel him in, but it was no good. Eight yards. Eight yards, *Eight yards!* The strain was apparent to those close to the track, on the exhale breath he made little gasps: *gahh! gahh! gahh!* His eyes were starting to squeeze up shut but he could hardly see through the white haze anyway.

The chant roared across the field, beseeching, hopeful, frenzied.

CASS-A-DAY! CASS-A-DAY! CASS-A-DAY!

Shut up! Shut up! I'm not your godamned hero! All down the back straight he stared at the fleeing black suit through the wrinkled slits he had left for eyes, stared at the black suit and wished they would all leave him alone. Just leave him the hell alone with his misery and defeat.

That's when he saw it.

Almost imperceptible, but there it was just the same: the left shoulder dipped suddenly, then the right leg shot out a little further than usual, and that was it: back to normal stride.

Walton was tying up too.

So that's the way it is. Not so casual after all.

Cassidy bore down, bore down, and finally began reeling him in, all during the final turn, all the way around he pulled him in, inch by inch, as his mouth was drawn more and more into the ugly grimace by the spastic neck muscles. Inch by inch the black suit came back until finally they broke clear of the turn and there it was: John Walton was three feet ahead of him with a hundred and ten yards of Tartan stretching out in front of them to the finish line. There was utter pandemonium in the stands as the chant degenerated into a howling, shrieking din.

Quenton Cassidy moved out to the second lane, the Lane of High Hopes, and ran out the rest of the life in him.

All through the last 50 yards he had looked through the two fogged slits of windows at the howling slow motion nightmare going on around him as he rigged up in true fashion, getting the jaw/shoulder lock and the sideways final straight fade as he began to lose all semblance of control; he peered out at all this as the orb was about to burst letting all the poison flood out, peered at it and quite calmly wondered: *when will it all end?*

He felt more than saw Walton come back up to his shoulder, entertained an idle curiosity about who would get it, but then went back to wistfully concentrating on those green inches of Tartan passing slowly, slowly beneath his feet.

The last 10 yards his body was a solid block of lactic acid, with those straining neck muscles pulling his lip down and his back arched, trapezia trying to pull him over backwards. And all the way Quenton Cassidy is telling himself:

Not now . . . it hurts but go all the way through do not stop until you are past it you cannot afford to give the son of a bitch anything . . . so holdit holdit holdit jesus christ hold it holdit holditHOLDITHOLDIT HOLD IT . . .

Finally with a scream and a violent wrenching motion he shook himself loose from this terrible force that gripped him, forced himself into a semblance of a lean and it was over . . .

. . . or at least he thought it was over if it was not all some bad dream and he is gasping simply wrenching air from around him feeling death surely imminent here beside him crying and going hands-to-knees, stumbling *please leave me, please I don't want, please I need to breathe . . .*

And then Denton has him around the waist and is lifting him up off the ground, please Bruce put me down I can't breath but Denton is taking him off, away from them, dragging the tall brown limp doll which apparently cannot stand on its own, holding him up painfully and saying: Remember it Quenton, godamn you better remember it because it doesn't ever quite get any better are you listening to me godamn you? and Cassidy forcing his eyes open finally and seeing Denton through the white haze and seeing that he is crying too. Oh Bruce I'm listening please let me go jesus it hurts and Denton lets him go hands-to-knees to pray to the runner's finish line god but Denton leans over and whispers: three fifty two five, Cass. He kicked from 500 yards out but it was you, Quenton Cassidy, it was YOU all the way. You know you beat him don't you, Quenton godamn it?

But Cassidy can't do anything but hold his knees and make his little gagging noises and nod, wishing everyone would just leave him the hell alone so he could see if he was going to live or not.

WHEELBARROW

Eddy Orcutt

(1936)

Except for some of the upper-bracket faculty members, and a Scandinavian gardener who confined his conversation to the language of the flowers and weeds, Coach Foley was the only person on the campus who didn't call Barrow Taylor by his nickname.

Everybody else—even Barrow Taylor's girl, when he had one—called him Barrow; and once in a while, jokingly or affectionately or both, somebody called him Wheelbarrow, which was the name's original form. But Coach Foley always addressed him just as Taylor, and let it go at that, because he and Barrow were strangers.

"All right, Taylor; I think I'll run you in the mile today."

A stranger can't call a man by his nickname—particularly if he happens to be the stranger who invented it.

Barrow's name in the registrar's card index was Austin Taylor, and he'd come to Paxton from some flag-stop high school up in the San Joaquin Valley. Somehow, from plodding around in country track meets where 5:30 was dandy time for the one-mile run, the boy had wanted to be a runner. He had that craving for the feel of a level track and the thrill of a race—however he'd come by it, he had it—and he'd picked Paxton for his college because Martin Foley was there. He'd heard about Foley. Foley had fought it out in his time with Bonhag and Lightbody and Mel Sheppard, and the little bronze Victory on his office desk was a trophy from the Olympic 1500 meters at London. When he went to coaching, he had built his rep on the distance runners he developed—Hal Brown and Kelly at Oberlin, and boys like Ray Adkinson and the Sturges brothers at Paxton. So Austin Taylor had come to Coach Foley's college, figuring that Foley could make a runner out of even a big-boned, six-foot kid with a build like a blacksmith. The kid was strong as a horse, a glutton for work, and he terribly wanted to run. He had the dumb notion that Martin Foley could do the rest.

Foley might have guessed at some of this if he'd been watching the boy's face, that first time they met, back in Barrow's freshman year. He might have read hero worship in the way the big boy looked at him, and he might have seen the glance Barrow gave the Olympic trophy on Foley's desk—the kid's look would have suited the Holy Grail itself.

"But what do you want cross-country for?" Foley asked. "You ought to be playing football, buddy."

The kid had come in with a batch of other freshmen to take a physical exam and sign for cross-country, and he had stripped to the waist for Doc Weymiller to lay the stethoscope on him. So Foley wasn't watching the boy's face. He was inspecting a chest and shoulders and a pair of arms that belonged on a heavyweight.

"I want to get ready for track," Austin Taylor said. "I want to be a runner."

Foley chuckled at the big boy's blush, because he figured Barrow was putting up a stall. In cross-country a lad can do as much or as little as he pleases for his physical-ed. credits—the only requirement is that he go out for a jog three times a week, and run all three of the interclass races at the end of the season—and it is often elected by boys who do not wish to dally with sterner forms of exercise.

"All right; have your fun," Foley said. "I just work here." The stall was particularly funny in Barrow's case—a boy with Barrow's build had no more business in a distance run than he had in a butterfly ballet.

The coach didn't see Austin Taylor again until track season began.

Probably the boy had already acquired the habit of laughing at himself a little when the going was tough, because he was terribly slow and he didn't want people to guess how hard he tried. In the cross-country finals he finished back in the column of squads with the gold-brickers who were just earning their credits, and nobody could have known that he was trying any harder than they were. They finished with a laugh, and he was always laughing, too, and nobody gave him a tumble. When the track season began, then, he dawned on Coach Foley as a complete surprise.

Foley wound up the first day of regular training with an eight-lap workout for the distance men. They'd all been out for cross-country and they'd had a week of light work, limbering up and getting used to their spikes, so he sent them through a full eight laps on the first day.

"Jog three," he ordered, "and run the fourth. Then jog the fifth, run the sixth, jog the seventh and run the eighth. Got it? Let's go!"

He sent the squad away, then strolled over to watch a couple of high jumpers while the men jogged the first three laps. At the end of the third, he turned and gave them the office to step out. He went back to the finish line, sat himself down on a lime barrel there and pulled out his pad of yellow paper and a stub of pencil. He sheltered the pad with his hand and made marks on it; the boys loafing around the finish thought he was making secret notes, but he was not. He was making marks.

Red Myer was the only freshman among the leaders when the runners came around. He was running easily, up with Cronin and Miller. Foley said: "All right, loaf a lap now!"

He stood up and stretched. He was a lean, brown, sardonic figure of a man, and he watched his runners with a kind of lazy shrewdness, barking a comment now and again in a voice that carried clearly. "You, Stitt!" he called, as the field came by. "Cut down that kickup!" There were five or six men running together—no new faces. "Murdock! You can't run with your hands in your pockets! Use your arms!"

Foley watched the stragglers pass—half a dozen freshmen and perhaps a hopeless half-dozen sophs and juniors. "All right; take it easy!" he ordered.

Then—

The coach was just lounging back onto the lime barrel when Austin Taylor hove up toward the finish line.

The leaders had gone on, and the field had gone, and the stragglers had passed. And then came Austin Taylor. Running alone. Whoofing the perspiration off his nose at every stride. Laughing a little at himself, with a grin of good-natured despair on his face. And because he was far behind, and he knew that Foley and the bystanders would be watching, he was trying to pump up a little speed. He was trying hard.

The big boy ran with a forward lean from the waist, like a large hussar beginning a bow. He held his big arms rigid and slightly bent, the fists clenched. He pounded along powerfully, picking them up and laying them down, but he lurched and floundered as though the running track had been freshly plowed. He looked fearfully like the slow motion of a man wheeling sand into a cement mixer.

And it was no part of Coach Foley's technique to be caught speechless. He stared suddenly, and he crumpled the yellow pad a little, but he retained the use of his voice. Self-defense, in a way. He spoke up.

"Come, come, buddy!" the coach cracked. "Where's your wheelbarrow?"

And you can get the same effect, if you want it, by walking up gently to a five-year-old child and slapping it suddenly in the face.

Of course, if anybody else had pulled that crack, Wheelbarrow Taylor would have joined in the laugh and gone on plugging—he was used to being kidded. But Martin Foley, Olympic runner—the boy had come five hundred miles to get Foley's help, and he was trying so hard.

Wheelbarrow Taylor kept on. But he gave the coach one brief, dazed glance, and Coach Foley knew suddenly and swiftly what that glance meant. And then the bystanders' cackle of laughter hit Foley at the midriff and sickened him a little.

The boy still wore that look of grim amusement when he finished; the leaders lapped him, and the bystanders kidded him good-naturedly, but he went on and finished. And Coach Foley waited for him. When he spoke then, his tone was the casual, serious one that he'd have used to the best man on the squad.

"Keep jogging. Get under the shower as quick as you can, and take a good rubdown afterward. Don't take a chance on stiffening up."

"Yes, sir."

And from then on, through all the four years of Wheelbarrow Taylor's hopeless clowning on the track, that was their formula. Barrow's running was a joke, but Foley pretended that he didn't see it. Barrow pretended that he didn't mind it. And up to the day of Barrow Taylor's last race, each guarded his pretense against the other; between themselves the two held strictly to the careful forms that strangers use.

"Taylor, I think you'll find it will improve your sprint if you can learn to keep your chin down, even when you're tired."

"Yes, sir. I'll watch it."

So finally they came to Barrow's last season and its end.

The conference meet was delayed that year because of the Far-Western A.A.U. and the Olympic trials, and on the sultry May afternoon of Barrow's last race the finality of college commencement was already in the air, like the summer heat and the aroma of parched mesa grasses in the faint breeze over Alumni Field. The kids in the training quarters felt it, waiting with Coach Foley for time to be called, and the crowds drifting into the bleachers felt it. And because of it—because a time was ending, and old Barrow Taylor would never have another chance to run for Paxton—the boys had ribbed it up for Barrow to win his final race.

Barrow didn't know about it, of course, but everybody else did. And Coach Foley knew about it in plenty of time.

They liked Barrow, there at Paxton. They'd taken up the nickname because it was absolutely pat, and they'd shortened it to Barrow, and most of the kids had forgotten that he had any other name. But long before he had a nickname and long before his running became a campus joke, people had liked the quick, bashful grin that Barrow had, and the pleasantly surprised look in his eyes when anybody said "Hello" to him. They'd liked him when he was a freshman, and when he was a senior he still had the same kind of a grin and the same look in his eyes, and everybody still liked him. Not just girls—everybody. Though by that time he did have a girl, as a matter of fact.

The kids had laughed at his running, because it was funny, but they liked him; and now that he was wearing the Paxton colors for the last time, they wanted him to win his race. And they had it all fixed.

The campus grapevine brought it to Coach Foley some hours before the men reported for early lunch at the training table, and he thought it over carefully while Oxy and Caltech and Whittier and S.C.U. began pouring their delegations into the college town, and the campus edged up toward suspense, awaiting the meet's first gun. It was Coach Foley's business to figure out what the score was, and he did. In the chill of the locker room, its air made ice-cold and nervous by contrast with the blazing sunlight outside, he came to his decision.

"Like hell," Martin Foley said to himself.

He, too, knew that feel of senior year and final things and last chances, and when his calm decision was made, the feel of those things reached him swiftly. That guarded pretense between him and Barrow Taylor had a deep tension in it, and now the feel of last things threatened to snap it into something like resentment, like anger.

It was true that Barrow had tried desperately hard, all through those four years, to learn to run. But it happened that Coach Martin Foley had been bearing down, too, almost as desperately.

"Look, Taylor. You've got to learn to use your arms. Pull straight ahead with them. Lift and pull with your stride. . . . Like this. You've got big arms, and all they're doing for you now is tie you up.

"Reach out— Listen, Taylor. Take a lap, now, lifting the knees and reaching for stride. Get the feel of it."

Casually, patiently, shrewdly—

"Never try to pass a man, Taylor, with a steady pull; you'll just carry him along with you that way. Pull up behind him, then cut out fast, see? Uncork all the sprint you've got. Cut out around him and get your six-foot lead and cut in again. Do it fast, before he knows what's going on.

"And if he tries to pass you, listen to his stride and try to outguess him. Just when you figure he's going to begin sprinting, lengthen out and pull away. D'y' see?"

And the net result of it all had been that Barrow laboriously mastered every detail except one—somehow he never could manage to put all the details together. What he had at the last was not running form but a parody on it.

Sheer strength and guts and long training finally got him a place on the team, but what he showed on the track was a burlesque of running. Perfect in every detail, but funny at every stage of a race.

Because he was strong as a horse, never quite managing to spend himself completely, even his hopelessness on the last lap was never pitiful. It was funny. Wheelbarrow Taylor himself laughed at it.

Those kids on the bleachers would have to laugh. They'd cheer him because they liked him, and because he was game and he'd been trying for a long time, but they'd have to laugh too. Even in that last meet, when it was all set for him to win a race, because it was his last and because he was going away soon, they'd laugh while they cheered him.

Foley's distance men had had things their own way that year. The only man who'd given them trouble was Dink Morosco, of S.C.U.—he'd beaten Red Myer once in the mile, and the conference race figured to be another tough battle. But Paxton figured to finish one-two-three in the two-mile, that last day—Ray Kane, George Kessler and Barrow Taylor. Kane, with his hard mile for an excuse, was going to get sick and drop out of the two-mile, so the grapevine said. Then Kessler would lag in the late laps, fall back, fake a cramp and give Wheelbarrow Taylor the office to pass him. It was all set. So Barrow would win a race finally, and have it under his belt, and the crowd would have the warm feel of laughing and cheering for a lad it liked. And this ending would be a happy one, among so many endings.

"Like hell!" Martin Foley said.

Because if Barrow Taylor won that kind of a race, it couldn't be long before the boy knew or guessed what had happened—everybody else on the campus would know it by nightfall, and somebody would talk. And then, instead of one win to remember from his four years of trying, Barrow would have to remember a fake. Another laugh. One more joke.

In the nervous chill of the training quarters, waiting for the call, Coach Foley looked carefully at his watch.

"All right, boys! We're due in three minutes! Shake it up!"

So the meet began and the teams gathered in a blaze of open sun that made the live oaks at the rim of Alumni Field seem shimmering with distance. Suspense tightened, and the hurry and shuffle of the crowd in the stands made a kind of callous obbligato to the blaring of the band and the bawling of the announcer's megaphone:

"In the first event—"

Foley sent his sprinters up to the start of the hundred, but he lagged behind them. He scratched a foolish design on his pad of yellow paper, while he watched Barrow Taylor stroll up the track and cross over to the stands. Then he followed.

Tousle-headed in his blue robe, Wheelbarrow reached the west end of the bleachers, and a girl in cool green came down to the rail to meet him. Catherine Leal, her name was, and she was going to get a diploma next month, along with Barrow.

"Hello, Cath!"

"Hello, Barrow. Good luck today!"

Others interrupted their little ceremony: "Hi, Barrow!" "Go get 'em, Barrow!" The handshake was brief. But that was what it meant to have a girl in senior year; Foley knew how those things were. She wouldn't mind coming down to meet a man and touch his hand and give him good luck before they called him out for his race.

Barrow flushed a little, smiling up at her.

Foley timed his move.

"Oh, Taylor!"

The kid looked around.

Foley's voice carried calmly across the track: "I think I'll run you in the mile today, Taylor. Better jog down to the turn and begin warming up."

"The mile?"

The megaphone boomed: "Last call for the hundred-yard dash! Sprinters at the start! First call for the mile! First call for the one-mile run!"

Foley glanced at the boy. "Yeh, better start warming up," he repeated.

He saw Catherine's eyes widen. He knew that she caught her breath. He knew that there was a little circle of stunned silence in the crowd across the track. But he made his glance careless, looked Barrow Taylor in the eye, and saw there the thing he had asked for.

Sheer anger—almost hate.

Barrow didn't know anything about a fix for him in the two-mile, but he did know that he could place in it, and that Foley suddenly was going to keep him out of it. Foley was going to shove him into a race where he didn't have a chance. And Foley was doing it for no reason, casually, at the last minute, without warning, like a little tin god who didn't give a damn.

But Foley turned his back.

Foley drew lines on his yellow pad and watched the sprinters fiddling at their marks. Barrow crossed the track behind him. Foley still had to be careful. It was all right for Barrow to hate him, and it was all right for those kids on the bleachers to buzz about him; Foley had asked for that, and there it was, and he didn't have to like it. But he had to keep his head.

"Timers ready!"

"Judges ready!"

When the hundred was over, Coach Foley went quietly through the push and excitement at the finish line, and met his milers at the turn of the track. Red Myer began: "Look, Barrow here says—"

Myer, with a tough race coming up, was a little white around the lips and there was a puzzled hostility in his eyes. Foley cut him short. "Listen, Red," he said, "I want you to get Morosco this time. He'll want to make the pace again; grab it away from him. The only way to win this race is to stick your nose out in front and stay there!"

Red wanted to say something, but it was Barrow who spoke. "Never mind it, kid," he said to Red.

Foley turned quietly to Ray Kane: "Follow Red's race as close as you can," he said. "The first lap will be too fast, but stick with it. If you're in sight at the three-quarters, you've got a chance." Kane's glance was angry. He said nothing.

At the starting line, the clerk was calling the roll:

"All right, you milers! This way!"

Foley said: "That's all. Good luck." And then, very carefully, very carelessly, he remembered Wheelbarrow Taylor. "Oh, Taylor," he said. He smiled. "You can run this any way you want to." His smile took on a brief edge of amusement. "Use your judgment," he said.

He turned his back while the men went to their marks.

Foley knew the dread of the slow minutes before a race begins—the draw for positions, the bumbling instructions from judge and starter, the final hush when the starter's commands begin:

"On your marks!"

Foley held the yellow pad in his left hand, the pencil under his thumb. He held a stopwatch in his right. He steadied it.

"Get set!"

Then—

Coach Foley clicked the watch with the crack of the gun, and he stared forward suddenly, sweating cold in the hot sunlight, watching Wheelbarrow Taylor lunge fiercely into the start.

The crowd's yell went up, swift and shrill, when the gun barked, and the runners' spikes scratched in the hard-breathing scramble of the start. And Foley, having seen what he wanted to see, blundered away, walking into the infield. He felt caved in, hollow, light-headed. Somebody bumped into him.

"Look at that! Gee, the fool!"

Foley, not seeing anybody or anything just then, spotted the voice—King, one of the quarter-milers. King was yelling, and the yell had amazement and a laugh in it. The yell of the crowd hit that same note. The fool. Sure. Gone hog-wild.

"Bughouse! Lookit! The guy's gone bugs!"

Foley said: "Shut up, King. Go on over and lie down. You got a race coming up in ten minutes."

"Did you see that? That—"

"Save it," Foley ordered. His voice was all right. He gave his quarter-miler the eye. And then he looked carefully over toward where the runners were coming out of the turn into the backstretch—Wheelbarrow Taylor was leading Dink Morosco by five yards. Red Myer was tying in behind Morosco, running smoothly. Kane was coming up on the outside, out of a pack that was already stringing out. Wheelbarrow Taylor was fighting with the lift and pull of his big arms, pumping, striding out.

Foley felt sick.

There it was. There was Barrow Taylor's last race. And Foley, playing the coach's role of Almighty God, had pushed the boy out in front to run his heart out. But the coach knew, too, what the end had to be. He felt sick.

Over in the backstretch, Morosco stepped it up a notch, as if planning to catch Barrow on the second turn; then gave it up, let Barrow increase his lead. Myer followed, Kane still moving up.

Foley was afraid to look at the stopwatch.

The crowd's yell continued; it was still high with a great, roaring laugh, but the laugh had a thrill to it. The men at the shot-put circle were standing still, watching; a man wearing the S.C.U. scarlet and gold held the sixteen-pound shot cradled in both hands, delaying his trial while he stared across at the runners. And in the little knots of men in blankets and bathrobes, scattered across the field—the athletes waiting to compete—the boys were scrambling to their knees, getting to their feet, watching.

Barrow Taylor led the field into the turn, around the turn, headed into the straightaway. The bleachers piled into a new uproar, and the yell along the running lanes drowned out the Paxton band.

Foley stepped toward the finish line. He watched the line, forced himself to look calmly at the dial of his clock. Barrow crossed—

Sixty-one!

The shape of laughter on Barrow Taylor's face was angry, and the crowd was not laughing at all. Barrow was pumping and pounding, as he always had, in that parody on form that he'd spent four years to learn. He was holding his chin down, staring straight ahead, stretching out in the precise long stride that was a burlesque of the runner's reach. But his laugh was angry, and the laugh had gone out of the crowd's yell.

Morosco was ten yards behind him, going into the turn again; running too fast, but grinning a little at all the clamor. He was not going after Barrow. He was not letting any decoy kill him off.

Sixty-one! Sure. The fool!

Myer and Kane followed smoothly, six yards behind the S.C.U. runner. Barrow plugged around the first turn again and banged his way along into the backstretch. There was a little breeze there, and he slowed, going into it.

Sixty-one is not fast for the big time, where the Venzkes or the Cunninghams, shading 4:15, will do even a third or fourth lap in an even minute; but Wheelbarrow Taylor was running his race in company where nobody yet has cracked 4:25—

"Get 'em, Barrow, old kid!" King, the quarter-miler, was standing and yelling. Foley only gave him a glance.

Barrow went on.

He pulled away farther on the backstretch, but he was very tired when he hit the turn. He wavered there; then pumped his heavy arms and reached out wearily, striding. He got to going again. He came into the straightaway once more.

The crowd's roar was tense, fierce; there were hundreds there, perhaps, who knew what the coach had done to Barrow Taylor, and there was nobody who could not see what Barrow was doing in return. The big fellow was making a bid. He was not decoying Morosco. He was not pacing anybody. He was giving all he had, in the only way he knew; he was going to run as fast as he could for as long as he could, and let it go at that.

The crowd rose to it. Automatically, Coach Foley looked at his watch—2:09 for the half. Within two seconds of the fastest half the big fellow had ever done. And he was going on.

Then Foley walked slowly along the pole of the track, looking across at the crowd—the scramble of colors, waving arms, white faces. The Paxton band was banging frantically at something, but Foley could not tell what the music was or whether there was any. The band had gone crazy too. And none of them over there were laughing at Wheelbarrow Taylor any more; he was standing them up. They were yelling for him. They were hoping against hope, screaming at him, clenching and straining and trying in a crowd's fool way to help him along.

Barrow's girl was up there, seeing this—and she'd have to see the rest of it too. She'd have to see it when the boy ran himself at last into a stumbling walk, dead-legged, not able to go on any more.

But she'd know, anyhow, that they weren't laughing at him. Nobody could laugh now. And not because of any anger at those yelling kids with their colors clashing but because he had to say something, Coach Foley cursed at the crowd. His eyes were burning and he had a lump at the throat to swallow.

"Damn you!" he said. "Let's see you laugh now!"

Because Wheelbarrow Taylor was pulling through the backstretch on the third lap—he was making it. Foley, not seeing it, saw the crowd seeing it and heard the crowd's yell.

Foley was looking for the doctor. Doc Weymiller with his little black bag. Sometimes you had to have a doctor. Foley found him. He was at the rail, a few yards up from the finish line, where he was supposed to be. Foley made sure. Then he turned back to the race.

Barrow was all gone now. He finished the backstretch all right; he was plowing heavily, but still reaching and pulling. He was going into the turn. Morosco was a good twenty-five yards back, with Red Myer dogging him. Kane was trailing, but Barrow stumbled at the turn. He caught himself.

And now, with the uproar from the stands rising swiftly again, Martin Foley kept himself from blubbering. He had to do it suddenly, with every angry, derisive check he could muster. Because very suddenly, from his own days on the track, Foley remembered what the third lap was like.

The third lap is the killer and the heartbreaker of the one-mile run.

A man has to spend everything he has there, holding up his pace for that quarter of a mile, and knowing at every dead stride that he will have still another lap to do when that is ended. He must go on while he knows that he can't, and while he knows that he must.

Foley wanted the boy to finish that third lap. He wanted it terribly and suddenly, remembering the feel of the race. Wanted it with a mist in his eyes, making it hard to see.

Barrow caught himself, stumbled again—he still kept his head down, as he had taught himself to do, and he still worked his arms. Even stumbling, he tried to reach out, pull forward.

Foley watched him.

The big fellow was finishing the turn, lumbering into the straightaway, but swaying there and fighting for balance like a desperately tired man bucking a blizzard. He entered the straightaway. He came on. Foley, jostled in the screaming crowd at the finish line, looked down at his own left hand. He clenched the yellow pad, crumpled it, threw it down and ground his foot on it. He looked at the kid again.

The boy's face was ash-pale and his lips, wrenched back from his teeth, were white. He was cotton-mouthed, racking for breath, but he was keeping his chin down. He was pulling with his arms. He was making every stride laboriously, in an agony of will power. But he was making it. He was running.

He did finish the third lap.

The gun cracked in the crazy tumult—the gun for the fourth. Foley looked at his watch, not believing what he saw there. And then, staring at Wheelbarrow Taylor again, he did not believe what he saw there either.

The Wheelbarrow was getting up to his toes for the last-lap gun. The fool kid was run out and finished and spent, but he was getting up to his toes because that was the thing to do when they gave you the gun for Lap 4. That was the thing to do, and he had learned all the right things, one at a time, desperately and hopelessly, over four years of trying. So he was doing it now. He was getting up on his toes and staggering into a rubber-legged sprint.

Martin Foley unclenched his right fist, feeling the stab of splintered glass. He slammed the stopwatch into the dirt too.

And then, not seeing anything clearly, he knew from the yell of the crowd that Barrow Taylor's race was almost ended—Dink Morosco was going into the last lap, too, with Red Myer pushing him, and the S.C.U. runner was out to catch that fool kid and stop the runaway. The yell from the crowd was frantic, edged with hysteria.

What had to happen couldn't be helped, but it was not going to be nice to look at. Barrow Taylor was due now to take his beating.

Morosco drove himself around the turn, picking up five yards, six yards, seven yards. Barrow swayed when he breasted the wind on the backstretch, and he was having to fight hard for every stride. He kept fighting. But Morosco drew up on him.

Foley watched. He may have been yelling too. There were men straggling across the infield now, waving their arms, shouting. Foley only knew they were there, did not see them, did not hear them.

Morosco moved up. Barrow wavered against the wind, but he reached out, pulling himself forward by main strength—the roar of the crowd, the yells of those men on the field waving at him, perhaps reached him distantly. Something spurred him, and for perhaps a second Morosco did not gain on him.

Then Red Myer lashed himself into the race, and with his move the crowd's noise took on still a new note. Myer cut down the distance between him and Morosco, cut it more, very slowly, but steadily.

So they fought to the end of the backstretch. Barrow still strode, but he could not hold the pace. Morosco gained steadily, with Red Myer creeping up behind him. Red failed a little. Morosco still moved up. Wheelbarrow Taylor gained the turn, and there, for the first time, he looked up despairingly, and the pull of his dead arms threw his head back, so that he seemed struggling for air.

Dink Morosco caught him at the turn.

Foley could not see that far, by then. The noise—the crazy noise—told him what was happening. Morosco, like the fighting thoroughbred he was, had sprinted on dead legs to make up that last impossible ten yards. He had reached the big fellow. He was veering out, now, away from the pole. He was fighting himself, punishing himself. He had to muster one more sprint. He had to spurt around the big man and pass him by two full paces before he could cut in to the pole again. He was trying it. Coach Foley saw the thing very dimly.

Morosco, too, was dead to the world. He had to take two strides to each ungainly, plunging step that big Wheelbarrow Taylor took. And Wheelbarrow was fighting him off. He would not be passed. He was falling at every step, but he was falling forward; he was pounding, stumbling, flailing his big arms, but he would not let the desperate little man pass him.

And so Dink Morosco hung beside him on the outside of the turn, with Barrow Taylor taking one drunken lunge to every two strides of the last spurt Morosco could summon. Morosco had spent himself in catching the big man. Instead, now, of sprinting, passing and cutting in, he was able only to hurry the pace a notch; and Barrow Taylor, with the terrible remnant of his awkward, sheer strength, was meeting that pace, one lunge at a time.

They came around the turn.

Barrow had a lead of one clear yard. Morosco veered still farther from the pole, trying by blind instinct to get out into the open, where his own drive would not help Barrow's.

And there Wheelbarrow Taylor recited his last lesson in the art of running. He staged a sprint for the tape.

Coach Foley saw it. The screaming, trampling mob on the bleachers saw it—a parody of the parody that Barrow had shown so often. A racking, staring, dead-legged imitation of a drunken man imitating a sprinter.

Barrow made it work.

Dink Morosco faltered. Barrow pulled away from him—and when that happened, Morosco was through. He was not yellow. He was through. The gap that Barrow opened—unreasonable and impossible and inexorable—hit Morosco like a shot. Still sheering off toward the stands, he stumbled and went down.

Barrow wavered toward the pole. He all but stepped off the track. While the crowd shrieked at him, he staggered away toward the center lane. He steered away from that. Still sprinting. Still sprinting like a man in a nightmare. Fighting terribly. Moving a little. Trying to fix his eyes on the finish line. Trying to make it.

Martin Foley tried to catch the time. Automatically, because it was part of his business to clock a runner. He looked at his right hand. Empty. A smear of blood on it. He tried to look at Barrow Taylor again.

And Red Myer was following in, trying his own sprint.

Barrow had nothing left.

Red Myer wouldn't have taken the tape away from that big boy for anything in the world, but Red didn't know anything either. He was just running a race, and there was a man ahead of him. He was trying to win.

Barrow lurched, wavered very slowly

Red was tied up, gasping, pumping with his fists and finishing the last ounce of drive left in him. He was going to catch that other man. He was going to beat that other man.

But at the end, when Wheelbarrow faltered for the last time and stumbled forward, he fell heavily into a strip of white cotton worsted stretched above the chalk line at the finish. He fell into it, hit it and let go. He fought feebly, like a tired baby. Men were holding him, lifting him, and while he groaned for breath he tried to fight them away.

Red Myer, Paxton, second. Ray Kane, Paxton, third.

And at that, Wheelbarrow Taylor came back to earth before Coach Foley did.

With a smell of earth and sawdust and rubdown in his nostrils, Barrow found out after a while that he could breathe all right. He got up off his blanket by the broad-jump pit. He found that his legs would hold him up. People crowded around him, still yelling, but Coach Foley seemed to be the only one he could see quite clearly—right then, suddenly, the boy saw Coach Foley a lot more clearly than he had seen him for long years past. Foley had him by the right hand, pumping at it. Foley was yelling louder than anybody else:

"Wheelbarrow, old son, by golly, you won it! By golly, Wheelbarrow, you won it!"

Then Barrow broke out that quick, surprised grin of his, knowing that he and Martin Foley weren't strangers any more.

Coach Foley already knew that, of course. He knew, too, perfectly well, that Wheelbarrow had won that race. But he kept on yelling at the kid, because his trouble was that he still couldn't make himself believe it.

THE OLYMPIAN

Brian Glanville

(1969)

[*Ike Low, lackadaisical quarter-miler for an English track club, meets his destiny.*]

The first time I met him, I thought he was a nut case, just a nutty old man hanging around the recreation grounds, leaning over the rails, shouting at people as they come by. Ah, shut up, you daft old bugger, that's all I thought about him. Next time I come around, he was still there, shouting, and I caught a word or two, "Elbows *down!*" What the hell was it to do with *him*? Running around, I suddenly laughed. I'd suddenly remembered this old man at home that used to wander up and down the High Street, shouting at cars and waving his stick at them like they were people. When I got around, I was still laughing and that made him furious; you ought to have heard him, yelling and carrying on at me, something about, "I'll bloody teach you to laugh!" and then, when I'd run past, something about I wouldn't win nothing.

I did two more laps and then I packed it in. In the showers there, in the dressing room, he come in to me. With his little white beard and this look in his eye, very pale eyes, pale blue, I'd never seen eyes like them, he was like a prophet, one of them colored pictures in the Bible at home.

He said, "What were you laughing at?" I said, "Me? I wasn't laughing at nothing." I'd have told him to fuck off, but somehow you couldn't, he was so intense. I said, "I often laugh when I train." "Well," he said, "you're not going to get much training done, not *good* training. Who's your coach?" I said, "I haven't got one. Just the club coach." He said, "Which club?" I said, "Spartacus," and he gave a little snort; he said, "Fifty years out of date. They couldn't teach a stag to run."

Just looking at him, listening to him, he seemed some sort of crank. In fact, it's funny the way things come full circle, because that's how I come to think of him, a crank, just like a lot of people did then; only there was the time in between, quite a long time, when I didn't think like that; and the time after. I suppose it was what Jill said; in a kind of way he hypnotized me. There were his eyes, for a start, like I've said, so pale, like he'd spent a long time staring at the sun, for a challenge, not willing to be beaten by anything. He hardly ever blinked, just stared at you, almost through you, like some sort of blowtorch, burning away at anything he didn't like, any kind of disagreement with what he believed. And the hollow cheeks and the white tuft of hair and the way he shoved his face forward, into yours.

Alan, that's the sprinter, the bronze medal one, used to call him the Ancient Mariner; he'd say, "By thy long gray beard and glittering eye, now wherefore stoppist thou me?" but not to Sam, not directly to Sam; it wasn't the kind of thing you could imagine yourself saying to him.

Then, of course, there was his rabbit. In a way, it was never so much what he said, but the tone of it, the rhythm of the words coming and coming at you, nonstop, like a torrent; you went with it, or it just swept you away, anyhow. Even now, I remember parts of what he said, then, standing in that little, dark, cramped dressing room, dripping water, just out of the shower, while he kept on and on at me. He asked, "What distance do you run?" I said, "Two-twenties, quarters," and he said, "You are built to run the *mile*. You are the perfect combination of ectomorph-mesomorph; long calves, lean muscular thighs and arms, chest between thirty-seven and thirty-eight, and broad, slim shoulders. A miler is the aristocrat of running. A miler is the nearest to a thoroughbred horse that exists on two legs. Look at me: a natural distance runner, wiry and muscular, trained down to gristle. We are the *infantry* of running. Your four-forty and eight-eighty men, these are your cavalry. The sprinters are your shock troops, your commandos."

One of the lads changing over in the corner, someone from another club, said, "What are we then, mate; the walkers?" and the old boy said, "The walkers are what Chesterton called the donkey; the devil's walking parody on all twofooted things," and he gave this imitation, strutting up and down the dressing room, sticking out his arse and waggling his shoulders, just like the walkers do, till all of us that was in there laughed, and even the walker had to smile. The old boy said, "I am not decrying walkers. Each man to the physical activity that suits him best. I would be prepared to award a gold medal even to *crawlers*. We already have hop, step and jumpers. But there must be a proportion in all things. Just as a child learns to crawl, then to walk and then to run, so there is a hierarchy in athletic locomotion."

To tell the truth, I didn't know what he was on about most of the time, leaving school at fifteen like I had, dead idle, never bothering; he was using words I'd never heard of. But it held you; that was the thing about him. He could hold you.

When I was changed, we went for a cup of tea, or rather I had a cup of tea, he had a glass of milk. It was at Lyons, in the Edgware Road; we went and sat at one of those stone-topped tables with the tea slopped all over it and teacups everywhere. He asked me why I drank tea; he said, "An athlete is as good as his diet. Tea is bad. Coffee is bad. Alcohol is worse than either. Do you drink alcohol?" I said, "Well, yes, I have a few beers, now and again," and he slapped the table so loud everybody looked around; it was embarrassing. He said, "You are deliberately poisoning yourself. You are weakening the natural stimuli provided by the nervous system. The human body provides its own stimulant, and its own stimulant is adrenaline. This stimulant can be induced. Fear produces adrenaline. Anticipation produces adrenaline. But alcohol will clog your brain; it will dull your reflexes; it will effect your lungs; it will undermine your heart. Do you smoke?"

I wanted to say no, which was ridiculous, because who was he, I'd only known him for an hour, and whose life was it, his or mine? Till I decided—mine. I said, "Well, just a little." He said, "There is no truce to be made with the cigarette. Tobacco is the body's enemy. What happens to a chimney when it's been used a long time?" I said, "Soot?" and he said, "If you smoke, your lungs are like a chimney. But you can't call the sweep. Have you any cigarettes on you now?" and, when I half nodded, held out his hand, thin with blue veins, like a claw, and God knows why, I put my hand in my pocket and took it out, the packet, with what I had left in it, four or five cigarettes, and put them in his hand, and he crumpled them, his fingers closed around them like the grab of them mechanical cranes they have there in the arcades, in the Charing Cross Road, screwing them up; I should have belted him. But I didn't. I just said, "Hey," then watched while he opened his hand and let them drop out, the scrunched up fags and the packet, onto the floor, like rubbish.

Then he got on to diet; did I eat meat. I shouldn't eat meat, he was a vegetarian, that and milk, only this wasn't *good* milk, it had been through too many processes, the best milk was the milk that was closest to the cow. I said, "A runner needs strength, doesn't he?" He said, "Press down on my arm," and rolled up the sleeve and held it out, his right arm, all knobs and cords and veins like the root of a tree, the kind that grows above the ground, gnarled and twisted. I looked at it, and I didn't feel like touching it. He said, "Go on, try." and I tried, I put both hands on his arm; it felt hard, like wood, no flesh at all, and I started pressing. I was only eighteen, but strong, very, very fit, and it should have been easy, I almost felt sorry for him. But I couldn't budge it, however hard I pushed, till in the end I was actually standing up; there was sweat running down my forehead, people were staring but it didn't worry me, or rather it did worry me, I had to do it; I was making a fool of myself, and when I looked down suddenly, into his eyes, they had this look in them, a sort of smile—of triumph really—and more than that, like he was saying, "There you are, I told you so, I knew you could never beat me," which made me press down all the harder, still looking at him, but it was no go, he just blinked once, that was all, and in the end, I gave up. I sat down.

I said, "I don't know how you do it," and he said, "Not bad on vegetables, eh? Vegetables prevail over meat!" and then, "Strength is not just the strength of the body; it is the strength of the mind. The strength of the will prevails over the weakness of the body. The will drives the body beyond what the body believes it can do. That is why a great athlete must feed not only his body but his mind. How big was Paavo Nurmi? How big was Sidney Wooderson? He was a solicitor, and in a running vest, he *looked* like a solicitor, but when he ran the mind was greater than the body." And on and on. And on and on and on.

"Why were the Greeks the true, original athletes? Because the Greeks were the inventors of the golden mean. They did not neglect the body for the mind. In our age we have neglected the body for the machine. What we have to do is rediscover the body, stop poisoning it with false stimulants, stop filling it with noxious substances, stop treating it only as a means of self-indulgent pleasure. A plant needs water, and a body needs exercise. If you do not exercise a body, it corrupts, and the mind corrupts with it. Look at the politicians and the scholars and the businessmen. Look at the people who rule our world and tell us what to do. What a travesty of logic! These people who *have* no bodies, only heads. And many athletes have no heads, only bodies. A champion is a man who has trained his body and his mind, who has learned to conquer pain and to use pain for his own purposes. A great athlete is at peace with himself and at peace with the world; he has fulfilled himself. He envies nobody. Wars are caused by people who have not fulfilled themselves; I have fought in two, and I know. Look—just here, above the navel; that was Flanders. And here, on the right shoulder. That was Murmansk. But I bore them no ill will, because I knew I would survive. You can kill the body, but you cannot kill the spirit. There are no limits to what the body can do when it is strong. Twenty years ago they said the four-minute mile was impossible. I told them then: 'We shall live to see it run in three minutes, forty seconds,' and they laughed. But what has happened? The four minute mile is now commonplace. Athletes run it every week. Even schoolboys run it. We shall see a three-forty mile and a nine second 100 meters and a nine foot high jump and a twenty foot pole vault. It all lies in the conception. Once these things have been conceived as possible, they are achieved. And that is why athletics are important, why records are important. Because they demonstrate the scope of human possibility; which is unlimited. The inconceivable is conceived, and then it is accomplished.

"Look at me. It was inconceivable that my one arm could resist the pressure of your two, and yet it did. Now it is inconceivable to you that your two arms could defeat my one. But all this is arbitrary. Matter is arbitrary. It is your will against mine, your spirit against mine.

Everything depends on the will. I have been in India and seen a fakir stab himself with knives, plunge knives into his body and pull them out again, without a mark. I have seen them walk on fire. If these men desired, they could lift weights which would make the strongest man in an Olympiad look weak. A man like Vlasov of Russia would look puny, although he was three times their size. So this is why I say to you, train. Look after your body. Temper it with pain. And your body will amaze you; you will do things you thought impossible. That is why running matters. That is why Olympiads matter. Not for gold medals, those little worthless disks, but for their inner meaning, what they stand for. The Olympic flame is sacred, because it is the flame of human aspiration."

I got excited, listening to him, understanding some of what he said, not understanding lots of it, but still like I said, being carried along, as much by how he said it as by what he said. I mean, I was eighteen; who had I ever heard who could talk like that, who could spout ideas like that, who could make you believe in what you could do and what you were doing, the way he did?

Up to then I'd just been running, something to do, a race here, a race there, won a few, lost most of them, not knowing what I really wanted—out of that or anything else. But hearing him in that tea shop, I knew what I wanted and I realized it had been there all the time, only, like, it had come and gone. Sometimes I'd felt it when I was actually in a race, when I knew I'd got it in me to win, when I'd feel this sort of current shoot through me, a sort of ambition; other times it was when I was training, usually alone, in Epping Forest or some mornings on the track, early, when I'd been on night shift and I was there alone; you'd be moving so well, so smooth, your body felt so good, that you knew you could beat anyone on earth, bring 'em all on: Elliot, Bannister, the lot. And now I felt it in me again, even without running, even just sitting; this *knowing* that I could be great, that I wanted to be great—and something else: that he could show me how.

Mind you, you might say that was him, that was his stock-in-trade, which I admit; but what I mean is, that was part of it; if he hadn't had one, he wouldn't have had the other.

Out in the street, the Edgware Road, I hardly noticed the crowds. I was in my blue track suit, very proud of it, just got it, with the club crest on the pocket, and Sam was wearing what he always wore off the track, this gray jersey and a pair of blue jeans—never mind what it was, sun or rain, snow or hail.

I remember as we walked across Hyde Park, with him still talking, and passing Speaker's Corner, where they was all talking, too, the blackies and the Irish and the nut cases, and him looking around and saying in this loud voice, "Lunatics, the lot of them, pouring out their prejudice and hatred," and it suddenly came to me that this was what he'd kept reminding me of all the time he was talking—the tone of his voice and the way it was one long speech with you the audience.

All the way across the park he was talking, I was listening; I think we both just took it for granted he was going to train me. He'd got three or four he was coaching, he said; one was a miler, one was middle distance, and the others sprinters. Sundays they trained on Hempstead Heath; other days it depended on the light and the time people could get off. He said he had this physical education job with the city council—it was long before he opened his gym for businessmen—and he'd done it a year, and when he got tired of it, he'd change. He said, "If I want money, I can always make it. Money is easy to make. Never let yourself be dominated or deluded by the importance of money; it is secondary. I've been a sailor and a soldier and a farmer and a postman and a travel courier. I have cooked in the finest hotels, and I have worked as a garage mechanic. I have written for newspapers and I have sold newspapers. My dear wife is dead, I have no children, and I can exist with perfect comfort in the open air."

Then he asked me what I did, and I told him I was working in this cardboard-box factory, knowing more or less what he'd say—partly, I suppose, because it was what I really felt myself—that it was the wrong job for an athlete, unhealthy, that it wouldn't get me nowhere. I must have had half a dozen jobs, anyway, since I'd left school; working in a bakery, then a butcher's shop, apprentice electrician, trainee telephone engineer, and now the factory—nothing that really interested me.

He said, "A job like that erodes the will and stultifies the body. Go out into the open air! Be a bus conductor or a park keeper or a swimming pool attendant or even a road sweeper! Do something that involves use of the body. How can you hope to run when you spend the whole day standing still? How can you hope to master your own body when your body is the slave of a machine?" And I agreed with him; it all made sense; I didn't see nothing funny in it, his taking it for granted this was what I wanted, to be a great runner, whereas up to now it had just been something I did, where in the winter I played a bit of football over the Marshes.

I promised on Sunday I'd meet him on Hempstead Heath to do some training with him. By this time we'd walked right across the park, over to the bridge across the Serpentine, stood there talking, looking at the water, all the willows hanging over it, then back again, to Hyde Park Corner. Once he'd gone it felt a bit strange to me; it wasn't my manor, this part of London, but while you were with him you could be anywhere, you didn't think of where you were. When he shook hands, he held onto my hand very tight and looked at me, like an animal trainer or something, right in the eye; he said, "I can make you a great miler. If you want to be a great miler," then left me standing there, all dazed.

I could have flown home, let alone run, and all that night I couldn't sleep; I was running races, winning medals, hearing his voice come at me out of the dark. I don't suppose I slept above an hour.

We met up by the pond there; I was a few minutes late, and he was sitting on this bicycle, which was something I hadn't expected: I suppose I'd thought that he'd be running with me. There was no one else, just him and me; I mean, none of the other runners he'd said he was training. I'd never seen the Heath before, and it made quite an impression on me, though by the time the afternoon was finished, I wouldn't have cared if I'd never seen it again. But the sun was shining and everything was this fresh, bright green—the grass, the trees, even the weeds. And not flat, like a park, but rolling—dips and hillocks and mounds and woods, very round and lush, more like the country. I wondered if he lived around there; he'd been very mysterious about where he lived; I imagined him living in a tent, or maybe a caravan.

We strolled across the road, him wheeling the bike, and as we reached the other side, the Heath, he took a stopwatch out of his pocket. He said, "Here is your enemy. Here is the beast you have to conquer." There was a course he wanted me to run, he said, one he'd worked out himself, all along the paths, so he could ride beside me. He told me, "We'll see what sort of stamina you've got; then, when we know about that, we can work out a training schedule for you. The needs of every athlete vary, not just between the distance runner and the middle distance runner, the miler and the sprinter, but from miler to miler, sprinter to sprinter."

So off we went, him on the bike with the watch in his hand, now and then telling me, "Sprint!" then, "Stop!" up and down the paths, dodging the little kids and the prams and the people, over stones and sometimes tree roots, till I wished I'd never worn my spikes, down steep slopes into little valleys, up them again the other side. I'd always hated cross-country, always tried to get out of it when the club was doing a cross-country run, and this was killing, the worst I'd ever known, no chance to slow down or take a breather because *he* was always there, sometimes beside me, sometimes behind me, sometimes just ahead of me, turning around and calling me on, talking and talking, telling me to go faster, to take longer strides, to hold my head higher, to use more arm action, to keep my elbows closer to my sides, until I hated him; I tried to block out the sound of his voice, just concentrate on a group of trees I could see, try and make out what kind they were, or a cloud with a funny shape, or try and guess how many strides it'd take me to an oak tree or a pond or maybe someone I could see walking.

But it never worked for long; he'd suddenly raise his voice, shouting, "*Sprint!*" or some other order, or else he'd suddenly ride out ahead of me so I couldn't ignore him if I wanted to, not with him there ahead, his hairy old face bent forward towards mine. Then, just as I was thinking all I wanted to do was catch up with him and smash him, he'd spin around and disappear behind me. To make matters worse, it was a warm afternoon, and I was in my track suit. I wanted to stop and strip it off, yet at the same time I didn't want to risk no favors, I didn't want *nothing* from him, just finish the bloody run and go home and never set eyes on him again. And then there was another feeling I had at the same time as *that*, that this was how he wanted me to think, he wanted me to hate him. I don't know why, but somehow I knew it from the expression on his face, a sort of mocking look, and when I couldn't see him, from the sound of his voice.

Once he asked me, "Are you hot?" and I said, "I'm all right," though the sweat was running down my forehead, stinging my eyes, dribbling into my mouth, all salt, trickling out of my armpits, inside my running vest. He said, "It's better for you than a Turkish bath, this is." Once I asked him, "How long we been running?" He said, "Thirty-eight minutes. Are you tired?" I said, "No, not tired," and I tried to kid myself I wasn't, but the longer I ran, the worse it got, my mouth so dry, my heart pumping away so loud I reckoned people must be able to hear it for miles around. Then he said, "Want a drink?" and honestly I loved him; he had this plastic water bottle in his hand; holding it out to me, he said, "Not too much." It was better than champagne. And then, "You'd better take your track suit off," and I did, I stepped out of it, it had practically stuck to me in places, and with that off and the drink, I thought I'd run for miles, I'll bloody show him, and for a while, maybe a quarter of an hour or so, it was a bit better, I was almost beginning to enjoy it, which he probably realized, because soon things started getting harder; there were many more hills to climb, even a run across the grass. He said, "Down into that bowl and up the other side. I'll meet you there, I'll time you," and cycled the long way around the path while I ran down into this dip, then had to climb the bleeding hill, like going through some bloody assault course. He was there at the top with his stopwatch, saying, "Very good, all right, come on," and cycling off, not looking back, leaving me to follow like a dog.

So all this feeling good wore off; and after a while I was back where I started, and worse, except for taking off the bloody track suit; my legs aching, my chest aching, my heart thumping and banging away, the only things to look forward to, the only things that kept me going, the drinks of water; but only when he offered them, I'd never ask for them, no matter how I felt, any more than I'd stop till the old bastard said I could stop. Except twice to be sick, while he just stood watching me while it all came heaving out, not saying anything; just standing, waiting for me to go on, while I thought *Christ I'll die, I'm going to die, my guts are coming out, I'll die.*

In the end it got darker and colder; I was swaying about almost bumping into people, just not seeing them until they was on top of me, and at last, right at the top of another bloody hill, or maybe one of the same bloody hills, God knows, hearing his voice behind me saying, "Okay, that'll do," and collapsing, bang, right where I was and bursting into tears, lying there crying and not being able to stop, not even caring, just lying there and crying. He didn't say a word, just stood there by his bicycle, with his back to me, waiting for me to finish, just like when I was being sick. I don't think I've ever hated anyone the way I hated him then—giving me nothing, when it was him who'd got me in this state. People were walking past, looking at me, one or two of them stopping, but I didn't care about that either. I heard one of them say, behind me, "Is he all right?" and Sam's voice say, "Yes, he's all right," and I thought, "*Who the hell are you to say I'm all right, you old cunt; whose body is it, who did all the bloody running?*" till at last I stopped crying, and then I felt ashamed; I didn't want to face him; I buried my head in my arms and went on lying there, hoping that he'd go away, but when I looked up, he was still there, still with his back to me, like he was prepared to stand there forever. So I got up, and as I got up, he turned to me; the watch was still in his hand. He said, "You have run for two hours and seventeen minutes. I would estimate that in the first hour you covered ten and a quarter miles, in the second hour, nine and a half miles, and in the final seventeen minutes, less than two miles, making a total of slightly less than twenty-two miles, which is four miles less than the marathon. That, of course, is only an estimate." Not good or bad or well done or how are you. And still up on his bloody bicycle as we went all the way back across the Heath, my feet so sore I could hardly take a step, my calves aching like someone had gone over them with a truncheon, and him saying, "I do not believe in training to exhaustion. The Zatopek training. Zatopek was a great champion, but his achievements have been surpassed. This was not training; this was a test of stamina and will. There were moments when I doubted your will, but I am satisfied that you gave your maximum. Your maximum can be increased, just as your stamina *must* be increased."

I don't even know how I got home, on a bus, I think, sleeping most of the way. That night I dreamt I was flying. He was in it somewhere. He was doing it.

* * *

I hated the weight lifting; I'd never bothered with it in the club; smelly old gymnasium and all the big men there, the shot putters and that, grunting and heaving away like they were having it off. To me it was like a fetish, everybody had to do it, whether they were throwing the hammer or playing tiddlywinks; it didn't make no sense.

But he insisted on it. He had me along to this gym that belonged to a school in Holloway, one where he was teaching phys. ed. I went one evening, and there was this ruddy great barbell on the deck with shining disks on it, so big I could hardly bear to look at them, and he said, "Right, watch me; this is a curl," and put his hands on the bar, bent down and came up again, bang, bringing it to his chest, arms like twisted rope, red in the face, his eyes practically popping. Then he put it down, one-two, and said, "Now you do it."

There was a few kids standing around and grinning, teenagers like myself, most of them, and I didn't fancy it. I hesitated for a moment. I'd never done curls before, anyway, only squats and presses, and a bit of clean-and-jerk, but in the end I bent down, just about got the bloody thing off the floor, then dropped it. He said, "Right, we'll make it easier for you," and took off the big disks and put on a couple of smaller ones, twenty-five pounds, and this time I managed it all right, except that right away he said, "Again!" and after that, "Again!" till I felt I was back on the bloody Heath, pounding away with my feet like lumps of raw meat and my legs feeling like they'd drop off. But when I'd done them, he said, "All right, rest," and immediately started clinking about with the weights again, saying, "This time the press."

He put seventy-five pounds on the bar and made me lift the bloody thing above my head till my arms ached, keeping the usual running commentary: "All training must be done under calculated pressure. The effort and the intervals must be exactly judged. Training which is not done under pressure is of no real value."

The others in the gym had all of them gathered around by now; they seemed to be a bit amused by him but to respect him. He loved them being there, I could tell that, clowning around, showing the right way and the wrong way to lift weights, but I didn't enjoying being part of the act, the stooge.

Two of the lads there that night were runners he was training, a quarter-miler called Tony Dash that I knew about, he'd come in third in the Southern Counties—he was from somewhere like Clapham—and a boy from Yorkshire, Tom Burgess, that run the longer ones, the mad ones, like three miles and the six. Tom said he'd come down to London because of Sam; he'd met Sam when he was running for his club, at Chiswick. He was very, very thin and all he lived for was athletics; everything he did was tied up with it—his job, where he lived, what he ate and drank, whether he got married. I said to Tony once, "I bet he doesn't even crap without thinking will it help me do a better time," and Tony said, "If he thought it'd help, he'd never crap at all."

We went out to a cafe afterward, the four of us, to have a cup of tea—milk for Sam—and Tom and Sam got to talking about times, overall times and lap times, what the Americans had done this year and what the Russians had done, what you ought to aim for in the first mile if you want to run an Olympic-qualifying time in the three miles, whether it was better to put in a fast second mile and try to kill off the field or to leave yourself something in hand for a spurt at the end, whether in a race you should concentrate on the time, rather than the other runners, till I wondered, *Is this how I'm going to get? Is this all I'm ever going to think about?* because it was like a religion; but once or twice I caught Tony's eye and seemed to see him smile, which made me feel better about it.

Sam was on about Tony's smoking, the same stuff he'd given me about the body turning into a chimney. Tony said, "Five a day, Sam, I cut it down to five a day; I've come down from twenty. I can't just cut it off completely, honest, I'd die." Sam said, "You'll die much sooner if you go on filling your lungs with that filth." He ran for Poly Harriers; Tom was with Woodford. Clubs didn't seem to make no difference to Sam; he seemed to take athletes where he found them. I heard him say once, "I will not attach myself to any clubs. My talents are available to the best, whoever they may be. An athletes' club is a contradiction in terms. Athletics is an individual sport, and a club is a collective entity. A club is like a convoy—everyone goes at the speed of the slowest ship—but the race is won by the runner who goes the fastest."

Tom was living over Chigwell then, and we went back some of the way together, on the bus. He said, "Sam's a genius, you realize that. He's years ahead of his time," and he was dead serious; in fact, you hardly ever saw him smile. I said, "He don't half drive you, though." He said, "You're lucky to get taken up by him at all. I know people that have come to him and begged him. If there was any justice he'd be coaching the Great Britain team. But they hate him; they're jealous of him, a lot of coaches are. You'll find that out; you'll see." And in a way, I did see, quite soon as a matter of fact.

The thing was, Sam wanted to see me in a race, and not just any race, a mile. So I went to our own club coach one day, Des Tompkins, and I asked him, I said, "I'd like to run the mile." He looked at me—he was a tall man with a mustache, always very dapper, a bit like a sergeant major, really—and he said, "You? What do you want to run the mile for? You can hardly get around the quarter." I said, "Well, it's an idea I had, that's all. I'd like to try it." He said, "Well, three of our milers are here tonight"—at Paddington, this was—"why don't you join in with them?" I said, "Well, frankly, I wanted to run it under competitive conditions, just so I could see how I went." He said, "And frankly, you're not going to run the mile for this club unless you can show me you're better than the boys I've got already," which I suppose was fair enough, though I didn't think so at the time.

So there was nothing else to do but go out and run against them, which I did, though I must say I didn't like the idea. Not that any of them was all that; they'd none of them broke four minutes, the fastest any of them had done was 4:08 or something like that, but it was a new experience. I'd no idea how to pace myself, and I could easily end up looking like a twot.

Anyway, I ran. Des said to them, "This is our new miler; he says he's going to leave the rest of you standing," which made it even more embarrassing; the three of them gave me an old-fashioned look, then looked at one another. I said, "Just to see, that's all," and one of them said, "You'll bloody see. It's not like poncing around with quarters." Then Des lined us up and we were off.

I'd reckoned that the best thing to do, the safest thing, was just to stay up with them, then see if at the end I couldn't find a bit of speed to beat them, and in the first lap, of course, it was dead easy, being used to the pace of the quarter; in fact, the difficulty was not to let yourself go shooting out ahead of the rest of the field. The second lap, one of them, Jack Brogan, a lanky bloke with red hair, suddenly spurted ahead of the rest of us, and I thought, *Do I catch him or do I stay with the others?* but as he got farther ahead, I started worrying. I thought I'd better catch him, and put a spurt on, though it wasn't easy; I was feeling it a bit, this second lap, that feeling in the lungs when they're starting to ache and you think about things like second wind, which is something you never think of in the quarter.

I caught him, all right, and once I caught him he seemed to let up a little, we jogged along side by side, but as soon as the third lap started, I began to realize they must have got together, because he dropped back, and another of them, a little short fellow, Roger Coomb, shot past me like a blue-arsed fly, and then I saw it: They were trying to kill me off. So realizing this, I let him go, just jogging with the others, running a much, much slower lap, and Jack turned round to me and said, "What's the matter, are you clapped out already?" I said, "You'll bloody see."

When Roger saw I wasn't following him, he dropped his pace, staying maybe twenty yards ahead, hoping I suppose that I'd come up and challenge him, but I didn't, I was waiting for the last lap, and when we reached it, Des was there at the side, yelling, "Last lap; ding-a-ling-a-ling," for the bell. I said to the fourth one, Charlie Cooper, "Come on, your turn now," and sure enough he went, but of course it was a little late now, they hadn't worn me out like they meant to, and suddenly I found I was starting to enjoy it, the challenge of it all, the working things out, and even the rest of it, the actual running, maybe because that run with Sam had done me more good than I'd thought it had; after that, nothing could be too bad.

So there we were, all in a bunch, everyone afraid to go, I suppose—I know I was—I felt I'd got something left but I couldn't risk breaking; I'd no idea what they'd got. And then Jack, the red-haired fellow, broke, about two-fifty yards from home, just ahead of me in the inside lane, and there was something about the back of him, his head and shoulders, something cocky, that got up my nose; I thought, *Right, you bastard,* and I went, all or nothing, and he half looked around when he heard me coming behind him, and I reckon seeing me made him all the more determined, because he put on even more of a spurt. But I knew I had him, I was closing in—I wasn't even worried about the others—and suddenly I was level with him, looking at his face, seeing it dead white and worried, then past him, and I wanted to laugh, knowing I'd skate home, that he'd never catch me. Around the last bend, feeling the cinders kick up against my leg, then into the straight, just starting to run out of breath, but keeping it up, keeping ahead, until there it was, the line, and I was over it, standing there sobbing and puffing away, Des with his stopwatch in his hand saying, "Not *bad*, 4:11," then Jack coming in, then the other two, and Jack collapsing on the grass lying there like he'd been shot.

The week after that, Saturday, I ran the mile at Eton Manor.

A sports stadium on the fringe of East London, urban and peripheral, lurking behind a high brick wall; the very grass appears to be growing on sufferance. A brick-red running track surrounds the field; on one side there's a modest wooden grandstand, on the other, a small collection of wooden huts, of the kind which appear, ephemerally, on building sites. There are, perhaps, a dozen spectators scattered around the grandstand in little knots and islands, like a metaphor of noncommunication. More are dotted about the field, behind the green railings which separate the track, the field, from its residual public. On the grass, a number of athletes in track suits—blue, green, purple, black—are limbering up; spurting forward in sudden, nervous, truncated bursts; standing, feet apart, patting the ground, sitting down, legs outstretched, their hands reaching elastically to their toes, or high-kicking like ballerinas. Others sprawl about the grass, relaxing; still others form groups around older men in blue blazers—the coaches.

There is nothing predicated here of triumph, medals, laurel wreaths, of great stadia full of chanting thousands. If the athletes have style, the occasion has none, and the athletes themselves have style, for the most part, only in movement. In repose, strong limbs hidden in their track suits, there's a suburban gaucheness about them. Yet from these drab crucibles, champions come, just as boxers come out of the slums, footballers out of coal mines. The difference for the athlete is that this and places like it are his milieu, for most of the year. Some will never go beyond it, others will do so infrequently, the luckiest more regularly, above all in the Olympic year, with its special transmuting alchemy. Then, briefly, they will turn into lions and roar in the arena.

In the middle of the field a tall young man in a pale-blue track suit is limbering up, gracefully, yet anxious, jogging, sprinting a few paces, only to stop, like a man suddenly aware he is going in the wrong direction, jogging again: IKE LOW. *His hair is dark and wiry; as a child's, it must have been curly. Now it gives an impression of being almost tiered. He has a fine, straight nose, but the youth of his face is mitigated by the hollow cheeks of the athlete in training. His mouth is wide, but narrow; his eyes, gray and rather small, deep-set and alert, look frequently across the stadium, where the entrance gate is just concealed from view. Even in these few, restricted movements, one divines an elegance, a nervous, thoroughbred power. His tension, indeed, is that of a racehorse at the starting gate.*

A voice sounds, over the loudspeakers.

VOICE: Competitors for the mile, please. Will competitors for the mile please go to their positions.

IKE LOW *begins abstractedly to peel off his track suit, revealing broad, slender shoulders, slim, muscular arms, a chest not large, but firmly developed. The body, though clearly fit and strong, gives the impression of still-unused potential; it remains a boy's body, not a man's, and the man will be bigger than the boy. Suddenly, he appears to see what he is looking for; his eyes focus on a lean, gray-headed man who has appeared at the entrance to the track, brisk and purposeful, walking as if to set the world an example; that all men his age should be as fit, as fast, as tautly preserved as he. The man—*SAM DEE*—is wearing a gray, turtleneck jersey, blue jeans and canvas shoes. He has a small white beard, neatly kept—an emblem of defiance, perhaps, or jaunty eccentricity.*

Pulling his track suit, now, down sinewy, functional thighs, hard calves, flecked only lightly with hair, IKE LOW *raises a hand as if to wave, then drops it again. A tall man in a blazer comes towards him, straight-backed, with a small mustache, a long head, sleekly brushed, a military air; the coach of his athletics club,* DES TOMPKINS.

TOMPKINS: Come on, let's have you, Ike. Not looking for anything, are you?

LOW (*a little uneasily*): No, I'm all right.

TOMPKINS: Walder's the one to watch; he always comes in with a strong finish. Don't burn yourself out on the first lap. And try not to get boxed in.

LOW (*abstractedly*): No. No. Okay.

TOMPKINS *follows his gaze and sees* SAM DEE, *who has now stopped, almost level with the starting mark, and is looking about him, for* LOW.

TOMPKINS (*suspiciously*): That's Sam Dee, isn't it?

LOW (*carefully nonchalant*): Yeah, I think it is, as a matter of fact.

TOMPKINS: What's he doing here?

LOW (*speculatively*): Come to watch.

Together, LOW *and* TOMPKINS *walk toward the start.*

TOMPKINS: Come to see if he can pinch someone else's runners, more like. You do the work, then he nips in and grabs the publicity. (*With a sudden look at* LOW.) He hasn't been after you, has he?

LOW (*restlessly*): I have been seeing him a bit.

TOMPKINS: That's why you wanted to run the mile.

LOW: Sort of.

TOMPKINS: I might have known you'd never have thought of it on your own.

LOW: Why wouldn't I, then?

TOMPKINS: Okay, I'll talk to you about him afterward. Only he'd better keep out of my way.

He walks straight past DEE, *who is now leaning over the railings opposite the start, watching him and* LOW, *and goes up to another of his runners, the red-haired* JACK BROGAN, *who is also to compete in the race.* IKE LOW, *with a quick, cautious glance at him, approaches* SAM DEE, *who is smiling.*

DEE: Didn't like seeing me, did he?

LOW: Not much, no.

DEE: No, they're all the same, these coaches. Little men. Little men. Obsessed with their own importance. Now I'll tell you how you're going to win this race. The best runner is Walder. He has speed but no stamina. The ideal way to beat him is to kill him off before the last lap, but this you're too inexperienced to do.

As he talks, he continues to smile, with the air of a conniving wizard. LOW *listens to him with his total attention; his whole wiry body seems to be hearing, absorbing, almost as if he were under a spell, the young body possessed by, in thrall to, the old.*

LOW: So what do I do?

DEE: The first lap will be slow. Probably about 58.5. The second lap will be slightly quicker. You will take on Walder not in the last lap but in the third. At the end of that lap I want you to be ahead of him, even if you aren't leading. In the final lap . . .

THE STARTER *speaks, somberly, pistol in hand, like a platonic executioner. He is small and squat, his blue blazer elaborately crested.*

THE STARTER: Get to your marks.

TOMPKINS: Get down there, Ike.

DEE *(giving* TOMPKINS *a disdainful glance):* In that last lap, go on the final bend. You'll hear me shouting.

He pats IKE LOW *on the arm, and* LOW, *taking his place in the second lane, beside the inside track, bends down with the others in the ritual starting position, hands to the ground, arms straight and parallel, one knee bent—like men frozen suddenly, unwittingly, in a posture from race memory.* LOW*'s tongue can be seen to move briefly across his lips, but his face is smooth.*

THE STARTER *points his pistol at the sky.*

THE STARTER: Get set.

BANG*: The pistol finally explodes, the runners rise from their haunches and are off to a thin, dispersed cheer, in which individual cries—"Come on, John! Let's have you, Ted!"—are clearly heard. Because there are four laps, four good minutes to run, the start has none of the drama, the irretrievability of the sprints; nor is it as casual as the ten thousand meters or the marathon, where the runners merely stand at the start, one foot in front of the other, in a ragged phalanx. The pace of the runners now is brisk rather than urgent, the interest, in these early laps, a connoisseur's: tactical, stylistic. Dotted about the track, the coaches watch anxiously, calling sharp words of advice.*

TOMPKINS *(as the group, still compactly together, passes for the first time):* That's right, Ike, stay with them!

DEE: (*as* IKE LOW *goes by him*): Now remember, remember!

TOMPKINS: Remember what? I'm his coach!

DEE (*impervious*): Remember, Ike!

TOMPKINS *looks at him with rage, his chest heaves, the blood springs cholerically to his cheeks, but in the end he says nothing.* SAM DEE, *meanwhile, is looking intently at his stopwatch, held in the palm of his hand like a charm or talisman.* TOMPKINS, *jerking away with a movement of exasperation, takes out his own stopwatch and regards it, as though in silent competition. As the milers come around for the third lap, both men look up. The red-haired* JACK BROGAN *is leading now, moving not gracefully but crisply, his knees rising a little too high, his elbows pointing slightly too far out, the expression on his face one of remote inner communion. Behind him, compact and contained, running in an almost palpable aura of optimism, smug expectancy, lies* WALDER, *a square-built man in a black-and-yellow vest, with the broad calf muscles of the sprinter rather than a miler. He takes short, swift, bouncing strides, which seem to reflect not merely his physique but his disposition.* IKE LOW *is running fifth; his action is rhythmic, feline, and economical. By contrast with the first two runners, it seems wholly unselfconscious. He simply and naturally runs; he has no concept of himself as a man running.*

TOMPKINS (*as* JACK BROGAN *passes*): Stay there, Jack!

DEE (*as* IKE LOW *passes*): Now, Ike!

At once, virtually from one stride to the next, IKE LOW *accelerates. The long, white, almost tubular legs which have been so effortlessly churning, suddenly gain speed and urgency, like a voodoo drummer abruptly raising the beat. From around the field there goes up a faint sigh of surprise. This new and hectic pace carries him past the fourth runner, then the third, until he is level with* JACK BROGAN, *and, at length, past him, as well. For an instant, a stride or two, his speed seems to relent, then* SAM DEE*'s voice is heard again.*

SAM DEE: Keep going, Ike!

At this, IKE LOW*'s legs resume their faster rhythm, and he draws irresistibly away from the other runners, like a man drawing on an endless length of elastic. Now the field, a shaken kaleidoscope, regroups, defining a hierarchy.* WALDER, *in his black-and-yellow, sets out in pursuit of* IKE LOW, *the elastic contracting, while he, in turn, is chased by* JACK BROGAN. *The other five runners straggle out in ones and two behind them.*

TOMPKINS (*in loud soliloquy*): He's daft. He'll kill himself.

DEE (*shouting*): Stay ahead, Ike!

TOMPKINS (*with a darting look at* DEE): Bloody insanity.

As the runners come around for the fourth and final lap, an official in a soft gray hat and a blue blazer pulls the rope of the bell, which responds with its cacophonous, ritual jangle, like a ship lost in the fog. IKE LOW *is still ahead, but* WALDER *is now only some fifteen yards behind him.* IKE*'s pace is the same, but he is clearly maintaining it on borrowed energy; the lolling of his head, the radically changed expression of his face, denote as much. His brow is contracted into sharp furrows of concern; his eyes have a look of anxiety premature for his years, as if on this third lap he has made bewildering discoveries.*

DEE: Keep in front, Ike!

TOMPKINS (*scornfully*): Him! He's got nothing left.

DEE: Go!

Now WALDER *is only ten yards behind* IKE LOW, *now five; now, as they go round the third bend, he is almost level. It seems a trial of will as much as stamina,* IKE LOW *willing his body to maintain its pace,* WALDER *willing him to fail. There are these few seconds in which the race is to be decided, in which* IKE LOW *will falter, fall behind, or* WALDER*'s challenge will evaporate. And in the event, it is not so much that* IKE LOW *moves ahead as that* WALDER *gradually falls back, the gap increasing from a hand's width to a stride, from a stride to two strides, till at the straight* IKE LOW *is two yards clear, moving inexorably away as* SAM DEE, *even* TOMPKINS, *shout him home; increasing it to three yards, five yards, and at the tape, which he breaks with a look of saintly anguish, suffering tempered by the joyful certainty of reward, it must be almost ten. At once there's a convergence of people and voices around him and upon him;* TOMPKINS *rushes up to him; a solicitous official throws a blanket around his shoulders,* SAM DEE *leaps the fence and comes dashing into the middle of the group.*

VOICES: 4:01! . . . Can't possibly . . . First mile he's run . . . I made it 4:01 . . . First competitive mile . . . Four and eight-tenths.

SAM DEE *and* TOMPKINS *confront each other over* IKE LOW *like two dogs over a bone,* TOMPKINS *the dog which lays the owner's claim,* DEE *the marauder who disputes it. Neither concedes; each decides, after a few silent moments, on a fragile truce.*

TOMPKINS (*with emotion*): Ike, you've run a 4:01 mile.

DEE: I'm proud of you, Ike. Proudest of all that you're still on your feet. (*He looks scornfully at Jack Brogan, who, comforted by sympathizers, has now reached a sitting position.*) A true champion never runs himself into exhaustion.

IKE LOW's *head droops to his chest; weariness and a sense of sudden anticlimax combine to wrap him in momentary isolation. When* WALDER *pushes through the crowd to shake his hand, he limply allows it to be taken. His lips move in some polite, reflexive formula, but his eyes remain focused on the ground.*

TOMPKINS (*proprietarily*): Okay, Ike. Let's get you into the dressing room. *An arm around* IKE LOW*'s shoulders, he steers him out of the crowd, towards a gate in the railings.*

DEE (*addressing those around him, as he turns to accompany them*): And this is only the beginning! Within a month he will break four minutes! Within six he will be running for Great Britain! When I first saw him training, I convinced him he was naturally adapted to run the mile!

Indifferent to a virulent look from TOMPKINS, *his aura of silent hostility,* DEE *hurries forward to take* IKE LOW*'s free arm.*

DEE (*to* IKE LOW): Remember! We are just at the beginning!

THE OTHER KINGDOM

Victor Price

(1964)

[*Colin Warnock, an Irish miling prodigy who has recently suffered a string of bad races and considered quitting the sport entirely, has a change of attitude during a bar-room brawl, and races as a new man.*]

Six of them lined up for the beginning of the mile, with the crowd emitting its regular subdued roar like a distant waterfall. It was a completely neutral day, making no impression on Warnock whatever: neither cool nor warm, neither wet nor dry. It was shorthand for weather.

There were two of the runners he had beaten three weeks before, Higgs and Longbottom, the outsiders; he spoke to them in the changing-room like an old friend. They had no chance of winning: "We've come for the trip," they said. But he wondered idly whether one of them had an arrangement to fix the pace for Galliver.

It didn't matter, though; a subtle shift had taken place in his character in the past day or two, one of those subsidences which produce new landmarks and alter the emphasis of the old. What now stood revealed was enjoyment: he realised that he was a human being well fitted to enjoy. Astonishing but true: in all his years of running he had never positively enjoyed a race. He had envied the sprinters, the shot-putters, the jumpers, all those whose event demanded less ascetic discipline than his. Between puts he had seen shot-men reading the paper or chatting with their competitors. And he had felt excluded. Now it occurred to him that he had been excluding himself.

But he wasn't excluding himself any more. And in a flash of intuition he realised why: he had renounced ambition, the tyranny of schedule and stop-watch, the profit-and-loss accounting of his training to date. He said to himself: I solemnly give up all side-considerations, all hopes of gain or celebrity, retaining one thing only: the satisfaction of doing the thing for its own sake. Foley was said to offer up his running to a saint; he could offer up his too, but to some divinity that did not need to be specified: to the spirit of running perhaps.

Horvath was beside him too, another old friend, smiling at him and running his hands up and down his bow legs, black with hair. And there were the two newcomers.

Lenehan was a stringy young American of his own age, with soft blond hair cut short and sticking out all over in a pad of floppy bristles. He had the engaging American monkey-face, the face one sees in films about teenagers. "I'm Irish too," he said. "Second generation American. My old man still marches in the Saint Patrick's Day parade. I'm going to have a look at the old country this trip."

And there was Galliver, the European champion. Colin looked at him with interest. He was a man of twenty-six, which was getting on for a miler these days, with a body like whipcord. Enormously talented, he had one all-important failing: his reflexes ran away with him. He had spoiled race after race through impatience.

Colin had seen the film of the 1500 metres at the last Olympics when Galliver was twenty-two and at the height of his powers. You could positively see the man getting edgier as they took the bell and swung into the long semi-circle leading to the back straight. At last, four hundred yards from home, he could stand the strain no longer and made his break, tearing away into the lead and electrifying the crowd. Of course he burned himself out before the finish and stumbled over the line in fourth position. But in the European Games, two summers ago, the miracle had happened: he had contained himself until fifty yards from the line and then produced an explosive finish to win. The film showed that he had been boxed in until then. He was an anarchic influence; other runners hated to have him with them in a race. He made everyone as jumpy as himself; they tended to lose their sense of pace through worrying about what he was going to do.

Waiting now for the race to start, he kept rolling his shoulder blades in a circular movement and wringing his hands. The skin of his square face seemed to be pulled too tight over his cheek-bones; his lips were fixed in an eternal convulsive smile. His hair was a curly brown and he was very popular off the track.

The starter had checked their identities now and was calling them to their positions; starting from the inside, Horvath— Lenehan— Longbottom— Warnock— Higgs— Galliver. Colin felt his chest constrict and his mouth dry slightly; he was suddenly keyed-up. But not unpleasantly. He was the warhorse when it hears the bugle: there was going to be a fight and he was going to enjoy it. His skin began to prickle.

"Take your marks!"

"Set!"

The pistol.

As he swept forward in line with the others a controlled jubilation came over him. Christ, I'm full of running! he thought. I'm absolutely full of running. He was a man embarrassed with the richness of his possessions, not knowing how to dispose of them all; he would have to spread them out over the full four laps.

Higgs had gone straight into the lead and was spanking along at a good pace. Colin reined himself in easily, lying last, floating round the track without any sensation of effort. He felt, in the narrow grey world he was now inhabiting: I am working up to an important conclusion, a moment that must on no account be spoiled. Technique was the important thing, the manner of doing, the professionalism of it: not any other considerations, whether economic, moral or aesthetic.

They completed their first hieratic circle, Higgs still leading, with Horvath trundling bandy-legged after him; then Lenehan, wiry and elastic; then the withdrawn Longbottom striding along in a solipsistic world; Colin saw that he was no racer but a runner, and a Narcissus among runners at that; he ran for the pleasure of watching himself move. Galliver was directly in front of Colin; he was able to watch him most clearly of all. The man ran with a crude, ill-contained energy, radiating nervous tension. Colin thought: a week ago I would have been affected by this.

They passed the finishing-line for the first time, and he said to himself: About fifty-eight seconds. Perfect pace. He shot a glance at the big dial with its sweeping second-hand, and confirmed the time. His edge of pleasure grew keener.

Yet there was something mesmeric about their movement. The others too had realised that the pace was right; there was no need to disturb the man who was doing the hard work. So Higgs pulled them round again. With each yard run, the inevitability of running in this particular race strengthened; they grew into it, felt at home together. Every inch of distance was a small bronze weight added to the force that pushed them forwards; momentum increased with the distance covered. This was one of the joys of doing anything difficult: each step taken over the elected terrain made the next one easier and more natural.

At the end of the second lap one sensed them realise that they had passed the summit, were now on the downward slope. Colin once more guessed the time right: fifty-eight again. This was almost dangerously correspondent to his own wishes. A tiny doubt came to him: was all this too good to be true? He brushed it aside as inessential. The essential was this living organism striding round a track and this poised personality, shorn of attributes, ready for its convulsion.

It was evident that Higgs was faltering. All the runners smelt it in the air; his very manner of running, the set of the man, betrayed uncertainty. He had gone out knowing he had one thing to do: he had to run a fast first half. After that he was free; he was free now with no shell of responsibility to fit himself into, like a hermit crab. He was divagating before their very eyes.

The pace slackened. The hypnotic effect slowed down, deprived of its rhythm; the runners and the crowd visibly came out of their trance and looked around for someone who would lead the way back into it. With what consciousness remained uncommitted to the pressure gauges of heart and lungs, the revolution counters of arms and legs, Colin wondered if he should take over leadership himself, but he desisted: why be impatient? Impatience was a characteristic of the Warnock of two days ago, not the new one.

Galliver too was somehow able to resist his own nature; so they entered into a period of temporary status quo: a caretaker period where things stayed as they were until the force of circumstance should alter them. At reduced speed they crawled their way round the great quarter-mile ellipse, ants on some pointless errand.

When the rate of advance seemed at last unbearably slow Lenehan skipped round the two men in front of him and set out on his own. It was a half-hearted action; you felt that he was looking over his shoulder all the time, waiting for someone else to take over so as not to hold the lead at the critical time, a furlong from home.

They came solidly down the straight to the bell, quickly resettled into the new scheme of things. The lap had cost them sixty-one seconds, and the clock stood at 2:57. That means fifty-five for the last lap, thought Colin. Very well; there would have to be a development soon, a break. Otherwise the time would be another slow one: a mere 3:56 again. He did not want it to be a three fifty-six, he had passed that stage. But once again he resolutely put such accountancy out of his mind. What did the time matter anyway? It was the race that mattered.

The brash clangour of the bell, riding over a slow crescendo of noise from the crowd, never went unnoticed. Change became imperative; the psychology of the race demanded it. Colin saw Horvath close up to Lenehan's elbow, to have his opponent as a springboard when he required him. And now Galliver too was making a move. In a couple of nervy strides he was past Higgs and Longbottom in third place. Colin, with a pang of excitement, said to himself: so be it. Better to have those two behind me, where they can do no harm. He passed them and was again in the tracks of Galliver.

They swept around the long swinging bend. It was a delicious moment—you knew yourself to be on the verge of the last act: comedy or tragedy? Did it matter anyway? Provided the great mechanism was wound up and given its freedom, the content was of little importance. They were in the play-realm now, the realm of experience heightened by its limitations, its selectivity, and the culminating point of that experience was at hand. They were part of a work of art.

Suddenly, without ceremony, they were in *medias res*. Galliver bolted round Lenehan and Horvath, a hare making a dash for safety. There were three hundred yards to go.

Immediate decisions were called for. Colin had no hesitation. He followed him. Horvath and Lenehan disappeared behind and to his left. His life had been tending towards this single moment. In the heat of action it was impossible, unnecessary, to disentangle motives, but he knew subconsciously that he was acting in accordance with his own estimation of himself. The risk was huge, but he claimed the freedom to take it. He was in effect saying: in this company I am the best man and I challenge you to dispute it.

Galliver ran, Colin behind him. They were moving very fast now, almost at capacity, he realised. How close to himself in ability this man Galliver was! They were both on the verge of total commitment, and the gap between them never altered. They flung themselves into the last long bend as though locked together.

The bend seemed endless; eternally they would be swinging slowly round, inches to the left with every stride, running just within exhaustion, and nothing would ever change. Colin knew nothing of what was happening to anyone save Galliver and himself. They were the only protagonists now; by his gesture he had dismissed the others.

As they entered the straight they crossed the boundary into a purely physical kingdom. Nothing mattered now but to keep going: intellectual and emotional commitment now became total, nothing remained but to carry out those commitments to the end.

Galliver was weakening! This *alter ego*, this twin, was giving up the struggle, prematurely worn down by his own psychology. He wavered where he ran by the kerb-stone; he was finished.

A twin realisation, experienced at the level of the blood, came upon Colin. This was the creative orgasm now, and there would be no delay. Simultaneously, there was the knowledge that a great release had taken place in him unbidden. He knew in theory what it must be—the tapping of the final reserve—but the fact obliterated all theory by its intensity.

It was a wave of feral aggression, a lust for power and at the same time a sacred terror as though he were pursued by some fierce and inescapable beast. He exulted and shook with terror at the same time.

Life existed now only as far as the finishing tape, seventy yards ahead. Reaching that he would possess himself of a glittering kingdom and put himself beyond the reach of what pursued him. But it must be done immediately, and he must destroy himself in the process. He must be burnt up in a pyre of his own energy. Shortening his stride, he ran easily past Galliver.

Now there were only himself and the line of white. He felt himself going faster and faster with every step: but at the same time he was slowing-up to motionlessness. He was a runner in a frieze, the lover in Keats' Ode, for ever astrain and for ever doomed to remain on the same spot. The element of time expanded and contracted simultaneously; in this heraldic play-world where all was pregnant with a momentous seriousness, a seriousness on the threshold of physical agony, where the actions of this one man who was himself in some way were determining the fate of all men, none of the rules of life applied any more. There was no good, no evil, no success, no failure. There was only the man eternally running, eternally motionless.

And yet somehow the tape approached him. He looked at one moment and it was a mile away; at the next it was before him, it was breaking against him, he was safe and in his kingdom. And his body was burnt away. It fell away from him, consciousness fell away from him in a change that might have been into life or death or into both. But he felt with his last remnant of awareness that arms were receiving him.

He came to into a world of human solidarity, where his fellow men were holding him, taking care of him. It was delicious to feel the texture of a track-suit against his face, feel a wiry arm holding him under the shoulders, hear with the return of that sense the tired voices of Lenehan, Horvath, Galliver congratulating him. Their faces were drawn and drained, their cheeks congested, their lips coated with a small white fur; but they were congratulating him. In his heart he said: I did it for you; in reality, only for you.

The loudspeaker penetrated to him: "First, Number Five, C. Warnock, of Queen's University, Belfast. Time: three minutes fifty-two point six seconds, which, subject to ratification, is a new United Kingdom National, United Kingdom All-Comers and European record . . ." A roar, obliterating the voice.

". . . Horvath, Hungary. Three minutes fifty-three point nine seconds.

"Third, Number Two, J. Galliver, of Birchfield Harriers. Three minutes fifty-four point five seconds.

"Fourth, R. Lenehan. . . ."

He hardly knew what these strange facts meant.

The Marathoners

SEE HOW THEY RUN

George Harmon Coxe

(1941)

The bus stopped at the side of the road opposite the country lane, and as he waited for the door to open, Johnny Burke could see the farmhouse and the sea of parked cars in the yard beyond.

"It's going to be hot out there today," the driver said. "And, brother, I sure don't envy you any. When I go twenty-six miles I want to do it sitting down."

Johnny swung to the ground, leather carryall in hand. The smell of the countryside was fresh and fragrant in his nostrils, but he knew the driver was right. It would be hot. In the seventies now by the feel of it. He was right about the twenty-six miles too. Why anyone should want to run that distance had always been a mystery that not even his father could satisfactorily explain.

Going up the lane he remembered the farmhouse from that other trip, years ago, but he did not remember the yard. Like a picnic ground or gypsy carnival, with the relatives of the contestants milling around and laughing and eating basket lunches. Already there were some who stood about in track suits and sweaters, and Johnny Burke smiled a little scornfully. Coming here that other time with his father he had been thrilled and excited, but that, he realized now, was because he had been so young.

On the porch of the rambling farmhouse which had for this one day been turned into the marathon headquarters of the world, the hubbub of voices lay thick about him. Inside there would be places to change, for his father had told him how the furniture would be carted to the barn beforehand. Somehow this seemed as fantastic as the crowd outside or the race itself. Why should the owner turn her house inside out for a couple hundred maniacs? A Mrs. Tebeau, the papers had said. And although she was seventy-three years old she had, with the help of her daughter, served as hostess to the marathoners for sixteen years, furnishing sandwiches and milk for all who wanted them.

He noticed the girl as he climbed the steps. She was standing a few feet away, talking to some man; a slim, straight, pleasant-faced girl, looking strangely out of place here with her trim, heather-colored suit. She glanced toward him as he stopped, and smiled, and it was such a friendly smile that he smiled back and felt a sudden tingling ripple through him.

"Aren't you Johnny Burke?" The man, moving forward now, was a lank, lazy-looking individual, all but his eyes, which were blue and quizzical and direct. "I thought so," he said when Johnny nodded. "I saw you at the Intercollegiates last year. That was a nice mile you ran. I'm Dave Shedden, of the *Standard.*"

Johnny shook hands and thanked him. Shedden glanced at a list in his hand.

"So you're the John Burke that entered this year? We thought it was your dad. This would have been his twentieth."

"He couldn't make it," Johnny said, and then, because he could not explain: "So I thought I'd come up and take his place."

"It'll take some running to do that."

"So I understand."

"And what about the invitation mile in New York tomorrow?"

"I'm passing it up."

"Oh? I thought that was supposed to be your dish."

Johnny began to dislike Shedden. There was an undertone of sarcasm in his words, a skepticism that Johnny found annoying.

"I'd rather win this," he said.

"Just like that?"

"Don't you think I can?"

"Could be." Shedden shrugged. "Only you're stepping out of your class, aren't you? You won't be running against a select little group of college boys today."

Johnny gave him back his sardonic grin. "Select, maybe; but they all know how to run or they couldn't get entered."

"They've got reputations, you mean," Shedden said. "Well, out here a guy needs more than that. It's pretty tough on prima donnas."

Johnny let it go and would have moved on had it not been for a sturdy, bronzed man of forty-five or so who bustled up to take the reporter's arm.

"Hey, Dave, where's Burke? You seen Burke anywhere?"

"This is Burke," said Shedden, and Johnny saw the man's wide-eyed glance and then his grin.

"Johnny Burke!" He was pumping Johnny's hand now and slapping his shoulder. "Young Johnny, huh? I'm Tom Reynolds. I've run with your old man for nineteen years. Did he ever tell you? Where is he? Is he quittin'? Old age getting him? Oh, Kay."

And then, miraculously, the girl Johnny had been watching was standing in front of him. Her hand was firm and warm in his and he saw that there were auburn lights in her dark hair, that her nose was cute and lightly freckled.

"I saw you in the meet at the Garden two years ago," she said. "And I think it's grand, your running in place of your father today. He wanted to make it twenty races in a row, didn't he? And I heard what you said to Mr. Shedden about the race in New York. Will you mind so awfully?"

Johnny Burke said he wouldn't. He was used to the idea now, but two weeks ago it had been different. He had not known until then that his father would never run again, and he remembered too vividly coming down the stairs with the doctor that evening and going out on the porch where, with the darkness masking their faces, they had talked of Johnny, senior, and the verdict had been given. No more than six months, the doctor said. Probably not that.

It had been a bad night for Johnny, and before he fell asleep at dawn he knew what he wanted to do. His father, not yet aware how sick he was, had entered the marathon months before, and so, the next afternoon, Johnny told him he was going to use that entry and run this year's race by proxy and make the record an even twenty.

Even now he could see the thin wan face brighten as his father lay there in bed with the pillows propping him up.

"You will? You'll take my place?" he'd said. "Honest, Johnny?" And then, thinking, the doubt had come. "But that race in New York you've been talking about? That's the next day."

"The invitation mile?" Johnny had said. "What's that? I've beaten all those guys before, one time or another."

"You could win that race, though."

"I'll win the marathon too."

His father had laughed at that. "You're crazy! I only won twice in nineteen years and I was better than most."

"Ah, you were never anything but a fair country runner."

"I could outrun you the best day you ever saw," his father had cracked, and Johnny had jeered at him past the hardness in his throat because he saw how good it made his father feel.

There had been but two weeks in which to train, and he had worked diligently, following the schedule his father mapped out, wanting to cry sometimes when he saw how thrilled and proud his father seemed when he listened to the nightly reports. Johnny had worked up to twenty miles the day before yesterday, and when his father heard the time he admitted that Johnny might have a chance.

"Only don't try to win it, Johnny," he said. "This is no mile. You've been running races where only the first three places count. In this one the first thirty-five get listed in the papers."

Johnny hadn't argued then, nor had he told anyone the truth.

He knew how the newspapers would pounce on the sentimental elements of the story if they knew his father had run his last race. Not even his father must know that. And there was no sacrifice involved anyway. He had looked forward to that New York race, but he was glad to run this race instead, for he loved his father and knew how much this day meant to him each year.

He saw that Shedden and Tom Reynolds had moved on and realized the girl was waiting for him to speak. "No, I don't mind," he said again. "I've been arguing with Dad for years about this race and now I want to find out for myself."

"Arguing?"

"I can't figure it out. Dad has won twice, but in the past ten years he hasn't even been in the first five."

"My father hasn't been in the first five lately either."

"That's what I mean. Twenty-six miles, three hundred and eighty-five yards is an awful grind. If a guy feels he can't win—"

"You think no one should enter unless he feels he can win?"

"Not unless he's young and on the way up. There's maybe a dozen runners in the bunch. The rest of it's a farce." She looked at him strangely, but he did not notice and waved his hand to include the yard and farmhouse. "Look at them," he said, and in his laugh there was something superior, unconscious perhaps, but noticeable, for his was the viewpoint of one who has been at the top. "Anybody can get in that mails an entry. Anybody."

"Yes," Kay Reynolds said. "It's a poor man's race. You don't have to go to college or belong to any club, and there's nothing in it but a medal and a cup if you win. And yet they've been running this race for over forty years. There have been marathons ever since the Greeks defeated the Persians."

"Sure," Johnny said. "But why do they let all the clowns in? I read in the paper about some of them that even smoke—"

"Benny 'Cigars' Kelly and Jim 'Tobacco' Lane."

"Yes," Johnny said. "And the papers say they flatfoot the whole distance, puffing cigars and making faces at the crowd."

"Yes," Kay Reynolds said, "there are clowns. There always are in any event that's truly open. And there is Clarence De Mar, who is fifty-two and has won seven times. And Kennedy. He's fifty-seven. He's run twenty-eight times and finished twenty-seven races. And Semple, who's been running for twenty-four years. And your father and mine. That's why the papers call this race the biggest and freest sport spectacle on earth. Did you ever run before a half-million people?"

Johnny looked at her then. Her eyes were steady now and she wasn't smiling. "That's a lot of people," he said, and grinned. "Let's settle for a spectacle."

"But still a little beneath you."

Johnny's grin went away and his cheeks got hot. Who did she think she was, bawling him out? "What difference does it make? If a couple hundred fellows want to come out and run twenty-six miles, that's their business. I didn't come up here to make a spectacle; I came to win a race."

"Yes," the girl said, not looking at him now, and distance in her voice. "And I can see why you think you will. You've had every advantage, haven't you? The best coaches, and trainers and special food and privileges and expense money. These others have nothing but enthusiasm and determination. They are self-taught and trained and what food they get they work for six days a week."

"Okay," said Johnny, "I'm a snob. I came up to run this race, but I don't have to like it." He turned away, stopped to say stiffly: "It's nice to know you'll be rooting for me."

"I will," Kay Reynolds said, "because I'll be remembering your father, like thousands of others. I only hope you can do as well today as he would if he were here."

Johnny went inside, red-faced and angry, and the sight that met his eyes served only to heighten the irritation and bear out his argument. Like a side show at the circus. Skins of every shade from skim milk to chocolate. Fuzzy-chinned kids, gray-thatched and bald-topped oldsters; fat boys with pillow stomachs and skinny ones with pipestem legs.

He made his way into a side room that smelled of wintergreen oil and stale perspiration and old shoes. He found a place to sit down and began to change, not listening to the babble about him until someone addressed him.

"Your first race?" The thin Yankee drawl came from a blond, shaggy-haired fellow beside him. "It's my fifth. My name's Bronson."

Johnny had to take the outthrust hand. "Burke," he said.

"Not Johnny Burke's boy?" Bronson's face lit up. "Hey, fellows! What do you think? This is Johnny Burke's boy."

They flocked about him then, fifteen or twenty of them, shaking hands and asking questions and wanting to know about his father and wishing him luck. And though he was proud of his father when he heard their tributes, he was scornful, too, because, of the group, only a few made mention of his own achievements; even then the others did not seem impressed, cataloguing him not as Johnny Burke who'd done a 4:10 mile but only as Johnny Burke's boy.

"I'd never forget him," Bronson said as they went out on the porch. "Hadn't been for your dad I'd never finished my first race. I was down around Lake Street, running about twentieth when your dad came up.

You know they got official cars that have paper cups of tea and lemon halves and things like that to hand out when you need 'em, but they're caterin' to the leaders mostly. And I think I'm about done when a car comes past and your dad hollers and they pull alongside to give him a cup of water and he douses it on my head." Bronson grinned. "I finished. Twenty-third."

Johnny looked at him. "Did you ever win?"

"Oh, no. Finished ninth once, though. Got me a medal for it. I figure to be in the first ten this year too. Look, I'd like you to meet my wife. She's heard me talk about your dad—" He turned and was waving to someone, and Johnny Burke saw the sturdy apple-cheeked girl on the running board of a five-year-old sedan. She had a child on her knee and waved back. Johnny drew away, confused and a little embarrassed.

"Thanks," he said, "but hadn't we better get along to the starting line? Where you from?" he asked, to change the subject.

"Over Pittsfield way. Got a farm there."

"That's quite a jaunt, isn't it?"

"Oh, no. Lots come from Canada, even. We make a day of it. Start early, you know, and stop for a bite somewhere."

"And drive back afterwards?"

"You bet. Alice now, that's my wife, will ride along after we start and find some spot down around Brookline to watch the fellows go by; then she'll pick me up at Exeter Street after I finish. The official car'll have our bags all there waiting for us; and say—" He smiled with some embarrassment. "I guess you know a lot more about running than I do, but if this is your first marathon—well, I don't want to try and tell you, but don't let these front runners bother you. It's an awful long haul and—"

Johnny sighed. "I guess I can make out," he said, and then Tom Reynolds was there, looking bronzed and sturdy and fit, Johnny thought, like his father before that illness came.

"Been looking for you." He took Johnny's arm and drew him aside. "Don't let any of those fancy Dans fool you after we start. They'll dance away from the rest of us for three or four miles and then they'll get a stitch and get picked up by the Red Cross car and watch the rest of the race over a tailboard. They're like some of the other phonies."

"I'll remember," Johnny said, but Reynolds wasn't through.

"Your old man and I've been doing this for nineteen years. This was to be our last—we're no Clarence De Mars or Bill Kennedys—and we're old enough to quit. But now you've got to take old Johnny's place. Stick with me. I know the pace."

Johnny nodded his thanks. "We'll see," he said. "I never ran the course, but I think I can go the distance all right." Funny. To hear them talk you'd think he wasn't even going to finish without everybody helping him. "I'll make out."

"Sure you will. And say, Coolidge Corner in Brookline was always a bad spot for Johnny and me. That's gettin' near the end, you know, with lots of autos around, and not bein' front runners we couldn't always count on an official car bein' near. So Kay's always been there since she was a little girl, with lemon halves in case we needed 'em. She'll have one for you today." He paused and Johnny's glance faltered before the steady eyes because it seemed as though Reynolds had read his thoughts. "But maybe you won't need anything," he said abruptly. "Anyway, good luck."

The starter got them away promptly at the stroke of twelve and down the lane they went, stretched clear across its width and fifteen or twenty deep. To Johnny, it was nothing but a mob and he moved out briskly to get away from the dust and jostling.

By the time he reached the main highway he was running fifth and satisfied with his position, and for a while then he did not think about the race, but only how he felt. He felt good. Loose, with lots of juice in his flat-muscled body and an easy animal grace that brought the road back under him in long effortless strides. He didn't think about his pace until he heard someone pounding up beside him and then a voice in his ear.

"Easy, son." It was Tom Reynolds and he looked worried. "This is no mile."

Johnny nodded, a little irritated that this man should tell him how to run. He shortened his stride slightly and fell off the pace. Two chunky individuals went by him, one young and one old, flat-footed runners, making it tough for themselves already. Another came alongside, a string bean with pasty skin and a handkerchief, knotted at the corners, on his head, to keep the sun off.

He saw that Tom Reynolds was at his shoulder and thought about his advice. He thought of other things Tom Reynolds did not know about. He'd grown up knowing of this hobby of his father's, and how he trained, and hearing over and over the details of all these B.A.A. marathons. As a boy the race had seemed a colorful and exciting climax that he might sometime reach himself, but later, as he grew older and there were no more victories for his father, the idea of this annual contest had become an object of secret ridicule. Even his mother had sometimes acted ashamed in those last few years before her death. It wasn't dignified for a man of his age, she said. And what did he get out of it? It was probably the other women in her bridge club, Johnny thought, who asked her questions that she could not answer because she herself did not know why her husband ran on, year after year.

His own training had started while he was a junior in high school, and he could remember his father making him jog along with him sometimes, short distances at first, and working up in easy stages until he could do three or four loping miles without too much uneasiness. He had never lost a race in high school, and in college, though he was the son of a machinist and had to earn part of his expenses, he had become a figure of some importance on the campus solely because of the training his father had given him. That's why he was running today: to pay back a little of what he owed while it would do some good.

He saw now that they were running through a town and knew it must be Framingham. About five miles, he guessed, and he still felt good and there was no tightness in his lungs. There were crowds along the curbing now and he could hear them yelling encouragement up ahead of him. Then he was going by the checking station and from somewhere at the side he heard a roar that made him smile.

"Yeah, Burke," they said, and he waved back, thinking of the times he'd heard that same cry in the Stadium and Franklin Field and in the Garden.

He thought then of Tom Reynolds and glanced over his shoulder. Runners were strung out behind him as far as he could see, but Reynolds was not among them and he knew he must have stepped up his pace while he had been thinking.

Well, that was all right. There were other things Reynolds did not know. He and Bronson and those runners who had shaken hands. Some had probably never heard of him because they had no racing interest but the marathon distance; the others who knew of his reputation—Shedden, the reporter, and Kay Reynolds included—did not give him a chance. To them he was just another miler, and a cocky one at that.

Perhaps he was. And this race was as he'd always maintained in good-natured arguments with his father: a bunch of screwballs out to make an exhibition of themselves for the most part, with a dozen or so real runners in the pack. Well, he was running this one race and he was going to win it and that would be that. What the others did not know was that even while he was in college he had often trained with his father during vacations, sometimes driving the car slowly behind him to protect him from the other cars along the road, and sometimes jogging alongside him, mile after mile. He knew what it was to go twenty miles—he'd once gone twenty-five. Today he was going to do twenty-six miles and three hundred and eighty-five yards.

He brought the race back into the focus of his thoughts and found himself approaching the center of Natick with perhaps ten miles behind him. Across the square some enthusiasts had stretched a banner as a token of encouragement for a local contestant and as Johnny drew near he heard his name called from the edges of the road and found the tribute a cheerful sound, warmly stimulating. But the race was already taking its toll of impudent front runners. Of the dozen or so who had been in front of him, seven had dropped out. Approaching Wellesley he saw the pasty fellow with the handkerchief on his head sitting at the roadside waiting for a lift.

"Blisters," he said as Johnny went by. "Terrible blisters," he said, and waved cheerfully.

Along by the college the girls were out in force. Bright-faced smiling girls in sweaters and gay skirts and saddle-strapped shoes. There would be girls like that in New York tomorrow night, and though he would not run he would be there for the meet and the parties and dancing afterward. He'd get the four o'clock down this afternoon, and Stan Tarleton would meet him, and with no racing tomorrow he could step out.

"Halfway," he said as he passed the checking station and took stock of himself and the race.

He was breathing pretty well, but he could feel his legs and the pounding of the pavement now, realizing that the roadbed was a lot harder on his feet than a cinder track. He lengthened his stride for a hundred yards to get a kink out of his right thigh and it went away all right and he dropped back to his former pace.

Between Wellesley and Auburndale, two runners passed him and he let them go. Like the third quarter in a mile run, he thought, when it's still a long way to the end, but you have to keep the pace up. He was conscious of the heat now and it was harder to breathe. The pain was coming slowly, not real bad yet, but frightening when he counted the miles. Eighteen behind him. The hills of Newton and eight more to go.

The first hill seemed endless, slowing him down until he was practically walking at the top. Then, not sure how much longer he could go, he gained the downslope and his strength came back and he was struggling upward again. Gradually, as he fought that rise, a curious giddiness he had never experienced before came upon him and he did not know he was walking until he heard someone speak his name.

"Come on, young Johnny," the voice said. "Only a couple more hills to go."

It was an effort for Johnny to put the voice and the tanned blond face together and then, through the curtain of his giddiness, he knew it was Bronson, and picked up his stride again to match the other. The car, coming up from behind, meant nothing to him until there came a sudden icy shock upon his head and the feel of water trickling through his hair and down his neck. Then, abruptly, his giddiness had gone and he saw Bronson grinning at him, an empty paper cup in his hand as the official car moved on ahead.

"Thanks," Johnny Burke said. "I guess it was the heat." And he was both grateful and angry with himself for not remembering that in this race there were accompanying cars and refreshments for those lucky enough to get them.

"Sure," Bronson said. "Let's go now."

He started out in front, grinning over his shoulder, and Johnny went after him, seeing the other draw ahead until he realized that a country boy from Pittsfield was showing him his heels; then he pulled his shoulders back a little and sardonic resentment at his near collapse kept him dogging Bronson's footsteps all the way up the College hill and down the long slope to Cleveland Circle.

Here it was flat and he knew there were only five miles to go. The pain was coming again and a numbness crept along his leg and he thought, *It's like the last lap,* and then a new and horrible awareness came to him and he forgot the man up ahead. This last-lap pain for him had never lasted longer than a minute or so; now it must go on for five more miles.

"You went out a little fast, boy. You got anything left?" Tom Reynolds was at his shoulder, though he seemed a block away. His face was twisted and set, too, but he was breathing all right, and his stride was firm and solid.

"Sure I've got something left." Johnny got the words out one at a time, laboriously, angrily.

"Show me. Come on. Match me for a hundred strides. Your old man could do it if he was here."

Anger drove Johnny Burke along for quite a while. He matched Tom Reynolds' pace, forgetting the torture in his lungs and the aching numbness in his legs. He wanted to talk back to this man who drove him on, but he knew he could not speak, and kept pounding on, not counting the strides any longer but always matching them until, somewhere down along the misty row of faces on the curbstone, Reynolds spoke again.

"This is the place," he said heavily. "This is where your dad and I always find out who's the better man each year. You're on your own now, Johnny Burke."

He moved out in front then, Reynolds did, an inch at a time, and Johnny saw the number on his back pull away and dissolve into soft focus. Somewhere, dim and thin and faraway, he could hear the voice of the crowd. "Come on, Burke," it said.

And he kept on, holding his own as a new nausea began to fasten about his stomach. Not cramps, but a simple sickness he could not understand until he realized that over the past few miles the poisonous smell of automobile exhausts had become much stronger as traffic increased. The thought that a contest must be run under such conditions infuriated him, and yet, even as he raged, he knew that this was but another hazard in the race to be shared by all who dared to try it.

For a step or two he ran bent over to see if this would help. There were more people here, he knew, and he could see some kind of square with shops and store fronts and streetcar tracks down the middle of the street. He staggered finally, fighting the nausea rather than his weariness. He looked about for an official car and found none near him. Then, his stride breaking now, he saw something loom out from the edge of the crowd. A hand found his and a girl's voice was in his ear.

"Suck on this," it said. "It's not far now. You can do it."

There was something in his hand and he put it to his lips and there was a tart strong taste of lemon in his mouth, laving his throat and starting the saliva again. He felt it going down his throat, the quick contraction of his stomach. He sucked greedily, breathing around the lemon, and gradually his head cleared and the nausea fled and there was nothing left but the pain and torment that come near the end for every runner who goes all out.

Someone drew alongside him. He could hear the slap of shoes against the asphalt pavement. The sound angered him and he pulled away, finding the strength somehow and knowing then that he was running better.

Up ahead he saw a bobbing figure and focused on it, watching it come nearer, drawing even and then hearing Bronson's voice as he went past: "Give it to 'em, Burke! Give 'em hell for me!"

Vaguely he remembered passing someone else, for the sound of labored breathing was not his own, and as he came into the approach of Kenmore Square he saw a familiar number just ahead and then he was matching strides with Tom Reynolds.

"Go on," the older man called, though it must have been an effort now. "What're you waitin' for? It's only a mile and you've got two ahead of you."

He saw them out in front as he pulled away from Reynolds. They were running shoulder to shoulder, raggedly, and he set out after them, blindly in his exhaustion, yet no longer worried or afraid. His running was detached, all but the torment of pain in his chest, and though below his waist there was nothing but fringe, he somehow found himself thinking with a curious clarity that explained many things in that last mile.

It was the cheering that started those thoughts. The sound of his name, like the pounding of rain, refreshing him, beating out a monotone of encouragement. "Burke . . . Burke . . . Burke!"

He remembered the cheering back in Framingham, the vague sounds of applause and enthusiasm that had accompanied him mile after mile. Not a brief, concerted cheer for a stretch run and victory that he had so often heard, but something new and different that he had never before experienced. For more than two hours he had heard these sounds, and the thought of this helped carry him now, filling him with wonderment until, struggling closer to those twin bobbing figures up ahead, the question came to him—how did they know him, this crowd? They had never seen him before. His name was in the papers' starting line-up. Number 18. Johnny Burke. And then, all at once, he knew. Those half million along the course who cheered were cheering a name, the memory of a name, the memory of other races back through the years. Not him, but his father, whom they had known and loved as a great competitor who always gave his best.

Here were twin shadows at his shoulder now and the blood was boiling into his eyes along with the tears, and under his heart were red-hot coals. Loose bird shot filled his throat and the faces of the crowd went swimming by like painted faces in a dream. He lifted his elbows a little higher to give his lungs more clearance. He made a staggering turn into Exeter Street for the last hundred yards, and the sound of his name beat against his eardrums and he knew, finally, why his father had come back to run for nineteen years, why the others, not the clowns but the good competitors, came out on this day each year. Whether he finished first or fifty-first, each heard, for a little while, the sound of his name, a bit of acclaim to treasure secretly, to set him apart from his fellow man and make brighter an existence that otherwise was humdrum and monotonous; not an easy thing for any man to give up, for there is a need of such tribute in all men of heart and spirit, and each must find his little share in whatever way he can.

They said it was the closest finish in many years, but Johnny Burke did not know it. He did not feel the tape at his chest and would have run on had not strong hands grabbed him, supporting his arms so that he stood straddle-legged in the street with a sick stupor enveloping him until someone threw water in his face. Gradually then, the opaque shutter of his vision lifted and he straightened, seeing other faces about him and the cameras of the press photographers. When he felt someone prying at his hand he opened it and looked down and found the lemon, now squeezed to yellow pulp. The reporters were kind to him as he stretched out on the white sheeted cot in the basement of the old brick building. They stood about patiently until his heart had slowed and the strength began to flow again along his muscles. When he sat up someone put the laurel wreath upon his head. He had to keep it on while the flash bulbs popped, and then he had to talk, though there was little he could say except that he was glad he'd won and he knew his father would be pleased.

Later, under the shower, he thought of all the things he might have said, and of them all the thing he most wanted to say could be told to no one but his father. He knew how it would sound to those reporters—falsely modest, pretentious; corny, they'd call it. How could he tell them that he had not won this race alone, could not have won but for his father? Oh, it was his legs and lungs that did the job, but, falling back there in the hills of Newton, it was Bronson who had pulled him through. Bronson, talking to him, getting water from the official car and reviving him. Not because Bronson liked him or cared particularly whether he finished or not, but because in him he saw the other Johnny Burke. And Tom Reynolds, taunting him into matching strides when he started to lag again, reminding him always of his father so that he would not quit.

These two who had helped him had been thinking of his father, and yet, even with their help, he could not have won without the lemon that stilled his nausea and comforted him. Now, letting the cold water play along his spine, he had to know whether this, too, had been offered because of his father or whether that gesture Kay Reynolds had made was in some part for him alone.

Upstairs in the corridors of the old clubhouse the wives and mothers and families of those who had already finished clustered about their men; others, still waiting, gathered round to greet the front runners with the camaraderie born of good-natured competition. None seemed disgruntled, and when Johnny Burke appeared they came to him with their congratulations as though he had long been one of them. He thanked them as best he could, the cords in his throat tightening as he spoke of his father and parried questions he could not answer.

How long he stood there he was never sure; he only knew that it was an anxious time because always he was looking over heads and shoulders for a dark head and a heather-colored suit. Then, finally, he was by himself and an official had come up to ask him how the cup and medal were to be engraved.

"The way the entry read," Johnny Burke said, and the official, not understanding, smiled.

"But you're Johnny Burke, Junior, aren't you?"

"Yes," Johnny said, and could neither explain nor say he wanted his father's record to read an even twenty races run. "Yes," he said again, "but I don't use the Junior much. John Burke is the way I want it."

Then a soft voice was at his elbow, and his heart skipped and went racing on as he turned and saw Kay Reynolds' friendly smile. He had to clear his throat before he could reply to her congratulations, but there was a curious glow in his breast now; for as he took her offered hand in his he found something in her eyes that made him forget New York, something that told him from here on he was on his very own.

THE LOVELINESS OF THE LONG-DISTANCE RUNNER

Sara Maitland

(1980)

I sit at my desk and make a list of all the things I am not going to think about for the next four and half hours. Although it is still early the day is conducive to laziness—hot and golden. I am determined that I will not be lazy. The list reads:

1. My lover is running in an organized marathon race. I hate it.

2. Pheidippides, the Greek who ran the first marathon, dropped dead at the end of it. And his marathon was 4 miles shorter than hers is going to be. There is also heat stroke, torn Achilles tendons, shin splints and cramp. Any and all of which, including the first option, will serve her right. And will also break my heart.

3. The women who are going to support her, love her, pour water down her back and drinks down her throat are not me. I am jealous of them.

4. Marathon running is a goddam competitive, sexist, lousy thing to do.

5. My lover has the most beautiful body in the world. Because she runs. I fell in love with her because she had the most beautiful body I had ever seen. What, when it comes down to it, is the difference between my devouring of her as a sex object and her competitive running? Anyway she says she does not run competitively. Anyway I say that I do not any longer love her just because she has the most beautiful body.

Now she will be doing her warm-up exercises. I know these well, as she does them every day. She was doing them the first time I saw her. I had gone to the country to stay the weekend with her sister, who's a lawyer colleague of mine and a good friend. We were doing some work together. We were sitting in her living room and she was feeding her baby and Jane came in, in running shorts, T-shirt and yards and yards of leg. Katy had often joked about her sister who was a games mistress in an all-girls school, and I assumed that this was she. Standing by the front door, with the sun on her hair, she started these amazing exercises. She stretched herself from the waist and put her hands flat on the floor; she took her slender foot in her hand and bent over backwards. The blue shorts strained slightly; there was nothing spare on her, just miles and miles of tight, hard, thin muscle. And as she exhibited all this peerless flesh she chatted casually of this and that—how's the baby, and where she was going to run. She disappeared through the door. I said to Katy, "Does she know I'm gay?"

Katy grinned and said, "Oh, yes."

"I feel set-up."

"That's what they're called—setting-up exercises."

I felt very angry. Katy laughed and said, "She is too."

"Is what?" I asked.

"Gay."

I melted into a pool of desire.

It's better to have started. The prerace excitement makes me feel a little sick. Tension. But also . . . people punching the air and shouting "Let's go, let's go." Psyching themselves up. Casing each other out. Who's better than who? Don't like it. Don't want to do it. Wish I hadn't worn this T-shirt. It has "I AM A FEMINIST JOGGER" on it. Beth and Emma gave it to me. Turns people on though. Men. Not on to me but on to beating me. I won't care. There's a high on starting though, crossing the line. Good to be going, good to have got here. Doesn't feel different because someone has called it a marathon, rather than a good long run. Keep it that way. But I would like to break three and a half hours. Step by step. Feel good. Fitter than I've ever been in my life, and I like it. Don't care what Sally says. Mad to despise body when she loves it so. Dualist. I like running. Like me running. Space and good feeling. Want to run clear of this crowd—too many people, too many paces. Want to find someone to run my own pace with. Have to wait. Pace; endurance; deferment of plea-

sure; patience; power. Sally ought to like it—likes the benefits alright. Bloke nearby wearing a T-shirt that reads "RUNNERS MAKE THE BEST LOVERS." He grins at me. Bastard. I'll show him: run for the Women's Movement. A trick. Keep the rules. My number one rule is "run for yourself". But I bet I can run faster than him.

Hurt myself running once, because of that. Ran a 10-mile race, years ago, with Annie, meant to be a fun-run and no sweat. There was this jock; a real pig; he kept passing us, dawdling, letting us pass him, passing again. And every time these remarks—the vaseline stains from our nipples, or women getting him too turned an to run. Stuff like that; and finally he runs off, all sprightly and tough, patronizing. We ran on. Came into the last mile or so and there he was in front of us, tiring. I could see he was tired. "Shall we?" I said to Annie, but she was tired too. "Go on then," she was laughing at me, and I did. Hitched up a gear or two, felt great, zoomed down the hill after him, cruised alongside, made it look easy, said, "Hello, sweetheart, you look tired," and sailed on. Grinned back over my shoulder, he had to know who it was, and pulled a muscle in my neck. Didn't care—he was really pissed off. Glided over the finishing line and felt great for twenty minutes. Then I felt bad; should have known better—my neck hurt like hell, my legs cramped from over-running. But it wasn't just physical. Felt bad mentally. Playing those games.

Not today. Just run and feel good. Run into your own body and feel it. Feel road meeting foot, one by one, a good feeling. Wish Sally knew why I do it. Pray she'll come and see me finish. She won't. Stubborn bitch. Won't think about that. Just check leg muscles and pace and watch your ankles. Run.

If she likes to run that much of course I don't mind. It's nice some evenings when she goes out, and comes back and lies in the bath. A good salty woman. A flavour that I like. But I can't accept this marathon business: who wants to run 26 miles and 385 yards, in a competitive race? Jane does. For the last three months at least our lives have been taken over by those 26 miles, what we eat, what we do, where we go, and I have learned to hate every one of them. I've tried, "Why?" I've asked over and over again; but she just says things like, "Because it's there, the ultimate." Or "Just once Sally, I'll never do it again." *I bet,* I think viciously. Sometimes she rationalizes: women have to do it. Or, it's important to the girls she teaches. Or, it has to be a race because nowhere else is set up for it: you need the other runners, the solidarity, the motivation. "Call it sisterhood. You can't do it alone. You need . . ." And I interrupt and say, "You need the competition; you need people to beat. Can't you see." And she says, "You're wrong. You're also talking about something you know nothing about. So shut up. You'll just have to believe me: you need the other runners and mostly they need you and want you to finish. And the crowd wants you to finish, they say. I want to experience that solidarity, of other people wanting you to do what you want to do." Which is a slap in the face for me, because I don't want her to do what she wants to do.

And yet—I love the leanness of her, which is a gift to me from marathon training. I love what her body is and what it can do, and go on doing and not be tired by doing. She has the most beautiful legs, hard, stripped down, with no wastage, and her achilles tendons are like flexible rock. Running does that for her. And then I think, damn, damn, damn. I will not love her for those reasons; but I will love her because she is tough and enduring and wryly ironic. Because she is clear about what she wants and prepared to go through great pain to get it; and because her mind is clear, careful and still open to complexity. She wants to stop being a Phys. Ed. teacher because now that women are getting as much money for athletic programmes the authorities suddenly demand that they should get into competition, winning trips. Whereas when she started it was for fun and for women being together as women, doing the things they had been laughed at for as children.

She says I'm a dualist and laughs at me. She says I want to separate body and soul while she runs them together. When she runs she thinks: not ABC like I think with my tidy well trained mind, but in flashes—she'll trot out with some problem and run 12 or 15 miles and come home with the kinks smoothed out. She says that after 8 or 10 miles she hits a euphoric high—grows free—like meditation or something, but better. She tells me that I get steamed up through a combination of tension and inactivity. She can run out that stress and be perfectly relaxed while perfectly active. She comes clean. Ten or 12 miles at about eight minutes per mile: about where she'll be getting to now.

I have spent another half-hour thinking about the things I was not going to think about. Tension and inactivity. I cannot concentrate the mind.

When I bend my head forward and Emma squeezes the sponge on to my neck, I can feel each separate drop of water flow down my back or over my shoulders and down between my breasts. I listen to my heart beat and it seems strong and sturdy. As I turn Emma's wrist to see her watch her blue veins seem translucent and fine. Mine seem like strong wires conducting energy. I don't feel I want to drink and have it lying there in my stomach, but I know I should. Obedient, giving over to Emma, I suck the bottle. Tell myself I owe it to her. Her parents do not want her to spend a hot Saturday afternoon nursing her games teacher. When I'm back in rhythm I feel the benefits of the drink. Emma is a good kid. Her parents' unnamed suspicions are correct. I was in love with a games teacher once. She was a big strong woman, full of energy. I pretended to share what the others thought and mocked her. We called her Tarzan and how I loved her. In secret dreams I wanted to be with her. "You Tarzan, me Jane," I would mutter, contemplating her badly shaved underarms, and would fly with her through green trees, swing on lianas of delight. She was my first love; she helped make me a strong woman. The beauty, the immensity of her. When we swam she would hover over the side of the pool and as I looked up through the broken sparkly waters there she would be hauling me through with her strength.

Like Sally hauls me through bad dreams, looming over me in the night as I breathe up through the broken darkness. She hauls me through muddle with her sparkly mind. Her mind floats, green with sequinned points of fire. Sally's mind. Lovely. My mind wears Nike running shoes with the neat white flash curling back on itself. It fits well and leaves room for my toes to flex. If I weren't a games teacher I could be a feminist chiropodist—or a midwife. Teach other women the contours of their own bodies—show them the new places where their bodies can take them. Sally doesn't want to be taken—only in the head. Sex of course is hardly in her head. In the heart? My heart beats nearly twenty pulses a minute slower than hers: we test them together lying in the darkness, together. "You'll die, you shit," I want to yell at her. "You'll die and leave me. Your heart isn't strong enough." I never say it. Nice if your hearts matched. The Zulu warrior women could run fifty miles a day and fight at the end of it. Fifty miles together, perfectly in step, so the veldt drummed with it. Did their hearts beat as one? My heart can beat with theirs, slow and strong and efficient-pumping energy.

Jane de Chantal, after whom I was named, must have been a jogger.

She first saw the Sacred Heart—how else could she have known that slow, rich stroke which is at the heart of everything? Especially back then when the idea of heart meant only emotions. But she was right. The body, the heart at the heart of it all: no brain, no clitoris without that strong slow heart. Thesis: was eighteenth-century nun the first jogger? Come on; this is rubbish. Think about footstrike and stride length. Not this garbage. Only one Swedish garbage collector, in the whole history of Swedish municipal rubbish collection, has ever worked through to retirement age—what perseverance, endurance. What a man. Person. Say garbage person. Sally says so. Love her. Damn her. She is my princess. I'm the younger son (say person) in the fairy story. But running is my wise animal. If I'm nice to my running it will give me good advice on how to win the princess. Float with it. Love it. Love her. There has to be a clue.

Emma is here again. Car? Bicycle? She can't have run it. She and Beth come out and give me another drink, wipe my face. Lovely hands. I come down and look around. After 20 miles they say there are two sorts of smiles among runners—the smiles of those who are suffering and the smiles of those who aren't. "You're running too fast," says Beth, "You're too high. Pace yourself, you silly twit. You're going to hurt." "No," I say, "I'm feeling good." But I know she's right. Discipline counts. Self-discipline, but Beth will help with that. "We need you to finish," says Emma. "Of course she'll finish," says Beth. I love them and I run away from them, my mouth feeling good with orange juice and soda water. Ought to have been Sally though. Source of sweetness. How could she do this to me? How could she leave me? Desert me in the desert. Make a desert. This is my quest—my princess should be here. Princess: she'd hate that. I hate that. Running is disgusting; makes you think those thoughts. I hurt. I hurt and I am tired. They have lots of advice for this point in a marathon. They say, think of all the months that are wasted if you stop now. But not wasted because I enjoyed them. They say, whoever wanted it to be easy? I did. They say, think of that man who runs marathons with only one leg. And that's meant to be inspirational? He's mad. We're all mad. There's no reason but pride. Well, pride then. Pride and the thought of Sally suppressing her gloating if I go home and say it hurt too much. I need a good reason to run into and through this tiredness.

Something stabs at my eyes. Nothing really hurt before and now it hurts. Takes me all of three paces to locate the hurt: cramp in the upper thighs. Sally's fault; I think of her and tense up. Ridiculous. But I'll be damned if I quit now. Run into the pain; I know it will go away and I don't believe it. Keep breathing steadily. It hurts. I know it hurts, shut up, shut up, shut up. Who cares if it hurts? I do. Don't do this. Seek out a shirt in front of you and look at the number. Keep looking at the number. 297. Do some sums with that. Can't think of any. Not divisible by 2, or 3, or 5. Nor 7. 9. 9 into 29 goes 3. 3 and carry 2. 9 into 27. Always works. If you can divide by something the cramp goes away. Is that where women go in childbirth—into the place of charms? All gay women should run marathons—gives them solidarity with their labouring sisters. I feel sick instead. I look ahead and there is nothing but the long hill. Heartbreaking. I cannot.

Shirt 297 belongs to a woman, a little older than me perhaps. I run beside her, she is tired too. I feel better and we run together. We exchange a smile. Ignore the fact that catching up with her gives me a lift. We exchange another smile. She is slowing. She grins and deliberately reduces her pace so that I can go ahead without feeling bad. That's love. I love her. I want to turn round, jog back and say, "I will leave my lover for you." "Dear Sally," I will write, "I am leaving you for a lady who" (and Sally's mental red pencil will correct to "whom") "I met during the marathon and unlike you was nice and generous to me." Alternative letter, "Dear Sally, I have quit because long-distance running brings you up against difficulties and cramps and I cannot take the pain." Perseverance, endurance, patience and accepting love are part of running a marathon. She won't see it. Damn her.

Must be getting near now because there's a crowd watching. They'll laugh at me. "Use the crowd," say those who've been here before. "They want you to finish. Use that." Lies. Sally doesn't want me to finish. What sort of princess doesn't want the quest finished? Wants things cool and easy? Well, pardon me, your Royal Highness. Royal Highness: the marathon is 26 miles and 385 yards long because some princess wanted to see the start of the 1908 Olympic Marathon from Windsor Palace and the finish from her box in the White City Stadium. Two miles longer than before. Now standardized. By appointment. Damn the Royal Princess. Damn Sally.

Finally I accept that I'm not going to do any work today. It takes me several more minutes to accept what that means—that I'm involved in that bloody race. People tend, I notice, to equate accepting with liking—but it's not that simple. I don't like it. But, accepting, I get the car out and drive to the shops and buy the most expensive bath oil I can find. It's so expensive that the box is perfectly modest—no advertising, no half-naked women. I like half-naked women as a matter of fact, but there are such things as principles. Impulsively I also buy some matching lotion, thinking that I will rub it on her feet tonight. Jane's long slender feet are one part of her body that owe nothing to running. This fact alone is enough to turn me into a foot fetishist.

After I have bought the stuff, I slaver a bit over the thought of rubbing it into her poor battered feet. I worked it out once. Each foot hits the ground about 800 times per mile. The force of the impact is three times her weight. 122 pounds times 800 times 26 miles. It does not bear thinking about. I realize the implications of rubbing sweet ointment into the tired feet of the beloved person. At first I am embarrassed and then I think, well, Mary Magdalene is one way through the sex object/true love dichotomy. Endurance, perseverance, love. She must have thought the crucifixion a bit mad too. Having got this far in acceptance I think that I might as well go down to the finish and make her happy. We've come a long way together. So I get back into the car and do just that.

It is true, actually. In the last few miles the crowd holds you together. This is not the noble hero alone against the world. Did I want that? But this is better. A little kid ducked under the rope and gave me a half-eaten ice-lolly—raspberry flavour. Didn't want it. Couldn't refuse such an act of love. Took it. Felt fine. Smiled. She smiled back. It was a joy. Thank you sister. The people roar for you, hold you through the sweat and the tears. They have no faces. The finishing line just is. Is there. You are meant to raise your arms and shout, "Rejoice, we conquer" as you cross it. Like Pheidippides did when he entered Athens and history. And death. But all I think is, "Christ, I've let my anti-gravity muscles get tight." They hurt. Sally is here. I don't believe it. Beth drapes a towel over my shoulders without making me stop moving. Emma appears, squeaking, "Three hours, 26 and a half." That's great, that's bloody great. I don't care. Sally has cool soft arms. I look for them. They hold me. "This is a sentimental ending," I try to say. I'm dry. Beth gives me a beer. I cannot pour it properly. It flows over my chin, soft and gold, blissfully cold. I manage a grin and it spreads all over me. I feel great. I lean against Sally again. I say, "Never, never again." She grins back and, not without irony, says, "Rejoice, we conquer."

LONG ROAD TO BOSTON

Bruce Tuckman

(1988)

[*Bradley Townes, a former Olympic-caliber swimmer, is consumed with guilt and grief at having (barely) survived the car accident which killed his wife and two children. After more than a year of painful therapy and fierce, lonely training, he runs the Boston Marathon, hoping thereby to exorcise some of the horror. He harbors a burning desire not just to finish Boston, but to win. The novel alternates race scenes with flashbacks chronicling Brad's progress from the accident to the starting line; asterisks indicate omitted flashback segments. Gus, Washington, and Sue are friends he has made in the last year.*]

There were only ten miles to go, but these would be, he knew full well, the toughest ten miles of his life. He was already climbing the first hill, then crossing the bridge that spanned highway 128 below. It was always a windy spot but today it was worse than usual; it chilled his wet skin. The uphill grind and the wind together added an extra quotient of stress and he began to feel a slight pain in his chest for the first time since the race began. He longed to sit down, wrap a blanket around his cold body, and drink a frosty glass of beer. But he knew that it would be almost an hour more before he could even think about such incredible pleasures.

Right now he pondered his problem. He had run this race a thousand times in his own mind, and he always saw himself chasing Rodgers and catching him. But now there was this Seko guy, this Japanese superstar. Brad hadn't planned on him. What if he couldn't catch him? What if the powerful little runner was just the machine he appeared to be? He knew little of the Japanese outside of the stereotypes. But there is truth in cliches, and he had read Seko trained with religious fervor. He was said to be fearless; he would run until he died.

The thought strengthened his resolve. He would beat Seko—even in a duel to the death. No, that's overly dramatic, he thought. A runner is a runner. We all hurt the same when we run this far, this fast. He told himself that, but he wasn't sure he believed it.

* * *

He climbed the first hill and was about to descend. He was clearly feeling it. His breathing was labored as he struggled to repay the oxygen debt. His chest hurt more. He was beginning to realize that these hills could only be appreciated—if you could call it that—during the race itself. They were not steep hills and not even particularly long and he had run them countless times in training, never with much difficulty.

But he had never blazed for 16 miles like this and then tried to climb them. The first one had definitely hurt him and there were still three more to go, including the infamous Heartbreak, which he knew could break more than your heart.

The pack was holding steady on the downhill side, except that they seemed to be closing ranks slightly. He was sure that there would be some changes before they were out of the hills. He only hoped that he could hold his ground through this murderous stretch. It was getting progressively harder to breath.

* * *

The leaders reached the bottom of the first hill and were turning the corner at the Newton Firehouse onto Commonwealth Avenue. He could see each of them at the turn—first Seko, then Bjorklund, then Rodgers, then Stewart and then a little space. Finally, he himself reached the bottom, looked over at the fire engines standing in the firehouse and then sped around the corner right behind Fleming.

What a sight! He was looking up at what had to be the steepest and longest of the four hills. It was lined with people; people who liked to watch runners overcome pain or succumb to it. Sadists! And they were cheering, screaming loudly, and what they screamed sounded like. . . . BILLY! The many portable radios in the crowd told him what was happening.

They're halfway up the second hill and Rodgers, who has just passed Bjorklund and moved into second, is trying to make up some of the ground that Seko opened up with his spurt at the bottom of the hill. The crowd is screaming for their boy to do it.

So Seko is turning it on, he thought. Forcing Rodgers to make a move just to keep close. I guess I'll have to make a move too or I'll get so far behind I'll lose contact. What a fucking time to have to speed up: going up the steepest hill on the course.

But he made up his mind and began to drive up the hill even harder, his arms pumping for leverage.

Stewart is making a move now too on this hill to try to stay close to the leader. He's passing Bjorklund who's now faded to fourth and someone else has just moved up and ducked in behind Bjorklund but I can't make out who it is.

Fleming was now behind him, Bjorklund in front. Bjorklund's breathing was ragged. He could tell the Midwesterner, who had led for so long, was now hurting. Brad was hurting too. A lot. A burning pain had begun at the back of his right shoulder between the shoulder blade and the neck. That was his point of vulnerability when it came to oxygen debt. Usually the pain went away when he slowed down. That's what happened when he ran intervals. But he had never, ever run like this before. He felt like he was killing himself.

Maybe the pain will keep getting worse, he thought, until I can't stand it any longer. Or maybe it'll ease up a bit on the next downhill. At the moment, though, it hurt so much that the sweat on his face was mixing with involuntary tears.

Marathon fans stood about two deep lining the last few yards of the second hill and its crest.

GO UNDERDOG! GO UNDERDOG! they screamed.

Christ! he thought, they're screaming at me. And as he turned his head to both sides to look at their faces he could see that he was right. They were screaming at him, exhorting him—a high-numbered nobody—to catch the favorites, the glamour boys. Win one for the anonymous, they were telling him. Prove to the world that an average schmo has a chance. They were clapping and cheering him as he went past.

They've crested the second hill, ladies and gentlemen, and are now in for a short breather after that painful climb. Rodgers is trailing Seko by about 25 yards now. He made his move on the hill, Rodgers did, just to keep Seko from getting too far ahead. Stewart and Bjorklund and one or two others are within striking distance but Bjorklund looks bad. Wait! There's a real commotion coming from back there. The fans are cheering furiously for one of the other runners. Must be a local favorite, or maybe Foster or somebody like that. I can't tell yet. Maybe on the way down I'll be able to figure out what's going on back there.

* * *

He was climbing the third of the Newton Hills now among incessant screams of GO! GO! GO UNDERDOG! He had been discovered. Curious, he thought, how the crowd has an emotional attachment to two runners, the favorite and the underdog. The first fulfills their expectations, their need for predictability and order. The second captures their imagination, their need for surprise and more importantly, for hope. First they have Rodgers and now me. If I disappoint myself, he realized, I'll also disappoint them. He clung desperately to Bjorklund's heels as they worked their way up this, the smallest of the four hills. The shoulder pain that he felt on the second hill, the steep one, returned to plague him and he forced his right arm behind his back and attempted to reach it with his left from over his left shoulder. It was one of his stretching positions and it now gave him some slight relief from the nagging ache. He felt as if he were climbing a mountain and grabbed at the air with his hands to pull himself along. If he could only slow down, he thought, relax for a few moments, then all the pain will go away. But a quick look up ahead at the fleeting figure of the Japanese runner cresting the hill with the floating blond fellow right behind told him that there could be no thought of easing up, no notion of relief.

He wondered if they too were feeling the same incredible distress as he, if it was as demanding for them with all their experience as it was for him, the novice.

* * *

Another slight breather descending the third hill. The leaders were already partway down and he concentrated to keep the gap from widening. Still it was easier to go down than up even if you were forced to accelerate on the way down.

Seko is still leading, with Rodgers running about 20 to 30 yards behind him. Stewart is back another 10 to 20 and then there's Bjorklund trailing him by about the same distance. There's a fifth runner right on Bjorklund's tail but I don't recognize him and I can't see his number. He must be well-known though because he's getting a hand from the large crowd as he passes.

They'll soon be at Heartbreak, folks, and anything can happen there. Get ready to cheer them on, all of you marathon lovers who are waiting on that ferocious hill.

Ferocious hill is right, he thought.

This downhill stretch eased the pain a bit but the worst was just ahead. He could see it stretched out before him, all sides bounded by excited onlookers, whose screams carried up to him.

Bloodthirsty sonsabitches, he thought. Here to watch us kill ourselves and loving every minute of it.

* * *

Heartbreak! The last of the hills and the meanest. Where would he find the strength?

Here comes Rodgers! Billy Rodgers is finally making his move!

Up ahead, already moving up the hill, Brad could see the lithe form driving upwards at such a pace that it appeared that Seko was moving down toward him. The crowd that lined the famous hill was shrieking encouragement and approval. GO GET 'EM BILLY! CATCH HIM, BILL! GO! BILL! came the urgent shouts.

Rodgers is moving up fast on Seko, folks, he's flying up

Heartbreak! I don't think the Japanese runner will be able to hold him off!

In front of him Bjorklund seemed to be wavering. Heartbreak was doing him in. Despite the intensifying pains in his own chest and shoulders Brad knew he had to push as Rodgers had if he meant to keep contact. With a short burst of energy from somewhere deep down he drove past the weakening Bjorklund and into fourth place. The crowd greeted his charge almost as fervently as they had Rodgers'. Loud screams and GO, 2022! ALL RIGHT, BUDDY! GO UNDERDOG! were his reward for this last bit of effort, and it buoyed him up and carried him to the middle of the hill where the ground leveled off a bit before sharply rising again.

Bjorklund has just been passed but we still don't know who that runner is. We'll just have to call him our mystery man. The crowds love him whoever he is.

Brad's momentum was carrying him up to Stewart now. I might catch him by the top of the hill, he thought. But jeez it hurts to breathe! He gasped hard to try to force air into his aching lungs. His mouth was like sandpaper and his ears were ringing, causing the crowd noise to reverberate inside his head. He must get to the top of this hill soon or he would surely collapse on the ground and die.

Rodgers has just caught Seko at the top of Heartbreak Hill. I repeat, with a terrific burst of speed, Bill Rodgers has overtaken Seko. He has passed Seko! Rodgers has just passed Seko! Bill Rodgers is now running in front. He's crested Heartbreak Hill and Bill Rodgers is now leading the Boston Marathon for the first time!

So, Seko was human after all. Maybe it was Rodgers who was a machine. But he looked so human, so childlike and friendly. Then he ran like a fiend.

Brad caught Stewart as they reached the top of the hill but didn't have the strength to pass him. As he felt the temporary relief of level ground he tucked himself in behind Stewart and gasped for air, gratefully drafting behind his competitor. Brad's chest made a wheezing sound like a steam engine as he struggled to regain his composure after the monster hill. It's more of a ballbuster than a heartbreaker, he thought, but it hurts everyone the same. And it's behind me now. Thank God.

* * *

Brad Townes glanced at fringes of the Boston College campus, hoping to catch a glimpse of Coach, but all he saw were undergrads whooping and hollering and offering the runners beer. A beer would taste great, he thought, but not just yet. There is still work to be done and somehow I've got to find the strength to do it.

It seemed that the whole student body was out here crowding the street, yelling at the top of its lungs. "Go, man! Go!" the students screamed at him and Stewart as they raced by the campus and then down the slight incline toward the Lake Street turn and the Brookline border. It's funny, he thought, as he passed the college, these last five miles are the part of the course I know least. He usually stopped his training runs at the college, avoiding the heavy traffic of Brookline and downtown Boston. It's simple, he thought. All you have to do is follow the press truck. Then you won't get lost.

* * *

Rodgers has just made the turn onto Lake Street. He seems to be running easily at this point. With only a little more than four miles left to go, Melrose Bill is going to be a hard man to catch.

Up ahead Brad could see a policeman blocking traffic to let the runners turn onto Lake Street. The book called this street "a most welcome sight," he remembered. What an understatement. But not as welcome as the yellow banner at the Pru will be.

His chest and shoulder pain had eased a little now that he had left the hills. He couldn't afford to coast, though, even though he longed for a break from the relentless pace. Any time he lost the slightest bit of concentration, the others would begin to pull away. Stewart and Seko were still up ahead, and the big man in front of them. It would take a lot to catch him. Must wait till Beacon Street, Brad thought. Try to overtake Stewart and then play it by ear from there.

His thighs were beginning to feel sore and one of his knees was tender. He had not thought much about his legs. His pre-race worries always focused exclusively on breathing and energy. He never imagined that his legs might give out under the pounding. Now he had something else to preoccupy his mind as he eased up to make the Lake

Street turn.

Here the crowd looked to be three or four deep and they all shouted encouragement to him and Stewart. They were running together but with Stewart slightly ahead. He could hear the noise but he couldn't make out exactly what they were saying because the ringing in his ears had returned. His head had become an echo chamber. I doubt if they're exhorting me to catch their hero, he thought. Besides, I'm sure no one thinks he can be caught anyway. For them the race is over; they're just cheering effort now.

He had also read that these were great fans, appreciative of all the runners, from the fastest to the slowest, willing to give everyone a hand. One thing he knew for sure: There were sure enough of them out here, spending their holiday in the rain.

It stopped raining but he was too spaced out to notice.

* * *

Lake Street was even more crowded than Commonwealth Avenue had been and much noisier than even the baseball crowds he remembered. But then he had been one of the crowd, not one of the entertainers. He knew he should be enjoying it more, these moments of triumph and exaltation, for he was up among the leaders in one of the world's greatest foot races. But the pain dulled all but the most abstract sense of satisfaction. The noise and the pain seemed to blend together somewhere inside his head to produce a pounding that at times made him feel physically sick. He suddenly wanted to vomit, to spill his guts right here on Lake Street in front of the thousands watching. But he managed to calm himself and the nausea passed. The pain he would deal with in his own way. He would surround it and contain it, carry it with the dignity and pride that is the long distance runner's only solace.

Rodgers is making the turn onto Beacon Street and the enormous crowd is chanting his name. He seems to have it all under control as he begins the trek through Brookline, the trek that will eventually take him to the Pru and the olive wreath waiting there for him. Brookliners are lining the street to cheer him on, chanting his name as he passes.

Brad Townes could hear it himself through his ringing ears. The ringing and the pain and occasionally the nausea persisted as he too approached the Beacon Street turn right behind the persistent Stewart.

Stay with him. Stay with him, he told himself over and over. Stay with him.

Seko has just made the turn but doesn't look as strong, from this vantage point, as Rodgers. I tell you, that Rodgers is simply amazing. He just floats along.

Floats along. Floats along. What he wouldn't give to just float along. He no longer had much feeling in his legs. They seemed to move of their own accord. All he really felt was the non-specific and all encompassing pain. But at least the ground seemed to slant slightly downward. He felt as though his weight were carrying him forward.

Now I can see Chris Stewart making the turn onto Beacon and there's that mystery man still right behind. Even with my binoculars I can't make out his number. He's tucked right in behind Stewart. He couldn't make it any harder to identify him if he were trying. I haven't gotten one clear view of his number. I'll try to get one of our spotters on the route to get it for us so we can tell you who he is.

On Beacon Street now he sucked up a little closer to Stewart as they ran alongside the trolley tracks. He stumbled slightly when they hit a stretch of broken pavement.

* * *

Brookline. He was in Brookline now—his adopted hometown—and it began to look familiar, even through the haze of his unfocused eyes. The grocery stores, laundromats, gas stations, ice cream parlors—these New Englanders were crazy about ice cream—were all familiar haunts to him. He would soon be running through his own neighborhood. His own neighbors would be lining the route and cheering. But he doubted they would recognize him. They only had eyes for Rodgers. They knew him only as another of those crazy runners who goes out every day to punish himself into a state of fitness. And to give the dogs and the motorists fits.

Besides, he knew that to his neighbors these runners all looked alike in their shorts and singlets. Or the later ones with tee shirts bearing the names of strange and exotic races: Falmouth, Bloomsday, Peachtree.

The shirts of those who were less serious must appear equally obtuse and disconcerting even when they simply said ADIDAS or NIKE or I RUN TO LIVE. And even their own children were beginning to bring home these seemingly meaningless shirts. His neighbors, he was sure, could not distinguish the fat fighters and dilettantes from the true believers. They referred to them all by the slightly pejorative term "joggers," which they pronounced "jawgers."

Wouldn't they be surprised, he thought, to know that their loony neighbor with neither job nor car nor suit of clothes was now running down their famous Beacon Street within striking distance of the renowned Rodgers? Why am I so hostile? he wondered. Where is this hate coming from? They're not booing me or ignoring me or mocking me. They're cheering me. They're applauding me. But they don't take me seriously. They're sure no mere mortal man can catch King Bill.

It must be myself I hate, he thought, as the crowd noise rattled in his head. I hate me! I hate running! I hate having to do this! It was making him angry. The crowd made him angry. Their willingness to accept his defeat was what made him most angry. Even the noise was making him angry. He was coming to a downhill.

* * *

He reached the downhill but the expected relief didn't come. He entertained the fervent wish that a bolt of lightning would shoot from the sky and strike him dead on the spot, ending his pain. But another part of him wished for the strength to accelerate, to take off like he did at the start of his morning runs, fresh and energetic after a night's sleep. But wishful thinking, magic and miracles were of no use here. He was surprised he could think at all, and indeed, every few moments he felt himself slipping into something like delirium.

But there was his anger. He could fall back on that, draw on it now to power his flight down the hill. He knew he had to make some sort of move soon. Time was running out. So he stared into the faces cheering him. The crowd was so thick at this point that they spilled over the sidewalk into the street, despite the continuing efforts of the police to hold them back. Brad thought: They don't even know who I am. I am nameless and faceless to them, just another body hurtling futilely through their town in an effort to finish this race. They know who's going to win it. The best I can do in their eyes is just finish. And, as he thought, he pounded his right arm against his side as a jockey would whip a horse to make it run faster. And somehow, some way, he felt himself pulling out and drawing alongside Stewart. And then, slowly, moving ahead of him.

Stewart has just been passed—here on this long hill. Our mystery man has just moved out in front of Stewart and maybe now we'll be able to figure out who he is. . . . Wait! He's got a four-digit number, a two thousand number, but I can't make it out. I don't recognize him, he's not one of the big names. He's somewhat taller and more muscular than most of the world-class marathoners but I don't know who he is. He looks something like the East German, Cierpinksi, but Cierpinksi is not entered. Wait, we've got the number now. It's two oh two two. Two thousand twenty two. We still don't know who that is but we're in radio contact with race headquarters at the Pru and they're looking it up in their computers right now. Whoever you are, 2022, you're running one hell of a race! Meanwhile, Rodgers. . . .

Brad could still make out snatches of the radio coverage over the crowd noise. So they still don't know who I am, he thought. They can just call me Mighty Joe from Hannibal, Mo, he chuckled to himself, despite the fire now spreading through his lungs and back muscles.

Twenty yards ahead he could see Seko and beyond him in the distance, Rodgers. In front of Rodgers was only the motorcycle policeman. Now if I can just tie myself to Seko with an invisible cord, and slowly start to pull the son of a bitch in, he thought, just like Bannister did to Landy. He focused on the rhythmically moving shoulders of the Japanese champion, established contact in his mind, and then grimly set about his task.

Rodgers has just passed the 23 mile point, folks, and still looks as loose and easy as he did when he took the lead back on the hills. Seko is behind him but looks tired. And then there's that mystery man. We still don't have . . . Oh, excuse me . . . They're trying . . . Uh, here it is, I have it. I now have the information! Number 2022 is . . . Bradley Townes . . . whose name is not familiar to me. Nor . . . I'm just checking now . . . No? Nor to anyone else on the press truck.

Repeating: Bradley Townes is in third place. He is from Boston. He is 28 years old, and his best previous time is 2:22:35. He is not affiliated with any club and he lists no sponsoring company or product.

I hardly need emphasize that he was not included in any of the pre-race publicity information handed out by the Boston Athletic Association. Again, I apologize, but that is all the information that has been released. We are trying to find out more and we'll let you know as soon as we do.

Brad reached the bottom of the hill and now was just three miles out. Twenty-three down and three to go, he thought. Good God! Just give me the strength. He gave Seko a little tug on the cord.

* * *

It was becoming a blur, a dull greenish-grayish-yellowish haze that filled his field of vision. His eyelids were starting to stick together and his ears clogged up. He sucked in air audibly and greedily now, making a tortured, rasping sound on each breath. He was a locomotive badly in need of lubrication. Yet he still ran at a pace that seemed fast enough to break him at any second. On he ran, past the thousands of onlookers who crowded Beacon Street, Brookline's main drag. He kept pulling on the cord, slowly reeling Seko in.

Above the clamor of the cheering throng the radio raved on and on about the incredibly competitive finish to this great race. The voice was becoming hoarse extolling the silky smoothness of Rodgers, the grittiness of Seko and the excitement of the mystery man in third place.

All this whirred by as he cruised through Brookline, still feeling detached from his legs. All he could really feel was his fire-filled, rasping lungs and his aching arms and shoulders. On he sped, glaring at the back of Seko's white singlet through his narrow eye slits, tugging steadily on the cord, reeling him in.

* * *

Bill Rodgers is approaching Coolidge Corner, where the crowds are gigantic, the largest we've seen so far. There must be five thousand people crowded into this small area to cheer

the leaders as they go by. In a few seconds you will be able to hear a great roar as Rodgers arrives. Everyone loves Billy, I can tell you. From here it will just be a shade over two miles for his third straight Boston victory. This is his race.

Come on back, Seko, you son of a bitch. Come on back to me, he thought, pulling on the invisible cord that he had lassoed around Seko's neck. Vaguely he thought he heard someone playing the theme music from "Rocky" in the background, probably on one of those big ghetto blasters the kids carry. Dah, dah, *dah*—dah, dah, *dum*. It was perfect inspirational music for a long-distance race, but he was long past inspiration.

Seko is running second, just managing to hold the twenty yards or so between himself and Rodgers constant. But get this! Bradley Townes, the unknown runner now in third place, is really charging after Seko! He's now really closing in on him as they approach Coolidge Corner! The crowd, as you can hear, is screaming!

* * *

Brad Townes was flying after Seko as they entered Coolidge Corner, passing quickly through the mobbed intersection on the way into Boston. The crowd screamed and shouted encouragement, apparently aware—if only dimly—that they were seeing something quite extraordinary: a challenge by a classic underdog, unknown and unheralded, hounding the heels of two of the great runners of the world.

Brad was only vaguely aware of his surroundings now. He was not even sure where he was, although he surmised that it was still Brookline. He sensed also that the crowd was cheering for him to catch and pass Seko. No Brookliners recognized him, although he had lived among them for over seven months, running the streets in plain view.

He was giving them what they had come out for on a holiday afternoon: a race and a drama. A nobody doing his best to overtake the somebodies. They loved it. They cheered until their throats were hoarse, filling the air with a continuous roar as he passed.

He flew on toward Boston. Soon there would be just a little over a mile left. Not much time, he thought. *Not much time at all.*

* * *

Brad Townes caught Toshihiko Seko at the city line. It was all the announcer could do to relay the information to the radio audience.

This is. . . . I don't. . . . Ladies and gentlemen, Bradley Townes, an unknown runner from Brookline, Mass has just caught Toshihiko Seko of Japan! Bill Rodgers has just turned his head to see what all the commotion is about. In a few seconds he'll see the new challenger but I doubt very seriously if he will know any more about him than we do.

He's right behind Seko now, right in his shadow. I don't believe it! The crowd is electrified! He's next to Seko now, shoulder to shoulder and the Japanese runner seems to be struggling to fight him off. They're neck and neck, the two of them, as they cross into Boston.

Now it looks as though. . . . Yes! He's passed him! Bradley Townes has just passed Seko. Oh, please forgive me, I think I'm losing my voice. . . . Ladies and gentlemen, someone named Bradley Townes is now running second to Bill Rodgers in the last mile of the 1978 Boston Marathon!

* * *

Up ahead through his mental haze Brad could make out the slight figure of Rodgers floating along among a flock of motorcycles. They're escorting his royal ass to the finish line, he thought bitterly. Boston's finest are leading their man home from his day's labors. How jaunty he looks up there coasting along. And everyone loves it. Only a mile to go but his vision was becoming increasingly foggy. Passing Seko had taken a heavy toll, maybe too heavy. He had not counted on Seko—one runner too many to overtake. But he was close, so damn close. He had to go faster, had to find just a bit more speed. He could still not feel his legs, just a formless, nameless, unbearable pain every time his weary feet struck the pavement. The fronts of his thighs had all the elasticity of wood. His calves were knotted and sore, and each foot-strike sent sharp, shooting pains into the center of his consciousness. He had never hurt like this before, not even after the car wreck.

The crowd roared its approval, urging, demanding, cajoling him to hurry, to speed up, to make a race of it. Give Billy a run for his money, they pleaded. But he was hardly aware of them, despite the incredible din. He had discovered the one force that could shut out everything else in the world: pain. Pain was insistent and it was absolute. It fed upon itself, and it fed upon him. It had begun to devour him, organ by organ, cell by cell. He was turning into a corpse, a skeleton, a cadaver. But still he ran.

One more mile, one more mile. Run you cocksucker, run you motherfucker. These incantations provided the cadence to which he ran.

* * *

Rodgers is just a shade over a half a mile from the finish of what will be his third straight Boston Marathon triumph! But mystery man Brad Townes has not gone away! He's still chasing gamely and has picked up some ground, but he's still 20 or so yards back. His problem now is the clock. There just doesn't appear to be enough time left to catch Bill Rodgers.

Brad could hardly see anything but the back of Rodgers' fleet, moving form. The haze constricted his vision so he was barely aware of the crowd on all sides, and even his ears were clogging up. The ringing in his head was now constant, so the crowd sounded eerie and far away. He felt his mental faculties ebbing away too, as his muscles greedily consumed all his oxygen, leaving little for his brain. He couldn't remember even recent, important details, like his last split times. He had lost them somewhere in the fevered haze of his mind. He wondered idly if he would soon lose consciousness altogether, and if so, whether his body would keep on running by itself.

His ears were opening and closing now, producing a vibrato of sound and silence which combined with the ringing to make his head spin. He was becoming dizzy and disoriented and had to concentrate on locking his cloudy eyes on the back of Rodgers' head. He imagined that he teetered as he ran and exerted some small effort to control the sway.

I've got to catch that sonuvabitch before he's home free, he thought. But his body refused to respond. All those miles, he thought, all those freaking miles. Don't you give up on it now! Don't you do it. Think of those miles, the intervals, the hills, the mornings, all those freaking miles. Christ knows it hurts! But that will pass. It's got to be now, now, now. . . . Got to find a little more. Got to.

* * *

He could see the Prudential Center towering above the skyline ahead. It looked close enough to touch. His lungs were on fire and every breath fanned the flames.

But I'm racing now, he thought. Or at least I seem to be. Can hardly make out anything through the damned haze, but that shadow of Rodgers ahead seems to be getting a little larger. Key now is don't let up. Don't, don't don't.

Every now and then he thought he could catch a whiff of the fetid fumes of the motorcycles. Police on foot were everywhere, holding the crowds behind the gray, wooden sawhorses. The crowd seemed to have quieted, as if holding its collective breath pending the outcome. They were not so sure as they had been a moment ago.

Rodgers is still in the lead as we come down to the wire, but Brad Townes has cut the distance to about ten yards! We're in the final mile and we've got a real horse race on our hands here! An unknown runner is chasing the favorite and closing in on him!

Rodgers has been. . . . Yes, there he goes again. Rodgers has been sneaking looks over his shoulder, and he knows Townes is there. Rodgers appears to have picked up the pace, but it still looks to me as if the challenger is bearing down on him! About a half a mile to go and it's an open race!

Brad felt as if he were falling forward now under the force of this latest drive. He could feel himself hurtling ahead as his arms and his legs pumped painfully. He adjusted his posture into almost a slouch to keep the chest pain from cutting through his lungs.

I can catch him, he thought for the first time.

* * *

They're almost to the turn and Brad Townes is closing fast! He's had a lot of ground to make up in the last mile, but he seems to be doing it. What an exciting race! I can't remember a

finish like this, certainly not since '71 when Mejia beat out MacMahon at the wire by five seconds. Looks like we may have another one like that today. This unknown runner is really making a race out of it. Rodgers has got to be worried. He's not noted as a fast finisher. He usually just grinds his opponents down. But this underdog did not cave in.

Brad was hurting like never before, like he never imagined before. No single part of his body was spared. His lower back was beginning to convulse, sending waves of torment along the tops of his hips. And the bruise on his hip, where he had fallen, was pulsating like a second heart, its reverberations mixing with the pain in his lower back. Too many accidents, he thought, too many lumps and too many skeletons and not enough sense to know where I'm going.

But he seemed to know where he was going now. It was just a question of whether he could get there before he fell apart completely. He was close to Rodgers now, closer than he had been since Rodgers had passed so along ago in one of the tiny towns. He could see Rodgers' body moving rhythmically, seemingly unfazed by the long race.

* * *

There's not much time left, folks. Maybe a quarter of a mile. We'll be turning off soon. Rodgers is holding the lead as he approaches the turn onto Hereford Street, but Brad Townes is less than ten yards behind! The mystery man is still making his charge here after nearly twenty-six and a quarter miles! He's come from a long way back and he's doing what nobody thought could be done. He's running down Bill Rodgers in the final mile!

Don't let up now, he thought. It would be so nice, so easy to let up, but you would regret it the rest of your life. Don't let up. Don't let up.

His body would beat out simple phrases like a drum over and over making them bounce through his head.

I must do it, must do it, must do it.

Then even short phrases became more than his dulled brain could manage.

Run, run, run, run, run. . . . He was ordering himself, commanding himself, imploring himself.

Run, run, run, run, run. . . . He was begging himself, pleading with himself.

Run, run, run, run. . . .

He was crying.

* * *

They're coming down Hereford Street now, Bill Rodgers and Brad Townes. Only five yards separate the two! Only five yards between them as they drive toward the finish! This will be closer than '71, when five seconds separated first and second. These two are much closer than that right now!

They're running down the middle of Hereford Street and they both seem to have slowed down just a bit as they get ready for the last burst on Boyleston. This race will be decided in the last quarter mile! Or less!

From the press truck we can see them quite well as they approach the turn onto Boyleston Street. I can see both of their faces clearly, and the incredible strain of this race is obvious in both. You can tell the price they've paid just by looking at them, particularly mystery runner Brad Townes.

His eyes are squinched into slits and his mouth is gaping as he tries to suck in enough precious air. His skin is quite red and splotchy.

The crowd here at the turn and along the ramp leading to the finish is enormous—there are thousands upon thousands of them packed in behind the barricades and they are screaming! I'm sure you can hear them behind me. They are screaming! Wow! They're witnessing an unbelievable finish!

He could tell thousands of people were staring at him and waving at him, but it was all blurry and muted, like an old washed-out color movie. But the oddest thing was the silence, the total silence. For a while, it had been silence punctuated every few seconds by a roar and then more silence. That was very disconcerting. But now there was no roar at all, as if he had closed a window through which he was looking and could see but not hear anything.

But if he couldn't hear them at all, why was it he could hear his feet striking the pavement? That too seemed odd. He could distinctly hear the WHOMP, WHOMP, WHOMP of his blistered feet striking the pavement, sending unpleasant tremors up through his legs. In fact, if he listened closely he could hear what it was the sound was saying. It was not saying whomp, whomp, whomp at all. It was saying ROMP, ROMP, ROMP or maybe it was CLOMP, CLOMP, CLOMP or even STOMP, STOMP, STOMP or something like that. He could hear it very clearly but he wasn't sure what it was saying. Maybe it was changing what it was saying like STOMP, ROMP, CLOMP or ROMP, STOMP, CLOMP but it was clear as a bell. Whatever it was, he liked it, liked it a lot, so much so that he sang along with it. "SOMP, ROP, CLOP. SOP, ROP, CLOP. ROP, SOP, CLOP." Like that. It was so nice to sing; he liked to sing. He had sung in the bath when his mother splashed the water all over his back to wash away the suds. He had sung then too. "SOP, ROP, CLOP. ROP, SOP. CLOP." He would sing now too to all these nice people in their gray shirts with their gray faces who were being so nice and quiet so he could sing.

They've rounded the turn onto Boyleston and into the home stretch. They're starting their final kick. The mystery man is pumping his arms furiously and driving ahead. He has the strangest look on his face—he looks like . . . he seems to be . . . smiling. He's actually smiling and his lips are still moving. No telling what he's saying, if he's saying anything at all. The crowd noise is incredible! They're screaming their lungs out! I'm sure you can hear it in the background! I have to scream myself just to be heard! And I'm sorry, I'm losing my voice!

Townes is now gaining on Rodgers! He's right behind him! He's practically touching him! He's almost alongside him! He's driving like a madman! Rodgers is trying to fight him off! Rodgers is driving frantically! They're neck and neck, shoulder to shoulder! They're coming down the ramp right together! Lord what a finish! Less than a hundred yards to go! They're both driving hard, dead even! Still even! Still even! Still. . . . It's. . . .

The roar in the background rose to a mighty crescendo, a waterfall of sound, stretching as high and as wide as the Pru itself and even higher and wider till it bounced off the cover of dingy gray clouds and came floating down like small droplets of rain.

Momma's gonna rock me in my cradle, Momma's gonna rock me in my cradle, Sweet cradle, sweet Momma, Momma's gonna rock me in my cradle, all the night long. . . . All the night long. . . . All the night long. . . . I'm falling, Momma, I'm falling, falling. I'm falling. . . . Wheeeeeeee. . . .

He knew he was down and he felt sick, terribly sick. His stomach was in violent revolt, and the rest of him felt sick too. He could hear sounds around him and something cold was pressing against his face, something cold and wet. He could feel a cold stream of water running over his eyes and down his cheeks.

His mouth was dry and tasted funny—like mustard. There was something on top of him; it felt rough and warm against his skin. His skin hurt. It was all prickly and raw. He wanted to see what it was that was dripping on his face and what it was that was making his skin feel prickly but his eyes were too heavy, much too heavy.

* * *

He dreamed of a street, a quiet, shady street like the one he had grown up on. Elm trees and maples, tall ones full of leaves. He was playing with the trees, running around and around them and running his fingers along their rough bark. There were no people in his dream, just him, and it was very quiet and very peaceful. So peaceful. The only sound at all was the faint rustling of the leaves as the wind passed through them.

It was summertime. He could tell because he was wearing short pants and the skin on his legs felt warm from the air. Even the breeze felt warm as it bristled the hair on the back of his neck.

Then there was someone else in his dream, far away at the end of the trees. He could not make out who it was, but it was a woman and she seemed to be calling to him. He could hear no sound but could tell that she was calling to him by the way she was waving her arm. He wanted to go to her, to run to her, past the giant trees, but something was holding him back. He wanted to run but he could not seem to move his body in that direction. He moved his arms and legs but his body stayed. It just stayed the same.

* * *

He opened his eyes. Everything was still cloudy and blurry and the colors were still faded. He could hear voices. Someone was looking down at him. A face. He knew that face. It was round and it was smiling at him.

"Hello, Brad. How do you feel?"

He knew that voice too.

"Gus! What are. . ." He was still gasping for air, and couldn't talk in sentences. ". . . you doing here, Gus. Glad. To see. You." Now a small smile crossed his own face. It was hard to smile.

"I came to watch you run, Brad."

"You saw it, Gus? You saw the race?"

"I was right here in the Prudential Center, Brad. Me and twelve thousand others. We all saw it. You ran a great race, Brad. I'm proud of you. I cried."

"You saw it, Gus? You saw it end? My God, you saw it end. I don't even know. . . ." He paused. He suddenly felt very tired again. He had to stop talking to rest, so he could continue. "Even I can't hardly run that fast, brother," another voice chimed in, a strange high voice with a familiar ring. Brad knew that voice. "With a little practice I could keep up with you, though, but who'd be crazy enough to want to?"

He looked up toward the voice. Washington?

"Is that you Washington? Are you here too?" He tried to get to his feet, but couldn't manage it yet. He sat back down.

"Gus," he said. "I don't even know. . . . Did I. . . ."

Gus cut him short. "We've saved one more surprise for you." The two friends stopped before a small figure in the crowd. He looked up into Sue's soft brown eyes. There were tears in them.

"Hello, Brad." Her sweet voice made his heart jump. "Hi, Sue. Sweet Sue." He could feel the tears welling up in his own eyes.

"Were you there, too?" he asked her. "Did you see it all?" She put her hand to his flushed cheek, stroking it tenderly.

"I wouldn't have missed it for all the tea in . . . in Boston. It was wonderful, Brad. It was the most thrilling thing I've ever seen. . . . When you crossed the finish line you all but passed out. Luckily a man caught you and they brought you here. You were out of it for a few moments."

It was all hazy to him, after the first turn. Well, at least I crossed the finish line, he thought. I'm glad to hear that. There was a loud commotion somewhere in his vicinity but he couldn't see much besides Sue's face. Suddenly another face was alongside hers and a hand reached out and took his. The face was pale and thin, almost childlike, crowned with a mop of straight blond hair, which was wet with perspiration. The bony hand felt small in his, but the grip was firm.

"You ran a great race, Mr. Townes," he said, and even his voice had a cheerful, boyish tone to it. "I don't know where you're from, or how you managed this, but you're a great competitor and a great addition to the sport."

"Thanks. That means something, coming from you. And Bill. . . ."

Rodgers looked up expectantly. Brad leaned close to the blond mop of Rodgers' hair so he could speak softly.

"You are a true champion, Bill. I didn't understand much about all that. Until today." Rodgers looked at Brad, smiling sweetly. "And I take back all the nasty things I thought about you those miles I stared at your backside," Brad laughed.

"Well, I wasn't in love with you either. Every time I turned to check, you were a little closer. It was like Butch Cassidy, you know, 'Who *is* this guy.' Matter of fact, I *still* don't know the answer to that." Rodgers regarded him curiously.

"That is sort of a long story," Brad said.

"Tell you what," Rodgers said, "Come by and see me at the store sometime when you're around. Maybe we'll take a run. We've got lots to talk about. Twenty-six miles worth." They shook hands again, and Rodgers left, taking a portion of the clamoring reporters and TV cameras with him.

Someone finally brought him a folding chair, and he sat down gratefully, still drawing air greedily into his strained lungs. Someone came up and told him he had about three minutes before he would have to talk to the press. They couldn't be held off much longer.

This was like a dream, he thought. If I close my eyes it'll all vanish into thin air. But he did close his eyes. He could feel Sue's hand take his and press tightly. Sweet Sue. When he opened his eyes she was still there, smiling prettily down at him. He would not let her go again. Never again. Gus was back at his side then, squatting down to get closer to his ear.

"There's somebody else here who wants to shake your hand, hero. And you oughta want to shake his cause he's the guy who caught you when you fell. Besides, he's the gentleman who runs this whole show. The kingpin himself." Gus moved aside for the newcomer. The man, older than Gus, was nonetheless stocky and powerful looking. He offered a strong hand.

"Ya' ran a fine race here today, son," the older man said with a Scottish brogue. "I've got to tell ya we had some unbelievers on the committee. But videotapes don't lie. You made all the checkpoints. We know your name, but we still don't know *who* you are or how you did it. I guess we'll all know soon enough. Now, do ya think you're about ready? We've been puttin' off tha' TV people and tha' rest a' the media."

"I guess so," Brad Townes smiled at him. "Oh, and thanks for catching me at the tape. I guess you saved me some road burns."

"All in the line of duty," the older man replied. "I do a lot of odd jobs around here, and I was glad to be of service." And then he too turned and disappeared.

"They'll have the mayor in here next if we don't watch out," Gus said, "Maybe even the President of the United States. You're a real celebrity, Bradley Townes. The whole world is waiting to meet you."

He sat for another moment, gathering his strength. But what of the race, he wondered. I seem to have lost some of it somewhere. It occurred to him that he really didn't quite know what had happened. Gus handed him a can of beer and he grabbed it eagerly.

"There's more where that came from," Gus said, as Brad quickly moved it to his mouth and proceeded to dribble the first sip down his chin. The cool liquid felt good on his face and even better as it trickled down his throat to the dry cavern beneath. He had suddenly discovered how thirsty he was and began to guzzle the beer as if it would be his last.

"Hail the hero," a new voice proclaimed, "who hath caused Pheidippides to rattle in his grave."

"Coach!" Brad grabbed his hand.

"Were it not for interval training you would be out on the course yet, laboring away in obscurity," the coach admonished, thrusting a pedantic finger at him.

"Hey, Coach! It's good to see you!" said Brad. The coach had his familiar pipe clenched in his grinning mouth. "It's nice of you to stop by. I thought you had given up on me."

"Given up on you. Ha! That's a laugh. I only give up on the ones who stop dragging their asses to practice, excuse the French. But I can tell a real runner when I see one. I saw one that first interval session with my boys. And I sure as hell saw one today." Brad lowered his head.

"Thanks, Coach."

"You've got a real future ahead of you son. New York, Fukuoko. Who knows, maybe the Olympics." The coach was expansive. "When you get your sea legs back and you're ready to go to work—well, you know where to find me." Then he disappeared into the recesses of the crowd.

"So that's what you've been up to," said Gus, admiringly. "You've been on the track with the college guys."

Brad reached down and felt his aching thighs and shins. Someone, probably Sue, had removed his shoes and socks and he could see the redness of his feet, the blood vessels standing out on them like the blue lines on a highway map.

Tomorrow I will hurt like hell, he thought, but today there's only joy. He reached over and hugged Sue, which surprised her.

"Don't go away," he said. "Don't any of you dare go away. Stay close to me where I can see you and feel you."

"We won't go away," Gus promised. "We've got lots of time to make up for later, when you're all through here. But we're going to have to wait. You don't know what's heading in our direction."

It was the promised TV cameras and the rest of the reporters, ready to ask a million questions. They zoomed and they faded and they baked him with their hot lights until he knew he could take no more. Finally, after what seemed like hours, they too left.

Then, finally, they were walking out of the building, he and Sue straggling behind the others, when she stopped him, kissed him, and pulled his head down so she could speak without being overheard.

"Tell me something. Confidentially," she said softly. "Winning wasn't all that important, was it?"

Then, for the first time he realized it was true. He had not won. And somehow it didn't seem to matter.

GOING TO RUN ALL NIGHT

Harry Sylvester

(1944)

They brought him in before the commanding officer, a lieutenant colonel, and stood him there, almost as though he were a prisoner, a slight man, whose face, they now remembered, had been curiously harassed and marked by strain before this campaign had begun. He noticed that they walked on either side as if guarding him, as if, indeed, he were a prisoner or someone valued. And since he could think of nothing he had done or left undone for which they should make him a prisoner, he was driven to the incredible conclusion that at last he had come to be of value.

He looked at the lieutenant colonel, seeing that the officer's face was hardly less harassed than his own. All day, in the midst of the danger which constantly encircled them and intermittently killed some of them, the new legend of the lieutenant colonel's irascibility had grown so that now, standing before the man, the corporal could wonder he was not ripped up and down with words as scores of men had been that day.

The lieutenant colonel looked at him, blinking and staring, as though making some kind of adjustment from rage to calm. Which it was, perhaps, for to Nilson's amazement he said rather mildly, "They tell me that you used to be a runner, Corporal?"

"Why, yes," Nilson said. "Yes, sir, I mean.

"You used to run distances? I mean road races and such?"

"Yes, sir."

"Ever run in Marathon races or anything like that?"

"Yes, sir," the corporal said. He was thinking: There is nothing "like" the Marathon. Just the figures alone mean something: 26 miles, 385 yards. "I run seventh one year in the Boston Marathon." Right after he said it, he could see that the lieutenant colonel was not impressed, that he did not know running seventh in the Boston Marathon was not the same as running seventh in another foot race.

"Well," the officer said, as though making the best of a bad bargain, rubbing his eyes tiredly and slowly with the heels of his hands. "Well, as you know, they've sort of got us over a barrel here. The one radio we still have that is working has been damaged so that we cannot vary the frequency enough to keep the enemy from picking it up rather often."

He went on like that, rubbing his eyes, explaining to the corporal as if the corporal were a general—someone who ought to be told of what the situation was. "We think we can break out at dawn, if we can synchronize our attack with some sort of aid coming from our main forces opposite the point of our own attack. Break through the ring," he said vaguely. Then: "Look! You think you could run across the hills by dark and carry them a message?"

Nilson began to think, for some reason, about how his grandmother used to talk about lightning and how you never knew where or when it was going to strike. Fear was not in him, although for a little while he would think it was fear. His gasp was silent, so that his mouth was open before he began to speak. He said, "Why, I guess so. I mean, I'm not in very good shape. I—"

"But in no worse shape than anyone else here," the lieutenant colonel said. "And you used to be a runner. How long since you stopped active competition?"

"Oh, I was running all the time. Right up until my induction, and even then, when I was still in the States and could get leave, I was competing some."

The officer nodded. "Well, that's about all. There'll be no written message . . . in case you might be taken. You'll be picked up by one of our own patrols probably. Just tell them we can't last another day here and that we're going to try to come through at dawn. It's possible they won't believe you. But that's a chance we'll have to take. If they have time, they can send a plane over with a message, to let us know that they understand, although it hasn't been very healthy here for planes. There won't be much trouble getting you through their lines at night. I'll send a guard with you until you're beyond their lines and then you'll be on your own. Just follow the road. The main idea is to get there before dawn. I figure it's thirty-five or forty miles before they'll pick you up. We won't attack for six hours. You think you could make it in, say, five hours?"

"Why, if I was in shape," Nilson said, "I could, maybe, easy."

"Still," the officer said, "you're the best we have. Good luck."

"Yes, sir," Nilson said, and saluted and turned.

Outside, the two sergeants stood on either side of him, and the tall one said, "Well, what are you gonna need?"

"I dunno," Nilson said. "I guess I won't need anything. Maybe I'll take a canteen, maybe not." He knew that thirst for water and the actual need for water were not necessarily the same thing; he was already weighing in his mind the weight of the canteen against the necessity for water.

"Well, let's get going, then," the other sergeant said.

The tall sergeant got Nilson a canteen filled with water, and they moved out into the darkness beyond where the tanks and cars stood in a shallow arc like great animals huddled in the dark.

They were more than halfway across the three-mile plain that separated them from the hills holding the enemy, when Nilson said, "Look, this isn't any good for you two, is it? I mean if they see us, three isn't going to be much better than one?"

"Stop being noble," the tall sergeant said "Someone's got to show you through the hills."

"I see what you mean," Nilson said.

It was simpler than he had thought it would be. You could neither hear nor see the enemy, who needed no pickets to hear tanks approaching, or a plane.

The three moved upward over the dry hills, the soil crumbling under foot as they climbed, so that at the crest the sergeants were bushed, panting in the heat and the altitude like animals, and even Nilson was sweating. In the moonlight, below them and to the west and right, they could see the road.

"I guess this is where we get off," the tall sergeant said. "You better get going."

"All right," Nilson said. "I gotta get ready, though."

He undressed in the cloud-broken dark, until he sat there in his underwear, his socks and shoes and his dog tag. The other sergeant handed him the canteen.

"I'll take a drink now," Nilson said, "and that'll have to hold me. The canteen's too heavy—"

"You take that canteen," the tall sergeant said. "You're gonna need it."

"Look," Nilson said, then stopped. He saw that they did not know about water and running or any violent exercise. You could be thirsty for an awfully long time without actually needing water, but this was no time to start explaining that to them. "Well," he said, "I'll go along then."

"Good luck," they said. They watched him move, still walking down the slope toward the road a half-mile away. They thought it was because he couldn't run down a slope that steep, but Nilson was walking until the water was out of his stomach and he could be sure he wouldn't get a stitch when he started to run.

Watching him, the tall sergeant said, "You think he's gonna do any good?"

"No, I don't," the other sergeant said. "Even if he gets through their patrols, he'll drop before he gets to our people—or quit and go hide."

"What do you say that for?" the tall sergeant said.

"Because you're probably thinking the same thing I am!"

In the darkness, the tall sergeant nodded. "We both know we could go along, too, now and hide until this is over, because they're not going to get through tomorrow morning."

"But we go back, instead," the other sergeant said. "And I don't know why."

"I don't know why, either," the tall sergeant said.

Then they turned and began to go back the way they had come.

Nearing the road, the feeling of great adventure began to leave Nilson. Not fear but a sense of futility took him—of his own littleness in the night and the desert that was also the enemy's country. At the edge of the road he paused, although he could not tell why and attributed it to fear. It was not fear so much as an unwillingness to undergo one more futility.

He had not been a very good runner, and he was now thirty-one. Like many of the young men of the Scandinavian colonies in Brooklyn, he had run more because it was a tradition among their people. He had liked it, although after almost fifteen years of little or no glory, he had begun to feel that he was too old to keep losing that often, had begun to realize that, after a while, it did something to a man. Not that it was any fault of his; after all, you'd have to be pretty special to run well Saturdays or Sundays after being on your feet all day as a post-office clerk.

He still hesitated on the edge of the road; there was in his hesitation a quality of sullenness, a vague, shadowy resentment against some large amorphous body or group that somehow had become identified with the long years of defeat.

Without quite knowing what the resentment was, he knew it to be, if not wrong, at least inappropriate now and here. He sighed and at the edge of the road did a curious little exercise that relatives of his also had done three hundred years before in Norway. He bent over, touching his toes five or six times and each time straightening up and flinging his arms wide. The idea was to open his lungs quickly and limber the muscles of his chest and arms. Although he was not a very good runner, he knew all about running; he knew that a man ran as much with his arms as with his legs.

He stepped onto the road and in a reflexive gesture pawed at the crude paving as though it were hard-packed cinders, and the heavy G.I. shoes were the short-spiked ones of the distance runner. He felt sheepish, and in the darkness his mouth twisted into a grin. He began to run.

Almost immediately he felt easier; felt confidence flow through him as though it were his blood; felt that now, at last, he was in his own country, or, more accurately, in his own medium. There are mediums of action that vary with the individual; some feel best moving in an automobile, others on a horse, some walking, a few running or flying.

As he ran, he felt with his feet for the part of the tar-and-gravel road that was best suited to him. The road was slightly crowned in the center and in places pocked lightly by machine-gun bullets from the planes that had gone over it. As on most roads, he found that the shoulder was best for running. It was softer, the spikeless shoes slipped less, and its resilience would save him from shin-splints tomorrow. He thought with irony that it was of no importance whether he got the little pains along the shin from bruising or pulling the tendons that held the muscle to the bone. Certainly he would run no more tomorrow, come what might; indeed, there might not be a tomorrow.

This started him thinking of what he called fear—but what was really an ennui, a saturation in himself of having for so many years done things to no purpose. He wondered if this, too, would be to no purpose; if some burial detail, an indefinite number of days from now, would find his twisted body some place along this road.

Then he began to think that it would be worse to get to where he was going and not be believed. There was nothing he could think of to do about that, so he stopped thinking of it. Like many Scandinavians, he was a fatalist, and the war had not helped overcome that.

The night—soft, warm and windless—was all around him. In its blackness, there was a quality of brown; or perhaps he imagined this, for all day the hills were brown, so that afterward you associated the color with thirst, with violence and with the imminence of death. He had discovered, only recently and to his relief, that he was not afraid of death; after all, he had no responsibilities in life, no dependents; disablement, though, was something else.

Then suddenly he began to think of the time he had run seventh in the Boston Marathon; the cold day and the girls unexpectedly lining the road at Wellesley, and the tremendous lift they had given his spirit, just standing there, calling to the runners, the wind moving their hair and their bright skirts.

He was running faster, too fast, he thought. He was beginning to breathe hard. It was too early to be breathing so hard; but he knew that would pass soon, and the thing called second wind would come to him. He slackened his pace a little, feeling the weight of the shoes and trying to reject the thought before it took too much form; trying not to think of it.

He began to think of the enemy and where the enemy might be; all around him, surely, but probably not too near the road, because, by night, planes could see a road. Still, there might be patrols knowing a man running steadily by night was a strange and unaccountable thing. But they might never see him; only hear him and the pounding of his feet on the road. So, deviously, his mind came back to the thought which he could no longer avoid: there was only one thing to do, take the G.I. shoes off and run without them.

He slowed gradually until he was walking, and walked perhaps thirty yards before he stopped. Then he sat on the ground and took off his shoes.

When he stood up, he hesitated again. Once, he had lost a shoe and had finished the race, but the cinders had taken their toll of that foot.

The road here was bad, but principally what he feared was stepping on one of the scorpions. He wondered if they were out by night—and then he began to run again.

Now the element of strangeness about this man running in the night, this Brooklyn Norwegian in a strange land, was intensified by the silence, in which only his regular, heavy breathing made a sound.

Without knowing it, he ran at times in a kind of stupor. The nights of little or fitful sleep, the days of too little food and water, were beginning to affect him, and he began to take refuge from exhaustion and pain in something at times close to unconsciousness.

Twice he passed tanks not far from the road, their crews sleeping, he himself not knowing he passed them. Like a dun ghost, he drifted with the short, effortless stride he had developed over the long years of competition and training. These little spells of semi-consciousness no longer occurred; effort was too much to permit them, too sustained and by now terrible, so that his senses became acute again, his thoughts long-ranging, sharp and filled with color. It was perhaps this return to acute consciousness, induced by pain, that saved him.

He had begun to think of the long dreams of his youth, of passing through lines of people at the end of the Boston Marathon, as he strode in, tired but easily first; of the Olympic Marathon and the laurel wreath he had read of.

Some place there was sound and a hoarse shouting. He could not tell for a moment whether they were in his thoughts or in the reality of the night all around him. Then the sound, now long familiar to him, but still terrible, of an automatic rifle coughing in the night.

He glanced about him, flinching, his eyes, already strained open by the night, trying to open wider, so that the muscles near them hurt. The shouting, the firing were above him—here the road was sunken—behind and to the right.

The firing sounded again, farther away. He neither heard nor felt bullets. In one of those sudden lifts of speed—instinctive and desperate now—with which a distance runner sometimes in the middle of race tries to break the heart of his opponents, Nilson started to sprint.

The road ran downhill here, and now through the warm, dark night, the little man let his feet shoot out ahead of him, carrying his legs out with the controlled abandon of the cross-country runner going downhill.

He ran with almost no sound, although he was not aware of this. The shouting and the sound of guns continued behind him. With a faint pleasure, he realized that it was his passing that had alarmed the enemy.

There was an eeriness about him as he moved in the night. Perhaps it was this, perhaps only the adrenalin further secreted in his body by his fear when the shots sounded—but he found a new strength. The legs, the rhythmically moving arms recovered the thing of which, in his boyhood, he and the other runners had made a fetish—the thing called form.

So, going downhill now, the enemy all around him, he experienced a sense of power, as though he were invisible, as though he were fleeter and stronger than anything that could seek to kill or hinder him.

Sweat bathed him, he glistened as though oiled, and there was a slight froth at his lips. He moved with a machinelike rhythm and his eyes—if they could have been seen—might have seemed mad.

The road leveled, ran flat for perhaps a quarter-mile, then began to mount again. He became aware of this only gradually. The first change he noted was in himself, first the mind, then the body. The sense of power, of superhuman ability was gone, almost abruptly, his lungs began to hurt badly, and the cords in his neck. He was, he suddenly realized, nothing special; he was Pete Nilson from Brooklyn, and he was bushed; he was just about done.

He shook his head, like a trapped, bewildered animal. The desire, the need to stop was extraordinarily strong in him. He tried an old trick: he tried to analyze his pain, knowing this sometimes made it disappear. There was the pain in his lungs, in his throat, in the muscles of his eyes, but not yet where his arms went into the shoulders, not yet just above the knees where the thigh muscles overlapped.

His stride had shortened with the hill and his body leaned forward. He had not been above quitting in a few races, when he was hopelessly outdistanced, when he had not been trained right, when he had not had enough rest the previous week to make him strong.

It seemed that he had never been so exhausted as now, and his mind sought excuses to stop. First, came the thought that if only he knew how long he had to run, he might endure it. Twenty-six miles, 385 yards—that was the distance of the Marathon, and in Boston, in Toronto, you always knew within a few hundred yards how far you had come, how far you had to go. But now, no one knew or had known, not within four or five miles. The enemy was in the hills, and the hills were all around the lieutenant colonel and his men, and beyond the hills that held the enemy were more of your own men, some place. So late in his life he learned that it is important to all men in their various endeavors to see an end, to know how far off that end is.

Fatigue blurred his vision and he started to deviate from a straight line, veering slightly from side to side. Although he did not know it, he was beyond the enemy, and had only to combat himself. But he had forgotten about the enemy, and his mind sought reasons to stop, old resentments that could possess the weight of argument. What the hell had they ever done for him? He should have been a sergeant by now.

Anger formed in him: he could not tell its nature or its object. He realized it might be at himself; then, that it was at himself. He must have been crazy, he thought; he supposed that, all his life, his efforts had been directed obscurely toward achieving a sense of usefulness, corrupted sometimes into what was called a sense of glory. And now, close to it, he had almost rejected it.

When the change occurred, the sudden insight, he was on top of a hill and looking down into a plain full of great shadows; there was a paleness in the sky over the shadows. He was on top of this hill, but whether he was running or standing still, he could not tell, for it was as great an effort to stand as to run.

He began to move downhill again, still veering. He sensed, if he did not see, that there were no more hills beyond and that his own people must be somewhere near, perhaps at the bottom of the hill he now descended.

As he staggered, half-blind in the dim light, to the foot of the hill, he thought of the Athenian runner finishing the first Marathon and, as he collapsed, crying, "Rejoice, we conquer!" Nilson realized how much that image, those words had been with him, influencing him all his life. They heartened him now, sealed the sense of meaning in him.

A sentry challenged as the road leveled out into the plain, and Nilson, not knowing the password, reasoned that this was the place for him to collapse. Pheidippides, finishing the first Marathon, had cried, "Rejoice, we conquer!" but Pete Nilson, thinking this, and finishing his own run, said in a kind of prayer, "Christ, buddy, don't shoot," knelt and quietly fell forward in the dust.

He didn't remember exactly what he said to them, but they took him to another lieutenant colonel. And the miracle was not over. He could not believe it then; all the rest of his life, he could hardly believe it. They believed him. They believed him, and some place near him as he sat stupefied on a canvas stool in a tent, he heard all around him, in the first light, the sound of armor beginning to move, the clatter and roar of the tanks.

A staff sergeant tried to explain. "Look," the sergeant said, "nobody comes down here in the shape you're in to lie to somebody else. You see?" Especially the feet, the sergeant thought.

But all Nilson did was sit on the canvas stool and stare.

"Look," the sergeant said again, "you'll get something big for this. Don't you catch?"

Nilson stared at him. He was beginning to catch, but it would be a long time, if ever, before he could make anyone understand. The big thing, the most important thing in his life, was that he had come down here, without credentials of any sort, and they had believed him. The citation, the medal, nothing was ever going to mean that much.

"Look," the sergeant said. "They're getting you a doctor. You want anything now, though? Coffee or something?" Don't the guy know about his feet, he thought.

The little froth still at his lips, Nilson shook his head. He looked like a madman, and the sergeant thought that maybe he was mad. But all Nilson was doing was sitting there listening to the roar and thinking that he, Pete Nilson, had set it in motion. He didn't want anything right then, only to sit there and listen.

The Sprinters

RAYMOND'S RUN

Toni Cade Bambara

(1971)

I don't have much work to do around the house like some girls. My mother does that. And I don't have to earn my pocket money by hustling; George runs errands for the big boys and sells Christmas cards. And anything else that's got to get done, my father does. All I have to do in life is mind my brother Raymond, which is enough.

Sometimes I slip and say my little brother Raymond. But as any fool can see he's much bigger and he's older too. But a lot of people call him my little brother cause he needs looking after cause he's not quite right. And a lot of smart mouths got lots to say about that too, especially when George was minding him. But now, if anybody has anything to say to Raymond, anything to say about his big head, they have to come by me. And I don't play the dozens or believe in standing around with somebody in my face doing a lot of talking. I much rather just knock you down and take my chances even if I am a little girl with skinny arms and a squeaky voice, which is how I got the name Squeaky. And if things get too rough, I run. And as anybody can tell you, I'm the fastest thing on two feet.

There is no track meet that I don't win the first place medal. I used to win the twenty-yard dash when I was a little kid in kindergarten. Nowadays, it's the fifty-yard dash. And tomorrow I'm subject to run the quarter-meter relay all by myself and come in first, second and third.

The big kids call me Mercury cause I'm the swiftest thing in the neighborhood. Everybody knows that—except two people who know better, my father and me. He can beat me to Amsterdam Avenue with me having a two fire-hydrant head start and him running with his hands in his pockets and whistling. But that's private information. Cause can you imagine some thirty-five-year-old man stuffing himself into PAL shorts to race little kids? So as far as everyone's concerned, I'm the fastest and that goes for Gretchen, too, who has put out the tale that she is going to win the first-place medal this year. Ridiculous. In the second place, she's got short legs. In the third place, she's got freckles. In the first place no one can beat me and that's all there is to it.

I'm standing on the corner admiring the weather and about to take a stroll down Broadway so I can practice my breathing exercises, and I've got Raymond walking on the inside close to the buildings cause he's subject to fits of fantasy and starts thinking he's a circus performer and that the curb is a tightrope strung high in the air. And sometimes after a rain he likes to step down off his tightrope right into the gutter and slosh around getting his shoes and cuffs wet. Then I get hit when I get home. Or sometimes if you don't watch him he'll dash across traffic to the island in the middle of Broadway and give the pigeons a fit. Then I have to go behind him apologizing to all the old people sitting around trying to get some sun and getting all upset with all the pigeons fluttering around them, scattering their newspapers and upsetting the waxpaper lunches in their laps. So I keep Raymond on the inside of me, and he plays like he's driving a stage coach, which is O.K. by me so long as he doesn't run me over or interrupt my breathing exercises, which I have to do on account of I'm serious about my running, and I don't care who knows it.

Now some people like to act like things come easy to them, won't let on that they practice. Not me. I'll high-prance down 34th Street like a rodeo pony to keep my knees strong even if it does get my mother uptight so that she walks ahead like she's not with me, don't know me, is all by herself on a shopping trip and I am somebody else's crazy child. Now you take Cynthia Procter for instance. She's just the opposite. If there's a test tomorrow, she'll say something like, "Oh, I guess I'll play handball this afternoon and watch television tonight," just to let you know she ain't thinking about the test. Or like last week when she won the spelling bee for the millionth time, "A good thing you got 'receive,' Squeaky, cause I would have got it wrong. I completely forgot about the spelling bee." And she'll clutch the lace on her blouse like it was a narrow escape. Oh, brother. But of course when I pass her house on my early morning trots around the block, she is practicing the scales on the piano over and over and over and over. Then in music class she always lets herself get bumped around so she falls accidently on purpose onto the piano stool and is so surprised to find herself sitting there that she decides just for fun to try out the ole keys. And what do you know—Chopin's waltzes just spring out of her fingertips and she's the most surprised thing in the world. A regular prodigy. I could kill people like that. I stay up all night studying the words for the spelling bee. And you can see me any time of day practicing running. I never walk if I can trot, and shame on Raymond if he can't keep up. But of course he does, cause if he doesn't someone's liable to walk up and to him and get smart, or take his allowance from him, or ask him where he got that great big pumpkin head. People are so stupid sometimes.

So I'm strolling down Broadway breathing out and breathing in on counts of seven, which is my lucky number, and here comes Gretchen and her sidekicks: Mary Louise, who used to be a friend of mine when she first moved to Harlem from Baltimore and got beat up by everybody till I took up for her on account of her mother and my mother used to sing in the same choir when they were young girls, but people ain't grateful, so now she hangs out with the new girl Gretchen and talks about me like a dog; and Rosie, who is as fat as I am skinny and has a big mouth where Raymond is concerned and is too stupid to know that there is not a big deal of difference between herself and Raymond and that she can't afford to throw stones. So they are steady coming up Broadway and I see right away that it's going to be one of those Dodge City scenes cause the street ain't that big and they're close to the buildings just as we are. First I think I'll step into the candy store and look over the new comics and let them pass. But that's chicken and I've got a reputation to consider. So then I think I'll just walk straight on through them or even over them if necessary. But as they get to me, they slow down. I'm ready to fight, cause like I said I don't feature a whole lot of chit-chat, I much prefer to just knock you down right from the jump and save everybody a lotta precious time.

"You signing up for the May Day races?" smiles Mary Louise, only it's not a smile at all. A dumb question like that doesn't deserve an answer. Beside's there's just me and Gretchen standing there really, so no use wasting my breath talking to shadows.

"I don't think you're going to win this time," says Rosie, trying to signify with her hands on her hips all salty, completely forgetting that I have whupped her behind many times for less salt than that.

"I always win cause I'm the best," I say straight at Gretchen who is, as far as I'm concerned, the only one in this ventriloquist-dummy routine. Gretchen smiles, but it's not a smile, and I'm thinking that girls never really smile at each other because they don't know how and don't want to know how and there's probably no one to teach us how, cause grown-up girls don't know either. Then they all look at Raymond who has just brought his mule team to a standstill. And they're about to see what trouble they can get into through him.

"What grade you in now, Raymond?"

"You got anything to say to my brother, you say it to me, Mary Louise Williams of Raggedy Town, Baltimore."

"What are you, his mother?" sasses Rosie.

"That's right, Fatso. And the next word out of anybody and I'll be *their* mother too." So they just stand there and Gretchen shifts from one leg to the other and so do they. Then Gretchen puts her hands on her hips and is about to say something with her freckle-face self but doesn't. Then she walks around me looking me up and down but keeps walking up Broadway, and her sidekicks follow her. So me and Raymond smile at each other and he says, "Gidyap" to his team and I continue with my breathing exercises, strolling down Broadway toward the ice man on 145th with not a care in the world cause I am Miss Quicksilver herself.

I take my time getting to the park on May Day because the track meet is the last thing on the program. The biggest thing on the program is the May Pole dancing, which I can do without, thank you, even if my mother thinks it's a shame I don't take part and act like a girl for a change. You'd think my mother'd be grateful not to have to make me a white organdy dress with a big satin sash and buy me new white babydoll shoes that can't be taken out of the box till the big day.

You'd think she'd be glad her daughter ain't out there prancing around a May Pole getting the new clothes all dirty and sweaty and trying to act like a fairy or a flower or whatever you're supposed to be when you should be trying to be yourself, whatever that is, which is, as far as I am concerned, a poor Black girl who really can't afford to buy shoes and a new dress you only wear once a lifetime cause it won't fit next year.

I was once a strawberry in a Hansel and Gretel pageant when I was in nursery school and didn't have no better sense than to dance on tiptoe with my arms in a circle over my head doing umbrella steps and being a perfect fool just so my mother and father could come dressed up and clap. You'd think they'd know better than to encourage that sort of nonsense. I am not a strawberry. I do not dance on my toes. I run. That is what I am all about. So I always come late to the May Day program, just in time to get my number pinned on and lay in the grass till they announce the fifty yard dash.

I put Raymond in the little swings, which is a tight squeeze this year and will be impossible next year. Then I look around for Mr. Pearson, who pins the numbers on. I'm really looking for Gretchen if you want to know the truth, but she's not around. The park is jam-packed. Parents in hats and corsages and breast-pocket handkerchiefs peeking up. Kids in white dresses and light-blue suits. The parkees unfolding chairs and chasing the rowdy kids from Lenox as if they had no right to be there. The big guys with their caps on backwards leaning against the fence swirling the basketballs on the tips of their fingers, waiting for all these crazy people to clear out the park so they can play. Most of the kids in my class are carrying bass drums and glockenspiels and flutes. You'd think they'd put in a few bongos or something for real like that.

Then here comes Mr. Pearson with his clipboard and his cards and pencils and whistles and safety pins and fifty million other things he's always dropping all over the place with his clumsy self. He sticks out in a crowd because he's on stilts. We used to call him Jack and the Beanstalk to get him mad. But I'm the only one that can outrun him and get away, and I'm too grown for that silliness now.

"Well, Squeaky," he says, checking my name off the list and handing me number seven and two pins. And I'm thinking he's got no right to call me Squeaky, if I can't call him Beanstalk.

"Hazel Elizabeth Deborah Parker," I correct him and tell him to write it down on his board.

"Well, Hazel Elizabeth Deborah Parker, going to give someone else a break this year?" I squint at him real hard to see if he is seriously thinking I should lose the race on purpose just to give someone else a break. "Only six girls running this time," he continues, his head shaking sadly like it's my fault all of New York didn't turn out in sneakers. "That new girl should give you a run for your money." He looks around the park for Gretchen like a periscope in a submarine movie. "Wouldn't it be a nice gesture if you were . . . to ahhh . . ."

I give him such a look he couldn't finish putting that idea into words. Grownups got a lot of nerve sometimes. I pin number seven to myself and stomp away, I'm so burnt. And I go straight for the track and stretch out on the grass while the band winds up with "Oh, the Monkey Wrapped His Tail Around the Flag Pole," which my teacher calls by some other name. The man on the loudspeaker is calling everyone over to the track and I'm on my back looking at the sky, trying to pretend I'm in the country, but I can't, because even grass in the city feels hard as sidewalk, and there's just no pretending you are anywhere but in a "concrete jungle" as my grandfather says.

The twenty-yard dash takes all of two minutes cause most of the little kids don't know no better than to run off the track or run the wrong way or run smack into the fence and fall down and cry. One little kid, though, has got the good sense to run straight for the white ribbon up ahead so he wins. Then the second-graders line up for the thirty-yard dash and I don't even bother to turn my head to watch cause Raphael Perez always wins. He wins before he even begins by psyching the runners, telling them they're going to trip on their shoelaces and fall on their faces or lose their shorts or something, which he doesn't really have to do since he is very fast, almost as fast as I am. After that is the forty-yard dash which I used to run when I was in first grade. Raymond is hollering to me from the swings cause he knows I'm about to do my thing cause the man on the loudspeaker has just announced the fifty-yard dash, although he might just as well be giving a recipe for angel food cake cause you can hardly make out what he's saying for the static. I get up and slip off my sweat pants and then I see

Gretchen standing at the starting line, kicking her legs out like a pro. Then as I get into place I see that ole Raymond is on line on the other side of the fence, bending down with his fingers on the ground just like he knew what he was doing. I was going to yell at him but then I didn't. It burns up your energy to holler.

Every time, just before I take off in a race, I always feel like I'm in a dream, the kind of dream you have when you're sick with fever and feel all hot and weightless. I dream I'm flying over a sandy beach in the early morning sun, kissing the leaves of the trees as I fly by. And there's always the smell of apples, just like in the country when I was little and used to think I was a choo-choo train, running through the fields of corn and chugging up the hill to the orchard. And all the time I'm dreaming this, I get lighter and lighter until I'm flying over the beach again, getting blown through the sky like a feather that weighs nothing at all. But once I spread my fingers in the dirt and crouch over the Get on Your Mark, the dream goes and I am solid again and am telling myself, Squeaky you must win, you must win, you are the fastest thing in the world, you can even beat your father up Amsterdam if you really try. And then I feel my weight coming back just behind my knees then down to my feet then into the earth and the pistol shot explodes in my blood and I am off and weightless again, flying past the other runners, my arms up and down and the whole world is quiet except for the crunch as I zoom over the gravel in the track. I glance to my left and there is no one. To the right, a blurred Gretchen, who's got her chin jutting out as if it would win the race all by itself. And on the other side of the fence is Raymond with his arms down to his side and the palms tucked up behind him, running in his very own style, and it's the first time I ever saw that and I almost stop to watch my brother Raymond on his first run. But the white ribbon is bouncing toward me and I tear past it, racing into the distance till my feet with a mind of their own start digging up footfulls of dirt and brake me short. Then all the kids standing on the side pile on me, banging me on the back and slapping my head with their May Day programs, for I have won again and everybody on 151st Street can walk tall for another year.

"In first place . . ." the man on the loudspeaker is clear as a bell now. But then he pauses and the loudspeaker starts to whine. Then static. And I lean down to catch my breath and here comes Gretchen walking back, for she's overshot the finish line too, huffing and puffing with her hands on her hips, taking it slow, breathing in steady time like a real pro and I sort of like her a little for the first time. "In first place . . ." and then three or four voices get all mixed up on the loudspeaker and I dig my sneaker into the grass and stare at Gretchen who's staring back, we both wondering just who did win. I can hear old Beanstalk arguing with the man on the loudspeaker and then a few others running their mouths about what the stopwatches say. Then I hear Raymond yanking at the fence to call me and I wave to shush him, but he keeps rattling the fence like a gorilla in a cage like in them gorilla movies, but then like a dancer or something he starts climbing up nice and easy but very fast. And it occurs to me, watching how smoothly he climbs hand over hand and remembering how he looked running with his arms down to his side and with the wind pulling his mouth back and his teeth showing and all, it occurred to me that Raymond would make a very fine runner. Doesn't he always keep up with me on my trots? And he surely knows how to breathe in counts of seven cause he's always doing it at the dinner table, which drives my brother George up the wall. And I'm smiling to beat the band cause if I've lost this race, or if me and Gretchen tied, or even if I've won, I can always retire as a runner and begin a whole new career as a coach with Raymond as my champion. After all, with a little more study, I can beat Cynthia and her phony self at the spelling bee. And if I bugged my mother, I could get piano lessons and become a star. And I have a big rep as the baddest thing around. And I've got a roomful of ribbons and medals and awards. But what has Raymond got to call his own?

So I stand there with my new plans, laughing out loud by this time as Raymond jumps down from the fence and runs over with his teeth showing and his arms down to the side, which no one before him has quite mastered as a running style. And by the time he comes over I'm jumping up and down so glad to see him—my brother Raymond, a great runner in the family tradition. But of course everyone thinks I'm jumping up and down because the men on the loudspeaker have finally gotten themselves together and compared notes and are announcing "In first place—Miss Hazel Elizabeth Deborah Parker." (Dig that.) "In second place—Miss Gretchen P. Lewis." And I look over at Gretchen wondering what the "P" stands for. And I smile. Cause she's good, no doubt about it. Maybe she'd like to help me coach Raymond; she obviously is serious about running, as any fool can see. And she nods to congratulate me and then she smiles. We stand there with this big smile of respect between us. It's about as real a smile as girls can do for each other, considering we don't practice smiling every day, you know, cause maybe we're too busy being flowers or fairies or strawberries instead of something honest and worthy of respect . . . you know . . . like being people.

TEN SECONDS

Louis Edwards

(1991)

[The entirety of this novel takes place in the memory of thirty-five-year-old Eddie Franklin—a man long past his glory days and mired in the tedium of domestic life—during ten seconds as he watches a 100-meter dash at a high school meet. This section is called "And He Was Eighteen Years Old . . ."]

He is on his mark, he is set . . . he is on his mark, he is set . . . he is on his mark, he is set. But what is taking so long? Why doesn't that fat sonofabitch shoot the gun, start this race! Everyone is waiting, waiting, waiting. The sun is kickin. It's already burning up, even this early in the track season. His body is covered with beads of sweat. He feels as though he has just emerged from a misty sauna. His muscles are still aching from the leg he ran on the 880-yard relay. And now here he is about to run this 100-yard dash. He doesn't mind, though. It's his favorite race. When he hears the gun, his muscles will automatically spring to action. He can almost feel the breeze that will flow smoothly over his face and arms and legs. His spikes will rhythmically splash cinder behind him and there will be cheering from the bleachers to his right.

This is his favorite meet of the entire year. The Jacob High School Relays. He likes it partly because it takes place at his school and he gets to show off in front of his friends. Everybody knows how good he is, how fast he can run, but they really believe it when they can see it with their own eyes. And he likes the meet because the competition is always tough. This year two teams from Beaumont and a couple more from Houston are here. These brothers can move too—and they know it. The one from Houston in lane two, the one who won the third qualifying heat with a record 9.8, is wearing a bad-ass pair of spikes. They're navy blue with a fluorescent orange swish on the sides. When Eddie told him how cool they were, he just sort of shrugged his shoulders and jogged on. A real snotty muthafucka. Still, Eddie promises himself to remember to ask Coach Tillis about getting him some new spikes before too much of the season passes. The competition is good, but it isn't frightening to Eddie. It only makes him run faster. When he ran in the first heat to qualify for this dash final, he finished in front of two runners who both had been timed before at under ten flat. Eddie ran a 10.1 to beat them, only two tenths of a second off his best time. He had clenched his fist high above his head as he crossed the finish line—partly for the crowd, but mostly for himself. He has to keep proving to himself over and over again how good he is at this one thing. No one can take this winning feeling away from him. Whenever he experiences it, he makes sure he relishes it. He can't tell when he'll stop winning. The winning could end today for all he knows—but not if he can help it.

He likes the sweaty smells mingling with all of the oils the runners use on their legs and the Icy Hot they rub themselves down with. He knows he'll never forget the smell of Icy Hot. Before basketball season is over and even before track practice begins, he can already smell it. It comes every year with the robins, like clockwork. His rubdown is starting to wear off now; he can tell that his muscles will be tense as soon as this race is over. He'll have to have another rubdown before he runs the mile relay, the race he hates. He has to run a quarter of a mile, and that just isn't his best distance. But since Coach really doesn't have anyone better to run the race, Eddie goes along with it. He usually runs the third leg of the relay. "Stick!" That's what you say while you are jogging around the track practicing handing off the baton in a team of four. "Stick!" you yell to the man in front of you. And he will reach his hand straight back toward you in a quick motion and you slap the baton firmly into his palm. During the race, he grabs it and he's off. There are teams on the infield going through these motions now. He's concentrating on the path in front of him and waiting for the sound of the gun, but he knows they are there. Some of them are in the periphery of his vision.

And there—well, what do you know (there he goes!)—also in the periphery of his vision, at the end of the field where the finish line is placed, is the high jumping pit. (From Eddie's perspective the pit is not far from the center of his vision, really.) He *sees* the action there, though it is his race that is commanding his attention. He sees it all. He sees Malcolm, back arched over the bar. It is a perfect pose, something to behold. Someone should take a picture. The bar must be set on at least six feet, eight inches. Malcolm is suspended high up in the air. When the man said "On your mark" just a moment ago, Malcolm was running toward the bar, making his approach. And when the man said "Set," he was planting his foot for takeoff. Now he is in this perfect pose. Not on his way up, not on his way down. Just hanging there gracefully. Malcolm, Malcolm, Malcolm, Eddie thinks. It's such a great act you have, the way you have all of these people convinced that you're just another high jumper. Boy, you're something else, hanging up there in that red tank top and those ballooning blue shorts. You really have them fooled. But not me. No, buddy. Not me. You see, I was there in the backyard with you sitting in the oak tree. I was there. I know all about your fantasies. I know all about your dreams. I'm on to you. You may have the rest of them fooled, but you can't fool me. Not me. Not your brother. You ain't just jumping. You think you can fly, muthafucka. You think you can fly. I know all about you and your flying Africans and how they could escape and be free. I know all about it. You told me, remember? I was the one you told in the oak tree. And I never told anybody else. It was our secret. I was scared they'd laugh at you. But look at them. Nobody's laughing at you now—and you're flaunting it right in front of their faces. And they're not laughing—they're cheering. I'm cheering too, Ace. You've got it now. Hold it. Just hold it right there. Don't come down yet. Hold it. We believe, we believe. I believe. Show me, Malcolm. Will you show me how to do it? I believe you. I want to come up there. Forget about this stupid race. I don't care about it. It's a bunch of bullshit, anyway. Like I really need another trophy or medal or whatever crap it is they're giving away this time. I want to come up there. Will you show me how? Please. I want to fly. I want to feel under my arms the force you talked about, the force that carried you in your dreams. I want the feeling that is like smelling freshly baked bread. I want to soar at night. I want to fly, Malcolm. What is the secret? Tell me. Show me. I am on my mark, I am set. Show me *now*. I want to fly. I want—

Pow!

The race begins, and Eddie sees (oh, no) Malcolm falling. Eddie runs.

GALLIPOLI

Jack Bennett

(1981)

[*Archy Hamilton leaves the family ranch to seek adventure and glory. The story does not have a happy ending.*]

Western Australia, October, 1914

Round-up days on Bindana ended at the dam: a great saucer of coffee-coloured water in a red clay hollow. The stockmen threw themselves into it gratefully, laughing and splashing each other like children. There were layers of water in the dam: the top inch or two, heated by the sun, was almost blood-warm: after that it got colder and colder and on the hottest day the lowest layer, on the mud ten feet down, seemed almost freezing. Archy dived to the bottom and came up spluttering. He swam to the bank and got out, bare feet squelching in red ooze. Zac, dripping wet, joined him. They sat in companionable silence for a while on a fallen tree trunk, watching the stockmen's horseplay in the water.

Les McCann, sitting nearby and rolling one of his interminable cigarettes, glanced sourly at them. He finished making the cigarette and put it between his lips while fumbling in his shirt for matches.

"Prefer the company of blacks, eh, Archy?" he said unpleasantly. The unlit cigarette jiggled on his lower lip, dribbling tobacco.

The stockmen abruptly stopped their roughhousing. The dam's

small ripples licked the mud with soft chuckles.

Archy looked at Les. Careful now, he told himself. You're the boss's son and he's an employee. Think of what Uncle Jack'd say. Or your Dad.

"Zac's my mate, Les," he said. "All right?"

Les shrugged and grinned.

One of the new stockmen chuckled quietly.

Old Coop stood up, frowning.

"Arch and I—we run together—" began Zac.

The stockmen laughed. The tension was broken.

But Les McCann never knew when to stop. He grinned again, showing his stained teeth as he blew a disdainful cloud of smoke.

"Fancy yourself as a runner, do you, Archy?"

Zac stood up, balancing himself on the log, and began to pull on his boots.

"He's more than a runner, mate," he said to Les. "He's a top bloody athlete!"

Les frowned. "Who're you mateying, boy?"

"Take it easy, Les," said Old Coop. "He's a good kid."

"Which one?" asked Les. "The boss's son, Coop, or are you a black lover too?" He spat out the damp remains of his cigarette as Old Coop opened his mouth to protest. "Anyway, girls run. Men box."

"Ah, lay off, Les," said one of the new men.

"Archy can run faster than you can *ride*," said Zac hotly, and all the stockmen, even Old Coop, laughed.

Les pretended to be engrossed in rolling another cigarette.

"That so?" he inquired idly. "That really so? You'll be going to the Olympics next, I guess, eh?"

Archy said, flatly: "Two to one I'll beat you to the home gate."

One of the stockmen gave a whoop. "Take him on, Les. Take him on!"

Les stopped making the cigarette.

"You mean me on horse, you afoot?"

Archy nodded. "Yeah. I run cross-country, you take the track."

Les hesitated. "Well, now, I don't want—" but one of the new men interrupted him, grinning.

"It's a fair bet, Les. It's a couple miles further by the track, but you've got a horse under you. Four legs agin two." Les thought for a few seconds.

"Okay," he said. The stockmen whooped again. Archy began pulling on his boots. Les pointed at them, shaking his head.

"Not like that. Barefoot."

Archy looked around. The ground was rough and stony. Les smirked and lit his cigarette.

Archy handed his boots to Zac.

"You're on," he said to Les. The stockman stared at him, then shrugged.

"You want anything on it?"

"I said two to one," said Archy. "I've got two pounds I've been saving, and a bit. You beat me to the home gate and I give you two. I beat you and you give me one. All right?"

"Can't say fairer than that," said Old Coop.

Les walked across to his horse and prepared to mount.

"Just one thing," said Archy, as Les put his foot in the stirrup. Les looked over his shoulder. "Yeah?" he said, impatiently.

"Bareback," said Archy. Zac and the stockmen hooted with laughter. "Barefoot, bareback," said Archy, smiling sweetly.

"Fair enough," said one of the new men.

Slowly Les unbuckled the saddle. He glared at the other stockmen.

"Thanks, mates," he said.

"I'll be starter," said Old Coop, pulling out a soiled handkerchief.

They told about that race for years afterwards. The story was passed from stockman to stockman. How Archy took off like a kangaroo, bounding away in great long land-eating strides until Zac caught up with him and told him to slow down, to save himself; how they ran, black boy and white, away from the dam, through the scrub, jumping stumps, raising great pink and white flocks of galahs and white clouds of screeching cockatoos; how Zac dropped out, almost fainting with the heat and the pace. How Archy ran with one eye cocked on the track, looking for the cloud of dust that would tell him that Les was overtaking him. They tell, with some exaggeration, how the rocks tore Archy's feet and how you could follow his trail by the blood splashes; which was not quite true, although the rocks and small hidden stones (they were the worst) damaged him cruelly.

They tell, too, how while Archy was hanging on the home gate, panting and bloodied, a riderless horse cantered up, reins trailing, followed by Zac, mounted now, carrying Archy's boots, and laughing until the tears ran down his face, pointing back down the dusty track where, ten minutes later (some even said half an hour) a dusty, dishevelled Les McCann appeared around the bend.

"Slid off that bare back soon's he started," explained Zac when he had controlled his laughter sufficiently to talk. "Got on again, and fell off again—I tell you, Arch, he's been on and off that horse twenty times 'tween here and the dam!"

("And all old Les got out of that caper," the tellers of the tale would add, years later, "was the sorest backside from here to Sydney —fair raw, it was.")

But that was later, when the dust had settled. On the day itself, while Archy was getting his breath back and Zac, no longer laughing, was clucking over his ruined feet, a furious Uncle Jack, attracted by their laughter, suddenly appeared at the gate.

"You bloody young fool," he shouted, pointing at the torn feet, "perhaps you'll tell me how you think you'll be running in the big race—the Kimberley Gift!—next week? Or will you pray for a miracle?"

"I—Oh hell, Uncle Jack," said Archy, his face falling. "I'd forgotten about that!"

"Forgotten about it! Forgotten about it! Come up to my room—Zac, give us a hand—we'll clean 'em up before your mother sees 'em."

Jack did not spare the hot water, carbolic soap and some generous splashes of iodine, and Archy had to grit his teeth to stop himself crying out.

"That's the best I can do," said Jack finally, to Archy's great relief. "What a bloody mess."

"Will they—be all right in time?" asked Archy. Jack shrugged.

"Maybe. You're young and fit. And they're pretty hard feet—like old leather, thanks to your running barefoot—" he looked up from his bandaging and grinned, "even after your father forbade it. But you're going to have to rest them for a while."

"What'll Dad say? It's a busy time."

"That is your problem, Archy." Jack looked at the poster-portrait of Harry Lasalles. "You know, Archy, I don't understand you. You've got the God-given ability to be one of the country's greatest runners—and I'm not just saying that—you could be up there with Harry Lasalles—

and I don't just mean on the wall of my room, Archy, I mean up there, among the sporting *greats*—"

"Uncle Jack," began Archy, embarrassed, but Jack cut him off, impatiently. "Yes! You could be greater than Lasalles. And three days before your first big race you go and do this."

Jack seized the bandages and glared at Archy. He saw the years of training and preparation—the dawn runs, the lectures on the finer points of style—"Elbows and knees, lad—concentrate on your elbows and knees"—the careful build-up to this first vital race, all put in jeopardy by one foolish and impulsive act.

"I'll still win," said Archy. "If you did a good job on those feet."

"I did the best I could," said Jack curtly. "I'm not a miracle worker."

"Anyway," said Archy, hesitantly, watching his uncle's face, "anyway, running's not all there is to life, is it?"

Jack looked up from the bandages and stared at Archy in disbelief.

"I mean," said Archy, "well, there's a war on—" Jack eyed him acutely. "Yes?"

"Peter Trevellian joined up last week. The Light Horse."

Jack hauled himself to his feet.

"Let's hear no more of that nonsense, Archy," he said firmly. "You're under age."

"You ran away to sea when you were young—"

"I was twenty-one. Of age. And I didn't run away to a war where I might get me head blown off! Or anything else!"

* * *

The Officials' Tent was hot and close.

"The main event," said the younger official to Frank, "is the one hundred yards Kimberley Gift. The prize is ten guineas and a gold medal, and the event is closed. Entries had to be in a week ago."

"I just got in from outback," said Frank.

"What's your name, son?" asked the official.

Frank told him.

"It's not too big a field, Lionel," said the older official mildly.

Lionel looked at Frank.

"You registered?"

Frank nodded.

"Where do you usually run?"

"In Perth."

The official's eyes narrowed. "I know you. Dunne, the stand-up start."

Frank nodded again.

"Give him a go," said the official's offsider.

"Anyone take bets?" asked Frank, smiling innocently.

Lionel whistled and looked knowing.

"It's against the law," he said, filling out an entry form. "How much were you wanting to lay?"

"Twenty quid," said Frank.

"You're pretty confident. Let's see it."

Frank put his money on the table. Lionel looked at the little pile of old notes.

"Even money?" he asked.

Frank nodded. "Fair enough."

Still Lionel hesitated. "I want to be fair," he said. "This is a lot of money. Young Archy Hamilton's running."

"Who's he?"

"Probably the fastest kid in Western Australia. If not the entire country." He put out his hand for the notes.

"What's he do the hundred in?"

"Under ten," said Lionel. "Don't want to take your money without warning you."

Frank considered for a moment. "What's my mark?"

"Same as the local lad," said Lionel.

"All right. You're on," said Frank.

Lionel scooped up Frank's money and put it in his breast pocket.

"Changing room's behind the grandstand."

"Thanks," said Frank.

Jack inspected Archy's feet and sighed.

"They're still a mess," he said. "I could wring your neck."

"They'll do," said Archy.

"They're still bloody raw."

"Don't worry. They feel fine."

"You're a liar, Archy Hamilton."

"Never, Uncle Jack."

Jack replaced the bandages, sighing again.

"Saw Les McCann in the crowd. Surprised your Dad gave him time off."

Archy shrugged. "Les's joining up. A surprise, eh?"

Jack grunted. "I'll be surprised if the army's desperate enough to take Les." He finished the bandaging and stood up.

"You can still pull out, Archy. Lasalles himself pulled out of the Barlow Cup and nobody thought the worse of him."

"I'm running, Uncle Jack," said Archy quietly. He cocked an ear toward the noise outside the first aid tent. "Listen. They're calling the race. Let's go."

Outside a slight breeze had risen. The gay bunting on the grandstand fluttered and the stand itself uttered wooden groans as the crowd stamped and cheered the runners.

"Frank Dunne?" said Archy as he walked up to the starting line with Jack. "Never heard of him. Not from around here."

"Don't worry about him, whoever he may be," said Jack. "Start your breathing, boy. Deeply, now. Get those lungs *full. Fuller!* Here—" he gave Archy's thighs two stinging slaps. "Brace them, flex them, boy—"

Some of the other runners, passing them to take their places, grinned, and Archy smiled back, rather embarrassed. Jack ignored them.

"They'll laugh on the other side of their faces soon," he snorted. "Come on. What are these, eh? These things in your legs?"

It was a ritual they had fallen into over the years, a question and response litany which set Archy's heart pounding.

"Springs," he said. "Steel springs."

The grandstand was a pink and brown wall of inquisitive faces.

"Again," said Jack. "Don't take any notice of those people. Again!"

"Steel springs!"

A murmur rippled through the crowd. The starter was strolling towards the line of runners, holding the small starting pistol.

"What are they going to do?" asked Jack remorselessly.

"Hurl me down the track!" Archy was trembling.

"How fast can you run?"

"Fast as a leopard!"

"How fast are you going to run?"

The starter was almost at the line. People were staring at Archy and the old man.

"As fast as a leopard!"

Jack slapped him on the shoulder.

"Go, then. And let's see you do it!"

Archy crouched as the starter consulted his watch and raised the pistol. The crowd fell silent. Archy glanced down the line. The stranger was looking at him curiously. Archy looked to his front, down the track. The pistol cracked.

The pain was there instantly, the very second his feet thrust into the gravel. Each footfall was a blaze of agony: he felt as though he was running on glass. There was blood in his running shoes: he could feel it squirting between his toes.

He clenched his teeth and felt his face twist into an ugly mask. The crowd roared, rushing past him in a great blur of sound and gaping mouths.

Someone was coming up fast beside him. The stranger, Dunne, running with his handsome head high, coming up, passing him, the crowd going mad, now, screaming standing up pounding feet roaring Archy! Archy! Archy! Yards from the tape. You're a leopard! Dunne's a gazelle! Catch him! Catch him! His lungs aflame, he drew level, overtook Dunne, passed him, feeling the skin on his feet tearing, the blood soaking through his running shoes. Then the tape was against his chest, snapped, and he was rolling, writhing on the ground, tearing off his bloody shoes, biting his lips to stop himself crying out with pain and the crowd was around him, hauling him up, half-carrying him. Then whispers, hushed, awed, "Jesus, look at them feet, eh? Mincemeat!" And Dr. Hedley Parker cluck-clucking and Jack bouncing around on the outskirts of the crowd like a buoy in a tide-rip, grinning and waving.

They gave him ten golden guineas, which he gave to Jack to keep for him, and a golden medal, which they hung around his neck on a watered silk ribbon. They gave him a glass of beer which he gulped so fast that it went down the wrong way and sent him spluttering, and the crowd cheered and gave him another and slapped him on the back and lifted him on their shoulders and carried him to the first aid tent, where Dr. Hedley Parker was waiting with bandages and bottles of carbolic and iodine and creams and ointments.

He saw Dunne in the crowd, and leaned across several people with his hand out, but the stranger pretended not to see him and, turning away abruptly, shouldered his way through the pressing throng. Archy watched him go, feeling suddenly deflated. Hell, the bloke had run a good race. A *good* race. Why suddenly go crook? It was only a race, after all.

Dr. Hedley Parker burned his ragged feet with one potion, and cooled them with another, wrapped them in clean bandages, and made cutting remarks about the mental competence of both Archy and his Uncle Jack.

Then, grudgingly, he said: "All right. You'll do. I wouldn't do any running on those feet for a while, if I were you."

"I won't, Dr. Parker," said Archy with a grin.

"Or marching," said Dr. Parker pointedly, looking at an infantry recruiting poster, exhorting young men to "Fall In!" pinned to the tent-pole.

"The infantry, Dr. Parker? No fear!"

"He's too young, anyway," said Jack.

"And with luck this war'll be over before he's old enough," said Dr. Parker, washing his hands in a tin basin.

"Well! I hope so."

Jack helped Archy hobble to a bench in the front row of the grandstand. Something was happening, or about to: the field was deserted, and all eyes were on the entrance to the oval, across which a gaudy banner proclaiming "The Kimberley Gift, 1915" strained in the wind.

A brass band struck up outside the gate and the crowd stamped and cheered. Whips cracked, harness strained and timbers creaked. Something moved in the shadows beyond the gate: something monstrous, twenty feet high. It lumbered forward, breasted the banner, sent the two pieces fluttering away—a giant, staring-eyed wooden horse. For a moment, the mere sight of it silenced the crowd: then the whips cracked, the carrying-wagon lumbered forward, and cheers broke out: across the huge beast's wooden chest hung a sign, lettered in crackling red: "THE LIGHT HORSE—JOIN NOW!"

After a moment of stunned silence the crowd erupted: dozens of young men, full of athletic fervour, patriotism and the Royal Hotel's keg beer, spilled across the oval, clambered aboard the wagon, fell off and clambered aboard again, snatching recruiting forms; while some quieter spirits soberly joined the squad of mounted Light Horsemen and recruits (enrolled during the horse's passage through the town to the oval) trotting sedately behind the wagon.

Dr. Hedley Parker, watching the scene from the door of the first aid tent, frowned.

"The last wooden horse was a bad omen for a lot of people" he said sourly to his assistant, a stoutish man called McClicker who bank-clerked by day and ran the Figtree Crossing Boy Scouts on Friday nights. "Let's hope this one isn't."

"Why, Troy was a glorious victory," said Mr. McClicker, bridling. "This horse is a *symbol*, Dr. Parker—a symbol of Empire!"

Any minute now, thought Dr. Parker, and he's going to give me a lecture about Mafeking and Lord Baden-Powell and I really would prefer a drink.

"Mind the shop for a while, would you please, Mr. McClicker?" he asked, and strode with determined tread towards the refreshments tent. Mr. McClicker, rolling bandages, watched him disapprovingly.

Jack tapped his stopwatch.

"Nine and five-sixteenths seconds, lad. You've equalled Harry Lasalles—cut feet and all."

"Uncle Jack—" began Archy, but Jack was in full flight and would not be stopped.

"No, lad, nothing can stop you now. Nothing!"

"Uncle Jack!" Archy was almost shouting. "Listen to me."

He put his hand on Jack's sleeve.

The old man looked at him, suddenly silent.

"I'm not coming home."

Jack looked at Archy and across the oval at the grotesque wooden horse. Some soldiers were pitching tents around it: their mallets rose and fell with a steady whok-whok.

"I knew it," the old man said. "I knew it all along. This bloody war. Your bag weighed a ton. What the hell you got in there, lad, bricks?"

Archy laughed.

"Books, mostly." He smiled. "And my lucky arrowhead—the one you gave me."

Jack shook his head. "You're only eighteen—a long way from twenty-one. How're you going to get them to take you? You'll never get your parents' approval."

"They won't ask me too many questions when they see how I can ride—and shoot." Then a thought struck him. "Uncle Jack—you wouldn't—"

Jack shook his head. "No. I won't blow the gaff, Archy. I promise you that. I was young, once—" he stopped, and his eyes became remote: looking at them, Archy imagined Jack gazing at long lonely seas under the moon, at Zanzibar at dawn, Hong Kong climbing around the Peak, swift dacoit canoes trailing a lugger in the Celebes.

He held out his hand. "Goodbye, Uncle Jack—and thanks. Thanks for everything. I'll write. I promise I'll write. Here—" he fumbled in his shirt pocket and produced a crumpled letter. "For Mum and Dad. Try to explain to them, will you."

Jack smiled grimly. "Your mum's always thought me a bad influence, Archy, but I'll try."

Archy turned away. It was suddenly hard to speak.

"And—say goodbye to Zac for me, will you? He was always a good mate. Say goodbye properly to him for me, Uncle Jack."

"I will," said the old man. "Don't worry."

He watched Archy shouldering his way through the crowd, surrounded by wellwishers.

"God bless you, boy," he murmured, "and look after you."

THE MEDAL

George Ewart Evans

(1959)

Peregrine stood on the kerb watching him and at the same time watching himself, and asking: "Why should I be here, out of my orbit and out of all reason, waiting for an old man who knows less of me than I of him?" But he stayed, in spite of his impulse to turn and walk away down the grey street whose flagstoned pavements glistened with a mercy of light after the quick shower of rain. He could not be wrong because of the old man's colour; but he would have recognized him apart from this. Although the fifteen years had whitened the old man's hair and bent his knees, the features and the straight back with the head well set on the shoulders were still the same. He wore a white coat; and this with his fringe of white hair and straggle of beard made his colour shout out. But the children he was shepherding over the road clasped his dark hands without hesitation; and kept hurrying across with his great-footed shuffle as they collected in groups on the opposite kerb.

He watched the old man's face, and the half-smiling absorption he saw there made him decide to stay. But how could he get into conversation with him; and—more difficult still—how could he bring the talk round to his own purpose? The old man glanced his way suddenly and nodded—not with recognition, but as he would have to any stranger who was interested in his task.

And it was unlikely that he would have recognized him: Peregrine was only a boy then, barely sixteen, when it happened; and it was unlikely that there was on the old man's side any impress of the event to make him remember. It had probably melted back into his sixty-odd years as easily as a flake of snow disappearing into the tightened surface of a pond. As he recalled the afternoon it happened he glanced up towards the hill. The field hung over the narrow valley a couple of hundred feet above them, a narrow strip of fairly level turf, lit up now to a yellowish-green by the fitful sunlight. Powderhouse Field they called it; and it was here that sports had been held and football matches played for as far back as he could remember.

But that afternoon had passed in another world. The sun had been a raging furnace, blistering across the sky, driving all the dark out of the valley, making the length of field a bright, torrid strip of scant shade with the air rising to the bare hilltops in quick, agitated ripples. The feel of that day was still in his limbs: he remembered the vague glow of promise, the sense of being released as he sped over the turf of the roughly prepared track—effortless, as though his body had lightened, brought to a pitch of harmony by the simple miracle of the up-drawing sun. His limbs still held that feeling of power, and he re-lived the experience so vividly that he paced restlessly about the pavement; until the old man glanced his way and looked at him curiously.

He did not know in what part of him the other feeling lay—the quirk, the twist in the fibre that the afternoon had also left. But this, too, had persisted with the years and had brought him here; powerfully causing him, in spite of himself, to wait on an old man who was now leading little children across a busy road.

They came now in a continuous stream that showed no sign of stopping; and he could do nothing while the old man was so occupied. He would have to wait until the whole school of children had crossed before approaching him.

The long-past afternoon held his mind again, shutting out the morning and the watery, ineffectual sun. He was in the first heat, and was pacing about waiting for the starter to order the runners to their marks when he saw a woman at the side of the track nudge her neighbour and heard her loud whisper:

"Look, there's Mr. Brown the Black. He's going to run in the race!"

The coloured man was standing near the start, his jacket under one arm, and his boots, stuffed with tattered socks, held in his other hand. He was trying to catch the starter's attention. Tommy John, handicapper as well as starter, shouted across to him: "All right, Lewis, we'll have you in the last heat."

He must have been at least fifty years old then; and the crowd laughed with good humour at the thought of Mr. Brown the Black running with all those young men: *Of course he was a champion runner in his own day; but now! What can you expect at his age?*

Peregrine had a very good mark and won his heat easily. Tommy John had whispered to him just before: "You got the best lane on the track, young 'un. Keep going!" He rose like a bird from the tremendous crash of the starting gun, became conscious of his light limbs, and felt the dark forms and the white faces of the crowd slip harmoniously past him. Then he felt the tight, momentary pull of the tape across his down-thrusting chest. As he paced luxuriously back to the start to get his sweater Tommy John gave him a nod and a smile he could not read.

Afterwards he stayed on the side of the track to watch the other runners. When it came to Brown's heat a man who stood on the track shouted down:

"Where shall I put the black fellow, Tommy?"

The starter waved his programme casually.

"Take him for a walk up the course will you, Seth?" Brown grinned as he was led to a mark ten yards in front of the others. He tucked up his sleeves, and then his trousers carefully above his knees, showing his lean, sinewy legs and his big feet shining with sweat. The women screamed with laughter. *Look! Mr. Brown the Black. He's black all over. Deerfoot they used to call him when he was a runner. But look at his feet now!*

Lewis Brown the Black paid little regard to this: he stood solidly on his mark in the standing start of the old-timer. When the gun went off he sprang forward, running with long, ungainly strides which nevertheless ate up the ground in front of him. He finished yards ahead of the nearest runner. As he came back the crowd shouted with delight; but he paid little attention to them as he paced down the track with a slow dignity.

There were no cross-ties and the final came an hour later—an hour that was filled with the tinny uproar of jazz bands. Peregrine was strung up and anxious to get it over with; and he was one of the first of the finalists to take his mark. Brown the Black was the next one to come out to the course: he halted yards in front of Peregrine and stayed there immovable while the other runners paced about him like restless colts prancing about an old warhorse. *Come on, Deerfoot! Show 'em your heels!* came a quick challenge from the crowd, and Brown grinned in answer. But the starter was nodding towards him; and the starter's man came purposefully up the track and gently caught Brown by the arm.

"Back you come, Lewis. By here your mark is," and nodded to a spot two or three yards to the rear.

"No, no!" Brown protested. "Here my mark is, for sure. Here I was standing in the heat."

"But here you got to stand now, boyo." The starter's man was firm. "There was some mistake, no doubt, the first time." And Brown shrugged and took up his old, dated stance on the fresh mark. It all happened so quickly that few of the crowd noticed it.

But Peregrine, standing a few yards behind Brown, took in every move of the incident; and the look of resignation on the coloured man's face hit him. It was wrong to pull him back! That was his mark in the heat: he was entitled to hold the same mark in the final. Peregrine was about to speak to the starter's man; but the man spoke to him first, whispering urgently without turning his head as he passed: "Keep going, young 'un. You can win it." Then came the compelling shout of the starter, "Get on your MARKS!" driving out all thought except the many-times rehearsed response to the signal and the low obeisance towards the tape stretched out across the field a hundred yards or so in front of them.

After the gun's report, Peregrine gained immediately on Brown's slower impetus; but it was a struggle, even so, to pass him. Then in the whole-bodied thrust forward he saw no other runner, but hearing behind him a persistent *tck, tck, tck*, a disembodied sound chasing him—the urgent and chilling challenge of another runner's feet gaining rapidly upon him. But he breasted the tape before the sound caught up with him; and then he became aware for the first time of the crowd and their loud cheering. Brown the Black—he learned afterwards—was third.

Back again out of the clear, blue-printed past to the urgent and disturbing present where right action is hidden in a mist of numberless possibilities: his hand closed round the medal they had given him on that day. He had often recalled how he had gone up for it before a crowd quiet in a precarious hush, and had heard a voice say, "Brown the Black should have won that. It's his by right. If he had his proper mark you never would have caught him!" And that voice had long echoes because it was his own voice, reminding him that he was not whole, that a part of him had been left on the field that afternoon, not to be recovered until he had tried to put things right with this old coloured man.

Then on his return after many years he had found the medal thrust away in the drawer, hidden from the light as he had often willed his memory of it to be; and hearing that Brown was still alive and living in the village the urge to seek him out had brought him to the edge of the kerb where he was now standing like a diver estimating the steel-smooth water which he sensed rather than saw below him. Brown the Black! Well, he had better tackle him and get it over: pluck out the small snag that had been irritating his self-respect for so many years. Besides, it would be rather pleasant to put this matter right; to give the coloured man his proper due, although the day was rather late for doing so. He watched the old man escort two other children across to the kerb. Would he remember? Or would Peregrine have to lead him laboriously back to the event on Powderhouse Field?

At that moment the stream of children suddenly ceased. He walked across to the old man and got into conversation with him. Yes, he remembered the afternoon well; even remembered his name and that he had won the sprint. And when Peregrine told him that he was not very happy about winning it, Brown shrugged his shoulders with the same gesture and said in the same high-pitched voice he so well recalled:

"You had to win it, mun. It was rigged."

"Rigged?"

"Ay, didn't you know? Perhaps you were too young: you were carrying a pile of money, most of it Tommy John's, the starter's. You had to win! All that money was betted on you."

Peregrine felt a jolt: he had gone to pick up an empty vessel and it turned out to be full. He was going to put things right, and now it seemed the old man was putting things right for him. He had been too eager for good works and had made a blunder. Yet as he watched the old man's lined face and friendly eyes he knew that was not his thought:

"It was a very hot afternoon," Brown said with a smile. "I remember it well." Then nodding up towards the cemetery on the other side of the valley: "Tommy John won't handicap no more: he's up there now, back right behind scratching himself." But he spoke without bitterness.

Peregrine's hand closed again around the medal in his pocket; and with a stubborn resolve to see his purpose through he took it out and showed it to the old man. He looked at it with interest:

"I knew there was a medal, but I never saw it."

"It's yours by right," Peregrine said with relief, and with the satisfaction of saying a long-rehearsed line. "Wouldn't you like to take it?"

The old man glanced up quickly and Peregrine immediately saw the look as refusal. Another false move. He saw his impulse to return the medal for what it was: his wish to right a wrong had been mixed with something less pleasant, and the old man had instantly spotted it; and he was now brushing aside the brash gesture with all the grace of natural good breeding. He wanted to snatch the medal from the old man's hand and return it to his pocket where it should have stayed. For a moment they both stood awkwardly on the pavement. Then a sudden clear note interrupted them: the sound of a boy's voice from the opposite kerb calling insistently:

"Mr. Brown. Mr. Brown the Black."

The old man looked up and held up his hand to signal the boy to stay where he was. Then after looking up and down the road he shuffled across, taking the boy's hand and bringing him over the road. They were both smiling as they reached the pavement where Peregrine stood: the old man out of natural pleasure, the boy with the satisfaction of a lesson rightly carried out.

When they stood near Peregrine, Brown—who was still holding the medal—asked the boy:

"So, are you the last today?"

The boy nodded, his hand still in the man's.

"Well, the last shall be first, so they say. And the first ought to have a prize, for sure."

And bending over, the old man pinned the medal on the boy's coat. The boy flushed as he realized that he was meant to keep it, and without another word he ran up the pavement as far as he could go—eager to bring his good fortune home to his family.

For a moment Peregrine stood amazed at the old man's action. But as he saw the little boy scuttling exultantly up the street a deep laughter took hold of him; and it was not long before the old man was laughing with him. Then the hard light of the too enduring past broke up instantly into a spatter of bright and quickly vanishing colours. And their laughter continued, long after the sound of the boy's footsteps had gone right out of the narrow, echoing street.

Young Runners

THE WINNING BUG

Jackson Scholz

(1926)

As the quarter-milers swung into the last turn, something peculiar happened which set me to thinking. It might easily have been an accident, with no significance at all, because a twelve-lap board track offers a ticklish bit of navigation, even for the experienced runner, and I had to admit that Sax was pretty green at this sort of thing.

But, at the same time, it's part of a coach's business to watch for just such little happenings of this kind, which might make or break an athlete if they're allowed to pass unnoticed.

It looked as though Sax had deliberately fouled Chris Leighton with his elbow as they swung into the last turn. Of course there were any number of things which might have caused him to lurch in Chris' direction, such as a loose board, plain leg weariness or inexperience, and, anyway, it didn't make a great deal of difference, because Chris had weathered too many rough races to be bothered by a little thing like that. He held his stride, without breaking, and they came into the home stretch shoulder to shoulder. Sax cracked about fifteen yards from the finish, and Chris romped home with a good lead.

I hadn't intended for them to make a race of it, because we'd only been on the boards a little over a week. We train for the indoor season on a twelve-lap board track, built just outside the gym. It was my idea to get away from the narrow, dangerous curves of the inside track, so, after yelling my head off for a couple of years, they finally gave me an outdoor track, just to keep me quiet. More later concerning this.

I had sent Sax and Chris out with specific instructions to turn me in a sixty second quarter, but, as it often happens with colts and athletes when you give them their heads, this pair got started, and before I knew what it was all about, they were running their fool legs off. I could have yelled to them to cut it down, but I'll frankly admit that I was curious to see how it would come out. I enjoy a good race as much as anybody.

I wasn't curious about Chris. He'd been my top-notch quarter-miler for the last two years, and I knew pretty well what stuff he had. But this was Saxon Demming's first season in competition, so I figured that this was about as good an opportunity as any to learn the material I had to work upon. The result of the race convinced me that he had plenty of natural speed, endurance which could be developed, and a good supply of courage. But the little incident on the last turn caused me to discredit all of these until I was a little surer of my ground.

Saxon Demming was still a rather unknown quantity. He had done a little track work as a freshman, but, inasmuch as he hadn't shown a great deal of promise at the time, I hadn't paid a great deal of attention to him. This year, however, he looked like the real stuff. He had filled out a lot, grown some, and taken on the keen, alert appearance of a man who knows what he wants. I liked his eyes.

And I learned, too, that he was pretty popular on the campus. He was dabbling a bit in politics, which was a tribute to his ability for making friends and, from reliable sources, available to all coaches, I learned that he was one of the best liked men in his class.

I proceeded to bawl out Chris and Sax for the exhibition they had staged against my orders. I laid it on pretty thick, merely for the sake of discipline, and for the benefit of the rest of the squad standing around. Chris had heard the same thing before, so he didn't pay much attention to it; and Sax, standing hunched over with his hands on his knees, was still too winded to care much what happened. I sent them both to the showers and transferred my attention to the hurdlers.

When I went down to the varsity room a little later, Sax was just lacing his shoes. I told him to drop into my office on his way out. I was waiting for him when he came up a few minutes later, and I didn't waste any words.

"What was the idea of staging a race out there today?"

Sax flushed a little, but didn't try to avoid the question or pass the buck. "Why, I—I don't know, coach," he said. "I just don't seem to be able to help it. I had no intention of racing when we started, but I was feeling so good, and—well, I guess I went a little faster than I intended. When I started to run I forgot myself altogether."

I let that pass, because it was a pretty good indication of a natural-born racer. "How about the little mix-up on the final turn?" I asked pointedly. "Why did you foul Leighton?"

Naturally I expected him to deny this, or at least to offer some good excuse, but instead he regarded me with a sort of lost, puzzled look in his eyes.

"I don't know," he said simply.

"You don't know?" I gasped. Sax shook his head dully. "But you knew you did it," I insisted.

He nodded. "Then why?" I demanded.

The expression in his eyes became stubborn and a trifle sullen.

"I—I don't know," he repeated, and, before I had a chance to question him further, he turned and hurried out of the office. I let him go.

The funny part of it was that I believed the kid, as much as I hated to do so. He had absolutely no idea why he had fouled Leighton on the turn. The whole thing was a mystery to him, and worried him all the more for that reason. If he had asked me for a solution, I could have told him, although I don't believe it would have helped a great deal. A coach, after twenty years of experience, gathers a lot of wisdom in spite of himself, and I don't suppose I'm any exception to the rule.

Sax Demming's problem was not a common one among athletes, but every coach runs up against it now and then. For convenience I'll call it "the winning bug." By that I mean that whenever an athlete is bitten by this bug, the idea uppermost in his mind is to win, regardless of all consequences. He attaches so much importance to victory that everything else dwindles to nothing by comparison.

It doesn't necessarily indicate a crooked streak in a man's character, because in every other way he may be square shooting and fine, except that under the excitement of competition he is not really himself. But, if such a thing is allowed to run, it may become such a fixture in a person's character that it pokes its head up in some of the problems of everyday life.

Athletics with such men is generally a passion, and when aroused to the fevered pitch of competition they are not responsible for their actions, inasmuch as their ideas are all centered on winning, and anything they do immediately before or during the race may be laid off to some automatic impulse.

I don't often preach on the subject of sportsmanship, because it's not becoming for a coach to shout about morals, ethics and such things. He's paid to deliver the goods, not talk about them, so the more he concentrates on the matter in hand the fatter and more regular will be his paycheck.

He's also paid to win, but at the same time there are various ways of winning, and I find that my men will win more regularly if they are right mentally, before and after a race. It pays in the long run to keep the minds of the boys clean and square. I teach my boys to give their last breath and to fight to the last inch, but to fight fair all the way.

In that way victories mean a lot more, and defeats hurt a lot less. If a man runs the best race that's in him and loses, he hasn't much to regret, but if he runs a crooked race and wins, well—think it over. If they lose they learn to grin and keep their mouths shut. No excuses, you understand.

Then, of course, there's the selfish, personal satisfaction I get out of developing a piece of raw material. The athletic field is a wonderful workshop, and a man can be analyzed there to a finer point than in any classroom in the world.

Some winning bugs are never cured. They continue their way through life, fouling on the turns. It's one of the most pathetic problems I'm faced with on the track, and I sure hated to see the symptoms cropping out in young Demming, because I certainly liked the kid.

So, because I realized what the trouble was and Sax didn't, I felt the responsibility to be mostly mine. Maybe I was assuming an obligation out of the line of duty, but I couldn't see it that way. It seems to me that a coach's duty is to the athlete himself, even though the school is paying his salary.

I was still mulling the matter over when someone rapped on the door. I yelled, "Come in!" and a couple of slick-haired, sailor-panted lads came in with their hats respectfully in their hands. They were clean-cut youngsters, and a trifle ill at ease, so I grinned and invited them to relieve their minds of whatever was bothering them.

"Well, it's this way, coach," one of them began. "We represent the Scroll and Quill—membership committee, you know, investigation and all that sort of stuff. We're considering Saxon Demming for membership, and—and we thought we'd better talk to you before deciding on him definitely. Can you recommend him, coach? Is he the sort of man we want?"

Now can you beat that? Of all the times in the world for the Scroll and Quill to take me into their confidence. It's true, they always ask my advice on any track man they consider taking in, and I've always tried to play square with them, and to advise them honestly on the man in question. But Sax Demming, just at this time—huh!

The Scroll and Quill, by the way, is a second-term sophomore organization which is composed of the most influential men in the class. The members are chosen irrespective of any other connection, and are considered for their capabilities alone. It's a mighty fine organization, perhaps the best in the school, with its ideals based exclusively on the welfare of the college. It is nonpolitical, but has an admittedly tremendous influence on school life, particularly toward the development of lower classmen. To be a member of the Scroll and Quill is pretty much of an honor, and gives a man a good running start for his entire college career.

You see, I realized what this membership would be to a boy, but, at the same time, I was unable to shake off the uncomfortable vision of two flying figures, coming into the last turn of the quarter, the deliberate foul, and—well, I wanted to be fair to both parties so the only thing I could do was stall for time.

"Well, now, I'll tell you, boys," I said. "It was mighty good of you to come to me for advice, but I'm afraid I'm not in a position now to give it. You see, I haven't had much of a chance to see much of the boy yet, but if you can wait till a little later in the indoor season, I can tell you definitely, one way or the other."

This seemed to be agreeable to them, although I'm afraid they had a hunch that something was wrong. At any rate, they decided to let it go at that, and left me alone once more to wrestle with my conscience, and a few other minor and major difficulties.

I'd told you before that I'd had a lot of trouble getting my outdoor board track, but I didn't mention any of the details, or the ticklish position in which the acquisition of this feature had placed me. Track athletics, in the first place, were none too popular with some of the old fossils in the faculty, but there was one old duck who was particularly rabid about the money spent for my track, inasmuch as he had wanted it spent for an original painting, by somebody or other, to be hung in the library.

At any rate, he raised a lot of fireworks, by virtue of the fact that he'd been on the faculty for so many years, and when the money was finally appropriated, this old boy, "Doc" Brown by name, had managed in some way or other to make my job hinge upon the big indoor meet. He figured that, as we'd been winning consistently in previous years with the old track, to spend all that money for a new track and lose besides, would be just cause for a new coach. The sad part of it was that he had rallied enough support among the other athletics-hating members of the faculty board to make my job hang by a thread.

Of course I didn't help things a lot by telling him a few of my personal views on the matter, which were pointed enough to cause the old boy to turn a dangerous shade of purple. At the end of our little interview, he tore his beard and swore a half dozen assorted kinds of vengeance. I'd have felt kind of sorry for him if I hadn't known that he'd accumulated enough money in his life to permit him to retire in comfort and quit pestering other people. Anyway, I didn't think much of his ravings at the time, but later learned I had reason to believe that the old cuss had meant every word of it, and was out for blood after all.

We worked out regularly every afternoon. Sometimes the weather was pretty chilly, and sometimes we had to sweep the snow from the track, but the boys were all supplied with sweat suits, and I made them limber up well indoors before taking a chance on pulling a muscle on the outdoor track.

I had a good likely bunch of material that year, and was bringing them all around in pretty fine shape. The outdoor work seemed to agree with them, and it looked as though the Indoor Valley Conference would be a repetition of the last few years. I didn't see how we could be whipped. But then, I figured without old Doc Brown.

I should have been warned when I noticed him snooping around the track several afternoons of the week. He seemed to have taken a sudden keen interest in athletics, and he used to stand in the shelter of the wide gym door, his old knit muffler wrapped around his neck, and his sharp little eyes peering from the sides of a hooked nose, for all the world like a vulture perched hungrily on a rock.

I wouldn't have been surprised to hear him croak, or whatever vultures do. At any rate, he sure devoted a lot of time to hate. A nice pleasant disposition. He worried me some, and I often wondered what friendly thoughts were fermenting in his fertile old brain.

But I had other worries, too, and I don't mind admitting that Sax Demming was my principal one. Every time I'd run him in any sort of race or a trial, he'd go plumb hog wild and do almost anything to cross the finish first. It was a case with him of win or bust, and there wasn't much danger of his busting. In fact, he developed into the fastest four-forty man on the squad. That was the irony of the thing, because, good or bad, I won't let a man compete for me if he doesn't shoot square.

I suppose I should have kicked him off the squad, but that would have ruined his whole career in the school, and might have had a serious effect on his life. Anyway, I liked the kid, and had a feeling deep down in me that there was some way out. I talked to him on several occasions, and he was always repentant and humble as the deuce.

But that's all the good it seemed to do. The rest of the squad liked him in spite of his tactics on the track, so I just let him stick around and worried my head off, trying to figure out some solution. Finally I hit on one which I thought might work.

Our indoor schedule was light this year, and aside from a few club meets, in which I entered a few individual stars, the Valley Conference was the first big meet of the season. It came earlier this year than usual, because the colosseum in Kansas City, where it was always held, was only available on this date.

The meet, through years of popularity, had come to be a pretty big affair—almost a social function—and all the seats were sold weeks in advance. True, we had won the meet for the last several years, but there had been some mighty tight squeaks, and the crowd always got their money's worth. It was the biggest track event, indoor or outdoor, on our sport calendar, so naturally we went after it with everything we had.

I held tryouts for this meet one week ahead, a regular track meet on a small scale, in which my boys fought for places on the team. I had started working them, a week before the tryouts, in smooth-soled shoes, because the owners of the colosseum refused to let us chew up the floor with spikes.

Some indoor meets, you see, are run in spiked shoes—tiny spikes which grip the boards and add a lot to a runner's speed—but in some meets spikes are prohibited and we have to use a flat-soled running shoe. As I said, I made the boys wear the plain-soled shoe a couple of weeks before the big meet, so they would be used to the things. I was trying out a new kind of shoe this year with little rubber pimples on the sole. They seemed to hold the boards fine.

We had a good day for the tryouts, and there was a fair-sized crowd on hand to watch the boys do their stuff. I had four pretty good quarter-milers, but one of them, Davis, also ran the half, so it made no difference if he qualified for the four-forty or not. Therefore, as I had to have four men for the mile relay, I had to pick three other quarter-milers from the tryouts. I had made the statement that I expected to take but four quarter-milers along.

Sax was, of course, the fastest man I had. The other two were Chris Leighton and Jack Wallace. These two I called into my office just before they went on the track. We had a short talk, and both boys protested at what I told them to do until I'd explained the matter and they saw things from my angle. They were grinning when I sent them out to warm up.

Six men started the quarter. Three were to be chosen for the team, and it meant a lot to represent the school in the indoor conference.

I brought the men to their marks, and Sax jumped at the gun—anything to win. I called him back and penalized him three yards. He took it without a whimper. The next time I got them off to a fair start. Three laps to go.

Chris shot out and took the lead, with Wallace at his shoulder. The rest bunched on the turn, and Sax brought up the rear. Sax let out on the back stretch and tried to take the lead, but as he was about to pass, Wallace swerved, apparently by accident, bumped Sax, and sent him reeling to the outside of the track. Sax recovered, ran wide on the turn, and tried to take the lead again on the home stretch, but couldn't quite cut it down.

As they swung in toward the pole on the curve, Wallace again stepped wide, and, as Sax fell in behind Chris, Wallace fell back beside Sax, and they had him in as neat a little pocket as you ever saw. They ran in this position for a lap, Leighton purposely slowing down the pace so that all the stragglers could catch up.

As they started the last lap, Sax became desperate and forgot himself, as I knew he would. He tried to fight his way out of the box, first shoving Wallace to one side, and then shouldering up beside Chris, but that was as far as he got.

No sooner had he come alongside, than Chris deliberately brought his elbow back and buried it in Sax's stomach. The race was over then, as far as Sax was concerned. He finished gamely, but only managed a poor fifth. Leighton had won it, Wallace was second, and a mediocre lad by the name of Bush came in third.

Sax was having a pretty hard time getting his wind back after the wallop he'd received. He was leaning against the wall of the gym with both hands over his midsection as though it were giving him some trouble. Leighton started toward him with the evident intention of apologizing, but I grabbed him in time and told him I'd do all the apologizing necessary.

I was watching Sax pretty close, because I wasn't quite sure what he was liable to do. I noticed a sort of puzzled expression come over his face when he started breathing regularly again, as though he was trying to figure out what it was all about.

As soon as he saw me standing by myself, he came over and stood at my elbow. I didn't encourage him any, so pretty soon he spoke.

"Does—does that race mean I don't get to make the trip, coach?"

He tried to keep his voice even, but it shook in spite of him. I didn't even turn my head.

"You knew beforehand that the first three men would be chosen for the team," I told him. "You finished fifth. Figure it out for yourself."

"But coach!" he pleaded desperately, "he fouled me! Leighton fouled me! You saw it yourself! He—"

"He *what?*" I whirled fiercely and glared at him. "He *what*, did you say?"

"Why, he—oh!" I saw a peculiar light come into his eyes. They widened with the scared look of a man who sees something astounding for the first time, and realizes that it's been under his nose all the while. His face went scarlet and his face dropped to the track.

"Oh," he said, just "oh," as he turned slowly and headed for the showers. At any rate, the kid was no fool, and I had a pretty good hunch that his first lesson had been learned.

The next week was one long nightmare, with old Doc Brown playing the heavy lead. The old scoundrel finally managed to get across some of the nice pleasant things he'd been threatening for so long, for, on the Thursday before the meet I received an apologetic little note from the dean, saying that Wallace and my sprinting ace had been reported by Doctor Brown to be flunking his—Doctor Brown's—class in philosophy, and that he regretted the necessity of declaring them ineligible for athletic competition until their work in his class showed a decided improvement. Now wasn't that nice? The old villain, I could have murdered him.

Of course you know what that did to my team. The loss of Wallace robbed me of some sure points in the quarter and knocked the spots out of my mile-relay team. The loss of my sprinter was the worst blow, however, because I had figured him as a sure first in the sprint and both the high and low hurdles. He was the most valuable man on the team, and without him in the line-up I figured my chances of winning the meet to be worth something slightly less than a cigar coupon.

I didn't mind the possibility of losing my job so much—there were plenty of jobs—and besides, I was sure the student body would stand behind me to the last ditch, but it was the idea of the thing. It had resolved itself into a sort of show-down between school athletics and the old anti-athletic element on the faculty, and it sure looked as though they'd handed me a loaded cigar in our first major encounter. There was nothing to do, however, but patch the team up as best I could, and then pray for a few breaks.

Thursday evening I stopped at Sax's fraternity house. The boys told me he was upstairs in his room, so I went on up and found him humped over a table under a big droplight, figuring something on paper. He looked up guiltily when I came in and tried to hide the paper.

"Writing to the girl?" I asked casually.

"Oh, hello, coach, come on in. Have a chair. No," he answered my question, a trifle sheepishly, I thought. "To tell the truth I—I was doping out the meet Saturday night."

"How do we stack up?" I demanded.

"Why, not so good, coach, I'm afraid. We need another—another—" he stammered in confusion.

"Quarter-miler," I helped him out. Sax turned and started making lines on the paper. "How would you like to go?" I asked suddenly.

He almost fell out of his chair, as he whirled around to see if I was serious.

"How would I like to go!" he shouted. "How would I—" He caught himself, settled back, swallowed a couple of times, and continued quietly, his voice husky. "I guess maybe you know how much I'd like to go, coach. I guess I'd like it more than anything else in the world, just now. I didn't think it meant so much until I found out that I hadn't made the team. And I—I believe I've learned the other thing."

"I hope so son," I said as I got up to leave, "but you can never tell until you're in actual competition. You're a different person then. We all are under that strain. I'm hoping for the best, and gambling pretty heavy on you. We meet at the station tomorrow at noon. Good night."

I left him staring soberly at his dope sheet.

We arrived in Kansas City Friday afternoon. I generally like to give the boys a complete day of rest before a meet, and don't like to have them do any traveling on that day. I chased them to bed that night at ten o'clock, but sat up for a couple of hours longer myself, doping out the events as best I could, and trying to figure my crippled team for as many points as the law of averages and a barrel of luck would allow.

I was just about ready to turn in, and was just about to pull down my shade, when a window suddenly lighted on a level with mine, just across the court on which my room opened. I stared for a moment, just like anyone would, without any idea of being impolite, and my conscience bothered me even less when I noticed that the room belonged to Sax Demming. He had just switched on the light beside his bed and was in the act of climbing out. I thought he might be sick or something, so I kept watching.

Somebody, however, had evidently rapped on the door. Sax opened it and stood staring sleepily at the man on the threshold, who proceeded to slide into the room in a slinky way, which made me jump for my own light to turn it out, in order that I could see better.

The newcomer had a bundle under his arm. He came into the room, apologizing, apparently, for his late call, and then started to talk to Sax in an earnest sort of way, at the same time starting to unwrap the bundle. I was all attention now, and Sax seemed to have waked up enough to take an interest in what the stranger was saying. The package finally revealed a pair of indoor track shoes. Sax's visitor was still talking to beat the band, explaining something about the shoes, which looked to me exactly like the kind we were already using. Sax took one of them in his hand, examined it, nodded his head, and said something to the other fellow, who smiled in a relieved sort of way, as though he'd just finished a tough job. He talked a minute longer, grabbed Sax by the hand in a hasty shake, and slid out the door like he was on his way to rob a bank or assassinate a child.

I didn't like this lad's looks a bit, so I hurried to the door and hiked up the hall in the hope of waylaying him as he was waiting for the elevator. He evidently, however, was in too much of a hurry to wait and had already left by the stairs by the time I arrived. When I got back to my own room, Sax's light was out, so I went to bed and laid awake for another hour, wondering what the devil I was up against now. It looked worse than I was willing to admit, but I decided to let it rest until morning.

I got up about eight o'clock, feeling a little ragged, and joined the great army of cold-bath takers. There's nothing like a cold bath in the morning, unless, possibly, it's a clout over the head with a baseball bat. Their chief value, as I see it, is to shrivel you up like a withered peanut, and give you something to brag about.

I routed the boys out and got them down to breakfast. When they were all accounted for I went to Sax's room and found the door unlocked. I had no difficulty in finding the package, in which the shoes had been loosely wrapped. I took one up to examine it.

As I had noticed the night before, they seemed to be identical to the ones I had chosen for the team, but, as I held the sole in the palm of my hand, and bent the rest to try the flexibility, I found that I was wrong. For, as I bent the shoe, I grunted with the pain of a sharp stab in my palm—spikes.

Yes, sir, spikes! Tiny little needle points, cleverly concealed in the little rubber pimples of the sole. Spikes which would allow the wearer to pass the test of stepping flat-footed on a piece of paper without leaving a mark, but would come into play the minute his foot was bent in running, and would grip the treacherous turns of the smooth track, giving him a tremendous advantage over his rivals.

Anything to win! I couldn't believe it, and dropped limply in a chair to reason with myself. But I had seen Sax accept them with my own eyes. I knew his failing under the excitement of competition, and just before a race, and yet—and yet—huh, I didn't know.

Then I recalled our conversation on the night I told him he would run. I recalled the pathetic light in his eyes when he learned I'd trust him in a race. And then I remembered what I'd said before I left. I had told the kid I'd gamble on him, and suddenly it came to me with convincing force that he was certainly worth gambling on. I could step in now, spoil everything, and prove nothing. On the other hand—

I arose and carefully replaced the shoes as I had found them. Five minutes later I was having breakfast with the squad.

I kept the whole team in bed most of the afternoon, and gave them a light meal around five o'clock. A couple of hours later, I bundled them into taxis and sent them to the colosseum. I took the last cab from the hotel, and, just before leaving, I made a rush trip to Sax Demming's room. The shoes had disappeared.

The crowd started to come early, and before the first event was called the place was packed. One of the more affluent alumni repeated his yearly practice of hiring a brass band to entertain the assembled multitude, and to follow him about the streets in full blast after the meet was over. This was always his big night.

Firemen patrolled the aisles, enforcing the "NO SMOKING" signs, which had been posted for the occasion. Not that there was any danger of fire, but because the coaches had got together and had originated this as an excuse to keep the building free from smoke, so the runners would have a fighting chance to get some halfway decent air in their lungs. The average spectator is pretty thoughtless after he's paid his admission.

The atmosphere of the dressing room was tense. I had every member of the team to a beautiful edge, and they all showed their excitement in different ways. Few of them would be recognized as the same individuals in everyday life. Some were talkative, others were sullen, some were pale, some flushed, some forced grins, while others sat tight-lipped and rigid. They took their rubs in the order of their events and the room soon reeked with the pleasant odor of hazel, alcohol and wintergreen.

Sax sat over in a corner by himself, his eyes a trifle glassy with the strain. His hands trembled as he hung his clothes in the locker, and he would stop every now and then to steady himself with a long breath. I watched him narrowly, and guessed the terrific tension he was under.

He wrapped his insteps with black tire tape, and removed it several times before it was fixed to suit. He adjusted his pushers and worked on a pair of new shoes, which fitted nice and snug, like gloves. All the squad were wearing new shoes that night.

I spoke a last word to several of the boys, and went up to the track, which looked, at first glance, like a society function of some sort, rather than a track meet. All the officials were strutting about in evening clothes, which contrasted strangely with the scantily clad athletes, flashing up and down the straightaway, and jogging around the track, warming up for the first events.

I got a slight shock when I bumped into old Doc Brown, wandering around in a rusty old swallowtail and sporting an official badge on one of his lapels. I'll bet it was the first track meet he'd ever attended, and how he'd ever managed to horn in as an official set me to thinking once more. I smelled a whole nest of mice, and my expression must have registered something of this sort, as I spoke to him.

"Well, doctor," I said, "you seem to have developed into a real track fan."

He glared at me out of his malevolent little eyes as though I'd accused him of stealing horses. He started to speak, changed his mind, and walked away. Nice pleasant chap. Personally, I believe he was a little cracked.

The meet started and the sprint heats thundered down the track, while the spectators yelled or held their breaths, according to their dispositions. I didn't score in the sprints nor in the hurdles, which followed next. My miler, however, came through with an unexpected win, and a youngster, whom I was merely running for the experience, nosed his way into third place, by some miracle or other.

The quarter mile came next, and my heart turned a flip-flop as Sax and Chris went to their marks. Chris drew the second lane from the pole, while Sax had a rotten break, and drew the next to last position on the outside.

The gun roared, and they all raced for the first turn, and the advantage of the pole. Naturally this resulted in a flying bunch of legs and elbows, with the almost inevitable result of a spill. The man in front of Sax slipped and tumbled, bringing Sax down with him. They both slid in a tangled mass, and brought up against the concrete railing of boxes.

My cuss word was lost in the groan of the crowd, but I breathed again when I saw them both get up, apparently none the worse for wear. I hiked over to find Sax a little dazed, but otherwise all right. I saw Doc Brown heading in the same direction, but bumped the old boy aside and rushed Sax down to the dressing room.

It was on the tip of my tongue to satisfy my mind once for all, but the same peculiar feeling held me back. The battle, after all, wasn't mine. All I could do was help, and I figured the best way I could do that was to keep my mouth shut, and go ahead and gamble as I'd promised the boy I would. He felt pretty bad about the quarter, so I talked to him quietly a while, then stretched him out on a table and told him to wait till I called him for the relay.

In the meanwhile Chris had won the quarter, and things were looking rather promising. I scored some unexpected points in the pole vault, and also in the shot put, and to make a long story short, I came down to the final event, the mile relay, just a single point behind the leaders, who, as luck would have it, were our choicest rivals in everything pertaining to athletics.

It so happened also that none of the other teams had a chance to win the meet by winning the relay so that we were the only teams entered. Both teams, I felt, were rather well matched, although I knew I would feel the loss of Wallace, thanks to Doc Brown, mighty keenly. As things stood the result was a toss-up.

I was on my way to the dressing room to get the boys out to warm up, when I passed the refreshment stand. I had almost gone by, when my attention was attracted by a strangely familiar face, partially obscured by a hot-dog sandwich. I waited till the sandwich had been lowered, then leaped to the side of its owner, and grabbed his arm with such force that the hot-dog hopped unnoticed to the floor. I dragged my prisoner to a corner and backed him into it.

"And now, my boy," I snarled in my most ferocious manner, "what were you doing in Sax Demming's room last night?"

The kid turned a pasty color, opened his mouth, but couldn't utter a sound. Finally he managed a couple of squeaks, which I took for a denial. I twisted his arm till he started to whimper.

"Don't lie to me, you little pup," I hissed, "out with it!"

"Oh, don't, coach, don't please," he whined. "I'll tell you, honest! It was Doctor Brown—yes, it was! He made me do it; said he'd flunk me in his class. He'd do it too, and—and I've never flunked. All I did was to take the shoes and—and—"

"That'll do," I cut in. "What's your name, and where do you live?"

He told me and I let him go. He was thoroughly scared.

I got the relay team on the track and made them warm up well. The crowd was jumpy and nervous for it was composed mostly of alumni and students of these two schools. Programs were crumpled and torn, serving the purpose of safety valves. A girl giggled hysterically every now and then.

I had decided to start Davis, the half-miler, first; Bush, my weakest man, second; Leighton third, and Demming anchor. All were drawn taut and quivering and I was in no better shape myself. My throat was dry as cotton, and the palms of my hands were wet and cold.

The starter called the teams to the starting post. Each man was to run three laps.

The gun roared, and the two figures shot from their marks, raced for the first turn and settled into their strides. Davis, slow on the start, swung in behind and stuck closely to the other's heels. They were well matched, and Davis, following my instructions, stayed close behind and swung even on the stretch.

Bush took the baton on a perfect touch-off, and gained just enough to put him in the lead. Then he proceeded to lose his head, and instead of coasting the turns and sprinting the straightaways, the darn fool tried to sprint the whole distance.

He opened up five yards before the inevitable happened and he began to tie up. He couldn't stand the pace, and our rooters raged and pleaded as his man slowly cut him down, passed him and handed the other team a ten-yard lead.

Leighton took the stick on a well-timed touch-off, and set out after his man in a businesslike way that made my heart swell at the courage the lad possessed. He ran his race like the great veteran he was, conserving every ounce of strength, studying every turn, slowly closing the gap, and finally fighting to within two yards of the leader before he passed the baton to Sax.

The crowd by this time was wild, but I could only clench my hands and pray.

Sax took out after his man with a careless fury that made me hold my breath as he leaned into the turn. But his shoes, by some miracle, held. He caught the leader as they came down off the first turn, and they both raced shoulder to shoulder down the stretch. I gritted my teeth as they came to the second turn. They were both going too fast to take it well, and Sax was on the outside. Why didn't the idiot slow up? My heart dropped with a plop as I realized that he intended to fight for the pole with his arms—anything to win.

I would have turned away but I couldn't possibly shift my eyes. They were glued to the two speeding figures, and for this reason I perhaps saw what no one else would have noticed. For, a split second before they reached the turn, I saw Sax's head jerk back slightly, as though a thought had jammed itself forcibly into his brain. At the same instant his stride faltered and he swung wide, shunning his opponent as though he had the plague.

Sax's momentum carried him into the concrete railing of the boxes. He warded himself off with his hand, and had just about floundered into his stride again when the crowd came to its feet with a great gasping groan. The other boy had leaned into the turn too far, had lost his feet, and had tumbled to the floor. The baton shot out of his hand and rattled across the track.

And the groan of the crowd turned to dead silence.

For Sax had heard the groan, had turned his head, and finally stopped. With the race delivered to him, bound and tied by the hand of fate, he stopped dead, recovered the baton of the fallen man, and handed it to him as he scrambled to his feet.

It was the most spectacular and cleanest piece of sportsmanship I had ever seen, but my own shout was lost in the din of the crowd. It was a great ovation to a great sportsman.

The race started again with the men in their original positions, side by side, but the other lad was too shaken by the fall to make much of a race of it. They finished five yards apart, and the crowd closed in on the victor.

That was the reason I didn't get to Sax for several moments. But when I'd finally wormed my way to the center of the circle, I found Doc Brown already there, together with several other officials. He was arguing.

"I insist that you examine this man's shoes," I heard him say.

My heart dropped like a chunk of lead, but bounced again like a rubber ball, as I noticed the expression on Sax's face. He was surprised at first, then grinned as he slipped off a shoe and handed it to Doc Brown.

The old boy bent it and prodded it a bit, and his face slowly took on an expression of blank surprise, followed suddenly by one of rage. He grunted something, handed the shoe back, but, as he turned to go I grabbed him, and whispered gently in his ear what I had already learned.

"You're a foxy old gent," I told him, "and crooked as they make 'em. You watched the team enough to figure Demming was the weak point, but your ignorance of that little thing called 'sportsmanship' has made an ass of you. Take my advice and resign."

A moment later I had dragged Sax off to one side.

"You see, coach," he explained, "I didn't want to tell you anything about it, because I was pretty much ashamed of the fact that they'd picked me for the goat. And besides, I figured that, by pretending to accept them, I'd learn who was at the bottom of it. It sure worked out that way, didn't it?"

I patted him on the shoulder and sent him down to dress. As I turned someone touched me on the arm. It was a lad from the Scroll and Quill.

"Congratulations on the meet, coach," he said. "Can you give us any dope on Saxon Demming yet?"

I regarded him fondly and patted him on the shoulder too.

"Take him quick, son, take him quick," I said. "You'll never get a better man."

THE LONELINESS OF THE LONG-DISTANCE RUNNER

Alan Sillitoe

(1959)

[*Sent to a Borstal, or reformatory, for having committed burglary, Smith—an extraordinary runner and the archetypal adolescent rebel—expertly wields the only power left to him.*]

The pop-eyed potbellied governor said to a pop-eyed potbellied Member of Parliament who sat next to his pop-eyed potbellied whore of a wife that I was his only hope for getting the Borstal Blue Ribbon Prize Cup For Long Distance Cross Country Running (All England), which I was, and it set me laughing to myself inside, and I didn't say a word to any potbellied pop-eyed bastard that might give them real hope, though I knew the governor anyway took my quietness to mean he'd got that cup already stuck on the bookshelf in his office among the few other mildewed trophies.

"He might take up running in a sort of professional way when he gets out," and it wasn't until he'd said this and I'd heard it with my own flap-tabs that I realized it might be possible to do such a thing, run for money, trot for wages on piece work at a bob a puff rising bit by bit to a guinea a gasp and retiring through old age at thirty-two because of lace-curtain lungs, a football heart, and legs like varicose beanstalks. But I'd have a wife and car and get my grinning long-distance clock in the papers and have a smashing secretary to answer piles of letters sent by tarts who'd mob me when they saw who I was as I pushed my way into Woolworth's for a packet of razor blades and a cup of tea. It was something to think about all right, and sure enough the governor knew he'd got me when he said, turning to me as if I would at any rate have to be consulted about it all: "How does this matter strike you, then, Smith, my lad?"

A line of potbellied pop-eyes gleamed at me and a row of goldfish mouths opened and wiggled gold teeth at me, so I gave them the answer they wanted because I'd hold my trump card until later. "It'd suit me fine, sir," I said.

"Good lad. Good show. Right spirit. Splendid."

"Well," the governor said, "get that cup for us today and I'll do all I can for you. I'll get you trained so that you whack every man in the Free World." And I had a picture in my brain of me running and beating everybody in the world, leaving them all behind until only I was trot-trotting across a big wide moor alone, doing a marvellous speed as I ripped between boulders and reed-dumps, when suddenly: CRACK! CRACK!—bullets that can go faster than any man running, coming from a copper's rifle planted in a tree, winged me and split my gizzard in spite of my perfect running, and down I fell.

The potbellies expected me to say something else. "Thank you, sir," I said.

Told to go, I trotted down the pavilion steps, out on to the field because the big cross-country was about to begin and the two entries from Gunthorpe had fixed themselves early at the starting line and were ready to move off like white kangaroos. The sports ground looked a treat: with big tea-tents all round and flags flying and seats for families—empty because no mam or dad had known what opening day meant—and boys still running heats for the hundred yards, and lords and ladies walking from stall to stall, and the Borstal Boys Brass Band in blue uniforms; and up on the stands the brown jackets of Hucknall as well as our own grey blazers, and then the Gunthorpe lot with shirt sleeves rolled. The blue sky was full of sunshine and it couldn't have been a better day, and all of the big show was like something out of Ivanhoe that we'd seen on the pictures a few days before.

"Come on, Smith," Roach the sports master called to me, "we don't want you to be late for the big race, eh? Although I dare say you'd catch them up if you were." The others catcalled and grunted at this, but I took no notice and placed myself between Gunthorpe and one of the Aylesham trustees, dropped on my knees and plucked a few grass blades to suck on the way round. So the big race it was, for them, watching from the grandstand under a fluttering Union Jack, a race for the governor, that he had been waiting for, and I hoped he and all the rest of his pop-eyed gang were busy placing big bets on me, hundred to one to win, all the money they had in their pockets, all the wages they were going to get for the next five years, and the more they placed the happier I'd be. Because here was a dead cert going to die on the big name they'd built for him, going to go down dying with laughter whether it choked him or not. My knees felt the cool soil pressing into them, and out of my eye's corner I saw Roach lift his hand. The Gunthorpe boy twitched before the signal was given; somebody cheered too soon; Medway bent forward; then the gun went, and I was away.

We went once around the field and then along a half-mile drive of elms, being cheered all the way, and I seemed to feel I was in the lead as we went out by the gate and into the lane, though I wasn't interested enough to find out. The five-mile course was marked by splashes of whitewash gleaming on gateposts and trunks and stiles and stones, and a boy with a waterbottle and bandage box stood every half-mile waiting for those that dropped out or fainted. Over the first stile, without trying, I was still nearly in the lead but one; and if any of you want tips about running, never be in a hurry, and never let any of the other runners know you are in a hurry even if you are. You can always overtake on long-distance running without letting the others smell the hurry in you; and when you've used your craft like this to reach the two or three up front then you can do a big dash later that puts everybody else's hurry in the shade because you've not had to make haste up till then. I ran to a steady jog-trot rhythm, and soon it was so smooth that I forgot I was running, and I was hardly able to know that my legs were lifting and falling and my arms going in and out, and my lungs didn't seem to be working at all, and my heart stopped that wicked thumping I always get at the beginning of a run. Because you see I never race at all; I just run, and somehow I know that if I forget I'm racing and only jog-trot along until I don't know I'm running I always win the race. For when my eyes recognize that I'm getting near the end of the course—by seeing a stile or cottage corner—I put on a spurt, and such a fast big spurt it is because I feel that up till then I haven't been running and that I've used up no energy at all. And I've been able to do this because I've been thinking; and I wonder if I'm the only one in the running business with this system of forgetting that I'm running because I'm too busy thinking; and I wonder if any of the other lads are on to the same lark, though I know for a fact that they aren't. Off like the wind along the cobbled footpath and rutted lane, smoother than the flat grass track on the field and better for thinking because it's not too smooth, and I was in my element that afternoon knowing that nobody could beat me at running but intending to beat myself before the day was over. For when the governor talked to me of being honest when I first came in he didn't know what the word meant or he wouldn't have had me here in this race, trotting along in shimmy and shorts and sunshine. He'd have had me where I'd have had him if I'd been in his place: in a quarry breaking rocks until he broke his back. At least old Hitler-face the plain-clothes dick was honester than the governor, because he at any rate had had it in for me and I for him, and when my case was coming up in court a copper knocked at our front door at four o'clock in the morning and got my mother out of bed when she was paralytic tired, reminding her she had to be in court at dead on half past nine. It was the finest bit of spite I've ever heard of, but I would call it honest, the same as my mam's words were honest when she really told that copper what she thought of him and called him all the dirty names she'd ever heard of, which took her half an hour and woke the terrace up.

I trotted on along the edge of a field bordered by the sunken lane, smelling green grass and honeysuckle, and I felt as though I came from a long line of whippets trained to run on two legs, only I couldn't see a toy rabbit in front and there wasn't a collier's cosh behind to make me keep up the pace. I passed the Gunthorpe runner whose shimmy was already black with sweat and I could just see the corner of the fenced-up copse in front where the only man I had to pass to win the race was going all out to gain the half-way mark. Then he turned into a tongue of trees and bushes where I couldn't see him anymore, and I couldn't see anybody, and I knew what the loneliness of the long-distance runner running across country felt like, realizing that as far as I was concerned this feeling was the only honesty and realness there was in the world and I knowing it would be no different ever, no matter what I felt at odd times, and no matter what anybody else tried to tell me. The runner behind me must have been a long way off because it was so quiet, and there was even less noise and movement than there had been at five o'clock of a frosty winter morning. It was hard to understand, and all I knew was that you had to run, run, run, without knowing why you were running, but on you went through fields you didn't understand and into woods that made you afraid, over hills without knowing you'd been up and down, and shooting across streams that would have cut the heart out of you had you fallen into them. And the winning post was no end to it, even though crowds might be cheering you in, because on you had to go before you got your breath back, and the only time you stopped really was when you tripped over a tree trunk and broke your neck or fell into a disused well and stayed dead in the darkness forever. So I thought: they aren't going to get me on this racing lark, this running and trying to win, this jog-trotting for a bit of blue ribbon, because it's not the way to go on at all, though they swear blind that it is. You should think about nobody and go your own way, not on a course marked out for you by people holding mugs of water and bottles of iodine in case you fall and cut yourself so that they can pick you up—even if you want to stay where you are—and get you moving again.

On I went, out of the wood, passing the man leading without knowing I was going to do so. Flip-flap, flip-flap, jog-trot, jog-trot, crunchslap-crunchslap, across the middle of a broad field again, rhythmically running in my greyhound effortless fashion, knowing I had won the race though it wasn't half over, won it if I wanted it, could go on for ten or fifteen or twenty miles if I had to and drop dead at the finish of it, which would be the same, in the end, as living an honest life like the governor wanted me to. It amounted to: win the race and be honest, and on trot-trotting I went, having the time of my life, loving my progress because it did me good and set me thinking which by now I liked to do, but not caring at all when I remembered that I had to win this race as well as run it. One of the two, I had to win the race or run it, and I knew I could do both because my legs had carried me well in front—now coming to the short cut down the bramble bank and over the sunken road—and would carry me further because they seemed made of electric cable and easily alive to keep on slapping at those ruts and roots, but I'm not going to win because the only way I'd see I came in first would be if winning meant that I was going to escape the coppers after doing the biggest bank job of my life, but winning means the exact opposite, no matter how they try to kill or kid me, means running right into their white-gloved wall-barred hands and grinning mugs and staying there for the rest of my natural long life of stone-breaking anyway, but stone-breaking in the way I want to do it and not in the way they tell me.

Another honest thought that comes is that I could swing left at the next hedge of the field, and under its cover beat my slow retreat away from the sports ground winning post. I could do three or six or a dozen miles across the turf like this and cut a few main roads behind me so's they'd never know which one I'd taken; and maybe on the last one when it got dark I could thumb a lorry-lift and get a free ride north with somebody who might not give me away. But no, I said I wasn't daft didn't I? I won't pull out with only six months left, and besides there's nothing I want to dodge and run away from; I only want a bit of my own back on the In-laws and Potbellies by letting them sit up there on their big posh seats and watch me lose this race, though as sure as God made me I know that when I do lose I'll get the dirtiest crap and kitchen jobs in the months to go before my time is up. I won't be worth a threpp'ny-bit to anybody here, which will be all the thanks I get for being honest in the only way I know. For when the governor told me to be honest it was meant to be in his way not mine, and if I kept on being honest in the way he wanted and won my race for him he'd see I got the cushiest six months still left to run; but in my own way, well, it's not allowed, and if I find a way of doing it such as I've got now then I'll get what-for in every mean trick he can set his mind to. And if you look at it in my way, who can blame him? For this is war—and ain't I said so?—and when I hit him in the only place he knows he'll be sure to get his own back on me for not collaring that cup when his heart's been set for ages on seeing himself standing up at the end of the afternoon to clap me on the back as I take the cup from Lord Earwig or some such chinless wonder with a name like that.

And so I'll hit him where it hurts a lot, and he'll do all he can to get his own back, tit for tat, though I'll enjoy it most because I'm hitting first, and because I planned it longer. I don't know why I think these thoughts are better than any I've ever had, but I do, and I don't care why. I suppose it took me a long time to get going on all this because I've had no time and peace in all my bandit life, and now my thoughts are coming pat and the only trouble is I often can't stop, even when my brain feels as if it's got cramp, frostbite and creeping paralysis all rolled into one and I have to give it a rest by slap-dashing down through the brambles of the sunken lane. And all this is another upper-cut I'm getting in first at people like the governor, to show how—if I can—his races are never won even though some bloke always comes unknowingly in first, how in the end the governor is going to be doomed while blokes like me will take the pickings of his roasted bones and dance like maniacs around his Borstal's ruins. And so this story's like the race and once again I won't bring off a winner to suit the governor; no, I'm being honest like he told me to, without him knowing what he means, though I don't suppose he'll ever come in with a story of his own, even if he reads this one of mine and knows who I'm talking about.

I've just come up out of the sunken lane, kneed and elbowed, thumped and bramble-scratched, and the race is two-thirds over, and a voice is going like a wireless in my mind saying that when you've had enough of feeling good like the first man on earth of a frosty morning, and you've known how it is to be taken bad like the last man on earth on a summer's afternoon, then you get at last to being like the only man on earth and don't give a bogger about either good or bad, but just trot on with your slippers slapping the good dry soil that at least would never do you a bad turn. Now the words are like coming from a crystal-set that's broken down, and something's happening inside the shell-case of my guts that bothers me and I don't know why or what to blame it on, a grinding near my ticker as though a bag of rusty screws is loose inside me and I shake them up every time I trot forward. Now and again I break my rhythm to feel my left shoulder blade by swing-ing a right hand across my chest as if to rub the knife away that has somehow got stuck there. But I know it's nothing to bother about, that more likely it's caused by too much thinking that now and again I take for worry. For sometimes I'm the greatest worrier in the world I think (as you twigged I'll bet from me having got this story out) which is funny anyway because my mam don't know the meaning of the word so I don't take after her; though dad had a hard time of worry in his life up to when he filled his bedroom with hot blood and kicked the bucket that morning when nobody was in the house. I'll never forget it, straight I won't, because I was the one that found him and I often wished I hadn't. Back from a session on the fruit-machines at the fish-and-chip shop, jingling my three-lemon loot to a nail-dead house, as soon as I got in I knew something was wrong, stood leaning my head against the cold mirror above the mantel-piece trying not to open my eyes and see my stone-cold clock—because I knew I'd gone as white as a piece of chalk since coming in as if I'd been got at by a Dracula-vampire and even my penny-pocket winnings kept quiet on purpose.

Gunthorpe nearly caught me up. Birds were singing from the briar hedge, and a couple of thrushies flew like lightning into some thorny bushes. Corn had grown high in the next field and would be cut down soon with scythes and mowers; but I never wanted to notice much while running in case it put me off my stroke, so by the haystack I decided to leave it all behind and put on such a spurt, in spite of nails in my guts, that before long I'd left both Gunthorpe and the birds a good way off; I wasn't far now from going into that last mile and a half like a knife through margarine, but the quietness I suddenly trotted into between two pickets was like opening my eyes underwater and looking at the pebbles on a stream bottom, reminding me again of going back that morning to the house in which my old man had croaked, which is funny because I hadn't thought about it at all since it happened and even then I didn't brood much on it. I wonder why? I suppose that since I started to think on these long-distance runs I'm liable to have anything crop up and pester at my tripes and innards, and now that I see my bloody dad behind each grass-blade in my barmy runner-brain I'm not so sure I like to think and that it's such a good thing after all. I choke my phlegm and keep on running anyway and curse the Borstal-builders and their athletics—flappity-flap, slop-slop, crunchslap-crunchslap-crunchslap—who've maybe got their own back on me from the bright beginning by sliding magic-lantern slides into my head that never stood a chance before.

Only if I take whatever comes like this in my runner's stride can I keep on keeping on like my old self and beat them back; and now I've thought on this far I know I'll win, in the crunchslap end. So anyway after a bit I went upstairs one step at a time not thinking anything about how I should find dad and what I'd do when I did. But now I'm making up for it by going over the rotten life mam led him ever since I can remember, knocking-on with different men even when he was alive and fit and she not caring whether he knew it or not, and most of the time he wasn't so blind as she thought and cursed and roared and threatened to punch her tab, and I had to stand up to stop him even though I knew she deserved it. What a life for all of us. Well, I'm not grumbling, because if I did I might just as well win this bleeding race, which I'm not going to do, though if I don't lose speed I'll win it before I know where I am, and then where would I be?

Now I can hear the sportsground noise and music as I head back for the flags and the lead-in drive, the fresh new feel of underfoot gravel going against the iron muscles of my legs. I'm nowhere near puffed despite that bag of nails that rattles as much as ever, and I can still give a big last leap like gale-force wind if I want to, but everything is under control and I know now that there ain't another long-distance cross-country running runner in England to touch my speed and style. Our doddering bastard of a governor, our half-dead gangrened gaffer is hollow like an empty petrol drum, and he wants me and my running life to give him glory, to put in him blood and throbbing veins he never had, wants his potbellied pals to be his witnesses as I gasp and stagger up to his winning post so's he can say: "My Borstal gets that cup, you see. I win my bet, because it pays to be honest and try to gain the prizes I offer to my lads, and they know it, have known it all along. They'll always be honest now, because I made them so." And his pals will think: "He trains his lads to live right, after all; he deserves a medal but we'll get him made a Sir"—and at this very moment as the birds come back to whistling I can tell myself I'll never care a sod what any of the chinless spineless in-laws think or say. They've seen me and they're cheering now and loudspeakers set around the field like elephant's ears are spreading out the big news that I'm well in the lead, and can't do anything else but stay there. But I'm still thinking of the outlaw death my dad died, telling the doctors to scat from the house when they wanted him to finish up in hospital (like a bleeding guinea-pig, he raved at them). He got up in bed to throw them out and even followed them down the stairs in his shirt though he was no more than skin and stick. They tried to tell him he'd want some drugs but he didn't fall for it, and only took the pain-killer that mam and I got from a herbseller in the next street. It's not till now that I know what guts he had, and when I went into the room that morning he was lying on his stomach with the clothes thrown back, looking like a skinned rabbit, his grey head resting just on the edge of the bed, and on the floor must have been all the blood he'd had in his body, right from his toe-nails up, for nearly all of the lino and carpet was covered in it, thin and pink.

And down the drive I went, carrying a heart blocked up like Boulder Dam across my arteries, the nail-bag clamped down tighter and tighter as though in a woodwork vice, yet with my feet like bird-wings and arms like talons ready to fly across the field except that I didn't want to give anybody that much of a show, or win the race by accident. I smell the hot dry day now as I run towards the end, passing a mountain-heap of grass emptied from cans hooked on to the fronts of lawn mowers pushed by my pals; I rip a piece of tree-bark with my fingers and stuff it in my mouth, chewing wood and dust and maybe maggots as I run until I'm nearly sick, yet swallowing what I can of it just the same because a little birdie whistled to me that I've got to go on living for at least a bloody sight longer yet but that for six months I'm not going to smell that grass or taste that dusty bark or trot this lovely path. I hate to have to say this but something bloody well made me cry, and crying is a thing I haven't bloody-well done since I was a kid of two or three. Because I'm slowing down now for Gunthorpe to catch me up, and I'm doing it in a place just where the drive turns in to the sportsfield—where they can see what I'm doing, especially the governor and his gang from the grandstand, and I'm going so slow I'm almost marking time. Those on the nearest seats haven't caught on yet to what's happening and are still cheering like mad ready for when I make that mark, and I keep on wondering when the bleeding hell Gunthorpe behind me is going to nip by on to the field because I can't hold this up all day, and I think Oh Christ it's just my rotten luck that Gunthorpe's dropped out and that I'll be here for half an hour before the next bloke comes up, but even so, I say, I won't budge, I won't go for that last hundred yards if I have to sit down cross-legged on the grass and have the governor and his chinless wonders pick me up and carry me there, which is against their rules so you can bet they'd never do it because they're not clever enough to break the rules—like I would be in their place—even though they are their own. No, I'll show him what honesty means if it's the last thing I do, though I'm sure he'll never understand because if he and all them like him did it'd mean they'd be on my side which is impossible. By God I'll stick this out like my dad stuck out his pain and kicked them doctors down the stairs: if he had guts for that then I've got guts for this and here I stay waiting for Gunthorpe or Aylesham to bash that turf and go right slap-up against that bit of clothes-line stretched across the winning post. As for me, the only time I'll hit that clothes-line will be when I'm dead and a comfortable coffin's been got ready on the other side. Until then I'm a long-distance runner, crossing country all on my own no matter how bad it feels.

The Essex boys were shouting themselves blue in the face telling me to get a move on, waving their arms, standing up and making as if to run at that rope themselves because they were only a few yards to the side of it. You cranky lot, I thought, stuck at that winning post, and yet I knew they didn't mean what they were shouting, were really on my side and always would be, not able to keep their maulers to themselves, in and out of cop-shops and clink. And there they were now having the time of their lives letting themselves go in cheering me which made the governor think they were heart and soul on his side when he wouldn't have thought any such thing if he'd had a grain of sense. And I could hear the lords and ladies now from the grandstand, and could see them standing up to wave me in: "Run!" they were shouting in their posh voices. "Run!" But I was deaf, daft and blind, and stood where I was, still tasting the bark in my mouth and still blubbing like a baby, blubbing: now out of gladness that I'd got them beat at last.

Because I heard a roar and saw the Gunthorpe gang throwing their coats up in the air and I felt the pat-pat of feet on the drive behind me getting closer and closer and suddenly a smell of sweat and a pair of lungs on their last gasp passed me by and went swinging on towards that rope, all shagged out and rocking from side to side, grunting like a Zulu that didn't know any better, like the ghost of me at ninety when I'm heading for that fat upholstered coffin. I could have cheered him myself: "Go on, go on, get cracking. Knot yourself up on that piece of tape." But he was already there, and so I went on, trot-trotting after him until I got to the rope, and collapsed, with a murderous sounding roar going up through my ears while I was still on the wrong side of it.

It's about time to stop; though don't think I'm not still running, because I am, one way or another. The governor at Borstal proved me right; he didn't respect my honesty at all; not that I expected him to, or tried to explain it to him, but if he's supposed to be educated then he should have more or less twigged it. He got his own back right enough, or thought he did, because he had me carting dustbins about every morning from the big full-working kitchen to the garden-bottoms where I had to empty them; and in the afternoon I spread out slops over spuds and carrots growing in the allotments. In the evenings I scrubbed floors, miles and miles of them. But it wasn't a bad life for six months, which was another thing he could never understand and would have made it grimmer, if he could, and it was worth it when I look back on it, considering all the thinking I did, and the fact that the boys caught on to me losing the race on purpose and never had enough good words to say about me, or curses to throw out (to themselves) at the governor.

The work didn't break me; if anything it made me stronger in many ways, and the governor knew, when I left, that his spite had got him nowhere. For since leaving Borstal they tried to get me in the army, but I didn't pass the medical and I'll tell you why. No sooner was I out, after that final run and six-months hard, than I went down with pleurisy, which means as far as I'm concerned that I lost the governor's race all right, and won my own twice over, because I know for certain that if I hadn't raced my race I wouldn't have got this pleurisy, which keeps me out of khaki but doesn't stop me doing the sort of work my itchy fingers want to do.

I'm out now and the heat's switched on again, but the rats haven't got me for the last big thing I pulled. I counted six hundred and twenty-eight pounds and am still living off it because I did the job all on my own, and after it I had the peace to write all this, and it'll be money enough to keep me going until I finish my plans for doing an even bigger snatch, something up my sleeve I wouldn't tell to a living soul. I worked out my systems and hiding-places while pushing scrubbing-brushes around them Borstal floors, planned my outward life of innocence and honest work, yet at the same time grew perfect in the razor-edges of my craft for what I knew I had to do once free; and what I'll do again if netted by the poaching coppers.

In the meantime (as they say in one or two books I've read since, useless though because all of them ended on a winning post and didn't teach me a thing) I'm going to give this story to a pal of mine and tell him that if I do get captured again by the coppers he can try and get it put into a book or something, because I'd like to see the governor's face when he reads it, if he does, which I don't suppose he will; even if he did read it though I don't think he'd know what it was all about. And if I don't get caught the bloke I give this story to will never give me away; he's lived in our terrace for as long as I can remember, and he's my pal. That I do know.

DECLINE AND FALL

Evelyn Waugh

(1928)

[*Sports day at Llanabba, a tawdry boarding school in Wales staffed by misfits and failures, precipitates a hilarious chaos. Paul Pennyfeather is a decent young man teaching there; Philbrick, the butler, is a con man; Grimes and Prendergast, sad eccentric characters, are also teachers. The "Doctor" is the headmaster.*]

Frankly," said the Doctor, "I am at a loss to understand my own emotions. I can think of no entertainment that fills me with greater detestation than a display of competitive athletics, none—except possibly folk dancing. If there are two women in the world whose company I abominate—and there are very many more than two—they are Mrs. Beste-Chetwynde and Lady Circumference. I have, moreover, had an extremely difficult encounter with my butler, who—will you believe it?—waited at luncheon in a mustard-coloured suit of plus fours and a diamond tie pin, and when I reprimanded him, attempted to tell me some ridiculous story about his being the proprietor of a circus or swimming bath or some such concern. And yet," said the Doctor, "I am filled with a wholly delightful exhilaration. I can't understand it. It is not as though this was the first occasion of the kind. During the fourteen years that I have been at Llanabba there have been six sports days and two concerts, all of them, in one way or another, utterly disastrous. Once Lady Bunyan was taken ill; another time it was the matter of the press photographers and the obstacle race; another time some quite unimportant parents brought a dog with them which bit two of the boys very severely and one of the masters, who swore terribly in front of every one. I could hardly blame him, but of course he had to go. Then there was the concert when the boys refused to sing 'God Save the King' because of the pudding they had had for luncheon. One way and another, I have been consistently unfortunate in my efforts at festivity. And yet I look forward to each new fiasco with the utmost relish. Perhaps, Pennyfeather, you will bring luck to Llanabba; in fact, I feel confident you have already done so. Look at the sun!"

Picking their way carefully among the dry patches in the water-logged drive, they reached the playing fields. Here the haphazard organization of the last twenty-four hours seemed to have been fairly successful. A large marquee was already in position, and Philbrick—still in plus fours—and three gardeners were at work putting up a smaller tent.

"That's for the Llanabba Silver Band," said the Doctor. "Philbrick, I required you to take off those loathsome garments."

"They were new when I bought them," said Philbrick, "and they cost eight pounds fifteen. Anyhow I can't do two things at once, can I? If I go back to change, who's going to manage all this, I'd like to know?"

"All right! Finish what you are doing first. Let us just review the arrangements. The marquee is for the visitors' tea. That is Diana's province. I expect we shall find her at work . . ."

Sure enough, there was Dingy helping two servants to arrange plates of highly coloured cakes down a trestle table. Two other servants in the background were cutting sandwiches. Dingy, too, was obviously enjoying herself.

"Jane, Emily, remember that that butter has to do for three loaves. Spread it thoroughly, but don't waste it, and cut the crusts as thin as possible. Father, will you see to it that the boys who come in with their parents come in *alone*? You remember last time how Briggs brought in four boys with him, and they ate all the jam sandwiches before Colonel Loder had had any. Mr. Pennyfeather, the champagne cup is *not* for the masters. In fact, I expect you will find yourselves too much occupied helping the visitors to have any tea until they have left the tent. You had better tell Captain Grimes that, too. I am sure Mr. Prendergast would not think of pushing himself forward."

Outside the marquee were assembled several seats and tubs of palms and flowering shrubs. "All this must be set in order," said the Doctor; "our guests may arrive in less than an hour." He passed on. "The cars shall turn aside from the drive here and come right into the ground. It will give a pleasant background to the photographs, and, Pennyfeather, if you would with tact direct the photographer so that more prominence was given to Mrs. Beste-Chetwynde's Hispano Suiza than to Lady Circumference's little motor car, I think it would be all to the good. All these things count, you know."

"Nothing seems to have been done about marking out the ground," said Paul.

"No," said the Doctor, turning his attention to the field for the first time, "nothing. Well, you must do the best you can. They can't do everything."

"I wonder if any hurdles have come?"

"They were ordered," said the Doctor. "I am certain of it. Philbrick, have any hurdles come?"

"Yes," said Philbrick with a low chuckle.

"Why, pray, do you laugh at the mention of hurdles?"

"Just you look at them!" said Philbrick. "They're behind the tea house there."

Paul and the Doctor went to look and found a pile of spiked iron railings in sections heaped up at the back of the marquee. They were each about five feet high and were painted green with gilt spikes.

"It seems to me that they have sent the wrong sort," said the Doctor.

"Yes."

"Well, we must do the best we can. What other things ought there to be?"

"Weight, hammer, javelin, long-jump pit, high-jump posts, low hurdles, eggs, spoon and greasy pole," said Philbrick.

"Previously competed for," said the Doctor imperturbably. "What else?"

"Somewhere to run," suggested Paul.

"Why, God bless my soul, they've got the whole park! How did you manage yesterday for the heats?"

"We judged the distance by eye."

"Then that is what we shall have to do to-day. Really, my dear Pennyfeather, it is quite unlike you to fabricate difficulties in this way. I am afraid you are getting unnerved. Let them go on racing until it is time for tea; and remember," he added sagely, "the longer the race the more time it takes. I leave the details to you. I am concerned with *style.* I wish, for instance, we had a starting pistol."

"Would this be any use?" said Philbrick, producing an enormous service revolver. "Only take care; it's loaded."

"The very thing," said the Doctor. "Only fire into the ground, mind. We must do everything we can to avoid an accident. Do you always carry that about with you?"

"Only when I'm wearing my diamonds," said Philbrick.

* * *

All the school and several local visitors were assembled in the field. Grimes stood by himself, looking depressed. Mr. Prendergast, flushed and unusually vivacious, was talking to the Vicar. As the headmaster's party came into sight the Llanabba Silver Band struck up *Men of Harlech.*

"Shockin' noise," commented Lady Circumference graciously.

The head prefect came forward and presented her with a programme, beribboned and embossed in gold. Another prefect set a chair for her. She sat down with the Doctor next to her and Lord Circumference on the other side of him.

"Pennyfeather," cried the Doctor above the band, "start them racing."

Philbrick gave Paul a megaphone. "I found this in the pavilion," he said. "I thought it might be useful."

"Who's that extraordinary man?" asked Lady Circumference.

"He is the boxing coach and swimming professional," said the Doctor. "A finely developed figure, don't you think?"

"First race," said Paul through the megaphone, "under sixteen. Quarter mile!" He read out Grimes's list of starters.

"What's Tangent doin' in this race?" said Lady Circumference. "The boy can't run an inch."

The silver band stopped playing.

"The course," said Paul, "starts from the pavilion, goes round that clump of elms . . ."

"Beeches," corrected Lady Circumference loudly.

". . . and ends in front of the band stand. Starter, Mr. Prendergast; timekeeper, Captain Grimes."

"I shall say, 'Are you ready? one, two, three!' and then fire," said Mr. Prendergast. "Are you ready? One"—there was a terrific report. "Oh, dear! I'm sorry!"—but the race had begun. Clearly Tangent was not going to win; he was sitting on the grass crying because he had been wounded in the foot by Mr. Prendergast's bullet. Philbrick carried him, wailing dismally, into the refreshment tent, where Dingy helped him off with his shoe. His heel was slightly grazed. Dingy gave him a large slice of cake, and he hobbled out surrounded by a sympathetic crowd.

"That won't hurt him," said Lady Circumference, "but I think someone ought to remove the pistol from that old man before he does anything serious."

"I knew that was going to happen," said Lord Circumference.

"A most unfortunate beginning," said the Doctor.

"Am I going to die?" said Tangent, his mouth full of cake.

"For God's sake, look after Prendy," said Grimes in Paul's ear. "The man's as tight as a lord, and on one whisky, too."

"First blood to me!" said Mr. Prendergast gleefully.

"The last race will be run again," said Paul down the megaphone. "Starter, Mr. Philbrick; timekeeper, Mr. Prendergast."

"On your marks! Get set." Bang went the pistol, this time without disaster. The six little boys scampered off through the mud, disappeared behind the beeches and returned rather more slowly. Captain Grimes and Mr. Prendergast held up a piece of tape.

"Well, run, sir!" shouted Colonel Sidebotham. "Jolly good race."

"Capital," said Mr. Prendergast, and dropping his end of the tape, he sauntered over to the Colonel. "I can see you are a fine judge of a race, sir. So was I once. So's Grimes. A capital fellow, Grimes; a bounder, you know, but a capital fellow. Bounders can be capital fellows; don't you agree, Colonel Slidebottom? In fact, I'd go farther and say that capital fellows *are* bounders. What d'you say to that? I wish you'd stop pulling at my arm, Pennyfeather. Colonel Shybotham and I are just having a most interesting conversation about bounders."

The silver band struck up again, and Mr. Prendergast began a little jig, saying: "Capital fellow! capital fellow!" and snapping his fingers. Paul led him to the refreshment tent.

"Dingy wants you to help her in there," he said firmly, "and, for God's sake, don't come out until you feel better."

"I never felt better in my life," said Mr. Prendergast indignantly. "Capital fellow! capital fellow!"

"It is not my affair, of course," said Colonel Sidebotham, "but if you ask me I should say that man had been drinking."

"He was talking very excitedly to me," said the Vicar, "about some apparatus for warming a church in Worthing and about the Apostolic Claims of the Church of Abyssinia. I confess I could not follow him clearly. He seems deeply interested in Church matters. Are you quite sure he is right in the head? I have noticed again and again since I have been in the Church that lay interest in ecclesiastical matters is often a prelude to insanity."

"Drink, pure and simple," said the Colonel. "I wonder where he got it? I could do with a spot of whisky."

"Quarter Mile Open!" said Paul through his megaphone.

Presently the Clutterbucks arrived. Both the parents were stout. They brought with them two small children, a governess, and an elder son. They debouched from the car one by one, stretching their limbs in evident relief.

"This is Sam," said Mr. Clutterbuck, "just down from Cambridge. He's joined me in the business, and we've brought the nippers along for a treat. Don't mind, do you, Doc? And last, but not least, my wife."

Dr. Fagan greeted them with genial condescension and found them seats.

"I am afraid you have missed all the jumping events," he said. "But I have a list of the results here. You will see that Percy has done extremely well."

"Didn't know the little beggar had it in him. See that, Martha? Percy's won the high jump and the long jump and the hurdles. How's your young hopeful been doing, Lady Circumference?"

"My boy has been injured in the foot," said Lady Circumference coldly.

"Dear me! Not badly, I hope? Did he twist his ankle in the jumping?"

"No," said Lady Circumference, "he was shot at by one of the assistant masters. But it is kind of you to inquire."

"Three Miles Open!" announced Paul. "The course of six laps will be run as before."

"On your marks! Get set." Bang went Philbrick's revolver. Off trotted the boys on another race.

"Father," said Flossie, "don't you think it's time for the tea interval?"

"Nothing can be done before Mrs. Beste-Chetwynde arrives," said the Doctor.

Round and round the muddy track trotted the athletes while the silver band played sacred music unceasingly.

"Last lap!" announced Paul.

The school and the visitors crowded about the tape to cheer the winner. Amid loud applause Clutterbuck breasted the tape well ahead of the others.

"Well run! Oh, good, jolly good, sir!" cried Colonel Sidebotham.

"Good old Percy! That's the stuff," said Mr. Clutterbuck.

"Well run, Percy!" chorused the two little Clutterbucks, prompted by their governess.

"That boy cheated," said Lady Circumference. "He only went round five times. I counted."

"I think unpleasantness so mars the afternoon," said the Vicar.

"How dare you suggest such a thing?" asked Mrs. Clutterbuck. "I appeal to the referee. Percy ran the full course, didn't he?"

"Clutterbuck wins," said Captain Grimes.

"Fiddlesticks!" said Lady Circumference. "He deliberately lagged behind and joined the others as they went behind the beeches. The little toad!"

"Really, Greta," said Lord Circumference, "I think we ought to abide by the referee's decision."

"Well, they can't expect me to give away the prizes, then. Nothing would induce me to give that boy a prize."

"Do you understand, madam, that you are bringing a serious accusation against my son's honour?"

"Serious accusation fiddlesticks! What he wants is a jolly good hidin'."

"No doubt you judge other people's sons by your own. Let me tell you, Lady Circumference . . ."

"Don't attempt to browbeat me, sir. I know a cheat when I see one."

At this stage of the discussion the Doctor left Mrs. Hope-Browne's side, where he had been remarking upon her son's progress in geometry, and joined the group round the winning post.

"If there is a disputed decision," he said genially, "they shall race again."

"Percy has won already," said Mr. Clutterbuck. "He has been adjudged the winner."

"Splendid! Splendid! A promising little athlete. I congratulate you, Clutterbuck."

"But he only ran five laps," said Lady Circumference.

"Then clearly he has won the five furlong race, a very exacting length."

"But the other boys," said Lady Circumference, almost beside herself with rage, "have run six lengths."

"Then they," said the Doctor unperturbably, "are first, second, third, fourth and fifth respectively in the Three Miles. Clearly there has been some confusion. Diana, I think we might now serve tea."

JOHN SOBIESKI RUNS

James Buechler

(1964)

One September afternoon the door of the cross-country team room at an upstate New York high school opened a little way and then closed again, admitting in that instant a very short boy who looked a little underfed even for his size. Nobody paid him the least attention. In the first place, there were only three people in the locker room. One was a member of the varsity, a dark, Italian-looking boy dressed ready to go out in sweat pants and a sweat shirt with a picture of a winged spiked shoe printed in red on its breast. He sat tying on his lightweight cross-country shoes in front of a star-spangled locker, sky blue in color and covered with white stars, with a red-and-white stripe running around the edges of its door. Most of the lockers were dark green, but there were a half dozen or so such splashy ones. The dark boy sat on one of two wooden benches running the length of the room, about two feet out from the lockers. On the opposite bench a boy in track shorts lay stomach down, his head to one side, his arms hanging, while a serious-faced man, an assistant coach, picked with his fingers very fast at the backs of the other's legs, snick-snick-snick-snick-snick. The liniment he was using smelled sharply above the prevailing, long-accumulated odor of sweat.

Turning from the door, the short boy stepped over one of the benches in a motion remarkably easy, considering his size. With his face in the corner made by the last locker and the wall, he began to undress. He had a blue looseleaf notebook with the name of the school on it, and he laid it on the bench. Then he took off a brown knit sweater, which he folded up on top of the notebook. Under that he wore a white shirt starched so stiffly that when he took it off it held the creases of his wearing and would only fold brokenly in a high springy pile. Now he simply stood for a moment in his undershirt with slender shoulders and brown hair about the color of his sweater, wearing a pair of darker brown pants. He looked like a boy who had been sent to the corner for something he ought to be ashamed of. He had been trying to get something out of his pocket that didn't want to come, but all at once, as he stood tugging, the thing gave, flew out—an ordinary piece of blue cloth—with a sweep and flourish that seemed to disconcert him. Immediately he loosened his belt and let his trousers fall to his ankles. He stepped out of them and into the blue cloth thing, a cheap pair of gym shorts with a string pull at the waist. These on, he was uniformed. The brown pants he rolled up with his little pile, bent and tightened the strings of his shoes, and, fixing his eyes on the door at the far end of the room, walked toward it between the lockers, a very thin boy who might have been called lanky if he had been a foot taller. He opened the door, looked out, and finding that it led to the playing field, disappeared through it, running.

In the locker room the varsity member, his dark hair hanging over his face in long Vaselined strands, had finished with his running shoes. With a shake he laid his hair back on his head in orderly lines and, at the same time, gave one single, sophisticated glance across at the coach.

Still picking away, the man said, "He could grow."

John Sobieski—this was the short boy's name—found himself running out of the school building's shadow into the warm sunlight, over hard, even ground covered with short grass which stretched away, from beneath his own thin legs, into the biggest flat field he had ever seen. Moving across it, he passed over gleaming lines of white lime powder and, except for them, did not feel he was moving at all, running though he was across the big green field in the sun. He saw, far away on his left, the football players, tiny, bright-colored people, hunching and waiting, rising and moving and entangling all together in waves, heard whistles, and saw before him, past many lines and various goalposts, more boys—the running team. Many were lying all about on the ground, but many were standing up too, all upright together in a tight kind of pack that vibrated and moved around like a thing in itself, something very bright, red and white, spinning there in the sunshine on top of uncountable bare legs. As he came nearer he saw that the people on the ground were only discarded sweat suits with nobody in them; the runners were all up and gathered around a very tall man who was waving a clipboard of papers in the air above his head as he spoke. The runners had on bright red shirts with lettering across the chest and white shorts edged in red, and they shifted and pranced on their slight little running shoes as on hooves, their bright uniforms blended and mingled to make up that whirling bright-colored thing which, idling nervous and impatient in place up to now, suddenly lurched and flexed and strained within, before extending itself loosely and easily away as, on its many legs, it began trotting off over the field. John Sobieski ran as hard as he knew how; as he pounded up, the big man flagged him on with the paper-fluttering clipboard, boomed, "Right there . . . after those men!" and John Sobieski was past and pounding after the pack of runners that stretched away loose and red and white in the sunlight toward a far fence bordering the field.

So they were running, and John Sobieski was with them. But already his legs felt heavy, and he was breathing faster than he had ever breathed in his life. He had come running all the way across the big green field, only to find that they had started already. The unfairness of it made him hot and sick. He had come out for cross-country knowing he would have to run miles, but they had started before he was ready. His throat ached; his feet he raised up and clapped down like flatirons. As he ran he thought to himself, "It's not my fault they started before I was ready. . . . I'll stop right here, somewhere."

They had come to the end of the field and passed through a gate; they were running on a sidewalk past houses. A boy in a red shirt was running not far in front of him. John Sobieski could see his own shoes hitting the sidewalk one after the other, while he himself seemed to ride above somewhere as on some funny kind of running machine. Bumping along in this way, he was interested to find, after a while, that his machine seemed to be moving a little faster than the other boy's machine. Fascinated, with curiosity and detachment mixed, he watched the increasing nearness of the other boy's white pants—for some reason that was all he could see—until gradually he came alongside the other. Both of them were bouncing up and down furiously, but the other boy seemed to bounce up and down in the same spot, while John Sobieski was very slowly moving, until, gradually again, he couldn't see the other boy anymore. But it didn't make any difference; there was another boy in front of him.

And this one approached and went by, and another one sprang up. Regular as telephone poles they went slowly by him until there had been six. He counted them because he didn't have anything else to do. Then everything grew dark, and though it was only because they had entered a park and were running on a path through woods, John Sobieski didn't know it. All he knew was that he was running after a strange white flag that moved before him in the dim. Fluttering and twinkling, always ahead, it dipped and wound with the path, and John Sobieski behind. At last, after a long time, they broke out into the light. There was the fence around the shadowed green playing field and, inside it, the football players, looking weary in their dirtied uniforms, and beyond them, far across the field, the high school building. John Sobieski's heart lifted. He saw that the white flag was nothing but another pair of the white shorts edged with red. The boy running in them was only strides in front, and, though he was tired, he set himself to beat this one boy at least. As he sprinted around the fence toward the school—which burned at its edges like a coal, blocking off the sun—it seemed to him he had just started, he was virtually flying, he would pass them all. And he did overtake the boy in the twinkling white pants, and another.

Standing up against the bricks of the school building, the assistant coach, who had just finished a rubdown in the locker room, watched the line of long-distance runners coming around the fence. They toiled with incredible slowness and suffering, each one preserving only the formal attitude of running. Long ago they had lost the speed the attitude is supposed to produce. He watched them toiling, one by one, and as he watched, one moving slightly faster than the rest strained painfully closer to the next man, painfully abreast, and in time came up behind the next runner, whom he would probably pass before reaching the school. The coach turned and walked swiftly toward a corner of the building.

Now the leaders had reached a gate by the school. There something halted them, making them run into one another in their weariness. As John Sobieski came up he stumbled and fell against the slippery neck of the boy in front of him. The boy's sweat came away on his lips, and as they passed through the gate a man shouted something at each one. John Sobieski felt his shoulder grabbed and squeezed.

"Thirteen!" the man said to him. It was the assistant coach.

Nobody was running anymore. They all walked around in circles. So did John Sobieski. He felt sick again. His chest and throat exploded every time he tried to breathe, and he was terribly hot. What he wanted most was just to be unconscious, but he couldn't bear to sit or lie down. He saw a boy crouching on the ground, retching onto the grass between his hands. Somebody had brought in the sweat clothes off the playing field, and boys were picking their own out of a pile. They hung their sweat shirts over their shoulders like capes and tied the arms in front. After a while John Sobieski began to feel better. He walked toward the locker room, more or less with five other runners. Just in front walked the boy who had vomited, with a friend supporting him on either side—a sweat shirt was thrown on John Sobieski's back; the arms came dangling down in front of him. He never saw who did it, because nobody seemed to look at him or pay much attention to him.

Back in the locker room it was strangely quiet, considering the place was filling with runners, who sat down on the benches or tinkered quietly at their locker doors. John Sobieski went to his own pile of things, turned his back, and let his blue shorts slide down to his shoes. Then, holding his brown pants open, he stepped into them, stuffed the shorts into his pocket, pulled the crackling white shirt over his undershirt and the sweater over that; and leaving the sweat shirt neatly folded on the bench, he turned around and stood, his back to the entrance door, surveying the room. It was as if he had only just come in and was looking for something. Now he smelled the perspiration smell fresh and strong and moist, mingling with the steam that clouded out from the top of the shower-room door, and mingling, too, with all the hubbub that had come up in the short time he was changing. Everybody in the steamy room seemed naked, and they all seemed unnaturally up above him, but that was only because nearly all the runners by now were standing on the two benches, which were two parallel pedestals for their sweating, moving nude bodies. John Sobieski moved between them in his brown sweater, looking very intently for something, and having no attention paid him. He even walked a little way into the shower room, clothes and shoes on and all, and peered through the steam at the runners there. But nobody seemed to notice this either.

Finally he went out by the same door he had first come in, passed through a few halls, and left the building.

"Thirty-four," he thought to himself as he stepped outside into the cold afternoon air. "I beat twenty-one at least."

He walked home. The night passed, and then the next day—but John Sobieski couldn't have said how. He was a small, thin boy sitting at back desks in various classrooms with a blue notebook open in front of him, but what he was seeing was not a teacher or a blackboard, but four or five boys in twinkling white pants running before him, and he himself coming up behind, planning how he was going to take them.

By four in the afternoon he was on the field again. The runners were warming up. Some were doing pushups; some were lying on their backs on the damp ground and springing up in quick little sitting motions; some just stood around with serious faces, paying no attention to others; some were rotating their torsos, with hands on hips. John Sobieski looked around carefully and did some of the same things. The tall man of the day before was nowhere to be seen, but after a few minutes the assistant coach came walking out toward them with a boy on either side. His face was hard and dark, but his eyes were large and white and serious, and appeared to be considering other things even as he said something brief and imperative to the boy next to him. This boy gave one single vigorous nod and without warning whirled, and was away. Instantly the others took after him, and John Sobieski, who hadn't been ready for it to happen so fast, was left doing pushups on the ground.

He jumped up and ran after them, though he knew it was hopeless;

he was already 50 yards behind the pack and at least 100 behind the leaders. For the second time, they had started before he was ready. Before they had even left the playing field, he felt sicker than he had at any time the previous day. His body was a misery to him. He ran along beside the endless steel wire fence crying to himself, "Why did I think I could run! I can't! I'm not any good!" He ran another hundred yards and he prayed, "Please let me just finish. I don't want to beat anybody. All I want to do is just finish." Because somewhere inside him was the idea that if he could endure it just this one time, then maybe he would get his fair chance, when he could really do something, tomorrow.

His father had warned him. At the end of summer, when John Sobieski came home one night and told his mother and father he wasn't going back to St. Stephen's anymore but was going up to the big city high school, his father had asked him: "What do you think you're going to get by going up there?"

"Everything," said the boy. "They got everything up there, so you can do what you want, when you get out. You can be whatever you want."

His father was smoking. At first he said something, muttering only to himself, while he shook out a long wooden match. "Nah—you can't do what you want, John Sobieski," he said then, and blew out smoke. "You just try it and you'll find out. You better stay around here. We'll teach you everything you need to know."

"No, I'm going up there."

His father looked straight at him over the table, with something ugly in his look. "Do you know who you are? D'you even know your own name?"

"Sure. Everybody knows who they are."

"No they don't. But you, you're John Sobieski. That was my father's name too. He came over here when he wasn't any bigger than you are. He was one of the ones that helped put up St. Stephen's in the first place. I went there myself and so did my brothers. That's where we belong—and you're just the same as we are. No use trying to be any different, because you belong around here. You ain't ever going to be any different from that."

"Yes I am," said John Sobieski. "Oh, yes I am."

And they looked at each other, the two of them almost exactly the same size except that the father was older, and so everything about him was somehow thicker, and more unwieldy. John Sobieski's mother kept out of it, away at the stove. The two looked at each other from opposing chairs until the father's expression broke, and he turned away.

"You think you can do what you want," he said, quite differently. "You start out all right with it too. You leave the house every morning and you only come back at night. You get pretty far away. After a while you think you don't have to come back at all. Then one day you get caught out there all by yourself—and you get licked, good."

"No," said John Sobieski.

"Stay where you are," his father pleaded. "It ain't so bad down around here."

"No, you talk like that because you're old. Well, I'm not old. I'm not going to listen to it!" He got up and went into his bedroom, where he could be by himself.

Struggling, spreading out, the runners pounded along upon a hard city sidewalk. They strained and reached, with knees and toes and shoulders; each step had only one job—to slide over as much ground as possible. Most of them could not see, and none paid any attention to the big car that followed along in the street keeping pace, but inside it the head coach, the tall man who usually carried the clipboard thick with papers, hovered just beyond the toil of the runners. Ahead of him, in the next block, he watched an indistinct cluster of legs and a flash of color separate themselves, as he came closer, into a runner in blue shorts and white top trailing a line of three abreast in the red-and-white uniforms. As blue-and-white closed with the red, the legs became entangled and inextricable again, until suddenly somebody got stepped on. A boy in red shirt and white pants reeled to the side, off the curb and into the road, where he fought to recover himself, climbing back to the sidewalk only to drop rapidly to the rear, his pace broken. Meantime blue-and-white had moved up between the other two, so that the three of them, bouncing up and down, remained for a long moment like a slot machine come to rest after changing, red-blue-red, until gradually blue-and-white disengaged himself again and moved out in front.

The coach accelerated and passed on, but John Sobieski didn't notice him. He had hardly even seen the three runners. His eyes were wet and partly closed as he ran, and all at once he knew that something was in front of him, preventing him. More or less, he saw them. But there wasn't anything he could do except keep running, because he knew if he were checked at all he would have to stop altogether. Then after a moment he was clear and by himself again. He ran on. No vision of the school building raised him. It was a gray, damp day. He didn't know how far they still had to go. He passed more runners, singles or straggling twos, without any struggle. He couldn't think about taking them, or of anything; they were just going slower than he was, and he moved by.

It was over abruptly. They passed through the same gate as yesterday, freely, without being stopped, the runners all streaming in and dispersing, and as soon as John Sobieski realized where they were and stopped trying to run he collapsed.

"Walk him around!" somebody shouted. It was the tall head coach. He had parked his car and now stood just inside the gate, wearing a long raincoat. "What's the trouble?"

Two runners had already lifted John Sobieski to his feet, but he was fighting them off, and they couldn't hold him; they were tired themselves.

"I don't know . . . he's talking to himself," one answered between breaths. "He's trying to say numbers."

"Walk him around," the tall man repeated. "That's the way to finish a run. There isn't a one of you should have anything left at all!"

The two of them took John Sobieski's arms across their shoulders and together they walked him around on the grass. After a while they had their own wind back, but as soon as John Sobieski got breath enough, he began to cough. The afternoon was chilly and damp. He took several wheezing breaths and then coughed again, badly. By the time the others had walked off the effects of their run, he was coughing steadily for long stretches.

The two boys took him into the locker room. They sat him on a bench in front of their own lockers and got his clothes off, while he continued coughing. They walked him with care through the jostling, sweating, strong-smelling runners into the steamy shower room, and one readied a shower while the other held John Sobieski. Then they put him under it and left him.

Later, when the two runners were dressed and ready to leave, they turned to find the small thin boy standing naked across the bench from them, dripping onto the floor.

"Feel better now?" the bigger one asked. "What's the matter, forget your towel?" He drew his own heavy damp one from his gym bag and took the one that his friend was carrying rolled up under one arm and hung them both over John Sobieski's shoulder. The small boy opened his mouth as if to say something, but instead he was overcome by a fit of coughing.

The two had to go. "Give them to us tomorrow," said the one, pausing in the locker-room door. He was a big, strong-looking boy with a very large head. "Ernest Borkmann and Joe Felice." Still John Sobieski stood, just looking at the two boys; he was fighting a rising cough, and the door had already closed before he called after them:

"John Sobieski!"

He went back to the bench with his towels. All the runners had left. He wiped himself, put on his clothes, and put his running shorts in his pocket. But he didn't leave the two towels behind; he took them along home with him. His second day's running was over.

When he reached his own street it was dark, and a cold, foggy rain was drifting down. By the light of street lights the wooden two-family houses rose high all around him, their thrusting, peaked roofs shoulder to shoulder, the mist falling from the darkness above upon their wet slate backs. Inside they were warmly lighted behind curtains.

John Sobieski went straight to his own bedroom. His mother and father, eating already, could hear him coughing behind the door. Finally he came out and sat down. A fire was going in the kitchen stove, since it was still too early in the year to light the furnace, and in the sudden, close warmth John Sobieski began to perspire and then to cough and cough. His eyes would become fixed, his face red and then contorted as he tried to stop himself, at least long enough to eat; but the thing would burst out at last and leave him shaking, his eyes watering. He drank cups and cups of coffee, which his mother poured out for him. His father read a newspaper on the other side of the table and glanced at John Sobieski when he coughed, but said nothing.

Later, as he sat on the sofa in the living room, wearing his heavy sweater, the cough subsided. His mother and father sat across from him on either side in upholstered chairs; his mother's fingers were crocheting something nimbly, and his father still had his paper. John Sobieski sat by himself on the sofa doing nothing, thinking about nothing, just sitting still under a lamp and gazing blankly at his parents. At one point, as his father folded over his paper to study the lower corner, he caught his son gazing at him.

"What now?" he demanded.

"Nothing. Can't I look?" said John Sobieski.

His mother, too, raised her head, worried-looking and sorrowful. She reminded John Sobieski of those old women with kerchiefs around their heads whom he used to see when he had been an altar boy serving early mass. They knelt and prayed, holding their beads, with a look upon their faces and in their eyes as though the whole world were filled with sorrow; and John Sobieski hated sorrow; he couldn't stand it.

"Oh, I don't like that coughing," said his mother, shaking her head.

But John Sobieski didn't mind even sorrow, now. All he wanted was to sit, just as he was, in his own house, doing nothing, thinking about nothing at all.

Then morning came again, and John Sobieski must go up to the high school. He took the two towels plus a third one for himself that he got from his mother, his running shorts, his notebook, his lunch bag, and a black umbrella of his father's, because the morning was dark and threatening rain again. By the time he reached the school his arms ached from carrying so many things, and when he thought of the running he would have to do that day he felt sorry for himself and thought, "No wonder I can't run. Nobody else has to wear themselves out just getting here!"

The rain in clinging drops or running down the panes of the windows, the shifting light and dark places in the sky—all were watched apprehensively by John Sobieski as he sat in the classrooms' dim electric light that could barely establish itself all day against the bleak light from outside. After his last class, as he walked among crowds of others through the dim and noisy corridors, Ernest Borkmann found him.

The big boy took him down to the wing of the school where the lockers were, past the door of the cross-country room and on to a further door where he left him. For one moment John Sobieski hesitated, but then he let himself inside quickly and faced the room.

In front of him, behind a desk, sat the tall man of the clipboard—a large and handsome-appearing man with long white hair combed back, seen now for the first time indoors, without his coat and hat. Leaning back with folded hands, he was talking to the smaller, darker, bony-looking young man who sat on the window sill with his back to the rain, his knees drawn up high and his feet on the radiator.

"Is that him?" the tall man asked. "The one that runs in the blue pants?"

The other coach only nodded gloomily, watching John Sobieski, the whites of his eyes showing in his dark face.

"What do they call him, anyway?"

A little smile seemed always to be hanging at the corners of the white-haired man's eyes and lips, as though to him things were always cheerful and a bit funny somehow.

"John Sobieski," responded the boy himself.

"John Sobieski . . . I hear that John Sobieski's a pretty good runner, Stan."

"He does the best he can."

"No, sir," said the white-haired man, "he's good, because he likes to run. He likes to go out there and beat those other boys. He likes to take 'em. Now, how's he going to do it the way he's been, Stanley? That isn't right. We have to give John Sobieski a chance, the same as everybody else. You come here, John Sobieski!"

The tall man reached forward and pointed to a box at the front of his desk. Of course it had been there all along, but for John Sobieski it only came into being at that moment. The boy opened it. Inside, under tissue paper, his hands grasped a pair of the spikeless cross-country shoes.

He lifted them out. They were small in size, for his own little feet, narrow and light and pointed, with hard and sharp rubber bottoms for digging in and starting; and he could see himself already, as from some distance away, the black shoes slashing like hoofs, slashing and slashing in arcs, the shoes of John Sobieski!

"John Sobieski's going to Utica with us," said the head coach, grinning. "John Sobieski's going to run at Syracuse—John Sobieski's going to New York City!"

"Well, you get a uniform and sweat suit from the manager, John Sobieski," the younger man told him more soberly. "Put a towel around your neck when you go outside and don't try to run very hard today. It's too cold for it."

The runners jogged across the field and gathered together under the drizzling clouds. Neither coach was anywhere around. John Sobieski had been one of the first ones out, and for once, at least, he was ready. Imperceptibly this time, without a signal of any kind, the runners began their run. They went off slowly, without making any sound, all the move and flash of their bright uniforms muffled within the heavy gray sweat suits. They moved at a shuffle just over a walk, then at a trot and then a little better. In the beginning they ran very close to one another in a tight pack, and yet in rigid silence, as though pushing together against some enormous burden, one so heavy that it might never be moved at all without an effort from each so intense as to isolate him from all the others.

Once outside the fence, John Sobieski found the pack lengthening. As it stretched out gradually, it seemed to snap in two. He was the last of the line that was moving ahead, and there were nine runners in front of him. He stayed where he was without working very hard. Then all at once, when he was scarcely tired, he spied the school building ahead of him, and he pulled out and ran as fast as he could. He passed the others easily, every one—not so fast as if they were standing still, but as if he were moving about twice as fast—and entered the gate first by a long interval.

Instead of stopping, he kept running straight on into the locker room. There he took a hurried shower and had already dried himself by the time the others began to come in, talking quietly, in twos and threes. John Sobieski dressed as fast as he could, his face buried in the new locker that had been assigned to him. He was afraid to turn around because they might all be looking at him, because he had come in first. He felt as though he were charged with electricity, and the figure 1 were shining out upon his back.

He was sweating again by the time he reached home. His coughing was so continuous that he knew he would not be able to stop it, or even halt it for a few minutes, until he had something to drink. But even so he went directly to his bedroom and carefully spread out on the bed his new running things, which were now all wrinkled and damp. The unfamiliar bright-colored things attracted his mother and father, and they came in to look.

"Where can I put these to dry . . ." John Sobieski demanded. But then he closed his eyes, grasping the long bar at the foot of his bed; his upper body leaned forward, the tears pressed at his shut eyes, and the cough came rolling out of him. ". . . where nobody will touch them?"

"Touch them," said his father angrily. "What are we going to touch them for?" And he left the room.

"We can hang them up over the stove," his mother assured him with bright, grieving eyes that only made the boy furious. "Come and eat with us."

"I'll be there!" he told her. "I have to see about this stuff first."

It was a Friday night. John Sobieski had the whole weekend to dry his running things, and on Monday he went to the school equipped just like all the rest—except that he had come in first the last time they had run. But that same day the figure 1, which he could almost feel burning upon his back once he was among the runners again, faded out. Nobody paid any attention to it.

Now every day was bright and blue. The cold air burned like alcohol on the skin of his arms and legs when he took off his sweat clothes and began to run in the afternoons. He was happy just to run with the others, keeping up with them along different streets of the city that he had not known anything about before. In the first time trials he finished twelfth.

The coaches took fifteen boys to run at Utica the following Saturday. They drove a few hours in cars, got out to warm up behind a strange and brand-new high school, gathered on a line in a bunch—one of a dozen such, each in its own bright colors—and then a gun was fired, a cloud of white smoke rose above the man who had fired it, and the bunches all sprang into a forward wave to cross the field together. John Sobieski was left behind, exhausted, right at the start. He decided he would just finish the race, this one last time, and then he would never run again. He felt that way all through the unfamiliar woods and as he came down out of them onto the field again, into the mouth of the bullpen between funneling ropes that crowded him against boys in front and on both sides until he stood still with one of the coarse-fibered ropes in either hand. Somebody wrote something on his back—a piece of paper with a number on it had been pinned to his red shirt—and then he staggered away, to walk around and begin coughing.

Riding home in the head coach's car, he learned their team had won the meet. Their first five men had come in second, fourth, fifth, seventh, and eighth for a score of 26. John Sobieski found the number 24 written in pencil underneath the big printed number on the paper he had torn from his back. Besides that, he had a blue satin ribbon. Two hundred boys had run, but only the first twenty-five received ribbons.

Monday his name appeared in the city newspaper. "A freshman, John Sobieski, was the Red and White's tenth finisher." Ernest Borkmann had cut the story out of the paper and showed it to him in the locker room before practice.

"Where did you come in?" John Sobieski asked him.

The big boy folded the clipping carefully with large strong fingers and put it away in his wallet "I got sick," he answered, frowning. "I didn't finish."

Saturday they ran at Syracuse, and there were twice as many runners. The high school placed second. John Sobieski, their seventh man in, finished thirty-ninth. It meant he had improved about nine places. And he beat three of their own runners who had finished ahead of him the week before.

This time he rode home with the younger coach. The other runners were subdued; John Sobieski's continual coughing was louder than all their quiet talk. It filled the car, though he strained to suppress it by sitting motionless with all the air breathed out of him, so that he would have nothing to cough with. But he had to breathe again sometime, and then the air would rush into his lungs, explode, and be thrown out once more. "Roll up your windows," the coach told the runners. Twice they stopped at gas stations to let him drink water, but even so he would only start coughing again in a few minutes.

Now John Sobieski began to notice that boys on the running team nodded or spoke to him when he saw them in the school's halls, and even a few others seemed to know who he was. He lived only for running. He got up in the morning and walked to the school for it, waiting all day for that living half hour when he emerged on the playing field and ran, suffering, until he swore he would never do it again, and at last finished somehow and returned to the locker room. His life was running. It was different now than ever before. "I only eat and sleep at home," he thought to himself as he sat and watched his father and mother in the evening. "They see me go away, and they see me come back—but they don't know what I do!"

It was five o'clock in the morning. New York City, the biggest city in America, lay more than 150 miles away to the east and south. The head coach had already driven off with five boys, and now the other coach and two remaining runners and a manager all got into a little car that stood by itself at the curb in front of the school. John Sobieski had the front seat. He hunched down inert and from there watched the dark houses, the peaking rooftops, roll by. Nobody said anything. The manager and the runner in the back seat were both trying to sleep. Once they were well into the country, John Sobieski sat up and looked out. It was just getting light. The sky was gray, as though cloudy. In the open fields there was light, but everything else remained shadowy. Buildings that they passed stood gray and chill-appearing, except for yellow windows distinct and square in a few isolated houses. The boy was glad to see them. It struck him as cheerful somehow, for it meant that people were awake within and beginning their work for the day. Something in him yearned toward them, but he was going to New York City; and he was glad to be going to New York, but he didn't want to run there.

The next time he looked out it was fully light; the day would clear. They were driving on a Parkway now, twin concrete highways that seemed to descend endlessly taking huge dips and turns. As the little car rose up with engine roaring to meet each new crest John Sobieski waited to see if the city were ahead, but the road on the other side only plunged them downhill again, twisting out of sight among hills and woods.

He couldn't sleep, but he closed his eyes for a long, long time, hoping that when he opened them again they would be there, and he would at least have rested a little.

What made him sit up again finally was a loud whining of tires. Then outside, all around, he saw more cars, a great many of them and all going to the same place. The young coach, sitting next to him, was very busy driving. John Sobieski saw that the man's face was now intent, his eyes fiercely concentrated ahead. He was passing the other cars as though they were runners. They went between some fairly high buildings and then ran downhill across a bridge; the coach paid money out his window, they went on down the ramp, blue water came around on the right, and immediately up in front of them, very high, a suspension bridge swung across to the other side. They drove underneath it and there were the tall buildings of New York standing out ahead as he had thought they would be—except that they weren't down close to the water, but were built on top of a steep hill rising on the left.

Just then the runner in the back seat—it was the same dark-haired boy who had been sitting on the bench when John Sobieski first entered the locker room—called out, "Hey, we're on the island!"

The older runner knew they should be running at a park somewhere back in the Bronx. The coach knew it too—he had run there himself when he had been a cross-country runner—but coming into the city he had missed his turn and was still looking for it when he had been caught among the cars rushing into Manhattan. He got off the parkway now and they ran steeply uphill between buildings, all of them bigger than John Sobieski had ever seen, but not what he had expected of New York either. They were big dirty boxes with innumerable windows in which, it looked like, people lived. It gave him a pang to think that.

They kept turning into different streets, driving fast, and then they were out of Manhattan again. All at once the coach turned off the highway and drove straight across a flat athletic field. Right where he stopped the car the runners were massed—bright-colored, moving and shifting by the hundreds, tightening up—and just as they went to get out, a shot was fired. The pack jolted, loosened, and stretched away like an expanding accordion, the farther edge moving rapidly over the field, while the near edge remained on the starting line playing out runners in waves. The coach swore aloud as he helped rip jackets and sweat clothes from John Sobieski and the other runner. Then the two of them were on the field running, before some had even left the starting line.

And if ever they had started before John Sobieski was ready, it was this time. Next to him, in front of him, behind him, shoving him, were runners; and he himself, short and thin, unable even to see above them. He felt as though he were dying, and as a drowning person sees his whole life, he saw his running. Then he knew he couldn't run at all; he was always sick, he only beat others by tormenting himself. And he hated it, because he cared only about beating the others and not all of them either, but just those on his own team, for of the rest there were so many as to make his own struggles seem feeble, indistinguishable.

Yet even now, as though it were a thing quite separate from himself, his small body was pressing forward through the thick of the runners. His eye was caught by the flash of a red shirt that he knew must be from his own school. Slowly, he was coming up to it. He made his way sideways between two larger boys, and when another boy just ahead stumbled, sighing, and gave up, John Sobieski dodged around him and into the free pocket, darting forward unhindered until he was running behind the familiar red shirt. When it found openings, he followed after. When it forced a way, shoving runners aside, he went through as though he had done it for himself.

They had passed over the Parkway on a bridge of stone arches and now they were running on a bridle path that turned and climbed upward under trees, around the bulk of a great hill on the other side. The stream of the pack had narrowed until it was only four to five runners wide, and at one edge the hillside fell away steeply—down to John Sobieski couldn't see what, though he was running on that side himself, just within the pack.

Twisting slowly uphill, flashing gay-colored, the pack surged over the crest of the hill and slid downward again, winding around, faster and faster. Somewhere John Sobieski had left the red shirt behind and now that the race was downhill, he tried to break out and pass runners, but he couldn't. It was impossible, with the runners pounding on all sides of him; he couldn't move from his place. He stood it until he couldn't any longer; then he pulled abreast of the boy immediately in front of him and went through diagonally to the right. He saw he was free. He let himself out, his feet smashing into the ground in long downhill strides. But while he was passing, exposed out there, an impulse that originated in an obscure movement somewhere deep inside the pack suddenly reached him and struck him through the elbow of the boy beside him. For an instant he continued to run wildly along the edge of the hill, with his arms waving and snatching for balance, but he was being toppled inexorably, and John Sobieski went down running, but he couldn't keep on his feet. A young tree caught him by the arm, spun him around and threw him, rolling, down the slope. He hit things; but the pain wasn't so great as the exhaustion and sickness that came on immediately as he ceased running. He lay on his side on dry leaves at the bottom, his body jackknifed and heaving. Overhead was the thunder of the passing pack, the rustle of their feet among fallen leaves, the muffled reverberations of the shocks of a thousand galloping legs all shod in the sharp-pointed running shoes like hoofs—passing by, pounding, and gone; a pause—a scattered hurry of stragglers, now one, now several; their breathing like the furious labor of bicycle pumps, their feet clumping—dying away; now all gone altogether—passed on.

He was left alone. Everything was quiet. A hot sickness, separate from the ache of lungs and throat, went back and forth over him, for the first time unmixed with the bustle of others walking around feeling the same way. He hated himself, he hated his body that gasped and gasped for breath among the crisp leaves. He could not bear to think that even though he had lost, he must still suffer for trying. For a while he did nothing; he didn't even try to get up, because there wasn't any use in it. But he started to feel the cold on his arms and legs and through his thin uniform. When he finally got to his feet he was so weak and listless he could hardly climb the steep bank. He pulled himself up from one young tree to another, and then clung to them on the uphill side, resting.

Up on the bridle path again, his coughing came over him. It began loud and wet, and would get worse, he knew, harsher and drier, as his running sickness improved, but now it was all the same to him. He walked downhill weakly, without purpose, staggering and coughing. As he came out of the woods, the dark-haired runner, recovered from his run, his sweat suit on, met him in the middle of the stone bridge over the parkway. Beneath them, the bright automobiles whined in both directions. John Sobieski leaned on the boy, and together they went down to the field, an enormous one big enough for twenty football games. On the far side of it the young coach's tiny car stood by itself, and, as they were crossing, the man got out and came toward them.

"Somebody pushed me. . . . I fell over," John Sobieski tried to explain, between fits of coughing, but the man only scowled, glanced briefly into the face of the other runner, and didn't answer.

They got him into his sweat clothes and inside the car. They rolled up the windows and laid him by himself on the back seat, with the coats of all three boys thrown over him. The coach and the other two rode up front, mostly in silence, while John Sobieski coughed with a horrible crouping dry sound all the way back to their own city.

From where he lay he could see it growing dark outside. The shapes of roofs were sharp in the cold sky. He was aware of the fits and starts of the automobile and the traffic sounds of the city outside; of the rush of cold air entering and the voices of the two boys briefly saying good-bye; finally of the emptiness of the car with only himself and the coach remaining—when at last the car stopped for good.

"Is this where you live, John Sobieski?" the man asked from out on the sidewalk. He looked up at the gray two-family house, while the boy was climbing out over the front seat.

"You listen to me now. I want you to get into that house and not come out of it for a month. You're sick. You belong in bed, for God's sake, and not out killing yourself running. It isn't running anymore, when you have to trade on your health just to get a place. That doesn't do us any good—it isn't reliable. You go in there and get better. Forget all about running, for a while."

The man spoke angrily. He held the car door open against the wind with his back and watched John Sobieski, but the boy just stood before him saying nothing. He got back into his car and drove away.

John Sobieski made his way upstairs. He went right to his room and to bed. His mother saw at once that he was sick and looked after him.

He stayed in bed three weeks. Most of the time he slept. There was nothing he wanted to get up for. After the first week he didn't cough anymore; as long as he didn't run it would be all right. His father came in to see him after supper. The older man seemed a little embarrassed. He would bring a kitchen chair and set it just inside the bedroom door, and talk across the space at his son, who would be watching him, lying deep in his bed, his brown head on a big pillow.

"How do you feel tonight?"

"All right."

The father nodded. He wouldn't smoke in the bedroom. He sat for a while. "The one time I was in New York," he said, "I went on the train with my father. When we got there we just stood up in some place and ate sauerkraut and frankfurts. That's all I remember about it."

John Sobieski listened, but didn't say anything. After a bit his father got up to go out. "Well, stay where you are now."

"Listen," John Sobieski called after him, "I'm still going back there, after I get better."

His father looked down at the linoleum. "They still want you, after you got licked like that?"

"I don't know. It doesn't matter if they want me, though—I'm going to go."

His father went away.

In the dark bedroom, John Sobieski closed his eyes. He could hear the wind blowing outside between his house and the house next door. A boy moved before him in the dark; John Sobieski was coming up closer, from behind. . . . He caught himself and swore, and thrashed in the bed with regret. He couldn't remember running without remembering his failure. Yet in twenty minutes more, going off to sleep, he would see before him a boy dressed in white shorts and a red shirt, and he himself, coming up behind, planning how he was going to take him.

Murder, Malice, and Madness

THE RUNNER

James Tabor

(1979)

Out of a silver heat mirage he ran. Two lanes of blacktop stretched straight and flat in front of him, straight and flat behind. August-tall corn walled in the road and its red-sand shoulders. A half mile away was a blue-dark wall of woods.

On the road it was neither cool nor dark. The sky burned, and under him the paving was a black mirror reflecting sun-fire. Sweat sprayed from his skin with each footstrike, so that he ran in a hot mist of his own creation. With each slap on the softened asphalt, his soles absorbed heat that rose through his arches and ankles and the stems of his shins. It was a carnival of pain, but he loved each stride because the running distilled him to essence and the heat hastened this distillation.

He wore a pair of blue Etonic Streetfighters, faded red gym shorts, a neck chain hung with two battered dog tags, and nothing else. The plates of his stomach muscles rippled with each stretched-out stride that floated him over the roadway. In the heat he heard the light *hsssss* of his own breathing, and the rhythmic *click-cleck click-cleck* of his footstrikes. Beyond these, in the sound-discouraging heat there were only snakes rustling in the rows of corn for something to kill.

He enjoyed running here, in the flat red corn country of Maryland's Eastern Shore. The roads were straight, traffic infrequent, problems few. And that was not unimportant to him. He wore his hair a little long for such original country, but he knew that the district's lone trooper was a whiskey drunk with all road love burned out of him. So here he could run without trouble, and he could rent a cheap clean room with a window over water, and he could make a few dollars working fishing boats that slid daily onto the Bay. That was all he wanted. He did not think it was too much.

From the distance a sound reached him, but he saw nothing. At first it was such a faint sound that he mistook it for the buzz of a diving bee, and prepared to swat it from his path. Then he saw a spot wavering on the horizon, and it grew larger.

A motorcycle. Jesus can't you keep them in the God-damned cities?

Rushing toward him, growing by the second, the cycle revealed itself: a fat chopped Honda, front fork pushed out, the frame an intestinal tangle of glistening chrome. He hated cycles, and not only for their buzzing snarls that fractured the peace of his running and filled the air with stink. Once, running in New Hampshire on the roads that coil around Winnipesaukee, he had been corralled by a gang from the Grafton races. For them at first it had been fun, circling their hogs around him on the dusty deserted road, spraying him with beer and urine, laughing, then readying to leave. But he was one of those men whose skin does not thicken into armor against the forces of lunacy. An eternal innocent, he existed in a state of near-constant amazement at the flaws in his universe. So he had cracked the throat of one with the flat edge of his hand, and then they had exacted a toll of torn flesh and splintered bones that had kept him from the roads for seven months.

The rider of this lone cycle reclined as though on a lounge, his back sloped against the sissy bar, his legs splayed and feet propped on high pegs. He wore tennis shoes and cutoff blue jeans and a yellow tank top. A full Bell helmet's black visor hid his face. When he roared by, blasting the runner with grit, scorched air, and exhaust stench, he made a languid salute: one middle finger, stiffly uplifted.

I seem unable to elude them. They cover the country like locusts, he thought, not only about the motorcyclists. But he could not really say to himself, as he ran between the green walls of corn, that he was surprised. Long ago he had realized that the world was divided, and he had begun trying to live his life free from the interference of a certain kind of people, who *drive station wagons, hunt deer, live near cities, watch television, mow lawns* (he ticked them off in rhythm to his foot-strikes) *read news-papers play softball go shopping buy insurance smile marry vote pay taxes pray.*

He was neither an indigent nor a criminal. In fact he was educated, and a decorated veteran of combat, and a man who had once fit comfortably into a satisfactory niche. In Vermont, he had taught in a college. But, finally unable to bear the dooming of rich young minds, he had abandoned that to teach skiing. Later, in Montana, he had trained sled dogs. In California he had rescued mountain climbers and worked in a sleeping-bag factory. In Florida he had guided men to good bonefish flats. In Maryland, now, he worked the high-prowed boats, and ran. He had always run for solace, even before the tide of things he despised began washing him from his progressively less satisfactory niches. Now he had stayed nearly a year in the cove-locked shore towns, liking the red country and the great Bay and the people whose faces, as flat and red and unkind as the land, asked him nothing. But he felt, as the dinosaurs must have felt, something troubling the air. And far into the darkness of certain nights, sitting with a candle and a bottle of Glenfiddich on the unvarnished table in his room, he wondered how long it would be.

He ticked off six miles with reaching strides, his rhythm rolling on itself, like coasting downhill on oiled bearings. He passed a narrow dirt lane, a channel for tractors, but he did not think of turning off. He did not want such lanes. They were thin and blocked at their ends. He ran on, settling back into himself after the motorcycle, filling his body with breathing. A mile, another, the rhythm hypnotic. And then he was startled by an engine close behind him.

Somehow he had not heard the car coming up. Either the hot breeze had been wrong, or he had been hypnotized by heat shimmer, or entranced by the smooth commotion of his muscles. But now he heard it, and glanced over his shoulder to see a wallowing Cadillac, its yellow paint new and bright. One green-tinted window powered down as the car came on. He saw a hand flash whitely against the dark interior. A full brown bottle of Budweiser, capped, shot toward him. It exploded against the pavement, spraying him with glass splinters and beer. Faces, tinted corpse-green by the glass, leered at him. As the car sped on he saw them, their features deformed by laughter.

"Screw you," he shouted, and hurled a rock at them. His rock fell far short and the Cadillac hurtled away, merging finally with the shimmering distance. Then he saw twin points of red light and a quick swirl, like the silver dart of barracuda in the flats he had once fished.

Coming back. They want to throw something else at me. Why don't they ever throw money?

He looked behind himself at the empty miles. Ahead, the Cadillac shot toward him down the straight black barrel of the road.

No more dancing. Jesus was a fool.

He picked up a baseball-sized stone, held it in his right hand, and kept running. *Come on.*

Come they did. Angling out of the center of the road so that its right wheels balanced on the pavement's edge, the Cadillac veered in toward him. When it was twenty feet away, he lofted his rock gently into the air. Then he dove into the corn. The Cadillac, roaring on, shattered its windshield against the languidly descending stone.

He reclaimed his road to the screams of skidding rubber. Without breaking stride, he glanced back at the giant car slewing sideways, its four fat tires spraying smoke. The car rocked to a stop. Three doors banged open. Two fat men and a woman labored out. Rolls of flesh jiggled on their bodies. Sweat darkened their clothing immediately. Their full lips spewed curses. The woman waved a bottle. One of the men lumbered to the car's trunk, threw it open, and lifted out a shotgun. He shouldered the weapon and fired. The runner saw a blue puff of smoke, then heard buckshot whistle by to his left. Anticipating the man's correction, he moved left and ducked again into the corn, running at an angle away from the road. Stalks hit his shoulders like slalom poles. The leaves, curling down like wide green ribbons, flicked his face as the shotgun fired again and he heard the *thack thack* of buckshot striking stalks. Then he heard doors slamming and the engine roaring and tires squealing and they were coming after him. He was not surprised.

Empty country. Clear and open and empty. Good country for killing. They do intend to kill me. The one cop asleep in his own puke. Come, then.

He ran out of the corn onto one of the narrow dirt lanes that crossed the main road. For an instant he did not move. At that same instant the Cadillac passed by on the road. He knew they had seen him. The car stopped, reversed, and turned down the tractor lane. He began running toward the dark woods that were another quarter mile away, looking over his shoulder once to see the broad car bulling its way down the narrow strip of dirt, spraying green stalks out from its fenders like water curving off the bow of a ship.

He entered the woods 25 yards ahead of them and ran on, hurdling fallen logs, twisting through brambles, padding silently on the pine-needle-cushioned floor. The woods smelled sweetly damp and ancient.

He heard their doors open and close, and he heard them enter the woods. He was kneeling behind a boulder, and the two men were walking straight in, about 25 feet apart, moving with noisy disdain. He drifted 50 feet to his left, lay flat on his stomach, and waited while they passed. They walked hunched over, like hunters, and the one who carried the shotgun looked as though he might actually have done some hunting. The other looked like a city man, hands nervously swatting at branches and gnats. Both of them wore loud sport shirts and fresh beach sunburns. They went on through the woods, making so much noise that he did not have to disguise his own as he slipped back from tree to tree and stopped at the woods' edge, not far from the car. He entered the corn rows, circled silently, and came up behind the woman, who stood facing the woods with one flesh-heavy hip propped against the car and a bottle of Almaden wine tilted to her mouth. She was swallowing noisily as he threw his dog tags and chain around her neck, garroting her, collapsing the larynx before she could scream. The bottle dropped from her hand but she tore at his eyes with her fingers. He had expected that and drove her face-first into the dirt, then planted both knees in the small of her back and hauled up on her slippery chin with all his strength until her neck snapped. Her toes, kicking reflexively, threw little spurts of dust behind her body. Voided urine stained a circle around her hips. He rested a moment, then lifted her into the back seat of the Cadillac and leaned her against the closed door so that she appeared to be asleep. With a flat rock he cracked the bottle of Almaden wine. When it broke well, with the slim neck and one long shard forming a dagger, he took it as an omen and went back into the woods.

He thought that the men would come out in thirty minutes, but they lasted only twenty. They were a hundred feet away when he heard them, cursing through the undergrowth, and when they clambered out blinking in the sunlight the one with the shotgun said, ". . . the hell is she doing? That God-damned wine put her to sleep?"

Both of their backs were to him as he made his rush focusing all his momentum into the flabby back of the one nearest, hitting him so hard that saliva burst in a white spray from the man's mouth. The glass dagger drove in as though into cheese, loosing a column of blood. The runner supported the fat man, so that he absorbed the buckshot when the second man fired once before he was knocked over by their combined impact. The runner watched the living fat man writhe beneath the dead wet weight of the companion he had just killed. When finally he struggled from beneath the corpse, he made no further move, because the runner was pointing the twelve-gauge shotgun into his face.

"You're crazy," the fat man whispered.

The runner's vision blurred from dripping sweat. Objects wavered before him now like plucked strings. Then, as he waited, everything clarified. The fat man was down on one knee, both hands flat in the dust, his head upraised. Dirt lined his flesh's creases. Sweat and new blood plastered his clothing to the rounded contours beneath. His eyes were soiled with hate and fury.

"Look what you've done. You're . . . you've killed two people. Jesus, you . . ."

"You're not people," the runner said. For a long time he had known that God was no more just than man was pure. He had sensed that the way to salvation was pain, and had run that road. Now his vision sharpened into an undeniable clarity. The air seemed to hum. Murder, he saw, was no longer the greatest sin.

He racked a shell into the shotgun's chamber and fired. Then he took off his shorts and wiped the gun free of fingerprints. He wiped his prints off of the shard of glass and the Cadillac. Then he put his shorts back on and ran out to the road, still shimmering under the afternoon sun.

THIRD WIND

Richard Christian Matheson

(1984)

Michael chugged up the incline, sweatsuit shadowed with perspiration. His Nikes compressed on the asphalt and the sound of his inhalation was the only noise on the country road.

He glanced at his waist-clipped odometer: Twenty-five point seven. Not bad. But he could do better.

Had to.

He'd worked hard doing his twenty miles a day for the last two years and knew he was ready to break fifty. His body was up to it, the muscles taut and strong. They'd be going through a lot of changes over the next twenty-five miles. His breathing was loose; comfortable. Just the way he liked it. Easy. But the strength was there.

There was something quietly spiritual about all this, he told himself. Maybe it was the sublime monotony of stretching every muscle and feeling it contract. Or it could be feeling his legs telescope out and draw his body forward. Perhaps even the humid expansion of his chest as his lungs bloated with air.

But none of that was really the answer.

It was the competing against himself.

Beating his own distance, his own limits. Running was the time he felt most alive. He knew that as surely as he'd ever known anything.

He loved the ache that shrouded his torso and he even waited for the moment, a few minutes into the run, when a dull voltage would climb his body to his brain like a vine, reviving him. It transported him, taking his mind to another place, very deep within. Like prayer.

He was almost to the crest of the hill.

So far, everything was feeling good. He shagged off some tightness in his shoulders, clenching his fists and punching at the air. The October chill turned to pink steam in his chest, making his body tingle as if a microscopic cloud of needles were passing through, from front to back, leaving pin-prick holes.

He shivered. The crest of the hill was just ahead. And on the down side was a new part of his personal route: a dirt road, carpeted with leaves, which wound through a silent forest at the peak of these mountains.

As he broke the crest, he picked up speed, angling downhill toward the dirt road. His Nikes flexed against the gravel, slipping a little.

It had taken much time to prepare for this. Months of meticulous care of his body. Vitamins. Dieting. The endless training and clocking. Commitment to the body machine. It was as critical as the commitment to the goal itself.

Fifty miles.

As he picked up momentum, jogging easily downhill, the mathematical breakdown of that figure filled his head with tumbling digits. Zeroes unglued from his thought tissues and linked with cardinal numbers to form combinations which added to fifty. It was suddenly all he could think about. Twenty-five plus twenty-five. Five times ten. Forty-nine plus one. Shit. It was driving him crazy. One hundred minus—

The dirt road.

He noticed the air cooling. The big trees that shaded the forest road were lowering the temperature. Night was close. Another hour. Thirty minutes plus thirty minutes. This math thing was getting irritating. Michael tried to remember some of his favorite Beatles songs as he gently padded through the dense forest.

Eight Days A Week. Great song. Weird damn title but who cared? If John and Paul said a week had eight days, everybody else just added a day and said . . . yeah, cool. Actually, maybe it wasn't their fault to begin with. Maybe George was supposed to bring a calendar to the recording session and forgot. He was always the spacey one.

Should've had Ringo do it, thought Michael. Ringo you could count on. Guys with gonzo noses always compensated by being dependable.

Michael continued to run at a comfortable pace over the powdery dirt. Every few steps he could hear a leaf or small branch break under his shoes. What was that old thing? Something like, don't ever move even a small rock when you're at the beach or in the mountains. It upsets the critical balances. Nature can't ever be right again if you do. The repercussions can start wars if you extrapolate it out far enough.

Didn't ever really make much sense to Michael. His brother Eric had always told him these things and he should have known better than to listen. Eric was a self-appointed fount of advice on how to keep the cosmos in alignment. But he always got "D's" on his cards in high school unlike Michael's "A's" and maybe he didn't really know all that much after all.

Michael's foot suddenly caught on a rock and he fell forward. On the ground, the dirt coated his face and lips and a spoonful got into his mouth. He also scraped his knee; a little blood. It was one of those lousy scrapes that claws a layer off and stings like it's a lot worse.

He was up again in a second and heading down the road, slightly disgusted with himself. He knew better than to lose his footing. He was too good an athlete for that.

His mouth was getting dry and he worked up some saliva by rubbing his tongue against the roof of his mouth. Strange how he never got hungry on these marathons of his. The body just seemed to live off itself for the period of time it took. Next day he usually put away a supermarket, but in running, all appetite faded. The body fed itself. It was weird.

The other funny thing was the way he couldn't imagine himself ever walking again. It became automatic to run. Everything went by so much faster. When he did stop, to walk, it was like being a snail. Everything just . . . took . . . so . . . damn . . . looooonnnngggg.

The sun was nearly gone now. Fewer and fewer animals. Their sounds faded all around. Birds stopped singing. The frenetic scrambling of squirrels halted as they prepared to bed down for the night. Far below, at the foot of these mountains, the ocean was turning to ink. The sun was lowering and the sea rose to meet it like a dark blue comforter.

Ahead, Michael could see an approaching corner. How long had he been moving through the forest path? Fifteen minutes? Was it pos-sible he'd gone the length of the path already?

That was one of the insane anomalies of running these marathons of his. Time got all out of whack. He'd think he was running ten miles and find he'd actually covered considerably more ground. Sometimes as much as double his estimate. He couldn't ever figure that one out. But it always happened and he always just sort of anticipated it.

Welcome to the time warp, Jack.

He checked his odometer: Twenty-nine point eight.

Half there and some loose change.

The dirt path would be coming to an end in a few hundred yards. Then it was straight along the highway which ran atop the ridge of this mountain far above the Malibu coastline. The highway was bordered with towering street lamps which lit the way like some forgotten runway for ancient astronauts. They stared down from fifty-foot poles and bleached the asphalt and roadside talcum white.

The path had ended now and he was on the deserted mountain-top road with its broken center line that stretched to forever. As Michael wiped his glistening face with a sleeve, he heard someone hitting a crystal glass with tiny mallets, far away. It wasn't a pinging sound. More like a high-pitched thud that was chain reacting. He looked up and saw insects of the night swarming dementedly around a kleig's glow. Hundreds of them in hypnotic self-destruction dive-bombed again and again at the huge bulb.

Eerie, seeing that kind of thing way the hell out here. But nice country to run in just the same. Gentle hills. The distant sea, far below. Nothing but heavy silence. Nobody ever drove this road anymore. It was as deserted as any Michael could remember. The perfect place to run.

What could be better? The smell was clean and healthy, the air sweet. Great decision, building his house up here last year. This was definitely the place to live. Pastureland is what his father used to call this kind of country when Michael was growing up in Wisconsin.

He laughed. Glad to be out of *that* place. People never did anything with their lives. Born there, schooled there, married there and died there was the usual, banal legacy. They all missed out on life. Missed out on new ideas and ambitions. The doctor slapped them and from that point on their lives just curled up like dead spiders.

It was just as well. How many of them could take the heat of competition in Los Angeles? Especially a job like Michael's? None of the old friends he'd gladly left behind in his home town would ever have a chance going up against a guy like himself. He was going to be the head of his law firm in a few more years. Most of those yokels back home couldn't even *spell* success much less achieve it.

But to each his own. Regardless of how pointless some lives really were. But *he* was going to be the head of his own firm and wouldn't even be thirty-five by the time it happened.

Okay, yeah, they were all married and had their families worked out. But what a fucking bore. Last thing Michael needed right now was that noose around his neck. Maybe the family guys figured they had something valuable. But for Michael it was a waste of time. Only thing a wife and kids would do is drag him down; hold him back. Priorities. First things first. *Career.* Then everything else. But put that relationship stuff off until last.

Besides, with all the inevitable success coming his way, meeting ladies would be a cinch. And hell, anyone could have a kid. Just nature. No big thing.

But *success.* That was something else, again. Took a very special animal to grab onto that golden ring and never let go. Families were for losers when a guy was really climbing. And he, of all the people he'd ever known, was definitely climbing.

Running had helped get him in the right frame of mind to do it. With each mileage barrier he broke, he was able to break greater barriers in life itself, especially his career. It made him more mentally fit to compete when he ran. It strengthened his will; his inner discipline.

Everything felt right when he was running regularly. And it wasn't just the meditative effect; not at all. He knew what it gave him was an *edge.* An edge on his fellow attorneys at the firm and an edge on life.

It was unthinkable to him how the other guys at the firm didn't take advantage of it. Getting ahead was what it was all about. A guy didn't make it in L.A. or anywhere else in the world unless he kept one step ahead of the competition. Keep moving and never let anything stand in the way or slow you down. That was the magic. And Michael knew the first place to start that trend was with himself.

He got a chill. Thinking this way always made him feel special. Like he had the formula; the secret. Contemplating success was a very intoxicating thing. And hyperventilation was heightening the effect.

He glanced at his odometer: Forty-three point six.

He was feeling like a champion. His calves were burning a little and his back was a bit tender but at this rate, with his breathing effortless and body strong, he could do sixty. But fifty was the goal. After that he had to go back and get his briefs in order for tomorrow's meeting. Had to get some sleep. Keep the machine in good shape and you rise to the top. None of that smoking or drinking or whatever else those morons were messing with out there. Stuff like that was for losers.

He opened his mouth a little wider to catch more air. The night had gone to a deep black and all he could hear now was the adhesive squishing of his Nikes. Overhead, the hanging branches of pepper trees canopied the desolate road and cut the moonlight into a million beams.

The odometer: Forty-six point two. His head was feeling hot but running at night always made that easier. The breezes would swathe like cool silk, blowing his hair back and combing through his scalp. Then he'd hit a hot pocket that hovered above the road and his hair would flop downward, the feeling of heat returning like a blanket. He coughed and spit.

Almost there.

He was suddenly hit by a stray drop of moisture, then another. A drizzle began. Great. Just what he didn't need. Okay, it wasn't raining hard; just that misty stuff that atomizes over you like a lawn sprinkler shifted by a light wind. Still, it would have been nice to have finished the fifty dry.

The road was going into a left hairpin now and Michael leaned into it, Nikes gripping octopus-tight. Ahead, as the curve broke, the road went straight, as far as the eye could see. Just a two-lane blacktop laying in state across these mountains. Now that it was wet, the surface went mirror shiny, like ribbon on the side of tuxedo pants. Far below, the sea reflected a fuzzy moon, and fog began to ease up the mountainside, coming closer toward the road.

Michael checked the odometer, rubbing his hands together for warmth. Forty-nine point eight. Almost there and other than being a little cold, he was feeling like a million bucks. He punched happily at the air and cleared his throat. God, he was feeling great! Tomorrow, at the office, was going to be a victory from start to finish.

He could feel himself smiling, his face hot against the vaporing rain. His jogging suit was soaked with sweat and drizzle made him shiver as it touched his skin. He breathed in gulps of the chilled air and as it left his mouth it turned white, puffing loosely away. His eyes were stinging from the cold and he closed them, continuing to run, the effect of total blackness fascinating him.

Another stride. Another.

He opened his eyes and rubbed them with red fingers. All around, the fog breathed closer, snaking between limbs of trees, and creeping silently across the asphalt. The overhead lights made it glow like a wall of colorless neon.

The odometer. Another hundred feet and he had it!

The strides came in a smooth flow, like a turning wheel. He spread his fingers and shook some of the excess energy that was concentrating and making him feel buzzy. It took the edge off but he still felt as though he was zapped on a hundred cups of coffee. He ran faster, his arms like swinging scythes, tugging him forward.

Twenty more steps.

Ten plus ten. Five times . . . Christ, the math thing back. He started laughing out loud as he went puffing down the road, sweat pants drooping.

The sky was zippered by lightning and Michael gasped. In an instant blackness turned to hot white and there was that visual echo of the light as it trembled in the distance, then fluttered off like a dying bulb.

Michael checked his odometer.

Five more feet! He counted it: Five/breath/four/breath/three/breath/two/one and there it was, yelling and singing and patting him on the back and tossing streamers!

Fifty miles! Fifty goddamn miles!

It was fucking incredible. To know he could really, actually *do* it suddenly hit him and he began laughing.

Okay, now to get that incredible sensation of almost standing still while walking it off. Have to keep those muscles warm. If not he'd get a chill and cramps and feel like someone was going over his calves with a carpet knife.

Hot breath gushed visibly from his mouth. The rain was coming faster in a diagonal descent, back-lit by lightning, and the fog bundled tighter. Michael took three or four deep breaths and began trying to slow. It was incredible to have this feeling of edge. The sense of being on *top* of everything! It was an awareness he could surpass limitations. Make breakthroughs. It was what separated the winners from the losers when taken right down to a basic level. The winners knew how much harder they could push to go farther. Break those patterns. Create new levels of ability and confidence. *Win.*

He tried again to slow down. His legs weren't slowing to a walk yet and he sent the message down again. He smiled. Run too far and the body doesn't want to stop.

The legs continued to pull him forward. Rain was drenching down from the sky; he was soaked to the bone. Hair strung over his eyes and mouth and he coughed to get out what he could as it needled coldly into his face.

"Slow down," he told his legs; "*Stop, goddamit!*"

But his feet continued on, splashing through puddles which laked here and there along the foggy road.

Michael began to breathe harder, unable to get the air he needed. It was too wet; half air, half water. Suddenly more lightning scribbled across the thundering clouds and Michael reached down to stop one leg.

It did no good. He kept running, even faster, pounding harder against the wet pavement. He could feel the bottoms of his Nikes getting wet, starting to wear through. He'd worn the old ones; they were the most comfortable.

Jesus fucking god, he really *couldn't stop.*

The wetness got colder on his cramping feet. He tried to fall but kept running. Terrified, he began to cough fitfully, his legs continuing forward, racing over the pavement.

His throat was raw from the cold and his muscles ached. He was starting to feel like his body had been beaten with hammers.

There was no point in trying to stop. He knew that now. He'd trained too long. Too precisely. It had been his single obsession.

And as he continued to pound against the fog-shrouded pavement all he could hear was a cold, lonely night.

Until the sound of his own pleading screams began to echo through the mountains, and fade across the endless gray road.

RUNNING

Joyce Carol Oates

(1992)

Here is what happened. Except, of course, nothing happened. Their third day out, they went running along a hiking trail beside Lake Mt. Moriah in the northeastern corner of the Adirondack Forest Preserve, running at a moderate speed, not pushing themselves, for they were not serious or obsessed runners, not marathon runners, neither in fact had been athletic or much interested in competitive sports in adolescence, she a slender dark-haired woman in her early thirties, he a tall, big-boned silvery-blond man a few years older, and she was running ahead since the trail was too narrow for them to run comfortably side by side, and he had to stop to retie a shoelace, he murmured, "Damn!" though good-naturedly, for he was a good-natured man, and she ran on, retaining her speed, she was in excellent spirits, as she often was at such times, sacred times, they seemed to her, the ease of running, the childlike pleasure, the illusion of being weightless, bodiless, without a name, as if, only at such moments, the physical being propelled through space, the soul, assuming there is a soul, defines itself *This is happiness!—my truest self,* and she was relieved that the sky had cleared, no rain clouds, it was a windy sunny brightly cool August morning, a day of aching beauty, the previous day they'd driven too long and much of the time in pelting rain, in close confinement in the car that, while technically his, they shared for ambitious drives, so the mere fact of a clear sky was a simple fact of happiness, she was one to be grateful for such things, and the sharp fragrance of the pine needles underfoot, and Lake Mt. Moriah, one of the region's numerous glacier lakes, that, the evening before, checking into their motel, they'd hardly been able to make out in the dusk, was so luminous as to seem unreal, a lake out of a dream, reflecting as in a polished metallic surface the sculpted sky and the dark serrated rim of trees, evergreens, birches, that surrounded it, she felt the blood beating hard and exuberant in her veins—*I can do anything! I need no one!*—and turning a corner she emerged into a grassy clearing of boulders, gigantic boulders that looked as if they were pushing up from the earth, covered with lichen, lichen like a man's beard, and deeply creased, like human faces compressed and distorted, and the wind in the topmost branches of trees was visible here, the effort, the seeming emotion, the trail divided into a broad, not very clearly defined V, the left branch curving back to the lake in the deep shadow of evergreens and the right branch, beyond several more boulders, into an unexpected meadow of tall grasses, Queen Anne's lace, milkweed gone to seed, dazzling goldenrod—*How beautiful: and if no one saw it?*—and she seemed not to hesitate, not even for a fraction of a second, it was as if gravity drew her to the right branch of the trail, and away from the lake, she was not thinking *How will he know which way I've gone,* nor was she thinking *Will he be puzzled, concerned, not knowing which way I've gone?* for she was a woman of moods and impulses and spontaneity, that was one of the ways in which, in the human world, she defined herself, and was defined, and she was curious, following the trail upward through the meadow, wondering where it would lead, guessing that, shortly, it would loop back to the lake, if it did not, and he didn't seem to be following her, she would turn back, return to the lakeshore trail, catch up with him from behind, as she sometimes did she would surprise him, playfully approaching him from behind—*Here I am! Did you wonder where I was?*—she was beginning to sweat inside her clothes, her khaki shorts, loose-fitting white shirt, a gauzy maroon-orange scarf tying her hair back from her face, but it was a good feeling, yes and the mild ache of her muscles, the calm hard defiant beat of her heart, she was thinking with pleasure too of returning to the motel room and showering and they would have their late breakfast, the routines of their lives together were comforting, yes, but they were confining, too, predictable and confining—*Are we addicted? To what are we addicted?*—thinking that they were a couple well matched, companionable, not married though they had been together for nearly four years and though they lived, at least much of the time (as on this eight-day drive through the Adirondacks, for instance: but often they traveled separately) as if they were married, yes, and married for years, casual acquaintances assumed they were a married couple, for there was between them an unstudied ease, a companionable cheerfulness, a manner suggesting familiar marital customs exercised without self-consciousness, or much emotion, they were professional people, she an administrator for a public school district, he an engineer at one of the Bell Laboratories, yes, but she wanted to return to graduate school to get another degree, in comparative literature, perhaps, and he was in his heart a purely theoretical mathematician, she was thinking of how strange it was, how simple a fact yet how strange, that he was the man who loved her and whom of all men she loved, how strange that they might be defined in that way, and, in another era, her mother's era, for instance, they would be married, would have married years ago, would have children, a child, at least, and if so who would that child be, for she had had an abortion once, and this was a secret from him, this was always to be a secret from him, as from her family, she told herself, *It matters to no one if it doesn't matter to me: and it doesn't matter to me*, and in truth she rarely thought of it, she never thought of it, she was not that terrified girl of nineteen, though terror surfaced in her sometimes, not that terror but another, she did not believe there was any connection, the girl of nineteen was vanished, forgotten, she could not remember the boy's face (and he was not a man, but a boy: her own age), but she knew she had not loved him, or, if she had loved him, it had been a mistake, just as, perhaps, the love she felt for the man who was not her husband was a mistake, a sickness of a kind, a sickness that had no name, because she feared losing him, he who was so good-natured, so kindly, so loyal a friend, a man of temperate desires and ambitions, a man so reliable, having no idea of the hunger she felt for him, her secret terror of being left by him, her terror even that he should know, should even suspect, though he was a man without suspicion, that she did fear losing him, that, sometimes, the terror woke her from sleep, her heart pounding erratically, a taste of something brackish at the back of her mouth while beside her, unknowing, the man who was not her husband slept his heavy, healthy sleep, drawing his deep rhythmic breaths undisturbed, yes, and had not one of her dream terrors wakened her only a few mornings ago, back in the city, the anticipation of this trip into the mountains, perhaps, had dislodged the terror, but of course she hid it from him, she shared everything with him by day, but really she shared very little with him, this too he did not know, he could not guess how by day, especially when she was running, she felt angry contempt for that other woman, that sick woman, that coward who was, yet was not, herself, for she was a wholly free agent, a woman with a career, an only moderately paying career but a career nonetheless, and hers, she was economically independent of any man, as her mother, and her mother's female relatives, had not been, why then did her mother express such worry about her, such disapproval, though reluctant to bring up the subject again, having once murmured, "If you love each other, I don't see why . . ." meaning *I don't see why you don't get married*, her voice trailing off into a painful silence, for there was no reply, only a stiffening of her daughter's shoulders, an angry hurt glistening in the eyes, and so, now, running, hearing the wind high in the trees, or was it voices, faint laughter, she told herself defiantly that she was not really certain, not really, that she loved him, this man with whom she loved who was not her husband, apart from the hunger that bound her to him she did not know if she loved him, or could love any man, though knowing that, however much she did, or did not, love him, his feeling for her was less intense than hers for him, less desperate, less hungry, and this was a fact about which she did not care to think, for it pained her, it was a hurt lodged deep in her, and in any case this was not the time for such thoughts, the happiness of this moment, flying weightless and bodiless and nameless along the trail that had now grown weedy thinking, *How different everything is, by day,* meaning *How different I am, by day,* she was a strong woman, really, buoyed by joy and defiance in equal measure, running now along what appeared to be a parkland access road into which the hiking trail had invisibly merged, Lake Mt. Moriah behind her and to the left, this road with a look of being abandoned, densely bordered by deciduous trees, many of them birches, striking clumps of birches with thick, sturdy, white-glaring trunks very different from the smaller birches downstate, she saw that some of their leaves had turned prematurely, yellow, wizened, the symptoms, she'd read in an Adirondack publication, of stress caused by acid rain, pollution out of Chicago and its industrial environs blown eastward to fall as poisonous rain in the Adirondack wilderness, wanted to cry with rage, she was furious, she was deeply wounded, one day soon she would break off her relationship with the man who was not her husband precisely because he was not her husband and he did not sense her need for him, her terrible hunger, how it demeaned her, when they returned to the city, perhaps, she was an independent woman, she was an ambitious woman, yes, she was willing to move to another part of the country and she was willing to move alone—*You don't love me as much as I love you, and so I hate you*—but of course she did not hate him, she loved him very much, unless that was simply her weakness, that love, of which, to him, she could never speak, and thinking of these things, vexed, disturbed, thinking of the very things she forbade herself to think of at this sacred time, this running time, this time of namelessness and flight and happiness, she drew the back of one hand across her forehead to wipe away the sweat, her scarf was damp, she heard laughter ringing on all sides, blinking to get her vision clear, she saw, ahead, several figures by the side of the road, young men they appeared to be, in their mid- or late twenties, campers, perhaps, hikers, they were dressed in shorts, or swimming trunks, barechested, they were talking and laughing loudly together, and then, noticing her, they quieted at once, the high-pitched laughter of one fading as, turning, he squinted in her direction to see what his companions had sighted, she would remember the sudden silence, and how, instinctively, hardly conscious of what she did, she glanced about to see if there were other figures close by, female figures, but there did not appear to be, she felt a stab of apprehension, thinking, *But I can't turn back, I won't turn back*, trying not to meet the men's frank rude assessing gazes, for she was not the kind of woman who anticipates harm from strangers, not at such a time, in a place of such natural beauty—*Not here, not now*—so she continued running along the road, the sun pounding at her temples, rivulets of chill sweat running down her sides, she did not consider herself a sexually attractive woman and she was several years older than these young men and once they got a clear look at her they would lose interest in her, she believed, her small, wan face, her over-large intense eyes, her sensitive skin that exaggerated any blemish, her narrow lips, small breasts, she told herself this even as running toward them, required to pass within a few yards of them since the trail led inexorably that way and to pause, to turn, to veer off suddenly in any other direction would be to acknowledge, to the men and to herself, that there was something between her and them to be acknowledged, she saw that they were staring with an unmistakable excitement, conferring together, one of them, thick-bodied, squat, his bare torso covered in coarse black hair, had already stepped quickly out onto the road as if to block her way, how very quickly he'd moved, by instinct, perhaps, sheer masculine instinct, the predator's instinct, yet, still, tasting panic now, she continued to run forward—*I can't stop, how can I stop: I will not*—she saw that one of the men had a growth of pale red whiskers, another, grinning, had fleshy lips, the one blocking her way was misshapen somehow, was he—a blunt hairless bullet head growing out of his shoulders, no neck, fatty-muscular upper arms, rolls of pale flesh at his stomach, the waist of his swimming trunks low enough to show his navel, a navel thickly whorled in dark hair, she saw his eyes, hot, derisive, hungry, in terror she was telling them, *I am not my body, I am more than a woman's body*, seeing the expectancy and arousal in their eyes, the crude appetite, the elation, how like dogs' mouths their grinning mouths, the teeth inside their grins—*Don't touch me any of you: God damn you!*—her vision blurred with tears of fury and helplessness and resignation as she ran into harsh sunlight as into oblivion, and then, so unexpectedly, she would recall afterward so miraculously, when she was within approximately twenty feet of the fattish young man blocking her way she saw how the expressions on the men's faces shifted, their eyes moving quicksilver in their sockets, their bodies too altering, almost imperceptibly, but unmistakably, they'd sighted something or someone behind her, in that instant she understood that the man who was not her husband and who did not love her with quite the hunger with which she loved him must have run into view, he'd known which branch of the trail to take, to follow her, very likely he'd been watching her all along, and so everything was changed—*I'm safe—saved*—as if the very sun had been extinguished and had then returned and all so instantaneously not a molecule in all of nature would register its unthinkable absence, let alone its miraculous return, she was safe, she was loved, not on her own terms but on another's, and this would be the terms of her life, these were the terms of her life, her eyes welled with tears that, undeserving as she was, she was safe and there remained no sign anyone might interpret to suggest that she had ever, for even the space of a minute, not been safe, for perhaps she had imagined everything? she had exaggerated the danger? for now the young men showed friendly faces, still watchful, but smiling, glancing from her to the man who ran behind her, judging, yes, this was a couple, the woman was under the protection of the man, yes, they understood, nothing required articulation, for instinct prevailed, instinct is all, the young man with the reddish beard lifted a hand in greeting, and the fattish young man blocking her way was no longer blocking her way, he stepped off the road, mock graciously, with a friendly smirk, even as, maintaining her speed, her face showing none of the emotion she felt, she too stepped off the road, on the other side, running in the grass to avoid him, courtesy in her gesture as well as caution, and then she'd passed him and the others and saw ahead only the narrow road, the intermittent blaze of goldenrod, the dense border of trees, and the sky a high remote blue marbled with cloud, that thin tracery of white that scarcely moves, like a frieze, and behind her she heard men exchange greetings, the man who was not her husband and the young men by the road, the murmured greetings common to joggers, hikers, bicyclists of our time—"H'lo! How's it going!"—and no replies expected, and so that was what happened. Except, what had happened?

WE CANNOT SAVE HIM

Lon Otto

(1988)

He was our friend, we miss him. But how were we to know when we laid our hearts in his hands, gave him our faith and admiration, that he would become what he is today, what we see already as we wait for him, half-asleep in these dew-drowned bushes?

We miss him, who still unseen approaches, running with calculated prissy breaths above the foggy river. Before he rounds the brushy curve, we see him, his French running shoes, his shorts, his naked legs, his T-shirt advertising something unimaginable, his terry sweatband, his stopwatch, his tiny nylon wallet fastened to his shoe ingeniously with Velcro—who once was never seen without a coat and necktie—hairy wool, rumpled linen, bleached-to-the-bone starched cotton broadcloth, stained shimmering reptilian silk—who hated zippers as much as polyester, snaps as much as leisure suits.

He was our friend, who traveled by a subway so dangerous and obscure that no one anyone knew had even heard of it, with whom alone we roared beneath the Mississippi, the ancient train crawling with the scum that cities full of hope and happiness generate according to some inverse law of social physics. With him we were horrified and unafraid. He was our friend, he led us clanking underground from the mildewed cavern of the old St. Paul Lower Market to the now-abandoned depths of the Fur Exchange in Minneapolis, and we miss him, who has a sticker on his car bumper, I'D RATHER BE RUNNING, who has a bumper now, who hated cars.

We miss a whole elegant landscape of decay, the rich overlay of stagnation. It was he, himself, who pointed out the first faint trail parting the grass of the hitherto untroubled parkway along dotty, lilac-lovely Summit Avenue. We see him still, as he crouched suddenly under the lamplight, directing our attention to the barely visible spine of earth showing through the grass. We touched the packed soil uneasily where he pointed out the ominous ribbed print of an early, clumsy running shoe. (This was before any of us had ever seen a "jogger," but we had heard of them and knew what their spoor must mean.) We wanted to smash the bottles we were carrying home, to sow the path with glittering denial, but he smiled his disquieting smile and led us away, knowing we were lost. Later, when the path had doubled, then doubled again under the tread of runners, had grown into a freeway of sappy health, then we discovered our defeat's full depth.

We miss him, who understood the secret night squalor of these too facile, too habitable two cities, who recognized by voice and vice the fierce-smelling grizzled crocks whose slapping overshoes crunch down the frozen alleys behind loft-converted warehouses where city planners toast their luck with California wine, where young architects and M.B.A.s and developers plot their clean and devastating lives over alfalfa sprouts and tofu.

He was our friend, we know he knows no fear and will not listen to the warnings we hopelessly recite: the jarred spine, ruined cartilage, wrecked knees and ankles, fractured shins, the mysterious sudden heart attack in the bloom of life, the neck broken on the expensive beach, the thugs waiting with chains and clubs in the inhuman, unmoving early hours of morning. And we whisper to ourselves, *He must not run along the river road at dawn, we cannot save him.*

We miss him, he was our friend, who spoke intelligently in the smoking darkness of the last free-lunch bar in South St. Paul, ripe with the reek of stockyards, spoke of Breton curb dancing, late Aztec erotic dentistry, the Parsee epitomes of the sixth century, who now subscribes to *Runner's World*, who jabbers eagerly about vitamins B and E, the relative merits of Tiger's Milk and Pro-Vita, about how good he feels about himself since he stopped smoking and drinking and eating red meat, who was our dark friend.

We have frozen in our heart's eye an image that humiliates and hardens our resolve: on the silent off-color television bolted above bottles, a mob of marathoners flows over the Lake Street-Marshall Avenue bridge, a river of specks streaming from nowhere to nowhere. Then, in close-up, we see him, captured randomly, neither first nor last, then gone, a number on his chest, who could explain with precision what went wrong with Horsley Beer after the retirement of brewmaster Koenigsberger and the ascendancy of Schlee, and who is now addicted to the mindless, unsubtle high of oxygen starvation and pheromones.

He was our friend, we would warn him if we could. Any moment now he will appear, cheerful in his shorts and flashy shoes against the gray dead end of night, obliviously trotting toward us where we wait, miserable, hidden precariously, the Mississippi's bank sloping treacherously away beneath our feet, our sticks and greasy chains and lengths of pipe oppressive in our hands, warning silently, hopelessly, *He must not run along the river road at dawn, he must not run along the river road at dawn, we cannot save him.*

Assorted Other Runners

THE TRACK

Walter McDonald

(1976)

By noon Bien Dien sweltered, the humid air heavy like deep depression. The clouds had not built far enough to block out the sun, which beat down almost too bright to see. For the first time since the rocket blast last night, the base was quiet, as if totally shut down. I could not hear a jet or bombs or gunfire anywhere. The whole war seemed to have been called off.

I felt my back baking already as Lebowitz guided me, jogging the three blocks to the track, a dirt oval bulldozed around a field laid out for football but covered now in dead yellow grass, a collapsing rusting goalpost at each end. Lebowitz said that in the old days, with a half million Americans in Vietnam, the base was famous as Bien Dien-by-the-Sea, its beaches a favorite R and R center. But after most of the troops were withdrawn, there weren't enough left for proper patrols, and the VC began mining the beaches. Now they were off limits, and jogging was the best hot way to relax.

A road paralleled the track and cut north to the flight line a few blocks away, hidden by hangars and quonset huts. Along the other side of the field were wooden bleachers built between the forty-yard lines, a platform at the fifty like a parade reviewing stand. Behind the bleachers a sagging cyclone fence ran the length of the field and on beyond were rows and rows of tin and wooden shacks where

Vietnamese airmen lived with their families. And at the far end of the field, beyond a great wall smothered with vines, there was a huge French mansion with a red roof and trees everywhere around it, like part of the jungle.

There were a dozen or more men in trunks already on the track, some of them jogging fast, some shuffling along with their heads down, their arms hanging. Lebowitz drew the towel from his neck and wiped his face and threw the towel on the field. His thin face was drawn, almost emaciated, and his eyes were deep set in dark hollow sockets, his stiff hair pepper white.

"Six times around for a mile," he said, not breaking stride.

"How many miles do you go?" I asked, my bones already heavy in the heat.

"Four, five, I'll let you know."

He ran light on his feet, a thin man with long muscles. He kept his fists straight out in front of him, knuckles up. He was taller than me by several inches, his long stride hitting three for my four. His high voice chattered like a separate thing that could not be winded.

"See that guy rounding the endzone? That's Fleming. He runs every day. The only guy here who can outlast me."

"Yeah," I said, still trying to fall in with his pace. "I see him."

Fresh from the States, I was used to handball and an indoor track, and running here in this humidity was like treading deep water with boots on.

I watched Fleming round the turn and enter the straightaway, running fast with determined desperate lunges past a group of slower joggers and along the row of Vietnamese shacks. Two or three children broke from the bushes and ran toward the track, whirling and darting away out of sight as Fleming ran past. When the children broke toward the group following him, one of the men lunged at them and the children scattered.

We approached the turn and the old wall of the French estate towered before us, lush with vines, shaded by the great limbs of trees beyond the wall.

"The Frenchman's place," Lebowitz said, tossing his thumb at the wall. "It's their private club, now."

I had read about Bien Dien before leaving Saigon. I knew it was one of the American bases built in the sixties, bulldozed not merely out of jungle but out of an old French colonial plantation on the bay by the name of Bien Dien. At the peak of United States involvement, eighteen thousand Americans crowded the base, along with a handful of French still running their plantation and a few hundred Vietnamese. Now, only four hundred Americans remained, and thousands of Vietnamese, and still the handful of French, who lived apart and never troubled themselves with Americans except invitations to the base commander and his staff at Christmas and the fourth of July and Bastille Day.

I heard a board thudding just beyond the wall and then a splash cut trimly into water.

"Swimming pool," Lebowitz said, his face parallel to the wall, his fists pumping. "Those cats still think they're in the Promised Land."

We turned down the backstretch and came even with the shacks. There was an awful smell, like rotten cabbages and wine.

"You numbah ten!" a child's voice screamed, the worst insult possible. "You 'mericans numbah ten!"

Lebowitz never turned his head toward that supreme insult, just kept jogging the same steady pace. And when the child screamed at us again, Lebowitz called back friendly, "You numbah one! You numbah one, boychild!"

He answered my silence as we jogged on. "Want to trade places with them?"

"No way," I said.

"You're right," he said. "If we can't be friends with the kids, there's no way."

Shackler and Malatesta arrived from the officers' hooches, and we fell in behind them as they entered the track, jogging heavily. Shackler lunged along, leaning forward like a heavyweight, but Malatesta brought his knees high and trotted with his shoulders thrust back as if he were marching.

"They hit the village again?" Lebowitz called.

"Naw," Shackler replied, not looking back. "Must be getting ready to hit the base."

Rumors. At breakfast someone had said three NVA divisions had crossed the demilitarized zone and were last detected twenty kilometers north of the base. Estimates of casualties from last night's mortar attack ran as high as dozens of Americans and hundreds of Vietnamese killed and god knows how many wounded. Someone said the VC had overrun half of Plei Nhon and massacred scores of villagers during the night.

I waited for someone else to speak, but all ran quietly, all alone. Now and then we would fall into step and there would be the thump thump thump of our running. Then the steps would syncopate and break rhythm and in the heavy depressing heat I would find myself having to concentrate to maintain stride.

Fleming caught us in the second lap and passed without looking, his breath heaving, the tendons in his neck stretched tight. He was a good-looking kid with blond hair and flushed cheeks and he looked too young to be out of high school. He raced on, as if trying to outdistance fear.

Each time we passed the great wall I would listen and once I thought I heard sensual laughter, and another time I heard music, slow and light and peaceful, like Paris in springtime.

A muscular, middle-aged man ran past us, deeply tanned, an old sergeant or a colonel, his stiff white hair glistening with sweat. Around his waist was a wide leather back support, gleaming black, a .38 holstered on one side and a knife scabbard stitched to the other. "Watch him," Lebowitz said. "He won't go near the shacks."

Sure enough, the man ran swiftly along the inside of the track, next to the football field.

"Hates kids?" I asked.

"Naw," he said, grinning. "Just afraid someone's gonna nail him before it's over. He's not the only one."

After three laps Shackler and Malatesta dropped out, panting heavily, but Lebowitz jogged on, staring ahead. I glanced at them walking slowly back towards the quarters, their arms limp. I felt more like that than running, but something in my legs kept going and after a few paces I caught up with Lebowitz again.

"It all counts towards DEROS," he said grimly. Date of Earliest Return from Overseas: months, impossible months from now.

We must have jogged around that track for an hour. One by one the others dropped out and returned to the quarters for showers and back to duty. After a while there were only Lebowitz and I and, lapping us every two or three rounds, Fleming, haunting the day with his fear.

Lebowitz paced me like a record spinning around and around, lap after lap. I caught my mind wandering off the track, dozing, drugged with fatigue and the heat. I no longer heard the children leering at us, only now and then a woman's high strange scolding from inside the shacks or a crying baby. I listened for the swimming pool to splash again or for music, but there were not even birds singing in the Frenchman's jungle beyond the wall. After a while even Lebowitz hushed and there was only the thump of our toes jogging on dirt.

My lungs numbed in the heat and my legs came to feel like things apart, able to go on and on. My eyes burned with sweat, and I squinted so tight I could hardly see anymore, and because they stung it was impossible to think. I was adjusting, though, lost in rhythm, like a mechanical animal caught on the rim of existence, going round and round, getting closer to DEROS. It felt good and I was slipping deep in dreams when I heard a noise with my name on it.

"Moose. It's time, Moose," Lebowitz called.

I jolted to a halt off the track and dropped my arms. My hands were numb. I heard jets roaring from the flight line. Drenched in sweat, tasting salt and iodine, I shuddered. It was overcast, the sky boiling with clouds, and in the distance there was thunder, or bombs, and I had the feeling there was still a long, long way to go.

CARBO-LOADING

Max Apple

(1980)

My first significant carbohydrates came from beer. Mom was a miler, but to nurture embryonic me she didn't even walk stairs. She spent eight hours a day in bed. While nursing she developed a taste for beer. Vaguely, I recall foam at the nipple. Dad sat beside us and sipped from long-necked bottles.

He'll be a hurdler, they thought, judging by my stride. As they cuddled me they stretched my tendons from the ankle to the knee. Dad wanted a sprinter, Mom hoped for distance. When I was thirty she got her way.

By then I had been a beer man for a decade. When I finally started to run I felt like a washing machine. The beer swirled within amid the colorful jungle of entrails. I had no stamina for a final sprint, no burst of glucose for the hills. I was always on rinse and hold.

My doctor said that because of my drinking I had developed little pockets of beer, not just the well-known belly but beer bulge at the wrists, behind the ears, between the vertebrae. As I ran, these bits of beer quivered like dangling earrings.

Dr. Isle is a runner too. He figures that if it increases his working life by just four years it will make him $1 million richer. So he cut the million from life insurance and added it to malpractice. He runs fifteen miles a day. Lots of times he's too mellow to diagnose. Tumors and arrhythmias float by as unnoticed as dull movies, but he perks up for a stretched Achilles tendon or a swollen knee joint.

After he drains my pouches with a long needle, Isle looks me in the eye. "Cut the beer," he says, "if you ever want to run a three-hour marathon."

Sweet Nurse Phillips bends to lace my Nikes. I hobble into the waiting room and crush my last six-pack in the wastebasket.

"Good for you," Nurse Phillips says. There are bright tears in her eyes. The patients cheer.

For the next two weeks I take Gatorade injections and run on a treadmill beside my bed. Then during my first outdoor ten miles my hair turns the color of autumn, my legs cramp, and my ankles crackle like chestnuts.

"Carbohydrate depletion," Dr. Isle says. He gets me into reclining position on the examining table. Nurse Phillips spoons dry Cheerios through my wind-chapped lips.

"Ten thousand cc's," he orders.

Her tender feeding revives me. The Cheerios that fall to my legs she spears on the point of a long fingernail. She does an impromptu cardiogram by putting her ear to nine different spots on my chest. Her tight curls tickle. When she embraces me, I respond.

"It's normal," she says.

Isle prescribes a box of unsweetened cereal for dessert every day. "Load up on carbohydrates," he says. "Protein will never get you more than ten miles. Amino acids are selfish. They want to stay the way they are. That's why I don't believe in life on other planets. Protein is insular and xenophobic. It's all left-handed. It's expensive and hard to maintain, I hate it as much as sugar, but what can you do? It's all there is. After twenty miles the body eats itself."

Nurse Phillips hands me a plastic packet with professional samples of bee pollen, desiccated liver, and body punch. I ask her to go out with me on Saturday night.

"The Boston Marathon is in two months," she says. "I'll be doing stretching exercises every spare minute until then."

"I'll see you in Boston," I say, "at the finish line." We make a date for the twenty-seventh mile.

"I hope you'll really be there," she says. "I hope you've got what it takes."

"I'll be there," I say. I pat the top of her nurse's cap.

What it takes, I learn, is more than what you have. I learn this from all the experts. The books confirm what Isle says. He has not deluded me. Carbo-loading will only get you twenty miles. For the last six you eat your heart out. In my training, even with Gatorade and bee pollen and seventy-dollar heel inserts, I can't make it past twenty miles.

I think of Nurse Phillips in Boston, moist and anxious at the finish, seeking me. Still I can't get past twenty. I think of Jesus on the cross, martyrs on the rack, witches at the stake, but my own misery is not diminished by the suffering of others.

In desperation I bone up on personal cannibalism. The prime minister of India drank his own urine, various women have sampled their breast milk, and all of us suck blood from our snakebites and swallow great quantities of phlegm and saliva. But none of this historicism helps.

Finally, on the advice of an experienced marathoner, I check into a running clinic. There I am immediately weighed naked under water and am relieved to learn that only 9 percent of my person is fat. This is better than average, so I have no excuse there. Furthermore, my resting pulse is forty and I can hit alpha waves at the mere mention of the word *peace* in any language.

I am a difficult case. The director assigns me to a running therapist. "Pick your speed," the therapist says, "stay comfortable, and don't try to impress me. You will for a while in middle distance try to model yourself after me. There may even be a passing boyish crush, a temporary identity crisis, Don't worry. By fifteen miles or so it will be over. You will learn to identify a stride and a gasping pattern that is totally unique."

The therapist has a gray beard, as I expected, and wears conservative dark gray shorts. He takes notes on a dictaphone no larger than a digital stopwatch.

My parents and childhood take the first five miles. We hit puberty at about thirteen. I talk on the exhale. Every three miles we take a two-minute break from analysis. During the rest I jog in silence. He encourages me to have pastoral fantasies during those intervals. "Pretend you are a gazelle," he says, "a gazelle along the verdant banks of the ancient Tiber, or a sleek antelope galloping toward some lush African watering place."

He is right. I do admire his long authoritative stride. I am enthralled by the way he hears me out, knowing exactly when to press the dictaphone. To him my lack of endurance is just a job. When I am finished he'll shower and take on someone else. What strength he has, what dedication. He reads the admiration of my silence.

"Look," he says, "body language aside, I don't think this should be a block for you. Let's just go on. By sixteen or seventeen miles it should be over. Believe me, it's just sort of Oedipal."

I get nostalgic then about my early training, my blue Adidas Dragons, the high school track, my first seven-minute mile.

"Speaking of time," he says, "you're doing an eight-fourteen pace and we're at the nineteenth mile." I know that he will stop at twenty. "The last six you're on your own. Even in therapy," he says, "I can't take you all the way. But I think you're ready."

At twenty miles an orderly in a golf cart is awaiting him. The orderly pours a bucket of water on my head, gives me a cup of Gatorade, and takes my therapist back to the clinic. "Good luck!" they shout.

I am in the deep woods now and it is almost dusk. Certain primal fears try to grip me, but my heart is too busy for fear. Twenty-one passes. This is all new territory. It's like suddenly growing four or five inches and having to relearn old habits like the length of a step. In my pride at having passed twenty-one miles I stumble on a tiny tree root. My ankle hurts. I'm unable to walk. When I'm not at the clinic as expected, the therapist himself comes out for me in the golf cart. He loads me onto the seat. "Nothing seems to be broken," he says, squeezing my right tibia and ankle. "There are obstacles in everyone's path. You'll have to be more wary in the future, but I think you'll make it."

And that, my friends, is as close as I came to 26 miles 385 yards until the day in Boston. Yes, I ran slow tens and twelves. I did sprints and fartleks. I ran hills and trained my breath on the steps of the football stadium. People who knew me in the beer days, even in the three-to-five-mile stage, were in awe of my leanness. At the track I lapped those who used to be my peers.

In Boston it's true I was alone and far from home. I had a bad night in a lumpy motel room. I was stiff and eager and maybe slightly overtrained. But I had eaten for the race. It was Monday. From the previous Sunday through Wednesday I had nothing but protein, meat at all three meals. At McDonald's I threw away the bun and held the double-beef patty and melted cheese in my bare hands. Instead of Coke I carried my own powdered beef broth, which I mixed with boiling water. Then from Thursday through Sunday I loaded carbos. With Dr. Isle's permission, of course, I had a six-pack on Sunday night. "Lots of carbos," he said, "and it will clean you out before the race." I ate miles of spaghetti and bought bread by the pound.

On Monday morning at the Hopkinton starting line I was ready. The stars of the distance world were all there pretending it was just another day. Frank Shorter ate a Ding-Dong and a banana, Bill Rodgers munched on gingerbread. Way up front, in the under- three-hour grouping, I thought I spotted Dr. Isle but I couldn't reach him in the throng. The one I really looked for, Nurse Phillips, was somewhere in the herd of four-hour women stretching their backs against trees, adjusting straps, fine-tuning themselves.

Well, I thought, I'll give it all I've got. Those were my big words to myself at the start. I said them over and over for the first four miles. I studied faces as they passed, then switched to subjects. I did philosophy from mile five to eleven, trying to form one discriminating sentence about Socrates, Kant, Spinoza, Kierkegaard, whomever. When I came to the authors of *How to Be Your Own Best Friend*, I knew my mind was wandering and let go of systematizing. I listened to the rhythm of my breath, which was unsteady as early as twelve miles into the race. By fifteen miles, lots of women were passing me and I understood that I might not make it. Without despair I continued step by step.

If not for the nurse's cap I might not have recognized Miss Phillips as she pulled alongside. Her stride was lively. The insides of her thighs puckered. "Take one of these," she said, slipping me a brown tablet. "Dolomite."

I hesitated.

"It's just magnesium and calcium. It will help with the cramps." Though I could barely talk, esprit de corps was in my eyes. She ran alongside me, my inspiration and my pacer, until I ran out of myself. She says it was after twenty-four miles. My feet just stopped taking orders.

In the sudden stillness I thought someone had put me into the sidecar of a motorcycle. I heard the static of a CB radio. Eight or ten horsepower seemed to be propelling me. It was Nurse Phillips. In charity she had entered my nervous system.

"Women have more stamina," she said. "I knew it before liberation."

I could feel that layer of feminine softness give of itself cell by cell. Her generosity moved my heart.

"Save something for later," I moaned, "for childbirth and famine."

She held my hand.

"I can't make it," I gasped.

"There's more to life than the marathon," she said. "There's the twenty-five kilometers, the hill climbs, the five-kilometer sprint, the half marathon."

"I'm too old," I said.

"There's the submasters and the masters. There's Golden Age jogging and, finally, trots in the sunset."

"Without you I couldn't make it," I said. "The therapist told me the last six miles had to be alone."

"There will still be loneliness," she said. "Swollen joints and arthritis, varicose veins, arguments over money."

The finish line was in sight—the Hancock Building, the great tower of insurance.

"For you," I said with my last breath. "I did it for you." At the finish line I collapsed in her arms. People all around were doing the same. It looked like World War I in underpants.

She doused me in Gatorade. "At any pace," she said, "there is infirmity and disease. Carbo-loading will never be enough."

We bronzed our shoes and toasted one another in Body Punch.

"When our electrolytes balance," she said, "we'll live happily ever after."

We showered and went into training.

STAYING THE DISTANCE

William R. Loader

(1958)

The stadium was packed. Forty thousand spectators were present. The noise of their talk and movement filled the oval arena. As the light clusters topping the four tall pylons were switched on, flooding the red track and the green middle with illumination, the noise rose in pitch and became a roar of excitement. There was an odd feel in the air. This wasn't just an ordinary athletics meeting that people had come to see. It was a battle of the nations, a clash of giants. Men and women who had never run a race in their lives could feel the tension mounting inside them. For weeks the press and the radio had prepared them for this encounter. Now that it was actually here, now that the athletes were assembling in their track suits for the ceremonial march past, people could hardly believe it was real.

The climax was to be reached at nine o'clock. Important though the other events were, and eagerly though British victories were applauded—with a polite, more restrained ovation for Russian winners—they were seen as a prelude, a build-up to the 5000 metres. The Race of the Century, newspapermen had been calling it. Golden Boy Somerford versus Iron Man Suvarov. In millions of homes all over the United Kingdom chairs were being drawn up to television sets. In the Dobson home in Steelbrough even Tigger's mother was fidgeting nervously, seized by the magnitude of the occasion, staring at the fourteen inch screen as if fearing that a moment's inattention might deprive her of a sight of her son.

In the British team's dressing-room at the White City men were also fidgeting. Rather, Somerford and Dobson were jigging round restlessly as they awaited the call to go out on the track, while Hooper was strangely calm. It was a bad sign, Tigger thought. Hooper was looking like a man who is already beaten before he starts running. Perhaps his crushing defeat at the hands of Suvarov in the European Games had knocked the spirit out of him. Certainly the spirit wasn't knocked out of Somerford. The Golden Boy was straining at the leash, desperate to get his revenge. In the past, Tigger's admiration of Somerford had sometimes been reluctant and tinged with personal animus, but now it was wholehearted. This man was a true champion. He deserved all the popular acclaim he'd ever had. It made Tigger oddly happy to admit it. He caught Somerford's eye, and smiled. The Golden Boy smiled in return.

"How are you feeling, Tigger?" he asked.

"Windy," Tigger said.

"Aren't we all?" Somerford glanced briefly and anxiously at Hooper. "I'm glad you've got your chance at last, Tigger. You've earned it. Jolly good luck."

"Thanks. Same to you."

"Five thousand metres in five minutes," an attendant shouted.

Now it was come. Now was the quickening in the bowels.

"How do you think we should work it, Gerry?" Tigger asked, as they went out.

Somerford shrugged. "I don't think there's much we can work with comrade Suvarov. The man positively enjoys front running. I've never seen anyone less affected by having to set his own pace. Our best bet is just to hang on and come at him at the finish." He laughed. "If we have anything left to come with."

"What about trying to break him up a bit?"

"You can, if you like, Tigger, but if I were to try it," Somerford confessed honestly, "I think I'd only break myself up."

They were across the bridge and on to the track now. A mighty roar of applause greeted the sight of Somerford's fair head. There was less applause, but equal interest, in the ash-blond Suvarov, whose hair looked white in the flood-lighting. Since the race was 188 yards longer than three miles the start was on the opposite side of the track from the finish. Television cameras followed the six runners as they trotted across the grass.

"There's our Tigger!" Johnny Dobson shouted excitedly, as he spotted his brother's tall, track-suited figure on the screen. "And there's Somerford! And I think that one's the Russian!"

"This is the race that everyone has been waiting for," the television commentator was saying, "the five thousand metres. And the big question is whether the British champion Somerford can avenge his recent defeat by Alexey Suvarov. The other two members of the British team are Hooper and Dobson, with Ruabin and Prasenko as the Soviet second and third strings. Without meaning any disrespect to the other competitors we can safely say this race is going to be a struggle between Somerford and Suvarov."

"The idea!" Mrs. Dobson said indignantly. "Does he think our Tigger is just going to let them walk away from him?"

"We might easily see a new world's record set up, bettering Suvarov's time of 13 minutes 54.4 seconds," the announcer went on. "Now the runners are stripping off their track suits. I've just been given the order of starting. On the inside of the track will be Dobson of Great Britain, next to him Suvarov of the U.S.S.R., then Somerford of Britain, then Ruabin, with Hooper in fifth position and Prasenko on the outside. I expect Suvarov will go with a rush right from the start, drawing Gerry Somerford after him."

On the track, under the floodlights, the two blond heads were prominent, the focus of everyone's attention. Having stripped off their track suits, the Britons and the Russians were shaking hands, the Russians giving a little bow as they did so. Tigger Dobson noticed that Ruabin and Prasenko were looking pale. They were men of no great reputation. Tonight they were out of their class. But Alexey Suvarov was a different proposition. An athlete of medium height, he looked the Iron Man the newspapers called him—under the red vest bulged a powerful chest, and it was matched by strong shoulders and muscular legs. Blue eyes stared vividly out from the broad, white face. He took Tigger's hand in a hard grip. Suddenly the Englishman recalled the only word of Russian he had ever heard. "*Tovarich*," he said.

A quick, surprised smile split the Russian's face, but he controlled himself instantly. He wasn't going to inject confidence into the opposition by any show of friendliness before the race.

"*Dobre vece*," he said curtly, and went on to shake hands with Hooper.

"Get to your marks!" the starter's voice sang out through the amplifiers. The noise of the crowd stilled at once. In silence they watched the red-vested Russians and the white-vested Britons take up alternate positions along the starting line.

"Get set!"

All eyes were on the two blond heads in the second and third positions. Even on the television screen, diminished by the distance of the cameras, they were easily identifiable. Spectators and viewers held their breath, waiting to see one of those blond heads break away quickly, wondering which it would be.

The pistol fired. A moment's silence as the tensed bodies sprang into action, and then a shout of disbelief went up from the crowd. The head that had broken away quickly, so quickly that the body which owned it was practically in a sprint, was dark, not fair. Tigger Dobson had stolen a march on the Russian. At the crown of the bend he was five yards up. Coming into the straight he was clearly increasing his lead. As he crossed the finishing line for the first time, having worked off the odd one eighty-eight yards and with three miles now to go, he was nearly ten yards in front of Suvarov and Somerford and going like a quarter-miler. In one brief dash he established his identity to millions of people. "Dobson!" the White City crowd shouted. "Dobson!" the television viewers echoed, either silently or aloud. "Come on, Tigger!" Jean Blackie called, in a small, stammering voice.

"This is fantastic, of course," the commentator gabbled into his microphone, adjusting himself to an initial race pattern which he hadn't expected. "Dobson can't keep it up. I remember he did something very like it in the A.A.A. three miles but eventually burst a boiler. Still, he's certainly going to shake Suvarov a bit."

Tigger was sweeping round the bend into the back straight. He could see the giant stop clock under the northwest stand. That first 188 yards must have been done in about twenty-three seconds. An extravagant expenditure of energy, but it might well pay dividends. He was slackening off now to somewhere in the region of a sixty-five second lap. He felt good. Not only did he feel good, he felt savage. His upper lip was curled back almost in a snarl. This was the night of his life. With mechanical ease and precision his legs oscillated from the hip. As yet there was no sensation of effort when he changed speed either up or down. He might have been advancing or retarding the starter handle of an electric motor. The roar of the crowd reached his ears as an amorphous rumour of sound. Impossible to hear the crunch as his spiked shoes bit into the cinder track. He was going to grind the opposition into the earth, and if he ground himself in the process, that was too bad.

The crowd noise swelled and changed in pitch when it was seen that Suvarov was going after the runaway Englishman. It was surprising he hadn't done so sooner. Perhaps he was taken aback by the defiance of his unknown opponent. As the Russian accelerated, so also did Somerford. The two blond heads advanced as if they were connected by a length of wire. Their sprint broke connection with the rest of the field. Even at this early stage Hooper was in distress, while the Russian second and third strings were lagging. Later, one of the Russians dropped out, but Hooper kept going at a dogged speed as if he were in a race on his own.

"Oh, look," Mrs. Dobson said, nearly in tears as she gazed at the television screen, "those other two are going to catch Tigger up. He isn't going to win after all."

"Hush, Mum," Johnny said impatiently, "there's another ten laps to go yet."

Where there had been one figure out on its own on the white-lined track there were now three together, the two taller Englishmen, and the shorter, burly Russian between them. They stayed in that order for a complete lap, taking it easy, each wondering who was going to make the next effort. Like a bush fire, excitement ran through the crowd. By heaven, this was going to be a race. The quality of the athletes they were watching was patent. Here were three young men, each superlatively fit, with his own reputation and his country's prestige depending on the power of his lungs and the strength of his legs. A man might not see another contest like this in ten years.

With a neat, swift movement Suvarov slipped past Tigger Dobson on the fourth lap, drawing Gerry Somerford after him. The crowd held its breath, expecting the Russian to make one of his spurts, but for the moment he was holding his fire. Not only had it taken a physical effort to come up with Dobson, but there had been a degree of mental stress as a result of being surprised.

"This is the pattern of the race we had been expecting," the television commentator said excitedly, "with Suvarov leading and Somerford trailing him. Dobson has served his team nobly over the first mile by taking the initiative from the Russian, but I doubt if he has much steam left now. I think he's looking a little weary."

On the back straight during the fifth lap the Russian struck. The crowd had been waiting for it. They saw the acceleration of leg movements even before Gerry Somerford did, and shouted their alarm. The Golden Boy was only caught off his guard momentarily. At once he answered speed with speed. The gap which had threatened to open between the two blond heads quickly closed. Going into the bend there was the same distance between them. Somerford had been foxed once by his opponent. He wasn't going to be foxed again.

"Som-er-ford! Som-er-ford!" the exultant, rhythmic chant rose from the stands.

"Su-va-rov! Su-va-rov!" the Russian's compatriots chanted back defiantly.

The heat was on now. The protagonists of Russia and the United Kingdom were at grips. On his back Gerry Somerford was carrying a great cargo of sympathy and exhortation lavished on him by millions of present and distant spectators. If he was feeling any mental or physical strain as a result of his efforts so far, no sign of it appeared in his face. With a grave, dedicated look he trailed the red vest, keeping near enough almost to touch it. His countrymen loved him. They loved his grace and his strength and his courage. He wasn't going to let them down. So concentrated was the gaze of the multitude on the two leading athletes that the man in third position was hardly noticed. Yet Tigger Dobson was lying not much further behind Somerford than Somerford was behind Suvarov.

At last the Iron Man began to test the opposition. For three laps in succession he burst away on the back straight, running with crucifying speed considering the distance that had already been covered. Each time he eased off as he entered the bend leading to the home straight, and each time he gave a quick glance over his shoulder to find that the Englishmen were still up with him. They hadn't been shaken off by as much as a yard.

"I think that Suvarov is getting worried," the commentator shouted hoarsely into his microphone. "I think by now he had expected to lose Somerford. But Somerford is still there, looking quite easy, and Dobson is there, too. My goodness, what a race this is. Just over a mile to go, and they are well inside the schedule for a new world record. Is it possible that Suvarov has shot his bolt?"

Down on the track, amid the billowing noise and the glare of lights, the three scantily-clad figures moved in harmony like the linked driving wheels of a locomotive. Tigger Dobson glanced at the placard showing "4" which an official was holding up. Dear God, another mile to go. He was feeling terrible. Outwardly he knew all was still well. His form was not going to pieces. His legs had answered all demands made on them. But how much longer could they keep on answering? These bursts by Suvarov were excruciating. They tore your body to bits. How was it they weren't tearing him as well? It wasn't human to run like this. He couldn't keep it up. If the Russian did another burst on this lap he wouldn't be able to respond. He would try, but already his mind was telling him it couldn't be done. In anguish he waited as they rounded the bend into the back straight. Any moment now that diabolical red vest would start going away again. Any moment now. Wait for it. Wait to be left standing.

The burst didn't come. Realization dawned upon Tigger slowly. Suvarov was human, after all. He didn't like the pace any more than his opponents. Even he had to take a breather sometimes. In fact, his speed on this lap was quite slow, slow compared with the others. And soon there would be only three laps left. A small flame of confidence began to burn in Tigger's mind. Physically he didn't feel any better, but it was a great mental comfort to know that he was showing himself as good a man as the Russian, as good a man as Somerford.

They came up to the finishing line with three laps to go. Hardly conscious of making the decision, Tigger suddenly pulled out from behind Somerford and forged up into the lead. The movement astounded everyone, not least the Russian. Owing to the position of the television cameras it was seen perfectly on the screen. Far away in Steelbrough Johnny Dobson went wild with excitement.

"Our Tigger's in front!" he yelled. "Mum! Dad! Our Tigger's in front! Did you see him go ahead just then? He's going to win!"

It was only a short and agonized burst round the bend, for there wasn't much left in Tigger to burst with, but it electrified the White City crowd. Going into the back straight the order was Dobson, Suvarov, Somerford. His two opponents came up with Tigger as he eased off, but they came up patently with an effort.

The B.B.C. commentator was stammering into his microphone. "This is unbelievable! Dobson is playing the Russian at his own game. I never thought this young fellow would stay the distance, yet here he is challenging the two finest three-milers in the world. But this awful pace must be sapping his last reserves of strength. There's just over half a mile to go. Has Suvarov got anything left up his sleeve?"

As the climax of the race approached, the crowd found the tension almost unbearable. The sight of the torture undergone by the three athletes worked upon the spectators' own bodies. Even upon the Russian's tough features the signs of strain were evident. But strained or no, he still had some steam in him. Down the back straight he drove himself into yet another sprint. The burst took him up into the lead past Tigger Dobson. For a few moments he gained a matter of five yards, and held the gain. Then Tigger, visibly summoning his resources, gradually pulled up. There was a gasp from forty thousand throats. But the gasp wasn't caused by Dobson's meeting of Suvarov's challenge. It was caused by Gerry Somerford's failure to do so. Men stared down at the arena, unbelieving. The Golden Boy had cracked under the terrible pressure. The idol of the track had blown up. His eyes half closed, Somerford kept going, but that was as much as he could do. Britain's hope had failed. The Iron Man had repeated his triumph of the European Games.

"Somerford's a spent force," the commentator groaned. "This is going to be a Russian victory. Where Somerford has failed, I cannot think that Dobson will succeed, magnificently as he has run tonight. They're coming up to the last lap now."

No one except the athletes heard the bell. Suvarov and Dobson went over the line separated only by a stride, with Somerford ten yards behind. The noise of the crowd had grown to a tremendous, hysterical roar. Men and women were standing and screaming, suffering with the runners below them, willing their own man to win. They were conscious of nothing except the titanic struggle taking place in front of them. Somerford, the pride of Britain, was forgotten. When the spotlight was switched on to two desperately weary men it illumined the blond head of Suvarov and the dark head of Tigger Dobson. The Golden Boy was in comparative dimness behind them. People who had never heard the name of Dobson before this evening would afterwards take years to forget it. On millions of television screens throughout the country the Englishman's effort was being registered and imprinted deep on the minds of the viewers. Women watched with tears streaming down their cheeks. Men pounded the arms of their chairs and uttered wild, nonsensical shouts. The agony of the runners was a visible, tangible thing. It was only courage and the deepest reserves of stamina that were driving them round the track, still competing, still fighting it out.

Caught in the bright pool of the spotlight, they drove. There was a horrifying moment when Dobson hit the board lining the inside of the track, and staggered. And he hit the board because he couldn't see where he was going. He was enveloped in a bloody haze, in which the red vest of this fiendish Russian kept merging. Long since he had passed the stage of fatigue, passed the stage of utter exhaustion. He was no longer conscious of his body, not conscious of it as a mechanism. Rather was it a ghastly and crushing weight which was grinding him to pieces. Why in God's name didn't someone stop this torture? Why didn't he stop it himself. The noise around him was excruciating. It drove iron drills into his brain. And then suddenly out of the shapeless din he heard a definite pattern of sound emerging.

"Dobson! Dobson! DOB-SON!"

As if they were fighting their way through a nightmare, in which no matter how fast they ran no progress could be made, the two runners rounded the last bend. They were nearly into the home straight. Less than a hundred yards separated them from the tape, a yard separated them from each other.

"He can't do it," Mr. Dobson was saying over and over to himself in a cracked voice, as he watched the anguish on the screen. "The lad can't do it. He can't do it, Mabel."

But Mrs. Dobson had hidden her face in her hands. She was only aware of the noise coming out of the set, a shrieking din surcharged with the rhythmic chanting, "Dobson! Dobson! DOB-SON!" It was her boy that they were shouting for. It was her boy.

Still caught in the pool of the spotlight, the two figures struggled into the home straight, the figure in the red vest leading the figure in the white vest. Jean Blackie could not see for tears. Someone near her in the crowd kept repeating, in a voice from which emotion had been exhausted, "It's going to be a world record! Just took at the clock! It's going to be a world record!" She heard the words, but did not understand them. Her father was uttering queer, choking noises beside her. All around the world was going mad.

Suvarov's head was back. His arms were thrashing wildly. He was a broken man. Only fifty yards left. Sweet Jesus, fifty yards of blood and fire. The spectators were no longer in possession of their senses. Dobson was coming up. It wasn't possible that he had anything left after that murderous race, but he was coming up. His countrymen saw him in the flesh, they saw his image on the screens. Like a man still crawling after he has been mortally wounded, he was inching up to the Russian's shoulder. The spectacle was unbearably poignant. It seemed to be taking place in slow motion. The thin line of worsted at the finish was almost within grasping distance. The two athletes were reeling under the cruelty of it all. It was horribly wrong that one of them should have to lose. The red vest and the white vest were level, and the white vest was still inching forward.

"He's going to win!" Jean Blackie's father screamed in her ear. The sweat streamed down his face.

"He's going to win!" Mr. Dobson croaked, staring at the screen with bloodshot eyes.

"Dobson! Dobson! DOB-SON!"

The great stadium was rent with noise. It was a mighty paean honouring courage and strength. The vision of two figures was burnt into the brain of every person present. And the figure in the white vest, eyes closed and face deathly pale, was crossing the line two feet in front of the figure in the red vest.

AN EVENING AT THE TRACK

Douglas Dunn

(1980)

Humphrey MacGibbon used to run the 400 metres hurdles and had been good at it by anyone's standards. At twenty-three, he broke his left leg in several places when he came off Harry Anson's prize possession, an old Matchless 1000 cc motorcycle.

When he was standing still, Humphrey looked every bit an athlete. He was tall, broad-shouldered and solid in the way 400 metres hurdlers usually are. It was only when he walked, with that jerking limp of his, that it became clear Humphrey was a man who had had an accident. "I'm the only man I know," he said, with a humour that disguised his disappointment, "who looks more like a one-lap man when he's sitting down than when he's walking about."

"Look on the bright side, for God's sake," said Harry Anson, who was usually in a bad mood, and who had never allowed himself to admit that either he or his collector's item of a motorbike was to blame for Humphrey's infirmity. "At least you don't need to feel guilty every time you go out for a drink."

"Is there anyone here, Harry, who seriously believes I could have taken my time down any more? I needed to lose another two seconds to be anywhere near world class." He looked at the others in the club's pavilion and dressing-rooms. No one else seemed to be listening. "It doesn't matter."

"Sure, sure," said Harry Anson. He had his special reason for wishing that Humphrey would stay away from the club. Everyone else was familiar with Humphrey's resignation, his good-natured acceptance of the worst that could have happened to him. But they, too, were less than delighted to see him, although they were welcoming when he arrived, as he did, about one evening a week. He had been the one outstanding athlete the club had produced.

They liked him. They admired him. It was not his presence so much as the presence of his limp that disturbed them.

Humphrey watched Harry Anson put on his tracksuit. "Why do you bother?" he asked, encouraging a laugh from the others.

"Keep the old belly in trim," said Harry Anson, tapping his stomach. He was an indifferent athlete in whom, they all agreed, natural ability had been allowed to go to waste because of indolence, nights out, girls, beer and cigarettes. He left the pavilion. In a few minutes the changing-rooms were empty.

Someone who had trained on his own earlier in the evening was in the showers. Humphrey could hear the water running. He pulled himself to his feet, and, hobbling with the walking-stick he still had to use, went out on the veranda. He leaned against the railings for a few minutes. It was a fine evening in late May, before the competitive season had properly begun. A couple of fixtures against other clubs was all that had been held, but the first important meet of the year was coming up that Saturday, the Western District Championships. Humphrey had always enjoyed it, in spite of having more celebrated championships and matches to look forward to later in the summer. Like most athletes, he had taken a sly if modest pride in being immeasurably superior to the best local opposition. A hard-earned third place in a classy time against international fast-men from the United States, Poland, or France, was satisfying to look back on; but he preferred to remember an arrogant fifty-five seconds in the heats of the Western District Championships—a time which the second- or third-placed men, in the final, would have done well if they had matched. Towards the end of that Saturday afternoon in late May, he used to anchor his club's 4 x 400 metres relay squad. Usually, he was faced with the prospect of overhauling a deficit of forty or fifty metres. He revelled in it. On only one occasion out of five had he failed to pull it off, and even then it had been a matter of a couple of feet, having provided the best race of the day.

A smell of cut grass from the centre and outside surroundings of the track was conspicuous in the still air. A cricket team was practising its nets. It was so still that in spite of the distance he could hear the smack of bat against ball. Five runners trotted through an open gate in the high hedge which hid the track from the road. They were the marathon and long-distance runners, setting off for their fifteen miles over the hills and lanes in the countryside beyond the edge of the suburb. Ferguson, the coach in charge of sprinters, was instructing junior members of the club on how to adjust their starting-blocks. Long-jumpers were high-kicking and bounding against space or stretching on the grass. High-jumpers were measuring high-kicks against a bar raised six feet above the ground. A dozen varieties of calisthenics were portrayed. Women athletes were coming out from their club-house on the other side of the track—always, for some reason, a few minutes later than the men. Humphrey waved, and they waved back. Round the track were three packs of runners, jogging, shuffling, warming up. A coach pulled someone out for a chat. A group laughed, sharing a joke.

Humphrey went carefully down the wooden steps to the level of the rolled cinders. Breaking into a caricature of his one-legged run, he hobbled across the track in front of a band of tracksuited runners. Peter Cairns, the club's senior coach, was consulting his clipboard. On sheets of tabulated paper, he had listed the names of his athletes, a sheet for each runner. Neatly typed were his notes on what he intended his charges to get through, day by day, week by week, various distances at various speeds, how much, how fast. All this physical arcana would be measured against one of his many stopwatches. He might have four or five watches running at the same time.

"Humphrey, would you hold that?" said Cairns, handing him the clipboard and its wads of training-schedules, leaving him free to shake an apparently deficient stopwatch against his ear. "Perfect conditions," said Cairns curtly.

"Yes. The wind's dropped for a change." The weather was the way it should have been and seldom was—no wind, no rain, and a clear sky. "I've been thinking," said Humphrey, "that I might do a little coaching. Have you any suggestions, Peter?"

"Later," said Cairns. He was a busy man. "But I don't see why not," he added, before he trotted over to where a group of athletes was waiting for him.

Humphrey followed him and stood for a few minutes listening to Cairns' pronouncements on the evening's work-out. A few runners protested, as they always did. One said he was too tense to train on the track. He set off for a run over the nearby golf course. The runner was a noted prima donna, a loner who found that the social endurance of training with other runners did not suit him. Cairns was angry and it took a few minutes for him to get rid of his petulance. He was fat, in his tracksuit. Humphrey suspected that Cairns' belly was as dead as his own left leg.

Dr. O'Neill, the club's secretary, was sitting on a camp stool on the veranda, pulling sheets of paper from his briefcase. They were entry forms for the open meets in which most of the club's runners would compete because they were not up to the standard of championship events. Humphrey was about to go and have a word with Dr. O'Neill when Cairns asked him if he would hold a watch on a young middle-distance runner. "Fine," he said, glad of the chance to be useful.

The young runner set off from the starting-line. Seconds ticked by on the watch. A good distance away, the runner who had been too "tense" to train on the track could be seen as a green-tracksuited figure climbing the first green incline of the links. Humphrey turned his attention to the young 1500 metres runner. Fluently, with a confidence that told Humphrey that the runner either had more natural ability than Cairns had noticed, or that he had trained hard before joining the club, he came up to the finishing mark. "Sixty-two!" Humphrey shouted as he passed him. "Dead on!" Cairns' schedule said that the runner should be doing laps in sixty-eight seconds, with a lap of four minutes in between each faster 400 metres.

"You're supposed to be doing sixty-eights," said Humphrey.

"I've done this before," said the runner. "You can tell him what you like," he said, meaning the coach, "but I'm doing twelve in sixty-two." He set off jogging a lap.

"Is that wise?" said Humphrey, but the young runner kept going, without an answer.

"Good evening," said Dr. O'Neill on the veranda. He had his medical practice in the same suburban district where the club had its pavilion. "These chestnuts," he said, pointing with his pen, "have come out since Saturday. Best-looking trees in the entire district."

A young sprinter, heavy about the shoulders, went striding past the veranda. "What's Ferguson thinking about?" said Humphrey. "That lad ought to move up to the four hundred."

"Twenty-two point five last night," said Dr. O'Neill, "on a grass track. He won the Inter-schools two-twenty. And I thought last night," he said, with a sly smile, "that there goes another Humphrey MacGibbon. I don't suppose you remember when I told you to move up to the four-forty." Dr. O'Neill's mind had failed to go metric. He still talked of furlongs, quarters, half-miles. To Dr. O'Neill, a middle-distance runner was still a miler or three-miler.

"Can he hurdle?"

"I doubt it," said Dr. O'Neill. "But neither could you until I taught you."

Humphrey snapped the stopwatch back into motion as the middle-distance runner set off on another lap. "I'm no expert on the long stuff," said Humphrey, "but he looks pretty useful."

"He's going too fast," said Dr. O'Neill. "Cairns'll just burn out young chaps like that. All these foreigners that Cairns gets his fancy ideas from."

"It's not Cairns' fault this time."

"Then you tell him, 'Make haste slowly,'" said Dr. O'Neill, reiterating his favourite maxim.

"Just under thirty-one at two-hundred. The lad can judge his pace," said Humphrey.

"Humphrey, we're having an argument," said a sixteen-year-old, from the cinders in front of the veranda.

"Was your best time," asked the boy beside him, "fifty point eight, or fifty-one?"

"Sixty-two!" shouted Humphrey, as the subject on his watch crossed the line again. "Fifty point five," said Humphrey casually, waving to his middle-distance runner, and switching the stopwatch back to its stopped zeros.

"What does it feel like? I mean, at the end, after a fifty point five?" asked one of the boys.

"It depends," said Humphrey, "on whether you've won or lost." He enjoyed saying such things to the young members of his Harriers club, having himself joined when he was fourteen.

"I mean, the exhaustion, what does it feel like?"

"You'll never know," said Humphrey, "until you've been there." Ferguson, the sprints coach, called the two boys towards him, and directed them, like truants, to two vacant starting-blocks.

"If there was one thing I hated," said Humphrey, "it was rehearsing sprint starts. Now, that I don't miss, not in the least."

"In my day," said Dr. O'Neill, "you scooped a couple of holes in the track, shoved your feet in them, and that was that."

The evening was now at its most animated. Cairns and others were calling out times. Jogging men athletes were making remarks to jogging women athletes. Long-jump and high-jump pits were busy. A lone hulk was shot-putting out of harm's way, on his concrete circle in the centre of the track. As always, the javelin thrower was being advised to see an optician."Sixty-two!" Humphrey called out again to the young middle-distance runner.

"You'd better tell him to slow it down," said Dr. O'Neill. "Cairns'll throw a fit if he notices what that lad's doing."

"Ach," said Humphrey, "it doesn't matter. The lad's obviously done this before. We'll see if he can learn the hard way."

Harry Anson, at the tail end of a pack, went round on one of his fast laps. Humphrey timed him, out of interest. The lap took sixty-seven seconds. Harry, bringing up the rear, did not look tired so much as bored. Cairns, his taskmaster, said nothing about it.

"Cairns," said Humphrey, "must know nothing, if he can't see that the lad's running sixty-twos instead of sixty-eights. I mean, the difference is visible."

"That's right," said Dr. O'Neill, who had never liked Cairns. "An unhappy man is Cairns. There are women now who can run a faster marathon than he ever managed."

"Talking of women," said Humphrey, "what's she doing here?"

"She," said Dr. O'Neill, "is a very promising shot-putter. That's how they build them these days."

"I can run faster than that."

"Not when you're carrying heavy weights, you can't," said Dr. O'Neill.

Humphrey looked and saw that, indeed, the shot-putter was carrying weights which, as she ran, she raised to the height of her chin, first one hand, then the other. "Good God!"

"They tell me she's nifty on the judo floor as well."

"What makes women do things like that?"

"What," asked Dr. O'Neill, "makes men want to run the four hundred hurdles in fifty point five?"

Before the light began to fade, at about eight-thirty, Humphrey's middle-distance runner finished his session. Only in the last three of his fast laps had he failed to be within a second of his ideal sixty-two seconds. "That," said Humphrey, "was terrific. Cheeky, but terrific. I'll look forward to seeing what you do on Saturday."

"I'm looking for a coach."

"Well, I'm no expert in middle-distance running, but I'll have a word with Peter if you like."

"Couldn't you bone it up?"

"I could, I suppose," said Humphrey, tentatively. "But the four hundred and the four-hundred hurdles were my races."

"I know. The thing is, you've been there."

The coaches and Dr. O'Neill cleared runners off the track. There was to be a race. The club's six 400-metres runners were to compete for the four places in the relay squad. They were already taking their tracksuits off at the start. Cairns, perspiring after his night's work, was examining his starter's gun.

"Will you think about it?"

"Sure. I'll tell you on Saturday," said Humphrey, as the middle-distance runner trotted away, thinking about his ambitions.

Humphrey hobbled over to the veranda from where he knew Dr. O'Neill would watch the race. Crossing the track, he wished the runners luck. He enjoyed his presence there, the way it acknowledged he had been faster than they could ever be, no matter how hard they trained or tried. He noticed that one of the runners was the tall broad-shouldered sprinter he had seen earlier in the evening, who had looked like an illusory memory of himself at seventeen. It made him stop. "I dare say you could still beat me, Humphrey," said one runner, bringing Humphrey back from whatever he thought he had seen and been absorbed by. "I don't know why I bother."

Light had faded into a cool greeny dusk in which birdsong was implicated, as well as a haze of late daffodils on the point of withering which grew against a bank. Cricketers were returning to their club-house, their whites greyed by the distance. There were a dozen people on the veranda, some in towels, others as they had come from the track. Peter Cairns held up his starter's pistol. He looked at it in his hand as if he liked the idea of himself as an armed man. "To your marks!" The competitors stepped into their blocks, apart from the man on the inside who, as an 800-metres runner, used a standing start. Two or three more athletes came out from the pavilion to the veranda. Some wives or girlfriends were standing at the nearest bend of the track, one with an agitated dog held tightly on a short leash. Cairns, losing patience, delayed the start until the dog had been shut up. On the other side of the track, on the veranda of their club-house, the women members of the club were gathered to watch the race. Dr. O'Neill stopped himself on the steps and waited to give the starter and the runners the silence they deserved. "Set!" ordered Cairns, in a high-pitched growl, drawn out and serious until it sounded like a threat. The gun went off.

Humphrey laughed under his breath with excitement. From the gun, the young sprinter whom Humphrey had said to Dr. O'Neill should move up to the 400 metres began to take yards out of the rest of the field.

As they raced round the first bend, the women who were standing there screamed at them with that feminine enthusiasm which, to any large crowd, adds a soprano pitch to the deeper-voiced roar of spectators. It was a sound Humphrey used to listen for in the days when he had been the centre of attention. The dog barked at the runners as their spikes kicked up cinders with each racing footfall.

"Well," said Dr. O'Neill, "it was you who said he should move up a distance." He had the pretended nonchalance of an old-timer who had seen too many runners come and go for him to have been able to take a race as seriously as they took it themselves. As he looked at Humphrey's tense enjoyment, he wished for the time when Humphrey, too, would join him as an interested cynic, fund-raising, organising the annual dances, distributing entry-forms and being invited to officiate at minor championship meetings. O'Neill's hero was Eric Liddell, who had won the Olympic 400 metres gold medal in 1924, because the final of his chosen event was to have been run on a Sunday, and to have competed would have been to break the Sabbath.

And so what, if Humphrey MacGibbon had run faster than Liddell, and on the club's own outdated cinder track?

Along the back straight, the young runner looked like a film of Humphrey. The others, by comparison, were clumsy, with their heads back, their arms flying across their chests. They were all effort and pluck and no style. They had nothing of the young runner's grace. His running had propriety, assurance; he possessed the event as, physically, his own. A distance, and speed, Humphrey knew, and as Dr. O'Neill knew, were part of a physical identity. They were not chosen.

Over the last sixty metres, the young runner began to slow down. His elegance was tortured into painful mediocrity. Humphrey yelled at him, "Fight! Fight it!" His face was as agonised as the runner's. Those who were also watching from the veranda were urging the runner on, too; but they were distracted by Humphrey's livid eagerness. As the winner broke the tape, Humphrey stopped his watch. Three others, at the finishing-line, were doing the same. Humphrey peered at the watch in the half-light. "Forty-nine six!" he read off. "Forty-nine six! Under fifty!"

Dr. O'Neill was scrutinising his own watch. "Five I made it. Forty-nine five."

"You should've told me," said Humphrey. "I could've had a word with him beforehand."

"I can still," said Dr. O'Neill, "spot the real thing when I see it."

"Trained properly, he could be doing forty-eight by the end of the season," said Humphrey, an emphatic pundit, speaking at first to no one, and then repeating himself to Dr. O'Neill, who, he found, was looking at him with pitiful benevolence, as if he understood how pleased Humphrey was to have been replaced. "That boy's a *natural* for the one-lap."

"Another Humphrey MacGibbon," declared Dr. O'Neill to the crowded veranda. "And I made it forty-nine five."

"Forty-nine six!" shouted Ferguson, the sprints coach, announcing the consensus of the three time-keepers.

Long-distance road-runners came in from the B-roads and bye-ways, smelling of sweat and dusk. Others crowded into the club-house. Harry Anson came out, already showered and dressed, having finished early and ignored the race. "Forty-nine six," said Humphrey.

"Good for him," said Harry Anson. "Well, I suppose you'll be there on Saturday to see me lapped in the usual fashion?"

"I wouldn't miss it."

"Thought not," said Harry Anson.

The new 400 metres runner was escorted to the veranda by Cairns, Ferguson and the other 400 metres men. There was a lot Humphrey wanted to say to him but the coaches were too full of recent stimulus to allow themselves to be interrupted.

From the car-park, behind the high hedge at the back of the club-house, Humphrey heard the roar of Harry Anson's motorcycle as he revved it up.

Steam came out of the club-house door. Shouting, laughter, and the sound of showers operating in spite of their antiquated plumbing were loud against Humphrey's ears. He did not go into the pavilion. He never did after an evening at the track. He had a dead left leg and it seemed cruel to remind everyone in there that they were susceptible to an accident. At the beginning of the evening that did not seem to matter; but after their exertions it did not feel right that he should remind them of how everything can be taken away in one sharp high-spirited surprise. "Good night!" he said to someone leaving.

"Night, Humphrey!"

The season now appeared as something definitely to be looked forward to. There was a new middle-distance runner, and there was a new one-lap man. Forty-nine point six! At his first race over the distance! Carefully he went down the wooden steps. From inside the door, where he was distributing the entry-forms he had sorted out during the evening, Dr. O'Neill could hear the tap of Humphrey's walking-stick on the steps. Then he could hear the limped rhythm of his walk over the spiked cinders.

Humphrey stopped and looked at the time registered on Peter Cairns' stopwatch. To take it back to him would have meant going into the club-house. He left the watch at the forty-nine point six seconds recorded on it and put it in his pocket and walked home.

"Good night!" he said to the wives and girlfriends waiting in the car-park. They all knew him, if only from his stick, his limp, or his blazer, with its flagged badge of the national team. He lived only a short distance from the track, a few streets, which he could cover in nine minutes and forty-six seconds, in the dark, when no one was looking.

Poems

FORM AND MOTIVATION

The Runner
Walt Whitman

On a flat road runs the well train'd runner,
He is lean and sinewy with muscular legs,
He is thinly clothed, he leans forward as he runs,
With lightly closed fists and arms partially raised.

Runner
W. H. Auden

All visible visibly
Moving things
Spin or swing,
One of the two,
Move, as the limbs
Of a runner do,
To and fro,
Forward and back,
Or, as they swiftly
Carry him,
In orbit go
Round an endless track:
So, everywhere, every
Creature disporting
Itself according
To the law of its making,
In the rivals' dance
Of a balanced pair,
Or the ring-dance
Round a common centre,
Delights the eye

By its symmetry
As it changes place,
Blessing the unchangeable
Absolute rest
Of the space all share.

The camera's eye
Does not lie,
But it cannot show
The life within,
The life of a runner,
Of yours or mine,
That race which is neither
Fast nor slow,
For nothing can ever
Happen twice,
That story which moves
Like music when
Begotten notes
New notes beget,
Making the flowing
Of Time a growing,
Till what it could be
At last it is,
Where Fate is Freedom,
Grace and Surprise.

This Runner

Francis Webb

This runner on his final lap
Sucks wildly for elusive air;
Space is a vortex, time's a gap,
Seconds are shells that hiss and flare
Between red mist and cool white day
Four hundred throttling yards away.

Each spike-shaped muscle, yelping nerve,
Worries, snaps at his stumbling weight;
He goes wide on this floating curve,
Cursing with crazy hammering hate
A rival glued to inside ground
Who flogs his heart, forces him round.

Friends, here is your holiday;
Admire your image in this force
While years, books, flesh and mind give way
To the sheer fury of the source.
Here is your vicious, central shape
That has no need of cheer or tape.

The Song of the Ungirt Runners

Charles Hamilton Sorley

We swing ungirded hips,
　　And lightened are our eyes;
The rain is on our lips,
　　We do not run for prize.

We know not whom we trust
　　Nor whitherward we fare,
But we run because we must
　　Through the great wide air.

The waters of the sea
　　Are troubled as by storm.
The tempest strips the trees
　　And does not leave them warm.
Does the tearing tempest pause?
　　Do the tree-tops ask it why?
So we run without a cause
　　'Neath the big bare sky.

The rain is on our lips,
　　We do not run for prize.
But the storm the water whips
　　And the wave howls to the skies.
The winds arise and strike it
　　And scatter it like sand,
And we run because we like it
　　Through the broad bright land.

Morning Athletes

Marge Piercy

Most mornings we go running side by side
two women in mid-lives jogging, awkward
in our baggy improvisations, two
bundles of rejects from the thrift shop.
Men in their zippy outfits run in packs
on the road where we park, meet
like lovers on the wood's edge and walk
sedately around the corner out of sight
to our own hardened clay road, High Toss.
Slowly we shuffle, serious, panting
but talking as we trot, our old honorable
wounds in knee and back and ankle paining
us, short, fleshy, dark haired, Italian
and Jew, with our full breasts carefully
confined. We are rich earthy cooks
both of us and the flesh we are working
off was put on with grave pleasure. We
appreciate each other's cooking, each
other's art, photographer and poet, jogging
in the chill and wet and green, in the blaze
of young sun, talking over our work,
our plans, our men, our ideas, watching
each other like a pot that might boil dry
for that sign of too harsh fatigue.

It is not the running I love, thump
thump with my leaden feet that only
infrequently are winged and prancing,
but the light that glints off the cattails
as the wind furrows them, the rum cherries
reddening leaf and fruit, the way the pines
blacken the sunlight on their bristles,
the hawk circling, stooping, floating
low over beige grasses,

and your company
as we trot, two friendly dogs leaving
tracks in the sands. The geese call
on the river wandering lost in sedges
and we talk and pant, pant and talk
in the morning early and busy together.

Strategy for a Marathon

Marnie Mueller

I will start
when the gun goes off.
I will run
for five miles.
Feeling good,
I will run
to the tenth mile.
At the tenth
I will say,
"Only three more
to the halfway."
At the halfway mark,
13.1 miles,
I will know
fifteen is in reach.
At fifteen miles
I will say,
"You've run twenty before,
keep going."
At twenty
I will say,
"Run home."

Out on the Course

William J. Vernon

On the roads, the race drew me outside
myself, running hills, fields and
woodlands, hearing both crow caw and
cow low, fearing that Doberman
growling across a front lawn,
rushing at me in a frenzy.

I was surprised by the beauty,
the sheer shapes of trees bared by fall
and the weather. My hungry eyes saw
it all, the deep ravines where creeks
were washing white rocks, and the steep
slopes were forested as densely
as they'd been in any century.
My cushioned soles felt the impression
of seeds, where corn and wheat had spun
out of combine or picker or loose-boarded

trucks. The homes were sleeping—or emptied
for going to church. A few people
waved from cars. Most stared at the simple,
half-naked men jogging in rain
in the forties, black numbers pinned
to their stomachs. I spoke at one

water stop. A shivering woman
gave me plastic cups. My voice, then,
hadn't worked as well as it should, when
I'd made a joke at twenty miles. My
mouth had stumbled. So I'd tried
again. The words had tripped over
themselves. Cackling, I'd run on, slower.

WINNING AND LOSING

The Service

Burges Johnson

I was the third man running in a race,
And memory still must run it o'er and o'er:
The pounding heart that beat against my frame;
The wind that dried the sweat upon my face
And turned my throat to paper creased and sore;
The jabbing pain that sharply went and came.

My eyes saw nothing save a strip of road
That flaunted there behind the second man;
It swam and blurred, yet still it lay before.
My legs seemed none of mine, but rhythmic strode
Unconscious of my will that urged, "You can!"
And cried at them to make one effort more.

Then suddenly there broke a wave of sound—
Crowds shouting when the first man struck the tape;
And then the second roused that friendly din;
While I—I stumbled forward and the ground
All wavered 'neath my feet, while men agape,
But silent, saw me as I staggered in.

As sick in heart and flesh I bent my head,
Two seized me and embraced me, and one cried,
"Your thudding footsteps held me to the grind."
And then the winner, smiling wanly, said,
"No dream of records kept me to my stride—
I dreaded you two thundering behind!"

If
Rudyard Kipling

If you can keep your head when all about you
  Are losing theirs and blaming it on you;
If you can fill the unforgiving minute
  With sixty seconds worth of distance run,
Yours is the earth and everything that's in it,
  And—which is more—you'll be a man, my son.

The Finish
Daniel Hoffman

The first runner reached us
bearing the news before
he was expected by
the camera crews—the instant
replay showed him strolling
by the roadside, sucking
half an orange. Who'd think
he had endured so many
miles? They demanded
he re-run the final
fifty yards while they
re-filmed him. While they filmed him
a second runner crossed
the line but by the time
the cameras turned to him
the second runner wasn't
running any longer
but sucking half an orange;
he too must re-enact
the second finish
since the public is entitled to the real thing.
Just as he recrossed

the line, finishing second
a second time, here comes
puffing up the hill
the third man, at his heels
the crazy crowd the first
runner had come to tell of
but had no chance to tell
anyone while cameras
caught his second first
finish and then turned
from him and scanned the second
finish of the second
finisher, the spent
third man with an orange
in his hand, the raggle-
taggle mob arriving
at the reviewing stand,
and soon there's blood all over
the finish line and no
reviewers and no stand,
but what viewer could
believe this, cameras still
following the third
man suck his orange? The crews
urge the crowd once more
to re-enact the finish—

Interview with a Winner

Donald Finkel

What was it like?
like losing
same bloody feet
blazing tendons
same sweet release
melancholia of exhaustion

What did you win?
a chance

For what?
to do it again
that wasn't it either

What did you get?
through

What's left for you?
tomorrow's race

losing is worse

Joan Benoit: 1984 Olympic Marathon Gold Medalist

Rina Ferrarelli

During the third mile
not the eighteenth as expected
she surged ahead
leaving behind the press
of bodies, the breath
hot on her back
and set a pace
the experts claimed
she couldn't possibly keep
to the end.

Sure, determined,
moving to an inner rhythm
measuring herself against herself
alone in a field of fifty
she gained the twenty-six miles
of concrete, asphalt and humid weather
and burst into the roar of the crowd
to run the lap around the stadium
at the same pace
once to finish the race
and then again in victory

and she was still fresh
and not even out of breath
and standing.

TIME, MEMORY, AND AGE

Running

Richard Wilbur

I 1933

What were we playing? Was it prisoner's base?
I ran with whacking keds
Down the cart-road past Richard's place,
And where it dropped beside the tractor-sheds

Leapt out into the air above a blurred
Terrain, through jolted light,
Took two hard lopes, and at the third
Spanked off a hummock-side exactly right,

And made the turn, and with delighted strain
Sprinted across the flat
By the bull-pen, and up the lane.
Thinking of happiness, I think of that.

II PATRIOT'S DAY

Restless that noble day, appeased by soft
Drinks and tobacco, littering the grass
While the flag snapped and brighted far aloft,
We waited for the marathon to pass,

We fathers and our little sons, let out
Of school and office to be put to shame.
Now from the street-side someone raised a shout,
And into view the first small runners came.
Dark in the glare, they seemed to thresh in place

Like preening flies upon a window-sill,
Yet gained and grew, and at a cruel pace
Swept by us on their way to Heartbreak Hill—

Legs driving, fists at port, clenched faces, men,
And in amongst them, stamping on the sun,
Our champion Kelley, who would win again,
Rocked in his will, at rest within his run.

III DODWELLS HILL ROAD

I jog out of the woods
To the crown of the road, and slow to a swagger there,
The wind harsh and cool to my throat,
A good ache in my rib-cage.

Loud burden of streams at run-off,
And the sun's rocket frazzled in blown tree-heads;
Still I am part of that great going,
Though I stroll now and am watchful.

Where the road turns and debouches,
The land sinks westward into exhausted pasture.
From fields which yield to aspen now
And pine at last will shadow,

Boy-shouts reach me, and barking.
What is the thing which men will not surrender?
It is what they have never had, I think,
Or missed in its true season,

So that their thoughts turn in
At the same roadhouse nightly, the same cloister,
The wild mouth of the same brave river
Never now to be charted.

You, whoever you are,
If you want to walk with me you must step lively.
I run, too, when the mood offers,
Though the god of that has left me.

But why in the hell spoil it?
I make a clean gift of my young running
To the two boys who break into view,
Hurdling the rocks and racing,

Their dog dodging before them
This way and that, his yaps flushing a pheasant
Who lifts now from the blustery grass,
Flying full tilt already.

100m Hurdles

William Borden

for Rachel

The runners
shake each foot,
loosening
gravity's tight jealousy,
before settling
into the blocks.

Fingertips on the line—
the starter's hand goes up.
The watchers wait
to breathe.

This is the moment
all time
rises on a toe.

It is this
that I remember, this
and the puff of smoke
that precedes the crack of the pistol,
the flurry of legs, the rocking
of hurdles grazed, the legs stretching,
the arms swimming, the crowd yelling,
as you clear hurdle after
hurdle, a dancer leaping
into the fine threads of the future,
faster than my heart, which
leaps everything for you.

The Sprinters

Lillian Morrison

The gun explodes them.
Pummeling, pistoning they fly
In time's face.
A go at the limit,
A terrible try
To smash the ticking glass,
Outpace the beat
That runs, that streaks away
Tireless, and faster than they.

Beside ourselves
(It is for us they run!)
We shout and pound the stands
For one to win
Loving him, whose hard
Grace-driven stride
Most mocks the clock
And almost breaks the bands
Which lock us in.

Running the Mile Relay

Ron Rash

Ours was an easy courage.
None of us college prep,
we did time in Crest High's
vocational wing,

learning nothing
that would save us
from trailer parks and mill work,
or even a winding-down war.

So we ran against time,
lived for stolen seconds, finding our measure
brassed in trophy cases.

Tight as the baton,
we gripped our certain knowledge:
this running in circles meant
more than anything coming.

His Running My Running

Robert Francis

Mid-autumn late autumn
At dayfall in leaf-fall
A runner comes running.

How easy his striding
How light his footfall
His bare legs gleaming.

Alone he emerges
Emerges and passes
Alone, sufficient.

When autumn was early
Two runners came running
Striding together

Shoulder to shoulder
Pacing each other
A perfect pairing

Out of leaves falling
Over leaves fallen
A runner comes running

Aware of no watcher
His loneness my loneness
His running my running.

At Guaracara Park

Eric Roach

(written after watching Kip Keino run)

the bronze god running;
beauty hurtling through the web of air,
motion fusing time and space
exploding our applauses . . .

speed was survival there in the green heat
where the lithe hero dashed
from the leopard's leap,
fled to cover from the feral fang
or ran the antelope across the plains

and speed and stamina were the warrior's pride
where impis of assegais and swords and shields
tore tigerish through the brush and raided
and bounced back upon the kraals
panting from wounds and weariness,
brandishing the trophies of their cradling war.

the slave ships could not break our bones
nor strip our tendons, nor the long slaving
years narrow our arteries nor disease
our lungs nor shrivel up our hearts,
but left love thundering to this running man.

not fame's wreath crowns him
but Ogun's aura now; that blaze of flame
that savaged history back beyond our memories
our dreams and searchings.
the blood of the fierce gods we lost,
the pantheon of the kraals made him immortal
or he would have been a scarecrow in the canes.

INJURY AND DEATH

Death of the Track Star

Bill Meissner

It all happens in a moment, telephone-still.
He leans backward across 30 years in his padded
swivel chair, back toward his high school track.

A magnet pulls at him again
from the finish line, the metal
of his legs is bending, churning.
He feels the choirs of wheezing,
a chestful of cinders.
This is real running, he thinks, his heart
beating hard in his heels.

No one can touch him, yet he touches
everyone: the crowd arches
as he breaks string after string
with his toughened throat and

For an instant he almost believes
he has lived the best possible life—
success pours across the desk in front of him, visible
as spilled coffee. It is the stain
of winning.
He feels a broken glass trophy putting itself
back together again
inside his body. And applause,
like a balloon of light,
surrounds each muscle.

Now his legs can soften into two blue silk ribbons
rippling in the breeze

he smiles, and suddenly inhales
all the breaths
he has ever exhaled in his life.

A Jogging Injury

Fleda Brown Jackson

All day I have lain, foot propped,
beating its shadow-heart
in time with the gods who stopped
my run midstride. Their art

stings less in my middle age.
At sixteen I would have cried
at my foot's carnage,
its quick turn from the right.

Now I am riddled with breaks.
Those I loved and others I turned from
have softened my bones to vague aches;
my original dreams come

into my thoughts like dried flowers
too tender for touch. Today blood
crowds and blooms its flower
under the skin, making a glad

try for total repair. The lame
foot struck a rock, innocent
on the path: its pain
is the rock's gift, a godsend.

Do We Need an Ambulance for Cross-Country?

question from the audience at a sports medicine seminar for coaches

Grace Butcher

And the scene comes unbidden into my mind:
the runners at the far turn of the course,
behind the roughest field and into the woods,
among the deepest trees left leaning
after last year's storm.

The alien colors trickle down the path:
the red & black, the purple & gold, the green & white.
We strain to see the first brilliant flashes
through the dying leaves, but must wait,
murmuring to ourselves, "Where are they?
Where are they?"

I know where they are.
I sent them there.
I know every stone, every rut and hole,
every root waiting to trap the delicate foot,
the feet of my slender animals,
claws scratching the dirt, striking sparks
from the flat rock on that sharp turn.
And I see one try to pass,
try to take the lead,
see the root reach for him
with a thin gray arching arm
that will not let go.

I hear the snap of something else,
the scream drift down the hill
through the golden leaves,
feel my face go white with fear.

I sent them there, sent all of them.
They go for glory
and because I told them to,
knowing all the while
how fragile the bones,
how fixed ahead the eyes are,
forgetting to look down, forgetting
in the beauty of the run
that anything can end in a second,
even when you are young
and protected by the names of fierce animals.

I hear the answer. It is yes.
My head swims. The auditorium
is too hot. I leave abruptly,
walk into the cool darkness,
look up, find the first star, make my wish.

Prefontaine
Charles Ghigna

He wore old Oregon on his chest,
a new mustache on his 24-year-old lip
and a scowl on his brow
that could jump out his mouth
quicker than that famous final kick.
We all agreed
he could run and run and run
after women and whiskey and ribbons,
a chip off the old lumberjack block.
We in the stands gave our clapped-red hands
to him and his victory laps.
We watched and prayed for his rugged runty form
under suns, gym ceilings and in television rooms.
He stood us wild after each mile
witnessing his sudden bursts of speed.
We now curse a coffin car we never saw.

The Iliad

Homer

(Robert Fitzgerald translation. Excerpt from Book XXII)

Then toward town with might and main he ran,
magnificent, like a racing chariot horse
that holds its form at full stretch on the plain.
So light-footed Akhilleus held the pace.
And aging Priam was the first to see him
sparkling on the plain, bright as that star
in autumn rising, whose unclouded rays
shine out amid a throng of stars at dusk—
the one they call Orion's dog, most brilliant,
yes, but baleful as a sign: it brings
great fever to frail men. So pure and bright
the bronze gear blazed upon him as he ran.
The old man gave a cry. With both his hands
thrown up on high he struck his head, then shouted,
groaning, appealing to his dear son. Unmoved,
Lord Hektor stood in the gateway, resolute
to fight Akhilleus.

. . .

Now close at hand
Akhilleus like the implacable god of war
came on with blowing crest, hefting the dreaded
beam of Pelian ash on his right shoulder.
Bronze light played about him, like the glare
of a great fire or the great sun rising,
and Hektor, as he watched, began to tremble.
Then he could hold his ground no more. He ran,
leaving the gate behind him, with Akhilleus
hard on his heels, sure of his own speed.
When the most lightning-like of birds, a hawk
bred on a mountain, swoops a dove,
the quarry dips in terror, but the hunter,
screaming, dips behind it and gains upon it,

passionate for prey. Just so, Akhilleus
murderously cleft the air, as Hektor
ran with flashing knees along the wall
. . .
the two men ran, pursuer and pursued,
and he who fled was noble, he behind
a greater man by far. They ran full speed,
and not for bull's hide or a ritual beast,
or any prize that men compete for: no,
but for the life of Hektor, tamer of horses.
Just as chariot teams around a course
go wheeling swiftly, for the prize is great,
a tripod or a woman, in the games
held for a dead man, so three times these two
at full speed made their course around Priam's town,
as all the gods looked on. . .

Great Akhilleus, hard on Hektor's heels,
kept after him, the way a hound will harry
a deer's fawn he has startled from its bed
to chase through gorge and open glade, and when
the quarry goes to earth under a bush
he holds the scent and quarters till he finds it;
so with Hektor: he could not shake off
the great runner, Akhilleus. Every time
he tried to sprint hard for the Dardan gates
under the towers, hoping men could help him,
sending missiles down, Akhilleus loomed
to cut him off and turn him toward the plain,
as he himself ran always near the city.
As in a dream a man chasing another
cannot catch him, nor can he in flight
escape from his pursuer, so Akhilleus
could not by his swiftness overtake him,
nor could Hektor pull away. How could he
run so long from death, had not Apollo
for the last time, the very last, come near

to give him stamina and speed?
                                        Akhilleus
shook his head at the rest of the Akhaians,
allowing none to shoot or cast at Hektor—
none to forestall him, and to win the honor.
But when, for the fourth time, they reached the springs,
the Father poised his golden scales.
                                        He placed
two shapes of death, death prone and cold, upon them,
one of Akhilleus, one of the horseman, Hektor,
and held the midpoint, pulling upward. Down sank
Hektor's fatal day, the pan went down
toward undergloom.

To an Athlete Dying Young

A. E. Housman

The time you won your town the race
We chaired you through the market-place;
Man and boy stood cheering by,
And home we brought you shoulder high.

Today, the road all runners come,
Shoulder-high we bring you home,
And set you at your threshold down,
Townsman of a stiller town.

Smart lad, to slip betimes away
From fields where glory does not stay
And early though the laurel grows
It withers quicker than the rose.

Eyes the shady night has shut
Cannot see the record cut,
And silence sounds no worse than cheers
After earth has stopped the ears;

Now you will not swell the rout
Of lads that wore their honor out,
Runners whom renown outran
And the name died before the man.

So set, before its echoes fade,
The fleet foot on the sill of shade,
And hold to the low lintel up
The defended challenge cup.

And round that early-laurelled head
Will flock to gaze the strengthless dead
And find unwithered on its curls
The garland briefer than a girl's.

ACKNOWLEDGMENTS

Max Apple: "Carbo-Loading," from *Free Agents.* Copyright © 1984 by Max Apple. Reprinted by permission of HarperCollins.

W.H. Auden: "Runner," from *Collected Poems*. Copyright © 1969 by W.H. Auden. Reprinted by permission of Random House, Inc.

Toni Cade Bambara: "Raymond's Run," from *Gorilla, My Love.* Copyright © 1971 by Toni Cade Bambara. Reprinted by permission of Random House, Inc.

Jack Bennett: excerpt from *Gallipoli* copyright © 1981 by David Williamson. Reprinted by permission of Collins / Angus & Robertson.

William Borden: "100m Hurdles" reprinted by permission of the author. Copyright © 1988 by William Borden.

James Buechler: "John Sobieski Runs," public domain. Originally published in *The Saturday Evening Post.*

Grace Butcher: "Do We Need an Ambulance for Cross-Country?" reprinted by permission of the author. Copyright © 1988 by Grace Butcher.

George Harmon Coxe: "See How They Run" copyright © 1941 by Curtis Publishing Company. Originally published in *The Saturday Evening Post.* Reprinted by permission of Brandt & Brandt, Inc.

Douglas Dunn: "An Evening at the Track" Copyright © 1980 by Douglas Dunn. Reprinted by permission of the Peters, Fraser & Dunlop Group, Ltd.

Louis Edwards: excerpt from *Ten Seconds* copyright © 1991 by Louis Edwards. Reprinted by permission of Graywolf Press, St. Paul, Minnesota.

George Ewart Evans: "The Medal" reprinted by permission of Faber & Faber (London). Copyright © 1959 by George Ewart Evans.

Rina Ferrarelli: "Joan Benoit" reprinted by permission of the author. Copyright © 1986 by Rina Ferrarelli.

Donald Finkel: "Interview with a Winner" reprinted by permission of the author. Copyright © 1975 by Donald Finkel.

Robert Fitzgerald: translation of Homer's *Iliad* copyright © 1974 by Robert Fitzgerald. Reprinted by permission of Doubleday, a division of Bantam Doubleday Dell Publishing Group, Inc.

Robert Francis: "His Running My Running" from *Robert Francis: Collected Poems 1936-76*. Copyright © 1976 by Robert Francis. Reprinted by permission of the University of Massachussetts Press.

Charles Ghigna: "Prefontaine" reprinted by permission of the author. Copyright © by Charles Ghigna.

Brian Glanville: excerpt from *The Olympian* reprinted by permission of Cedarwinds Publishing Company. Copyright © 1969 by Brian Glanville.

Daniel Hoffman: "The Finish" from *Hang-Gliding from Helicon.* Copyright ©1988 by Daniel Hoffman. Reprinted by permission of Louisiana State University Press.

A.E. Housman: "To an Athlete Dying Young" from "A Shropshire Lad," from *The Collected Poems of A.E. Housman.* Copyright © 1967, 1968 by Robert E. Symons. Copyright © 1939, 1940, 1965 by Henry Holt & Co. Reprinted by permission of Henry Holt & Co.

Fleda Brown Jackson: "A Jogging Injury" reprinted by permission of the author. Copyright © 1986 by Fleda Brown Jackson.

Burges Johnson "The Service," public domain.

Rudyard Kipling: "If," public domain.

William R. Loader: excerpt from *Staying the Distance* reprinted by permission of Jonathan Cape. Copyright © 1958 by William R. Loader.

Sara Maitland: "The Loveliness of the Long-Distance Runner" reprinted by permission of Curtis Brown, Ltd. (London). Copyright © 1983 by Sara Maitland.

Richard Christian Matheson: "Third Wind" reprinted by permission of the author. Copyright © 1984 by Richard Christian Matheson.

Walter McDonald: "The Track" reprinted by permission of Texas Tech University Press. Copyright © 1976 by Walter McDonald. Originally published in *Sam Houston Literary Review.*

Bill Meissner: "Death of the Track Star" reprinted by permission of the author. Copyright © by Bill Meissner.

Lillian Morrison: "The Sprinters" reprinted by permission of the author. Copyright © 1965 by Lillian Morrison.

Marnie Mueller: "Strategy for a Marathon" reprinted by permission of the author. Copyright © 1986 by Marnie Mueller.

Joyce Carol Oates: "Running" reprinted by permission of Ecco Press. Copyright © 1992 by the Ontario Review, Inc.

Eddy Orcutt: "Wheelbarrow," public domain. Originally published in *The Saturday Evening Post.*

Lon Otto: "We Cannot Save Him," from *Cover Me.* Copyright © 1988 by Lon Otto. Reprinted by permission of Coffee House Press.

John L. Parker, Jr.: excerpt from *Once a Runner* reprinted by permission of Cedarwinds Publishing Company. Copyright © 1978, 1990 by John L. Parker, Jr.

Marge Piercy: "Morning Athletes" from *Circles on the Water.* Reprinted by permission of Alfred A. Knopf, Inc. Copyright © 1982 by Marge Piercy.

Victor Price: excerpt from *The Other Kingdom* reprinted by permission of the author. Copyright © 1964 by Victor Price.

Ron Rash: "Running the Mile Relay" reprinted by permission of the author. Copyright © 1992 by Ron Rash.

Eric Roach: "At Guaracara Park" Copyright © 1971 by Eric Roach.

Jackson Scholz: "The Winning Bug," public domain.

Alan Sillitoe: excerpt from *The Loneliness of the Long-Distance Runner* reprinted by permission of Alfred A. Knopf, Inc. Copyright © 1959 by Alan Sillitoe.

Charles Hamilton Sorley: "The Song of the Ungirt Runners," public domain.

Harry Sylvester: "Going to Run All Night" reprinted by permission of Henry Holt & Co. Copyright © 1948, 1976 by Harry Sylvester.

James Tabor: "The Runner" reprinted by permission of the author. Copyright © 1979 by James Tabor.

Bruce Tuckman: excerpt from *Long Road to Boston* reprinted by permission of Cedarwinds Publishing Company. Copyright © 1988 by Bruce Tuckman.

William Vernon: "Out on the Course" reprinted by permission of the author. Copyright © by William Vernon.

Evelyn Waugh: excerpt from *Decline and Fall* reprinted by permission of Little, Brown & Co. and the Peters, Fraser & Dunlop Group, Ltd. Copyright © 1929 by Evelyn Waugh, renewed 1956.

Francis Webb: "This Runner" reprinted by permission of Collins/Angus & Robertson. Copyright © 1969 by Francis Webb.

Walt Whitman: "The Runner," public domain.

Richard Wilbur: "Running," from *Walking to Sleep: New Poems and Translations*. Copyright © 1968 by Richard Wilbur. Reprinted by permission of Harcourt Brace & Company.

About Breakaway Books

Breakaway Books was founded in the belief that sports and literature need not be separate domains. We hope to publish fiction, nonfiction, and poetry of a high literary standard relating to all competitive and recreational athletic pursuits. Writers are hereby encouraged to submit their work—of any length—for possible publication. Breakaway Books will also pay a small fee to the first person recommending a particular sports-related story, poem, or passage from a novel which we subsequently include in an anthology. The mailing address for Breakaway Books is Box 1109; Ansonia Station; New York, NY 10023. The phone number of the editorial offices, for questions, complaints, or suggestions, is 212-595-2216.

Finding Books Excerpted Herein

If you wish to read the entirety of any novel excerpted in *The Runner's Literary Companion,* here are some tips. *The Other Kingdom, Staying the Distance,* and *Gallipoli* are out of print, but may be found at your library. For *Once a Runner, Long Road to Boston,* and *The Olympian,* try your local bookstore. If they can't procure a copy for you, call the publisher, Cedarwinds Publishing Co., at 800-548-2388. *Ten Seconds* is available from your bookstore, or from Graywolf Press in St. Paul, Minnesota. *Decline and Fall* is available from your bookstore or from Little, Brown & Co. in Boston. *The Loneliness of the Long-Distance Runner* is available from your bookstore or from Plume, a division of Penguin USA, in New York City.